HIS
TIMING

JOE PAOLI

TATE PUBLISHING
AND **ENTERPRISES**, LLC

Published by Tate Publishing & Enterprises, LLC
127 E. Trade Center Terrace | Mustang, Oklahoma 73064 USA
1.888.361.9473 | www.tatepublishing.com

Tate Publishing is committed to excellence in the publishing industry. The company reflects the philosophy established by the founders, based on Psalm 68:11,
"The Lord gave the word and great was the company of those who published it."

Published in the United States of America

ISBN: 978-1-68142-254-1
Fiction / Christian / General
15.06.19

HIS
TIMING

CHAPTER 1

Sam couldn't hold it in any longer. He had just walked his date, Rachel, to her third story apartment, and he was finally alone in his car. *Had she heard all the grumbling my stomach was doing?* he wondered. From the moment he had picked her up that evening, he had been holding back his gas. Sure, his trip to the restroom had offered some relief, but even then, he wasn't without the threat of someone walking in on his toxic discharge. The trip down the stairs had been an opportunity to release some of the pressure, but he hadn't been sure she wouldn't wonder out onto her balcony and catch him in the act. Alone in his car, he was finally free to cut it all lose and was he ever.

Sitting there alone in the pungent smell of his sweet relief reminded him of something he had thought to himself many times before: being alone has its privileges. As he drove away from Rachel's apartment, he opened all of his windows and started poking around in his nose for that big lose, crusty sucker that had been driving him nuts most of the evening. He had swiped and pulled at his nose all night long in an attempt to dislodge his tormentor, but he hadn't had the chance to do the job properly with Rachel sitting across from him all night. With his finger two knuckles up into his nose and his gas blowing at full steam, his cell phone started to vibrate in his pocket. As he pulled it free, he wasn't at all surprised to see that it was Joe.

"Hey, Joe," Sam answered.

"What's up, Sambo? Are you still with the hottie?" Joe Morgan's tone and pace led Sam to believe he may have been drinking. In actuality though, Joe, being an athlete, rarely drank. He fooled people easily as he always seemed to be in such a good mood, most just assumed he was drunk. If you knew him well though, you were never sure if he had been drinking or not. Though few people knew it, Joe practically never drank. Tonight was another one of those nights. Joe was putting out an exceptional amount of joy, yet he had not been drinking, not one drop.

"No, I just dropped her off." Sam really wanted to head home for some alone time and, hopefully, for some texting with Rachel. He was still amazed that someone as beautiful as her would even consider dating him. From the second he had seen that it was Joe calling, he had begun praying that he wasn't calling to ask him to go to some party or something as it was the last thing in the world he wanted to do. Though Joe had been a great friend, he was also a bigger-than-life personality that always seemed to be in a crowd somewhere. Joe never seemed to be very far from the ladies either. He and Sam were opposites in many ways. Though they were both outgoing, they were opposites.

"Can you pick me up, dude? I got left at a party, and it's too far to walk home."

"Wow, eleven thirty and you are ready to go home? I've never heard anything like that before. Where are you?" Joe always knew he could count on Sam. Sam was a rock. He didn't drink; he was always there for his friends; he did all of his school work and got great grades; and he always seemed to care more about other people than himself. Joe admired all of these qualities in Sam and, deep down, actually looked up to him.

"Where else, I'm at Kevin's. I just got off the phone with your date, and I need to talk to you." Joe had introduced Rachel to Sam. She and Joe were first cousins, and the two had practically grown up in the same house. He loved Rachel like a sister and couldn't have thought any higher of her as a person than he already did. Sam was the first and only guy he had ever introduced Rachel to. Actually, Sam had been the first guy Joe had ever felt was good enough for her. Though he had been in several classes with Sam, they had not been close friends until recently when they had begun to spend quite a bit of time together. They often studied together, and Sam had even talked to Joe about his faith once.

"Is everything okay with her? I thought we had a really good time tonight. I hope I wasn't wrong about that?" *Why would Rachel call Joe so quickly after I left, and what could she have said that made him want to leave a party to talk to me about?* Sam wondered.

"It's pretty serious, dude. We need to meet right away. I may even let you buy me something to eat." Joe was almost never serious. He was very smart and possessed an uncanny ability to read people quickly and almost always correctly. Joe was fun to be around and had always been popular. Being a great athlete and a good student seemed to most to be mutually exclusive qualities. However, for Joe, this combination of desired qualities and abilities, along with his magnetic personality, made him the envy of most guys and the desire of most girls.

"I'll be there in about five minutes. Meet me outside. I don't want to get sucked into anything. I'm picking you up, but I'm not coming to a party." Now that he was aware that Joe had spoken with Rachel after their date, he had to speak with Joe right away. However, he knew there was always the chance that Joe would try to pull him into something that would keep him out for hours. For this reason, he set the ground rules.

Sam earnestly felt with every part of his being that Rachel had felt comfortable and enjoyed his company just as much as he had felt comfortable and enjoyed her company. She was very attractive, almost too attractive, and she seemed to have a great sense of humor. In spite of the high bar Joe had set with his buildup of Rachel, she had not only lived up to the hype, she had completely surpassed it.

Joe had spoken in glowing terms about her personality, her sense of humor, and her intelligence. He had sold Rachel so hard to Sam that Sam's expectations had been so high that he had been worried that he may go into their first meeting with unrealistically high expectations about how great she was going to be, which could leave him underwhelmed if he saw any flaw in her character.

Their first meeting had only been two days before tonight's date. Joe and his girlfriend, Ally, had brought Rachel to meet Sam at the McDonald's by the baseball stadium for lunch. The attraction had been immediate for both of them. They were both good-looking people. At twenty-one years old, most people are at or near their physical prime. Rachel and Sam were no exception.

"I'm already outside, gangster. If you are not here in five though, I'm making you come in to get me." Joe liked to play around. Sarcasm and humor were simply part of who he was. He could tell that Sam was already hooked on his beautiful cousin, and he was quite sure knowing that Rachel had called him so soon after their date was likely driving Sam crazy. Joe was sure he could go bunker down in the house, and Sam wouldn't even think twice about getting out of his car to come in to hunt him down. There was no chance Sam was driving home without hearing what Rachel had called him about. No chance at all.

"I'm on my way. Stay put. I mean it!" Sam immediately put his windows up and began to fill the car with his deadly gas. *I'll teach Mr. Funny Man,* he thought.

Before he got to Kevin's to pick up Joe, he sent Rachel a text. "I had a great time tonight, Rachel. I'm looking forward to the game tomorrow night." They had agreed to go watch Joe pitch for the Houston Cougars the next day. Joe was the ace of the team, and Rachel always went to his games. Sam had seen Joe pitch a couple of times, but since he had never known who Rachel was, they had never met. However, when he came face-to-face with Rachel at McDonald's during their introduction meeting, he recognized her right away. He remembered seeing Joe talk to her and her friend before a game and even remembered wondering what it would be like to be Joe. He couldn't even imagine what it would be like to have girls who looked like her and her friend wanting to talk to him. In contrast, Rachel had no recollection of ever seeing Sam. She felt an immediate attraction and quickly began to feel comfortable around him though.

A response to his text to Rachel came quickly. "Me too. I had fun." Even her response seemed cute to him. Though she was fairly tall, five foot seven inches tall, she was very slender. Her personality was a really good contrast for Sam's friendly outgoing style. In contrast to his, her personality was much more reserved. She had few friends, but the ones she did have were very close. Sam was much more outgoing but not at all on Joe's level.

Sam began to overthink her response almost as soon as he read it. *Why didn't she mention our date tomorrow? Maybe she's just being nice? Maybe she told Joe to tell me the bad news that she didn't want to see me again?*

As he pulled up to Kevin's house, he noticed Joe standing out front as promised. Before he stopped the car, he blew out another prize winner. It was a stinker that really filled the car. It was a real eye waterer.

The instant the car stopped, Joe jumped in. In classic Joe style, instead of complaining about the smell, he leaned over and cut one of his own. Unbelievably, its smell immediately overtook Sam's best effort.

"Are you kidding me?" Sam screamed at him.

"I always fart when I'm in the crapper, and that's what this place smells like." Joe was smiling ear to ear as if he actually enjoyed the deadly odor.

Sam held down the power window buttons, and all four windows started their decent.

"Come on, Sam, be a man. I ate yours."

"I'm glad you think this is funny." Actually, he thought it was pretty funny too, but there was no way he was going to admit it. He could hardly breathe.

"I do. Farts is really funny." As usual, Joe was enjoying himself. "I've never seen Rachel so into anyone, especially not this quickly.

What did you do to her?" As much as he had built Rachel up to Sam, it was nothing compared to how much he had built Sam up to Rachel. Joe was tired of seeing Rachel go from one jerk to the next. He knew Sam was different. He knew Sam was waiting for marriage to have sex, and he knew that Sam was going somewhere in life.

Sam had told Joe that he was waiting for marriage in response to Joe's questions about faith and Christian living. He had explained to Joe that pleasing God by living according to his word would always be his number-one priority. Sam openly told him that he constantly failed to live up to the standard, but that wasn't okay.

From the time they first met Joe quickly began to admire Sam for living according to his beliefs and for his willingness to tell others why he believed what he believed. It took courage to stand up for God's ways, and Joe was quite sure most people teased Sam for his stance. Not only did Sam believe, but also, he lived in accordance to what he believed. It was very uncommon.

It hadn't taken Joe long to figure out that Sam had the type of character that any brother or father would want in a boyfriend for their sister or daughter. With each interaction, Joe became more and more convinced that Sam was perfect for Rachel. He was tired of seeing her unhappy, and he knew Sam would be the answer.

"I didn't do anything to her. She is great. She's more than great and more than you said that she was. I wish she wasn't so dang good looking, though. I'm a little intimidated by that." He really was intimidated by her looks. *How could someone that good looking like me?* he wondered. Sitting across from her at dinner that evening, all he could think about was how amazing she was. He couldn't help but realize that she could have any guy she wanted. Her dark-brown hair and olive skin seemed richer and fuller in color than was naturally possible. It seemed as if she had no makeup on, and he wouldn't have added a thing to that face. Her body was just as perfect as her face to him, and he had struggled not to stare at it all night. He forced himself to stare only into her eyes all night long. He even noticed himself missing part of the conversation from time to time due to the distraction of her beauty. Their conversation had been deep and easy, and she seemed to be both bright and thoughtful. He was absolutely smitten from the first moment he saw her, and each moment they had shared since had only increased his hopelessness of ever forgetting her.

After an odd moment of silence while he thought about Rachel's beauty and without a word in response from the impulsive Joe, Sam continued, "Quit messing around and tell me why she called you. I'm thinking all the worst. What's going on?"

"When she called me, you had just left. She sounded like a little schoolgirl. She was so excited about how great you are. Then she started to get emotional and asked me to do her a favor." Most of it sounded good to Sam. It assured him that things had gone the way he had felt that they had. The big question was about the emotions and the favor. *What could that possibly be about?* he wondered.

"Do her what favor?"

Sensing Sam's vulnerability, he decided to have a little fun with him. "She asked me to gently break it to you that she is carrying my baby and that we need you to be the daddy so our family doesn't go crazy." It was just too ridiculous that even he, the father of practical jokes, couldn't keep it together. Before he even finished the sentence, he started to laugh.

"You are such a moron, Joe. Just tell me what she asked you to do for her." Sam had always loved the lighter side of Joe, but now just wasn't the time.

"Okay, I'll give it to you straight. It's her dad's baby." Again, he was laughing hysterically.

"Ha-ha," Sam forced out. "I'm glad you're enjoying this." Sam was starting to get a little restless now. In his mind, it had to be something Rachel was embarrassed of or something bad.

"Sorry, dude. I don't think you will have a big problem with this, but she's really scared that you might."

Oh no, Sam thought. He could feel inside how attached he had already become. At this point, she was absolute perfection to him. What was he about to hear about her?

"What is it?" His face was flushed with fear as he spoke. Joe never missed nonverbal signals or actually any kind of signals. He could see what was going on in Sam's mind, and he lived for these types of opportunities.

"She used to be a dude and still has a dork." He was really enjoying himself. He loved having information that people wanted, and Sam was giving him all he needed to feed the fire.

"Look, Joe, I really like her. Please stop doing this to me. I'll buy you some food, if you'll just tell me what favor she asked from you and quit messing around." Sam knew Joe was always up for food, and he had even mentioned it earlier during their phone conversation. *Maybe the offer will get him to stop messing around,* he reasoned.

"Yes, food would be good. It would definitely help me sing." Joe wasn't holding out for food but certainly wasn't going to turn the offer down. What he had to share was a big fear of Rachel's. He fully understood how important it was to her that Sam knew about it before he got sideswiped with it. He agreed with Rachel that Sam needed to know and that it had to be right away. Though he was making Sam work for it, there was no scenario in which he wouldn't have shared Rachel's concerns with Sam before their next date the following day.

"I will feed you then. Quit fooling around, and tell me what favor she asked of you."

"All right, you've earned it. She is worried that you will find out that she used to date Kevin Todd and that it will make you uncomfortable at the game tomorrow." Kevin was only an acquaintance to Sam. It was actually Kevin's house that he had just picked up Joe from. It was Joe and Kevin who were very close. Kevin had been Joe's primary catcher for three years, since they had come in as freshmen together. Sam knew Kevin's family had some money by the way he lived and by the car, he drove, but he knew little else. The only other thing he knew about Kevin was that he was a big-time ladies' man.

Sam pulled into the all-night taco stand he had been heading for, parked, and began to sit back into his seat to let the information sink in. Immediately, he began to feel a sinking feeling. Kevin was better looking, had more money, and surely had been having sex with Rachel. Quickly, he decided that it didn't matter since it was in the past. The future would be Rachel and his, if things worked out. Still, it hurt to know she had been with Kevin; it hurt more than Sam felt was appropriate for where things currently stood between them. He had always wanted to find someone that had not been with anyone sexually, but his only real criterion was that they were a Christian. If God had forgiven them, so could he.

"What can you tell me about it? How long has it been over? Is she over him? Is he over her?" He needed to know where things stood. Sam had never been the jealous type, but now, he was feeling very inadequate. Though he had dated girls before, he had always done his best to stay somewhat safe. He knew he was getting closer and closer to being ready for marriage, and his only interest in dating was to find a wife. *Is Rachel only getting my consideration because she is so beautiful?* he wondered. He didn't even know what she believed in yet, though he knew she was well aware of his beliefs, as Joe would have certainly told her. His only criterion for a wife was that she must be a born again, Bible-believing Christ follower. At this point, he had no clue where she stood spiritually. If she weren't a Christian and was not willing to investigate what the Bible had to say, it would be something he could not accept. He would either have to share his faith and see what God's plan was based on her response, even if it wasn't immediate, or he could just move on. From the way he was already feeling about her, he would soon share his faith to see where things would lead.

"Kevin wasn't that bad to her. He's just a guy having a good time. Unfortunately, he really hurt her by running around on her.

Rachel only had one serious boyfriend before him, so she's pretty torn up over him. Her previous boyfriend was a guy she dated the last couple of years of high school. He was a year ahead of her in school, and when he went off to college, it didn't take him long to start cheating on her. When she first met Kevin, I knew she was in trouble. Kevin is really good with the ladies, and Rachel has always liked guys like him. She likes good-looking popular guys, and unfortunately, she's good-looking enough herself to get them. I know she knows who Kevin really is now, and I guarantee that she is over him. She really learned a lot from their relationship, and she doesn't want to make the same mistake ever again. However, I know she still has feelings for him." He hoped he wasn't burying her with Sam, but he wanted Sam to understand her past so he could buy into the fact that she now had her eyes open.

Sam felt angry hearing about Rachel being used and cheated on by both guys. *What a selfish terrible world we are living in*, he thought. *How could anyone hurt such a wonderful person? Why cheat on her?* He was sure no one was better than her.

"When she finally got the courage to walk away from Kevin about a year ago, she swore off shallow, good-looking guys. Seeing Kevin with other girls had really taken its toll on her. He fed her lies every time she suspected that something was going on, but she never really believed him. Their relationship was never really very good as it lacked trust from the beginning. I had warned her to stay away from him, and when they got close, she and I actually drifted apart a bit. Though we were often both around Kevin, she knew how I felt about her dating him, and it drove a bit of a wedge between us." Joe loved Rachel with everything he had. He had tried to protect her all of her life, and he hated that she had always gone after the wrong guys.

Sam was perfect for her, and Joe knew it. He was everything Joe wanted for her, and for the first time in her life, Joe was sure Rachel was ready for a relationship with someone as worthy as Sam. To make sure Sam didn't focus on Rachel's mistakes, he added, "She's too good to be treated the way Kevin treated her.

She's smart and funny, and if she weren't my cousin, I'd date her. She is marriage material." That last part was sure to get Sam's attention. Joe knew Sam would only date someone that he could see himself marrying.

"Are you saying I'm not the good-looking type?" Sam had been told that he was attractive a few times, but he was fully aware that he was not in Kevin or Joe's class. At not quite six feet tall he had been a fair athlete most of his life, but he had never been the star. He liked to work out, but in the weight room, he could only marvel at how strong some guys were. No matter how hard he worked at it, his body never seemed to improve much. Not that he was chubby or anything. He just couldn't strengthen or tone his body the way he noticed some of the guys in the weight room seemed to be able to do.

"Come on, dude, when was the last time anyone asked you to pose for a calendar? You know you're a good-looking guy, but I'm sure you also know you're not Mr. America. You're a great guy in every way, and there is no one I want married to Rachel more than you. I know you wouldn't even go on a date with her if she weren't marriage material. She and I have grown up together, and you know how highly I think of her. You know you're my hand-picked perfect man for her. Just so you know, I was there when she accepted Christ. We both did it. We have both done things we regret since that day, but she will mature into a great Christian wife for you." Joe had a way of saying things like this. He knew what people wanted to hear, and he could shape his message well to scratch their itch. When it was the truth, he never had trouble saying it, and he always said it well.

Sam was really excited to hear that Rachel had already accepted Christ into her life. He knew many examples of good people that had God's calling on their lives but had fallen back into sin. He knew he wasn't without sin either and that his continual urges toward sin caused him to stumble often. It was his desire to be more like Christ that had afforded him a measure of success in his attempt to turn from sin. He was painfully aware that he could stumble at any time though. It kept him grounded and guarded against sin.

Knowing that Rachel had given her life to Christ made it far easier for him to forgive her. If she was a believer and had already confessed her sin to the Lord, she was forgiven by the only one that can forgive sin. While he reasoned within himself, he suddenly caught himself and realized that he had no right to feel that he needed to forgive her for anything. She had done nothing to him. It was between her and God only. He would need to get over what she had done with Kevin, but he didn't need to forgive her, though the knowledge of it would force him to live with it.

As far as Rachel accepting Christ, he decided he had no idea how real her surrender to Christ had been. He would definitely need to investigate but knew that only God would know for sure. Her words and actions would be clues, but her conversion would always be between only her and God. Still, hearing Joe say she had invited Christ into her life was like a shot of adrenalin to Sam. He was already praying that she was the one God had picked out for him. If it were all in his hands, she would be.

Sam had grown up in the church and had seen many young-and-old believers fall into sin. More than once someone close to him had succumbed to the sin nature and shocked him, their families, and the church. As he had learned, all sin was eventually exposed. Thankfully, God loves everyone, even sinners. If he didn't love sinners, he would have no humans to love.

Sam's ability to forgive came from his desire to be like Christ, as did his ability to love others. Through surrender to the Lord, the study of his word, and constant prayer, Sam was being shaped into Christ's image. His desire to be more like Christ required him to be forgiving, but his forgiveness was not the forgiveness she needed as atonement for her sin. That could only come from God, and he prayed she had asked for it already.

Sam had seen several examples of fallen Christians turning from sin and being restored by God. He had even seen sin in people without any sort of hurt in their lives, and he was aware that not all sin and brokenness had an external cause that we could see and prevent. In some cases, small surrender to our sinful nature is all that is needed to lead to a great fall. For these reasons, Sam was very forgiving and always erred on the side of believing people could turn from their sin. He firmly believed that everyone makes mistakes, especially young people. We are all flawed and make mistakes. He was by no means an exception.

"I'm glad you think so highly of me, Joe. I don't like the thought of her dating me because I'm not a good-looking guy, but I guess I can get over it. Yes, her being a Christian is a prerequisite for marriage. You've done your homework. We are a long ways from marriage, but I have to admit, she is great. She's funny, good looking, smart, and I really like her personality. She is amazing in every way. I can't and won't hold her past against her. It's over and done, and you say she has seen the error of her way and intends to change. I wish it hadn't been someone I know though. It will be harder for me to not hold it against Kevin." Sam was always straightforward. He never played games. His way was direct and straightforward. He was always friendly and honest to everyone, as he understood that God loves them all.

"So you won't hold me getting her pregnant against her either then?" The smart-ass smile was back now.

"You have got to be kidding me? Are you sure you're okay?" This guy was amazing to Sam. How could he take nothing serious yet be so dang good at everything?

"I'm actually pretty sure something is wrong with me, Sam," Joe answered.

"Do you think I should call or text her to let her know I'm okay with everything?" As usual, Sam's thoughts returned to those he cared about.

"Well, it's midnight now, but knowing Rachel like I do, I'm sure she's lying there, thinking about you. A text would be really nice. You would get some great points for letting her off the hook so quickly." Joe knew Sam would know what to say without his guidance, but he was more than willing to help if Sam asked.

"I just want her to know that she and I are starting from a clean slate and that I can't wait to see her tomorrow." Though Sam had been attracted to several other girls in his life, he had never felt what he was already feeling with Rachel. He had fiercely avoided any premarital sexual activity of any kind to this point in his life, though it had not always been easy. There were many times he had to simply remove himself from relationships and situations by asking friends to help him or actually changing classes or quitting youth groups.

Sam had even avoided dating all the way through high school, though that hadn't been a huge struggle for him as he had been a very late bloomer, and not many girls were attracted to him through his high school years. Until he was about eighteen, he was exceedingly skinny and was nothing special to look at. His complexion had also led to some fairly serious acne issues that had actually helped him repulse the ladies. Since he had graduated high school, he had grown almost four inches and filled out quite a bit. Girls were only beginning to find him physically attractive.

"You got it, buddy. Send her that." Sam had impressed Joe from day one, and Sam's response to hearing about Kevin was exactly what he had expected it to be. Joe's number-one criterion for pairing someone with Rachel was character, and Sam had it.

Sam quickly prepared the text as they ate. "I'm eating a very late meal with Joe. He told me about your concerns about Kevin. Please don't even think about your past. I am interested in our future. You and I have just started. I think you are great! I can't wait to see you tomorrow." As he pressed *send*, he could feel an immediate sense of relief.

Like Joe had predicted, Rachel was lying in bed, tied in knots over her fear of how Sam would take the news. She really liked Sam, but the shame of her past was getting the best of her. Sam was nice and funny just like Joe had told her he would be, but there was something in his way that had made her feel safe like she could trust him.

For months, Joe had been telling her that he could fix her up with someone who wouldn't hurt her, someone who would treat her the way she deserved to be treated. Now, after only one date with Sam, she knew Joe had been right. Their time together had been so easy and natural that she was starting to think that he could be her soul mate. She was petrified by the thought of losing him before they had really even started. Joe had told her all about Sam's faith, and she couldn't help but feel dirty and unworthy. She needed him to know about Kevin, and she didn't want it to come up later in a way that would make him think she had been hiding anything from him. Telling him was very difficult, but she knew it had to be done. Doing it through Joe was the easy way, and she hoped Sam wouldn't hold that against her.

Rachel was lying in bed with her cell phone in her hand, in case Sam or Joe sent her a text, when she heard the beep of the incoming message. With the sudden buzz, she went from the edge of unconsciousness to fully awake and partially startled all in a flash. Hoping it was Joe with an update about Sam, she quickly tapped the button that would illuminate her screen. Seeing that it was from Sam himself was even more exhilarating. She felt fear and excitement both at the same time.

Sam's text brought her immediate relief. Her hope for their future together immediately reduced her to tears. That she cared so deeply already told her this was definitely something special. While she was reading his text, it had felt like a weight being lifted from her. Her embarrassment about her sexual relationship with Kevin had left her feeling violated and angry toward the world. Knowing what type of guy Sam was, she couldn't help but feel unworthy. *Why hadn't I been wiser with my boyfriend choices?* she wondered. It was painful for her that she couldn't offer the purity that Sam had to offer her. Now that she was seeing things more clearly, she understood why her parents and church had always stressed staying pure.

Knowing Sam had never been with anyone and that he was waiting for the woman God would bring him made her feel like such a dirty rag. The feelings were actually upsetting her stomach. Thankfully, Sam's text had helped her through those feelings. It had immediately taken the focus off of her failures and directed her every thought to their future. It was so relieving that Rachel's admiration and attraction to Sam actually made her body tingle. This was something special. She was sure of it.

Rachel had intended to keep herself pure until she got married. Unfortunately, in her senior year of high school, her boyfriend succeeded in taking her purity from her. He didn't exactly take it from her as she had a big part in allowing it to happen, and she knew it. Since she was convinced they would marry someday, she had rationalized it in her head and decided that it was *okay* as he would be her only partner. Her boyfriend had helped convince her that they would always be together by constantly telling her that he planned to marry her. Whether he ever believed that, she would never know. Even after he had gone off to college, she had believed that they would one day be married. When he eventually broke up with her, he admitted that he had not only slept around since he had left for college but that he had even cheated on her several times in high school. The betrayal just didn't compute in her mind. For more than a year after the breakup, she refused to date. She took all of the blame for being such a fool, and the feeling that she should have known better dominated her thoughts for months.

Joe had been there telling her Jason was a jerk and that he wasn't a good guy. He heard the rumors about him running around with girls from other schools, and several girls had told Joe that Jason had hit on them. He confronted Rachel, hoping she would listen. Unfortunately, she wouldn't, believing Jason really loved her and that he was all hers.

Not even her Christian friends were living celibate lives when she was in high school. Well, at least not the ones she was hanging out with. They all seemed to think they would marry the guy they were with. One of them even told her, "It's just like any other sin. God will forgive you if you ask him to." That seemed too simple to Rachel, and she knew it was wrong. Also, her heart was telling her there was more to it than that. She had asked for forgiveness, but she wasn't feeling any. She felt alone, foolish, and violated.

After more than a year of absolute seclusion from all men but her cousin and best friend Joe, she began to feel a strong attraction for Kevin. He was such a great-looking guy with so much going for him. Everyone she knew would have loved to be his. When Joe started spending lots of time with Kevin, Rachel began to find herself in his presence almost every weekend. It didn't take long for Kevin to make his move. Her swearing off of men ended the day he kissed her. Though it was only lust Kevin had for her, she again mistook a player's moves for love.

Kevin was clearly cheating on her from day one of their relationship. Though she suspected it from the very beginning, she didn't have evidence until she saw him passionately kissing a girl at a party he didn't expect her to be at. It hurt her so badly that she left without confronting him. Even then, it took her several weeks before she had the courage to leave him.

Joe had warned her that Kevin would hurt her, but she chose to ignore him the same way she had when he had warned her about Jason. Even after she had seen Kevin in action with her own eyes, she had trouble letting go. She struggled internally believing all of the things he had told her about his love for her. She wanted to believe he really loved her, and she even considered forgiving him for kissing that girl, but with lots of support from Joe, she eventually came to the realization that he wouldn't change. Sadly, when she told him she couldn't keep dating him because she knew he was fooling around on her and she didn't believe he really loved her, he told her, "Don't sweat it. We can still hang out." The fact that he wasn't hurt at all practically destroyed her. She immediately swore off men again, and her feelings of rejection and betrayal kept her awake at night for months.

Rachel wanted to be loved more than anything. She needed someone to be in this life with her. She felt empty and alone without a man loving her, though neither of her boyfriends had actually loved her. The emptiness of being alone felt unnatural to her. She knew she couldn't do life alone, and she dreamt of finding someone who would truly love her. After Kevin, she began to fear that she was incapable of finding the man she longed for.

She knew that her attraction to men who other women desired was a big part of the problem, and she knew that physical appearance and popularity should not be qualities or requirements for finding her soul mate. She had grown up in a loving household with parents who loved one another. It was actually someone like her father that she now knew she needed to find. He was a very loving father and husband, and she truly admired him. He was an attractive man, so she decided good looks wouldn't disqualify a man, though she now knew it wouldn't make him either. Though she knew down deep they still would, she told herself, *Going forward, looks simply shouldn't matter.*

Girlfriends were dear to her, and she had several very close ones in her life, but she knew she needed more. She needed the man her mother had always told her that God would bring her. She needed the intimacy of a loving relationship built on trust and commitment. Her dad had been a great father, and she wanted a relationship like he had with her mother more than anything. Unfortunately, after Kevin, she had lost all faith in her ability to find a man like her father. The more she thought about how much Joe loved her, she began to believe that he might actually be able to help her find the right guy. He had been telling her he could for months now. After all, he loved her, and he had always sized up people better than she had. Now that she had met Sam, she knew Joe had been right, and after only one date with Sam, she knew she had finally met the right guy. It was a feeling almost too big for her to process.

Sam's text was just what she needed to know. The way he had responded right after talking with Joe made her feel that he could understand how she was feeling. His sense of urgency about how she was feeling really mattered to her. She was tired of being used, and she was becoming hypersensitive to the signs of some-one who would use her again. She was also relieved that he was good looking. *Could I have accepted him had he not been attractive?* she wondered.

Rachel really liked how Sam had responded in person rather then simply telling Joe that he was okay with her past. She wasn't okay with it, and she wanted Sam to understand how embar-rassed she was. Not only had she been foolish in dating someone like Kevin, for the second time in her life, she had allowed her-self to have sex before marriage again. There was no way she was making that mistake again. It pained her that she no longer had her purity.

In response to Sam's text, she tapped out, "Thank you for being so understanding, Sam. I feel much better now. I can't wait to see you tomorrow either." As soon as she hit *send*, she could tell that she would be able to fall asleep. The relief was immediate, and a peace swept over her as her eyes began to feel heavy.

Sam had been waiting almost ten minutes for a reply. Had he not gotten one, he would have assumed she was asleep. Something inside of him told him, like Joe had suggested, that she was lying there, waiting to hear how he took the news. Seeing her response, Sam couldn't help but tell Joe. "She's just responded. I think you were right. I am going to like her. I'm going to like her a lot." He was feeling really good about Rachel now, even with the news of her almost certainly sexual relationship with Kevin, he was able to see past it and believe she had learned from her mistakes. What he didn't understand was his desire to take care of her and to not hurt her feelings. He only wanted to comfort her, and he couldn't stand the thought of her feeling ashamed of her past. It was as if he had known her much longer, almost as if they already knew each other much deeper than was possible from the two face-to-face meetings they had shared.

"Good night. I'll come get you about an hour before the game tomorrow. Sleep well. I'll be thinking about you." With that text, Sam was ready to take Joe home so he too could go home and lie in bed and think about how great Rachel was. It was almost scaring him how fast this was going. She was perfect in every way in his eyes. While they were together, he had felt as if they could communicate without even speaking.

Almost the second his butt hit his seat, Joe cut another prize winner.

"Are you serious? We were just sitting outside, and you waited until we got back in the car for that nasty crap. What's wrong with you?" It smelled even worse than the last one. Though he was angry, Sam really enjoyed all of the fun he always had with Joe, and deep inside, he knew Joe was becoming one of his best friends. Whatever it was Joe had, Sam couldn't resist it. No one seemed to be able to resist liking Joe.

"I didn't want to waste it on strangers. This one is for you, buddy. It's a reward for you taking on my tragic cousin." Joe was flying high inside. He loved that things were finally working out for Rachel. Sam would treat her right, and she would finally be happy. He was sure of it.

Joe's apartment was in the same complex as Rachel's. Dropping him off made Sam yearn to visit Rachel, but as late as it was, he knew that was out of the question. Though they lived in same complex, they lived in the extreme opposite ends of the complex. It was a good half mile from one side to the other.

With Joe dropped off, Sam headed home with nothing but thoughts of Rachel in his head. "Why didn't I take a picture of us together?" he asked himself.

CHAPTER 2

Sam was off Saturday morning as he had given up his usual Saturday hours to be with Rachel. Since he was a full-time student in his junior year of college, he only worked about twenty hours a week. He'd had his current job, working for the church since he was a junior in high school, so they were very flexible with his hours. They had hired him to do maintenance and all kinds of physical labor around the church campus initially, but as he became more and more computer savvy, Sam began to help with the sound system, PowerPoint presentations, and had even become the go-to guy for all sorts of computer issues. Since college was only about fifteen or twenty minutes away from his church and home, he chose to continue working for the church while he attended college. He definitely needed the money.

Living at home while attending college wasn't the coolest thing, but it was definitely the most affordable route to take. Sam never thought of it as any sort of handicap. He lived a responsible life, and his parents treated him like the mature adult he continually proved to them that he was.

Money had always been tight in Sam's family. He planned to be the first in his immediate family to graduate from college, and the financial burden college presented was almost completely his own to bear. Between an academic scholarship and his job, he was barely able to squeak by.

His academic scholarship had been earned through lots of hard work. Sam was a smart guy, but he always had to put in more time than anyone else to keep up with the top of the class. He was always up to the task and stubbornly refused to do poorly in any class due to a lack of effort. His hard work had paid off in the form of admittance to the University of Houston's electrical engineering program and in the academic scholarship that his grades and test scores had earned him. The scholarship paid for his books, tuition, and his fees if he could maintain his grade point average above the program's minimum requirement. For almost three years now, Sam had maintained a grade point average over 3.5. It had not been easy for him.

Sam's car was more than ten years old, and he did all of his own maintenance on it. His father was an automobile mechanic, so he often leaned on his dad for help with the car. Though his father did not own the shop he worked at, he had put in more than twenty years there and was treated like family by the owner. Due to his father's strong relationship with the owner of the garage, Sam was allowed to use the shop when they were closed. On one such occasion, Sam broke an expensive piece of equipment. As the owner expected any child of his father's to do, Sam worked in the garage to earn enough to replace the piece of equipment he had broken. No one had to ask him to do it. He suggested it, did the work without any direction, and paid off his debt to the owner. It was who he was.

Sam had two younger brothers: Jack who was fifteen, and Tim who was twelve. He also had a baby sister, Katie, who was ten years old. His mother worked at a daycare where she had worked since Sam was two years old. They were a close family who spent lots of time together. Everyone went to see the others' sports and other extracurricular activities. Sam had never been without an audience for any sport or any other activity he had done while growing up. Even now that he was in college, he almost never missed his brother's games. Most importantly, Sam grew up knowing that he was loved.

More than anything, Sam's parents were proud of him. They knew he was grounded in God's word, and they never worried about his decision making. He never gave them a reason not to trust him. Though he had made mistakes, he remained honest with his parents about them. They never heard about anything he had done wrong from anyone before Sam himself told them about it. Sam knew that he could hide things from his parents if he wanted to, but he understood that he could never hide anything from God. For this reason, he held himself accountable to God first. This accountability to God made it easy to honor his parents with the truth. Sam understood that God would use his mother and father to deliver the consequences of his sin. He never saw his parents as the bad guys because he knew it was actually him that had sinned when they were angry, and that it was their God given responsibility to punish him.

Sam's family was deeply invested in their church. Mom and Dad always stressed reading God's word and finding one's place as a member of the church family. They believed heavily in a literal translation of God's word, and they clung to the Bible's teaching. Each family member used their strengths to contribute to the body of the church, and they all supported one another in doing so. Due to the leadership of their parents, the entire family lived their lives to find God's will.

The kids grew up watching their father love their mother while always honoring God's word. Dad never cared much about worldly possessions. Instead, he lived his life in moderation with a focus on God and his family. It was his strong belief that chasing the things of this world separates man from God. Though he never felt worldly possessions were evil or that people with wealth were living in sin, he did feel that the way of the world had a way of shaping us to be something that did not look much like Christ. For this reason, the kids grew up understanding that they were living on the enemy's territory where deception and distortion of the truth were winning the battle for young people's minds. Most professing Christians were caught up in the ways of the world to such a degree that they were simply unaware of their unhealthy desires for the things of this world, which will someday be burned up.

Dad lived his life in total accountability to the Lord. He constantly told the kids that his joy in life came not from any success of his own but from the blessings of his loving heavenly Father. They all adored their father, and each would pursue the gifts they saw their father enjoy with the rest of their lives. Through thick and thin, Dad never lost his focus. When things got bad, he humbled himself and prayed to God alone, with his wife, and even with the kids. All of his prayers centered on God's will for their family.

Though they never had worldly wealth, they had riches in joy and love in their home. As things would turn out, Dad's leadership would yield tremendous results for God's kingdom through everyone he touched, especially his children.

Though Sam was convinced through his father's example that his first priority in life would always be to become more like Christ, he was by no means perfect. He had trouble from time to time with his language and, more than anyone would ever know, he had trouble with his thoughts. All through high school, like most young men, Sam found himself fantasizing about girls. He learned not to tempt himself and chose not to date to keep himself from stumbling. His refusal to date had gotten him teased even at his church. Some of them had even accused him of being gay.

When Sam's senior prom came around, he chose to take a close friend from church. Though she was attractive, she had a very serious boyfriend who had joined the military and was away fighting in Afghanistan. His date's boyfriend was a year older than her and had graduated the year before. Sam and he were close friends, and they spoke several times before Sam took her to prom. They planned to take out any probability of anything inappropriate happening between them by going with another couple. The other couple would take them home immediately after the prom ended. Everything went as planned, and Sam had kept himself from stumbling once again.

Now, three years into college, Sam had been on several dates. None of them had felt like a good match to him until last night though. Rachel was easily the most attractive of the girls he had gone on a date with. He was still concerned that her outward beauty was making him feel the way that he was about her. He feared that her looks alone were causing him to think of her constantly the way that he was. He had been thinking about what he wanted in a wife for years now, and though he knew he needed to be physically attracted to her, he didn't want that to be his number-one criterion. *Am I doing that with Rachel?* he kept asking himself. *If she weren't so perfect physically, would I still be thinking of her constantly?* He needed to find out who she really was to answer these questions, and he couldn't wait to start.

Sam was on schedule to graduate in just over a year, and he was finally allowing himself to start preparing for the life he had been working toward. Life without the pursuit of girls had been far easier, but he knew it was time to start seriously searching for a wife. He couldn't keep doing life without at least the hope of marriage upon graduation. That had always been his plan.

Since he had first laid eyes on Rachel, he had thought of nothing else. The attraction had not only been immediate, it had also felt inescapable as if he was meant to be with her. Though he feared it was her beauty that was making him feel the way he was feeling, something was telling him that it was much more. *Is God in this?* he wondered.

CHAPTER 3

Rachel was the older of two daughters. Her sister had just turned eighteen and was about to graduate from high school. Rachel, Joe, and Sam were all the same age. Joe and Rachel had grown up as very close friends. Their fathers were brothers, and they lived within walking distance of one another. Actually, their father's both worked for Grandpa Thomas, who also lived in the same general area. Their hometown was about an hour away from the University of Houston's campus when the traffic was light, and both Rachel and Joe had moved out when they started college three years earlier.

Rachel lived off campus in the same apartment complex as Joe. She lived with her best friend Heather. The two had been best friends since they were kids. At one point, Heather and Joe had actually dated one another. Their dating was ancient history, and since they had dated way back in junior high, it never really was a distraction for them.

Heather was in the same class as Rachel when it came to looks, and the two of them seemed to have the same bad taste in guys. Because of her height and curves, Heather tended to get far more attention than her quiet friend Rachel.

Heather was a communications major, while Rachel was majoring in biology. Rachel had not yet decided if she wanted to be a nurse or a doctor, but she figured the biology degree would give her a good base for either one. While Heather was a very average student, Rachel was an excellent student. She carried a high grade point average, and she had scored very high on the SAT. Rachel also had a high IQ, but her calm, quite, introverted personality made it difficult for her to show it off.

While they were growing up, Rachel always followed Joe around. He was so popular and good at everything that she just wanted to be a part of it. Joe always treated her like a sister, and they got along like best friends. Heather too was part of their entourage. She was never far off. Joe treated them both like close friends, and it was like they were all part of the same family. Though he was close with Heather, Rachel actually was family, and he always felt like she was his little sister even though she was a month older than he was.

In high school, Joe had been a star athlete. He had been so popular that he was actually prom king his senior year. The biggest advantage of being around Joe was his ability to take all of the attention away from her. Rachel had no interest in being the center of attention, while Joe couldn't help but steal all of the limelight.

Joe almost always drew a crowd. He was funny, good looking, popular, and really loud. Rachel was funny as well, but she had a very dry sense of humor that very few people got. Joe definitely got her, but he was in the minority. Most people actually thought she was a little slow or stupid when she was being funny. It took a sharp mind to catch her humor, and most people simply missed it. Her skepticism of others allowed her to make funny observations that Joe always found amusing. What he couldn't understand was her inability to pick good guys as boyfriends. How could she see the character of others so quickly and easily to be able to make such accurate comical comments while being so incompetent at sizing up her love interests? The answer to that question eluded Joe.

More than anything, Rachel wanted someone like her dad to come sweep her away and take care of her. She had accepted Christ into her life when she was young, and though she had drifted away, she knew she belonged to the Lord. She often wondered why his love had not been enough for her though. Why had she rushed into unhealthy relationships with imperfect guys? Her failures with the opposite sex had filled her mind with guilt and doubt that she would ever get it right. She never realized that her inability to forgive herself for what she had done was creating a barrier between her and God. If she would have asked him for forgiveness and believed in his authority to forgive and forget sins, she would have been forgiven, and the condemnation she was feeling would have gone away. Instead, she unwittingly allowed the evil one to use her mistakes against her in convincing her that she was a failure.

It was Rachel's looks that had always gotten her attention from guys. With Sam though, she could sense that her looks weren't all that mattered. Not once did she notice him looking at her body or anyone else's either. She really liked feeling like who she was inside actually mattered for a change. She was fed up with herself for her foolish relationships, and for the first time in her life, she felt that she was ready for a relationship built on more than looks and feelings. Sam was already making her feel like more than a pretty face with a good body. She could tell that he wasn't at all like the two previous loves of her life. Maybe she was finally getting it right?

CHAPTER 4

Sam was so excited to be headed to Rachel's apartment that he sent Joe a text telling him he was on his way to get her. When Joe responded that Rachel had already told him he was on the way, Sam was thrilled. *She must be pretty excited if she sent Joe a message about me coming to get her,* he reasoned.

How could things feel so right with this girl so quickly? He had been questioning his true motives the more he thought about her beauty. The fact that his infatuation with her had kept him up most of the night kind of scared him. He had never felt so overpowered by his interest in anyone. Since their first meeting, he had thought of nothing else.

Then another text came in from Joe. "I hope you two will raise my baby like it's yours?" Sam couldn't help but smile. Joe could push things too far sometimes, but you couldn't help but smile when he did. In spite of his often off-color sense of humor, his heart for others overshadowed everything else. During their date, Rachel had gone on and on about how great a friend and protector Joe had always been for her. The fact that they both agreed that Joe was a great friend gave them a point of commonality.

"We will love him even if he's a retard like his father." Sam typed back. He could hardly believe he had just sent that, but he knew Joe would think it was funny.

"If he is, I guess we'll know for sure that it's not mine. I've got to put my phone away and start getting ready for the game. We are going out after the game. Go get Rachel!" That was just like

Joe to set something up that no one could say no to. They would have no choice but to go out with him after the game.

Rachel's beauty kept going through Sam's head. He had to dig deeper to answer his questions about the strong feelings he was having for her. What bothered him the most was that everything seemed so right about her. It all felt right to him. Since he had first laid eyes on her, he had almost been in a trance. Everything she said was funny to him. Her smile and deep blue eyes had been so inviting that she didn't even have to speak to impress Sam. Her quite and soft-spoken personality was a perfect complement to Sam's outgoing style. It was as if she was an angel from God.

Rachel was standing on her third-floor balcony with Heather when Sam pulled into the apartment complex. "There he is," she told Heather. "Are you sure you don't want to ride over to the game with us?" She regretted not asking Sam if Heather could come with them to the game. She hadn't even thought about it until she started getting ready for the game. She and Rachel had never been to a game without the other.

"I'll meet you there. If he asks me to come with you guys, you'll know how nice he really is. If he doesn't ask, I'll just meet you guys there. Don't ask him. Let's see what he does." Heather was very skeptical of all men. She grew up in a house with three brothers, so she knew what most guys were really all about. Unfortunately, she, like Rachel, had a major attraction to good-looking popular guys.

The biggest difference between Heather and Rachel was that Heather had dated a lot more guys. She had been intimate with five different guys and had even had an abortion that even Rachel didn't know about. The other big difference was her personality. Heather was very strong willed and confrontational. So much so that she often made Rachel uncomfortable.

As Sam jogged up the three flights of stairs, he noticed the two girls leaning over the balcony and was sure he heard them giggle a bit. Though he knew Rachel had a roommate, he had never met or even seen her. Rachel had told him that they were best friends, but that was all he knew at this point. Before he reached the door, he realized that Rachel's roommate would be left alone if he took Rachel to the game. He quickly decided that they likely went to games together and was sure inviting her to join them was the right thing to do. Perhaps, she was the girl he had seen Rachel with at the game he remembered seeing Rachel at before they had met. He remembered wondering what it would be like to be Joe when he had seen them talking to him at that game. From what he remembered, the girl with Rachel that night had been a knockout as well.

The last flight of stairs ended, and he turned to head to Rachel's door when he noticed she had come out to meet him. Though he had just seen her the night before, it felt as if it had been ages since they had been together. Everything inside of him wanted to hold her, but he knew it was too soon and that he had no business touching her. This was trouble, and he knew it. It pained him that it seemed wrong to rush into her arms. He prayed that she was good for him because he was sure that he had already fallen hard for her.

"Sorry about the stairs, Sam. At least we don't have to hear anyone above us up here. I'm so glad you're finally here." She let the door close behind her as she came toward him. His heart seemed to speed up as she approached in all of her perfection. In the seconds that it took for her to get to him, his mind recorded her every move and analyzed all of her facial expression. Everything told him she was just as happy to see him as he was to see her, and he was very thankful for that.

She was on him before he could even pretend to resist. Since she had initiated it, the embrace didn't feel out of place at all to him. What was a bit surprising was the tenderness and length of the hug. It felt like she already had deep feelings for him, and he absolutely loved it. As he held her tightly to his body, he took in her smell, which he promised himself he would never forget. It was a mix of her laundry detergent, perfume, and just enough of what he knew was simply her scent. His heart was filled with a hopeful joy he had never felt before, and all he could think about was how perfect she was and how great they were going to be together.

"I'm so glad to be back with you, Rachel. You are all I have thought about since I dropped you off last night." He wasn't the type to hold back his feelings, and he never worried much about exposing himself to anyone. This time was no different.

When they finally broke from the hug, Rachel backed up about half a step as they pulled apart. They were now holding hands at arm's length and staring into each other's eyes without speaking. Both of them were feeling things neither had ever felt, and their smiles were unforced.

After what felt like a few minutes but was only a few seconds, Rachel spoke, "You've got to meet my roommate Heather. Please come in for a minute." She turned and let go of one of his hands while tightening the grip on his other hand to pull him toward the door and into the apartment.

Heather was sitting on the couch, fully dressed to go to the game. He could tell she was planning on going to the game by her ball cap and team jersey. Heather stood as soon as they entered the apartment. Sam couldn't help but notice what a knockout she was. She had blonde hair and the body of the captain of the cheerleading team. Though Rachel was tall, Heather had to be at least two inches taller. He could tell she was used to guys looking at her body, so he did his very best to maintain eye contact with her. *Do not look at that*, he told himself.

Rachel pulled him close to her side and put her arm around him almost as if she were trying to protect him from Heather. "This is my best friend and roommate Heather."

"Hello, Heather," he had to pull away from Rachel to offer his hand.

"Hi, Sam. So you're the guy she won't stop talking about." She reached for his hand and gave him a limp-wristed shake as if she was annoyed at being asked to shake hands.

Sam immediately saw the differences between Rachel and Heather. Heather was a strong person with a confrontational personality. He could see that she was used to guys checking her out and decided no one could misread her flirtatious nature. Rachel was quite the opposite, as it seemed she would rather not be noticed. She was quiet and avoided attention, while he was guessing that Heather needed to be seen and appreciated. Though he could tell Rachel had a great body, although it was nowhere near as curvy as Heather's, she did nothing to draw attention to her figure. His early impression of Rachel was that she dressed very conservatively as to not draw attention to herself; he really liked that about her. Heather, on the other hand, did nothing to hide her figure. Even in the jersey she was wearing, Heather found a way to show off her figure by tying a knot in the shirt to draw it tightly to her frame. She had also chosen very short shorts to highlight her finely toned tan legs. Sam would take Rachel over Heather any day; it was no contest.

"She's all I've been talking about lately as well." He looked over his left shoulder to see Rachel smiling up at him. Her eyes spoke volumes. She clearly loved hearing him admit that she was always on his mind. Sam could sense that she knew he would never hurt her and that she would always be safe with him. His response had been in defense as it felt as if Heather was disapproving of Rachel's affection for him. His early opinion of Heather was that she was the type of jealous person that would put down a friend if it felt like that friend was happier than she was. *Why would Rachel have a friend like Heather?* he wondered.

"I hope you two love birds have a good time."

Sam could sense the sarcasm in her voice, and he knew exactly what she was doing. Her flirtatious style was repulsive to him, and her lack of joy over her best friend's newfound happiness made him doubt that she could be a very good friend for Rachel.

"Is there any way we could convince you to come with us to the game?" He knew it was the right thing to do whether he liked her or not. She was obviously a big part of Rachel's life.

A smile came to Heather's face. "I guess I could go with you guys. Let's get going so we can get good seats." Sam noticed the smile and began to wonder if she had only been testing him? Maybe she really wasn't so bad? Then he noticed her wink at Rachel. They were definitely testing him he decided.

Rachel pulled him in for another hug. This time, she really gave him a squeeze while she laid her head up against his neck and shoulder. Since it was right after Heather's wink, he assumed he must have passed the test.

All of the hug initiation was out of character for Rachel. Usually, she waited for the guy to make all of the moves. Things were different with Sam though, and she knew it. She had never felt this comfortable with anyone, especially not this soon. She could tell how much he liked her, but knowing what she knew about him, she knew he wasn't after her looks, and that helped make her feel safe. For the first time in her life, she was attracted to someone's character above all else. She liked his looks as well, but she was aware that he had been getting better and better looking to her every minute she was with him.

Rachel was feeling like she was in control over how much touching went on. Sam was so much the gentleman that she could tell that he would never press her to do anything she didn't want to do. From what Joe had told her, she believed that Sam was very likely a virgin. She absolutely loved that about him but regretted that she could not be that for him. Surely he knew about her mistakes, but his interest in her showed he was okay with it.

CHAPTER 5

Joe had pitched the game of his life in his previous start. It had been a complete game shutout, and he had only given up two hits with no walks. His prospects for being drafted early in the major league draft were bumped up another notch with the outing. Actually, every outing had been a boost to his draft status. Though he had been drafted late in the major league draft out of high school, the signing bonus wasn't much, and the money wouldn't have been there. He chose to go to a division-one school near home, which made him ineligible for the draft until the end of his junior year. Though ideally, he would play his senior year before entering the draft, he had done so well over the last two years that he was getting advice from everyone to consider going pro now rather than later. His last few outings had been so good that he was now being advised that he could only hurt his prospects by playing another year.

Joe had grown about two inches in college. He was now six foot three inches tall. Additionally, his high school velocity of 82 mph had improved into the low nineties. He had also improved his off-speed pitches and was now far wiser about what he threw to hitters. Simply put, he had improved everything considerably since high school. Now with the draft only weeks away, his performances seemed to get better and better with each start. He was now sporting a 2.08 ERA over his junior season. His talent was good enough to get him selected in the early rounds; the only questions were how high would he go, and how much would he be offered?

Though he was excited about his prospects of playing in the majors, deep inside, he really wanted to finish his senior year of college. After all, he was actually on pace to graduate with his engineering degree along with Sam the next fall. Though he didn't have Sam's GPA, he was expecting to earn his bachelors of science in electrical engineering right on schedule. School had been a struggle for him, but he was very proud that he had stuck with it and was on track to graduate. Sam had been a huge help to him over the past couple of years, and his admiration for Sam had brought him back to the realization that he too was a Christian. He didn't live like it, but he always knew in his heart that he belonged to Christ, and he was always aware when he was sinning.

Joe was beginning to seriously examine how he was living his life. He saw the way Sam lived his life as an example of how he should be living. After all, he had meant it when he accepted Christ into his life as a junior high student. He had given his life to the Lord and was positive that he believed that he was a Christian. Unfortunately, he had put his Christian life on hold and had been living for his own pleasure for several years now. Lately though, he was feeling a heavy pull to return to Christ. It was really weighing him down, and he was beginning to realize there was no way to escape it. God is everywhere all the time.

From the time that Joe and Sam started to have classes together, Joe saw Sam as being true to himself and to God. What he saw in Sam was something he had once committed to being. In all the time he had known Sam, he had never seen Sam lose focus. Sam was focused on his goals, but even more so on the preservation of his character. Though Sam had only gone out with Joe a few times outside of all of their study time together, he had never seen Sam drink, talk about girls, or even be unkind to anyone. It was Sam's life, not what he said, that was stirring something inside of Joe.

Joe's girlfriend, Ally, was all about fun. She had grown up outside of the church, and actually had told Joe that she didn't believe in God. He always had fun with her, and they were intimate several times a week. Her body was unbelievable, and Joe knew that it was her looks, along with her party nature, that kept him with her. They never really talked about anything the way he did with Rachel.

In Joe's discussions with Sam, he began to realize that he should be with someone he was friends with like he was with Rachel. Seeing Sam avoid the things he was engulfed in made him begin to realize that he was doing life wrong. He had never really dated anyone who he respected the way he respected Rachel. Physical attraction had always been his number-one criterion for a girlfriend, with fun being the second. Someone he respected or at least someone he would consider a friend had been way down the list.

For some reason, Joe was growing a conscience. He was becoming convicted that he needed to change the way he was doing life. The more he thought about it and began to accept that he was choosing pleasure over God's ways, he began to feel sick about his relationship with Ally. Lately, he was actually beginning to feel depressed, which was something his personality had not ever exposed him to previously. His nature had always been to fight and stay positive, but that was changing. He was now beginning to lose that battle, and he wasn't able to ignore his conscience anymore.

Things had been going great with Ally up until the point when he had decided to introduce Rachel to Sam. Since the day of that introduction, only a couple of days ago, Joe was regretting his relationship with Ally so deeply that it was affecting his demeanor. Several of his friends had even asked him if something was wrong. Joe had not been able to give them a good answer, but he knew exactly what it was that was eating at him.

Joe and Ally partied like crazy, but they really weren't friends. Their relationship reminded him of Kevin and Rachel's relationship. Though he didn't run around on Ally like Kevin had done behind Rachel's back, everything else was about the same. She was attractive, and he was only having a good time with her with no intentions of anything permanent. Though he hated seeing Kevin do the same thing to Rachel, he was definitely in the same boat with Ally. The difference was that Ally was doing it right back to him, while Rachel was being used.

Joe's thoughts had gone to the emptiness of his own dating life during the introduction meeting he had set up for Sam and Rachel. As he sat in the booth alongside Ally, with the love connection he was trying to orchestrate between Rachel and Sam across from them, all he could think about was how great it would be to be sitting there with someone he could truly love. Sitting there thinking about how pure Sam and Rachel's relationship could be, Joe began to think about his own situation. Then it dawned on him that though he had been very judgmental of Rachel's choices of boyfriends, he, in fact, was using the same criterion she used to select her boyfriends to select his girlfriends. Why was Rachel's choice of boyfriends wrong, while his girlfriend choices, which were based on the same things, not wrong? It defied logic, and Joe felt like he had been hit with a truth hammer as it sunk in.

Though he never admitted it to anyone, Joe had always wanted to be with Heather. It was her who had dumped him when they were in junior high, not the other way around. She had dumped him for an older kid when they were about to go into high school. They managed to remain close friends after the breakup as Rachel and Heather were always together, and Joe was Rachel's closest relative and protector. Joe's feelings for Heather never subsided. Actually, deep down, she had always been the one for him. Though he never asked her out again, he always thought about her and knew that one day, they would be together. She was the love of his youth, and in spite of how hard he had tired, no one had ever replaced her in his heart. All of the girls in his life had been temporary as he had always held out hope that one day, Heather would return to him.

Whenever they were together, Joe imagined that he and Heather would eventually be together. Although he thought about her good looks, it was who she was and his history with her that he really loved about her. The previous night when Sam had mentioned that he wished Rachel wasn't so beautiful so he would know that his attraction to her wasn't just physical, he couldn't help but answer the question in his head about his feelings for Heather as he knew his attraction to Heather was far more than physical. Heather was the standard by which all others had been measured. Even if they were beautiful, they would never be his precious Heather.

Joe was pretty sure Rachel knew how he felt about Heather though. She always seemed to know what he was thinking. For years now, Joe and Heather did nothing but argue and get on each other's nerves. Heather always complained about Joe, but they both went out of their way to be at the same place at the same time. Rachel was always saying things about how they acted like a married couple, and she always teased them about their obvious attraction.

Now that Joe was opening his eyes to what he really wanted in a relationship, all he could think about was Heather. He knew that his dreams of marrying her were still there, but he felt really uncomfortable thinking about telling her how he felt. She was so strong and overbearing that he almost feared that she may reject him again like she had in junior high. He didn't think it was likely though as he was pretty sure she had the same feelings for him; he just couldn't prove it.

Even though Heather was always tough on him, on many occasions, he had noticed her protecting his image in public and going out of her way to make sure he had a ride home or that he was feeling okay. She had been there for him after breakups as he had been for her. If he had a bad game or was down, she was always there for him. He treated her the same way, and though he was far closer to Rachel, Heather was his destiny. She had always been the wife of his dreams.

The fact that he had become such a superstar in baseball and that he had such a bright future led him to believe that she may value him for that more than for the right reasons. He had seen who she had dated over the years, and he knew she chose boyfriends based on looks and their stuff. There was no way he wanted her to want him for anything other than who he was. If he did reveal his true feelings for her and she responded positively, how could he know it was him and not his potential she was after? How could he be sure that he was opening his heart to someone who was able to open hers for him? He wasn't sure how he would do it, but he was sure that he had to try.

The more he thought about it, he began to reason with himself that she couldn't possibly love him for the wrong reasons. They had known each other for too long for that. She knew who he was down deep, just like he knew who she was down deep. If she admitted to loving him the way he had always loved her, it would be real and permanent. He decided it would also be very intense.

Almost immediately after the setup date between Rachel and Sam, Joe decided he had to break up with Ally and stop wasting his time. He hoped he could do it without hurting her in any way, but he feared it would be very difficult for her to understand. They had been together for most of the school year, so he did have some fairly deep feelings for her. He didn't want to hurt her at all, but he knew he didn't want to waste any more of his life with someone that wasn't ever going to be his wife.

Once Ally was out of his life, he would figure out a way to talk to Heather. She was the one, and he had always known it. He had loved her since they were little kids. It had taken Sam and Rachel's connection to show him what he needed to do. He wanted to be in a relationship like the one he was sure Sam and Rachel were headed for. Heather was definitely his Rachel, and he was pretty sure he was her Sam. He couldn't wait to start his life with her. If she were to reject him, he was sure it would be devastating.

CHAPTER 6

The threesome arrived at the ballpark in time to get good seats down by the home team dugout. Joe spotted them right away and gave them a wave on his way into the dugout. He was happy to see the three of them together and couldn't help but think about his impending revelation of his true feelings for Heather. Seeing her actually made him feel nervous and anxious. As usual, she was wearing the jersey he had given her. It was one of his, and he had even signed it for her. Seeing her in it confirmed in his mind that she was already his. His heart was hers, and her stare and smile reassured him that her heart belonged to him as well. *Wow, she's so beautiful*, he thought. *Why have I waited so long?*

From the first pitch, it was easy to see that Joe was on again. Inning after inning, he mowed them down. After each inning, he would smile and wave at his loved ones. They all appreciated the acknowledgement, especially Heather. *Had she always looked at me like this?* he wondered. *How could I have been so blind to this?*

Sam quickly realized that Heather knew about half the crowed, while Rachel never broke her attention from him to acknowledge anyone. Being with her in public was almost as if they were at home, watching the game alone, and he loved it that way. Having all of her attention helped him feel sure that she was actually into him. He was still struggling a bit with her beauty. Not just his worry about his attraction to her being primarily physical but also that she was too good looking to be seriously interested in him. He kept thinking that she could have anyone she wanted. *Why me? How can she be attracted to me? She's a ten, and I'm about a seven or maybe even a six. What if she wakes up and realizes that?*

In spite of Sam's concerns, Rachel clung to him throughout the game. She held his hand the entire time they were seated. They celebrated together and even hugged a few times after big plays. Rachel had never felt so natural with anyone. Sam just felt so easy to trust. It was something she wasn't used to. Her boyfriends had always been confident, attractive guys who other girls wanted to be with. Sam just wasn't that type of guy. He somehow seemed above all of that. He wasn't' looking around at other girls or hoping to be noticed; he was just happy to be there with her, and she could tell. She was pretty sure he noticed no one else. It was a feeling that put her at ease. She was sure he would never hurt her.

Sam was amazed that someone as beautiful as Rachel could be this into him. He had never taken someone this good looking on a date or even imagined that he could. He had certainly never held hands with or hugged anyone like her. He couldn't help but notice the other guys checking her and Heather out though. It made him feel some pride that he quickly dismissed. There was also some jealousy there, which he didn't like at all. Jealousy wasn't a feeling Sam dealt with often. Just feeling the smallest amount made him realize how dangerous an emotion jealousy could become for him. Being around Rachel would surely bring some new emotions into his life. Just the thought of that struggle triggered a short prayer for help with his emotions.

The more time Sam spent around Heather, the more he began to see who she really was. She was strong and a little pushy, but he no longer had any doubt that she cared for Rachel. Whether she was jealous of Rachel's newfound happiness or not, he hadn't yet decided. What he knew for sure was that Heather wasn't at all who he had initially feared that she was. If anything, she was guilty of caring enough about her friend to put him through the test for Rachel's own good. He admired her for that.

At one point during the game, Kevin actually waived at the three of them. He looked perfectly happy as if he either didn't know that Sam and Rachel were on a date or as if he did know and was fine with it, and he was even happy for her. As soon as Kevin disappeared into the dugout, Heather said, "What a jerk." Rachel shyly looked up at Sam with a look of embarrassment in her eyes and then quickly looked down. He could tell that she was uncomfortable, so he reached over and gave her a big squeeze, which made her smile and brought her eyes right back to his. He noticed a single tear, but her smile told him she was okay.

"That is over, Sam. It's you and me now," she whispered in his direction. Sam felt an immediate rush go through his body and couldn't help but smile. Hearing her say "it's you and me now" was a surprise. It made him feel like he was in some sort of fairy tale. *How could this be real?* he wondered.

After the Kevin incident, Sam's mind began to run wild. What if Joe expects them to hang out with Kevin after the game. Could he handle that? Could Rachel handle that? Though he had no fear of any sort of an altercation with Kevin, in spite of the fact that he was quite sure Kevin would give him a beating if something did go down, his real concern was for Rachel. He could tell she had been deeply affected by Kevin's little wave and was sure she would not want him in any room with them. Surely Joe wouldn't put them in that situation.

Rachel's mind was racing even faster than Sam's. She too was afraid that Joe would want to hang out with Kevin and that whole gang. She didn't want Kevin around at all. Heather was right; he was a jerk. She wished it wasn't so hard for her to move on, but it was. Why did she still have such strong feelings? *It was because we had been intimate*, she finally decided. Never had she felt so convicted of doing something wrong as she did at that moment sitting next to the nicest, smartest, and possibly the most Christlike guy she had ever dated. The condemnation she was feeling was overwhelming, and though she fought to move on, it continued to affect her so much that she was sure Sam would notice.

Not that Sam was making her feel the way she was feeling as she was actually amazed at how he had gone out of his way to make sure she didn't feel like that. The condemnation was coming from within. Though she had known it was wrong to have a sexual relationship outside of marriage, it had never occurred to her that it would become such a barrier when she met the right guy. The regret she was feeling was something new to her. It suddenly felt to her that she didn't deserve someone like Sam.

Sam sensed her struggle and knew there was nothing to be said. When he had hugged her right after Kevin's wave, he actually felt her tremble a bit. The hug had been the proper response to her body language as he had been moved to comfort her, knowing that she would understand that he was there for her. It was almost as if they were communicating at a very deep level without saying a word. His heart was going out to her, and he hoped she could feel his acceptance.

Thankfully, Rachel did feel his forgiving heart in his touch and in his facial expression when he had put his arm around her and in their ensuing eye contact after the hug. The kindness in his eyes had taken off some of the pressure, but her conscience just wouldn't let it go. She felt so dirty, knowing that Sam knew what she had done with Kevin. She hated herself for it. The longer she sat there, even though they had connected through the hug, the more her failure to keep herself pure got to her. Soon, she wasn't even watching the game, and Sam could tell he needed to do something.

Sensing her pain, he leaned in and said, "I'm going to go get a drink. Would you like to come with me?" He assumed she would come if she wanted to talk to him away from Heather and the crowd. If not, he would give her a chance to talk to her best friend by leaving them alone. Rachel didn't answer but nodded yes instead. When he noticed that she was on the edge of tearing up, he took her by the hand and stood up. He needed to get her alone so he could assure her that everything was going to be okay, and he didn't want her to be uncomfortable due to her emotional state.

His concern for her was intense and filled with urgency. He felt a bit of an adrenalin surge as he instinctively began to protect her.

"Heather, we are going to get a drink. Do you want anything?" Sam spoke up as there was no way Rachel was ready to speak. "Sure, could you please get me a bottle of water?" Heather knew what was going on, and Sam could tell that she did. He was impressed that she was allowing him to talk with Rachel alone rather than trying to tag along or even to try to take over the situation. Heather really wasn't at all who he had initially thought she was. He was very thankful for that.

Rachel slowed the pace when they got to the exit ramp as if she wanted him to close the gap between them. In response, he put his hands on her shoulders and led her past the crowd all the way to the fence that surrounded the ballpark. Once they were alone, he relaxed his grip, and she turned to face him. Her face began to quiver, and the tears began to flow.

"Hey, everything is okay," he told her as he pulled her into his chest. He could feel her deep sobs in every breath she took, and his heart was going out to her. He began to pray out loud, just loud enough for her to hear. "Heavenly Father in the name of Jesus, please hear our prayer. We pray for your forgiveness and for freedom from the grip of our sins, Lord. We know you love us, and we praise you for bringing us to each other. You are an awesome God, and we are in awe of your grace. Take this condemnation from Rachel, Lord. Give her peace, Father." He hadn't planned to pray, but it definitely was what was needed.

Hearing Sam pray was so powerful to Rachel that she completely crumbled. She was feeling so dirty and so condemned from her sinful choices that she just couldn't bear it. Now that it was right in front of her face, she had to deal with it. She wanted to be forgiven. She was truly sorry, and she hated the sinful life she had chosen. She wanted to cry out for help. Through her sobbing, she managed to say, "Can you ask him to forgive me? Can you tell him I love him and that I'm sorry that I messed up? Will he still save me?"

"Heavenly Father, we know that you know our hearts, Lord. Before we ask, you know our needs. We are all sinners, but you tell us that you will forgive us our sins if we trust in your son Jesus for our salvation, turn from our sin, and choose your ways, Lord. Jesus paid the price for our sin, and we need this type of forgiveness now, Lord. We need you to heal us and forgive us, Father. It's in Jesus name we ask these things. Amen." It felt so good to be praying for her to his heavenly Father that he too began to cry, though he was happy inside. He had never felt God's presence more than he was right then. He could tell that Rachel felt it too.

"Rachel, you will be saved if you believe in your heart that Jesus has paid the price for your sins. The Bible tells us that Jesus is our savior as he lived a perfect sinless life and then gave that life to pay the penalty of our sins. All we must do is accept his payment by confessing with our mouth that he is Lord and believing it in our hearts. If you have already done this, you will be saved. Only you and God know if you did it in earnest. Just because you have fallen back from his standards does not mean you have lost your salvation. However, if you never really believed in your heart, you will need to do that for real now. The fact that you are so convicted of your sin leads me to believe you are in fact saved, but it doesn't matter what I think. What do you think?"

After almost five minutes in each other's arms, Rachel started praying, "Thank you, Lord, for bringing me Sam. He is a gift straight from heaven. Please forgive me, and take me back, Lord. I want to be yours, and I want to be done with this evil world. Please make me pure for you and for Sam. I believe you died for my sins, and I want you to be the Lord of my life. Please save me, Lord." With that, her tears of sorrow and pain turned to tears of joy. The feelings of failure and that she was a filthy person left her, and she became full of hope and joy. She knew it was God's forgiveness, and it would be a feeling she would never forget. It was a far more meaningful encounter that her first confession of faith had been, but she was pretty sure the first had been real as well, and it had all led to this moment.

In only their third face-to-face meeting, Rachel had rededicated herself to Christ and had decided that Sam was a gift
from God. She decided right then that he was the one, and she
began to pray that he would want her the way she wanted him.
Something was telling her he would. Had he not, she would have
been completely lost.

Sam felt the same way that Rachel did about their future. She
was it for him. This would be his wife, whatever that took. He
would treat her the way his father treated his mother, the way
God told all men to love their wives. It had to be her.

The two exchanged a very light kiss and a knowing hug before
heading to the snack bar to pick up Heather's water. They had
been gone for quite a while now, and they knew the game would
be ending soon. The kiss was their first, but it was the first of many.

CHAPTER 7

When Sam and Rachel finally returned to their seats, the game was in the final inning. When it was through, Joe had won in another, dominating nine-inning performance, 2-1.

Upon their return, Heather could tell that something was different with Rachel. She seemed to have a glow about her, and she was holding onto Sam like he was a life preserver. Rachel seemed full of joy and almost bubbly after leaving in a fragile state. That simply wasn't who she normally was. Something had definitely happened between them; she was sure of it.

When the game ended and Sam excused himself to go to the bathroom, Heather finally got her chance to corner Rachel.

"Okay, what happened between you two out there? It feels like you guys have been together for years now. When's the wedding?" It was true; they were acting as if they had been together for a very long time. They leaned all over each other, stared into each other's eyes, and seemed to be alone even in the crowed. When Joe's girlfriend, Ally, had come by in the middle of the ninth inning to say hello, she even commented that they looked like a happy couple already. When confronted about it, they just smiled at each other and offered no explanation.

"I recommitted myself to Christ, and I'm in love with Sam like you wouldn't believe. It's very serious. He's amazing." Rachel was so happy and knew it was so right that she just said it. Her way had always been direct, and being a person of so little words, her best friend expected nothing different from her now. Rachel wasn't even worried what Heather might think. She knew she was finally doing dating right, and she didn't care what Heather had to say about it, though she did hope she would be happy for her.

"Are you kidding me? You haven't even been to church in years, and you hardly even know this guy." Rachel had first accepted Christ into her life on the same day Heather and Joe had. The three of them were actually baptized together. Since then, they had all attended church with their families intermittently until they had all left home for college. Since they had been in college, the only time they were ever in church was when their parents had forced them to go for a function of some kind or a holiday. None of them had been accountable to their faith, though they had all struggled with feelings of failure and helplessness due to their sin. Each had a different level of struggle associated with their sin, but all three were being convicted by the Holy Spirit. Unfortunately, they had all done the best they could to ignore him.

"We aren't getting married right away, but I'm telling you this is the guy. God brought him to me. I know it. I've never felt this good about anything or anyone. I know I can trust this guy. He would never hurt me. I feel safe and know he will always love me and protect my feelings. I knew it instantly when I met him. I'm not sure why, but the more time I'm with him, the more sure I am. If you care about me, you will trust me on this." Hearing all of that come out of her mouth made her realize how quickly this was all moving and how strange it must sound. *Am I being crazy and jumping the gun on this?* she wondered. *No, I'm right about this guy,* she quickly decided.

"I want to be happy for you, but it may take me some time, Rachel. I can tell he's a good guy too, but I need more time to accept this. What about all of this recommitment to Christ stuff?" Heather and Rachel were both believers, but they had been living like everyone else for so long that no one could have possibly discerned what they believed in. Hearing Rachel claim to have returned to Christ was a shock, especially since she knew about everything Rachel had done that would surely be considered sin. However, she too had accepted Christ and truly believed, and yet, just like Rachel, she had been living like everyone else. She too felt like she was failing God, and she hated who she had become much the same way Rachel did.

"Sam prayed for me when we snuck out earlier, and I actually felt the Lord forgive me. I bet I could even be around Kevin without feeling bad anymore. I've always believed that God loved me, but I could actually feel it when Sam and I prayed together. Believe me, Heather, my life changed less than an hour ago. Don't you remember when we all accepted Christ that summer? We were in eighth grade, and we all took a pledge to not have sex until we were married. We all failed, but God will forgive us if we ask him to. He alone can forgive our sin and change our lives. He can set us free. We used to all believe that. I know it's true now because I'm feeling a relief from my sin that I have never felt before. I'm feeling joy that I haven't felt in years, and I'm really excited about Sam and getting closer to God." She hoped Heather would also want to return to the Lord. Confronting her like this was way out of character for Rachel. It was usually Heather who stood up to her and everyone else for that matter.

To Rachel's surprise, Heather began to tear up. "I know," she said as she tried to hide her tears. "I feel like I'm lost and that I'll never be happy. I think I need God too. Nothing else has worked."

Sam walked up behind Heather while she was still trying to pull herself together. "Is everything okay?" he asked.

"Can you pray for me, Sam?" Heather asked. Rachel couldn't believe it. This was becoming the happiest and strangest day of her life. Her salvation was now set, and she could feel God's forgiveness relieving the condemnation she had been struggling with for so long. Now her best friend was asking Sam to pray for her too!

The stands had nearly cleared out at this point, so Sam asked if they were comfortable sitting down right where they were to pray. They all agreed, and Sam sat down next to Heather who was in the middle seat. "Heather, what is it you need prayer for? Do you want to make Jesus, Lord of your life?" He decided to make it easy for her by suggesting she pray to accept Christ into her life.

"I accepted Christ when I was young just like Rachel, and Joe did. None of us have kept our end of the deal though. I want to recommit my life like Rachel just told me you helped her do. I don't want to live like I've been living anymore." She was beginning to break down now and didn't even seem to care that they were in public.

"I've done some things I regret, and I know I've been doing things my own way and seeking pleasure and happiness in the wrong places. I feel like I've failed God. I've been with five different men/boys, and I hate myself for it. I even had an abortion last year." She was sobbing loudly now. It was the type of scene that would usually make Rachel very uncomfortable. On this occasion, none of them cared who was looking, though a few people were.

Rachel was stunned to hear Heather admit to having had an abortion. She felt really sorry for her as she could see the pain it had caused her, but felt a little betrayal over not being told previously. Rachel believed terminating a baby's life at any point after conception was wrong, and she and Heather had even spoken about this belief. Heather had always agreed with her, which made this confession even more difficult to hear. *How had she pulled that off without me knowing?* Rachel wondered. Thinking about it made Rachel feel horrible for what Heather must have been going through. *Why hadn't she told me?* she wondered.

Joe came back out onto the field to see if they were still there to find the three of them in a huddle in the stands where they had been sitting. His intent was to let them know he would get a quick shower before the four of them would go get a late dinner. He had decided to ditch Ally so he could be alone with them.

Ally had seemed fine with it, and Joe knew just where to find her if he needed to. She would be at Kevin's place with everyone else.

Seeing the way they were huddled up caught him by surprise. He immediately recognized that they were praying. It looked to him like they were praying for Heather since she was in the middle of their huddle. Without even thinking, he ran and quickly scaled the fence into the stands. In seconds, he was in the seat in front of Heather on his knees.

The group was startled at first until they realized it was Joe. "Sorry, guys. It looked like you guys were praying for Heather. I wanted in on it. Is everything okay, Heather?" His concern for her was impossible to hide.

Heather was touched to see Joe's obvious affection for her, and it showed. She acted on impulse and reached out for him so he leaned over the seat to embrace her. Being invited in to embrace her was something Joe had been dreaming about for longer than he could remember. She was more than someone he was attracted to; she was the one he loved. He had finally come to grips with it and was ready to confess it all to her. The emotions flowing through him as she let go and leaned away from him and back into her seat so she could speak to the group were overwhelming. *How did I ignore my feelings and the truth for so long?*

"I'm rededicating my life to Christ like Rachel just did." Tears were all over her face, and she truly looked broken. Joe wanted to comfort her with everything he had but understood she needed the prayer she was about to get more than his hug.

"That is great news! I thought someone had hurt you. I was ready to throw down." His fear for her well-being was gone, but he was now full of another emotion. *Is this love I'm feeling?* He was consumed with feelings for her now, and all he could think about was how precious she was. Something was telling him her rededication was a necessary step for their future together.

Joe was also very excited to hear that Rachel had already recommitted her life to Christ. He figured Sam would get them all there, but this was ridiculously quick and certainly exceeded his expectations.

As he knelt there smiling ear to ear, he continued, "Rachel, I'm so happy for you. This is great news. Now Heather too. This is great!"

"You are more than welcome to join us, Joe," Sam calmly said.

"I've been thinking a lot about this too," Joe admitted. "I know I want to rededicate my life to Christ. I've been a piece of trash morally for years now, and it's been really bothering me. My two girls here and I all made a commitment to Christ once upon a time. We accepted his free gift of salvation and his forgiveness of our sins, and then we simply walked away and ignored him.

"Maybe we were too young to realize we were living in a world like this, but we are now all adults, and I know we are all aware that we are doing life the wrong way. I've done too many things I regret to list right now, but I do want to admit to drinking, doing drugs a couple of times, lying and cheating, and too much sexual immorality to admit. I wish I hadn't done any of it, and I don't want to live that way anymore. I know I can't stop being who I've become on my own. I'll need help from God and accountability to my three closest friends. I'll also need to break up with Ally to do this. One of my biggest reasons for doing this now is that I've decided that I need to be a rededicated Christian before I ask Heather to be my girlfriend." He was now looking Heather right in the eyes with a huge smile stretching out his face.

Heather's face was blank in unbelief. "Are you screwing around, Joe?" she finally asked.

"Absolutely not. I've had a crush on you all of my life. When you left me in junior high, it crushed me. I've been paralyzed ever since, thinking that you may someday hurt me like that again if I ever made a move on you. I always think about you, and I compare every girl I date to you. You are my dream girl, Heather, and you always have been. I want to be your boyfriend more than I want to play pro baseball. I've even considered passing on the draft just so I can be around you for another year." *Man, that felt great to say.*

He was tired of holding back his true feelings for her. Sure, she could reject him again, and that would surely destroy him again. However, the upside was too important for him to not go for it. He needed her. She was the one, and he had always known it. He was sure that she was the one he wanted to spend his life with, and he was tired of pretending otherwise. He decided it had all been ego. He feared her rejection too much, but that was over now.

"I accept. Let's go on a date tonight." The stone face was gone, and her strength appeared to be back. "You are an idiot for not telling me how you felt. I dumped you when we were little kids. As soon as Jim and I broke up, I knew I had messed up. I've been in love with you forever. You realize we cannot even have sex if we are serious about rededicating our lives to Christ, right?"

She said it as if maybe they should put off the rededication until after they had a chance to sleep together. To avoid any confusion, she added, "Just so you know, I can't wait to rededicate my life to Christ. If you want me, you will have to do this with me and wait until we are married to sleep with me." She may have gained her composure back externally, but she was absolute mush inside. She couldn't believe this was happening, though it was a dream come true for her.

She always thought about Joe. She admired him, but she feared he had moved on and would never have interest in her romantically ever again. They always seemed to argue, but it had always been obvious to Rachel how the two felt about one another. They always asked about the other, and they would do anything to help the other. All of the complaining was only a façade that Rachel had always seen through.

"I know. Let me have a minute to think it over." He looked up and to the left, and then he continued, "Okay, I guess I can do that. You do realize that we will end up getting married if we go on this date tonight, right?" Sam and Rachel were only bystanders for all of this. They were both enjoying it though. Sam had even reached across Heather's back to take Rachel's hand when Joe had begun spilling his guts. That move won him even more points.

"I do. So you are really asking me to marry you? We will be engaged after tonight if I agree to go on this date?" She knew it was true. Neither of them was joking. You can't know someone as well as they knew each other without knowing you cannot date each other without being deadly serious.

At this point, the two were locked into one another's stare so intensely that they wouldn't have noticed if the place was on fire. It was the most beautiful moment Rachel had ever seen as her two closest friends were finally doing what she had been wishing they would do for longer than she could remember.

"I have no ring, but yes, that is exactly what I am saying. Do you accept?" He knew she was going to say yes at that point, and he was fully enjoying himself.

"You got a deal. As long as you promise to break up with Ally tonight. I can't deal with any drama there." It was true. Heather was direct and to the point. Drama was never her thing, and she had no sympathy for anyone who was looking for attention. If Joe wanted her, he had to be totally free from Ally tonight. She wasn't kidding, and knowing her like he did, Joe knew she meant it.

"Done. She's out, and you're in permanently. Can we get rededicated now so I can get to the showers? After our date, I'll go talk to Ally." Though he didn't look forward to breaking up with Ally, he knew he had to. There was no use in putting it off. It was already over as far as he was concerned.

"I can't believe I'm agreeing to make you an honest man." She was smiling hard now, and she had scooted up in her chair to the point where they were almost touching noses.

Joe reached out and gently drew her in for a sweet little kiss. "You are worth it, Heather," he told her as they separated from their kiss. Then he added, "I love you." None of them had ever seen him cry, but it actually looked like he was about to.

"I love you too you dumb jock." She knew he was no dumb jock, but she had called him that for so long it had become a term of endearment to him.

Then it happened; Joe actually cried. It was the "dumb jock" comment that got him. It was a very happy and heavy moment for all four of them.

Sam led the group in a prayer that brought everyone to tears. Both Joe and Heather joined Rachel in rededication. Before they knew it, twenty minutes had gone by. "I better go get a shower before it's too late. Can you guys wait for me by the gate where I always meet you?"

"We'll be there." Heather boldly proclaimed.

CHAPTER 8

Heather stood alone at the place she and Rachel always met Joe after his games, while Sam and Rachel stood by the car, talking and holding hands. Heather was working through things in her head as she waited. She could hardly wait for her relationship with Joe to leave the friend zone and enter the love-connection zone. The more she thought about the past, the more apparent it was to her how much he had always cared for her. The way he had always criticized her boyfriends should have been a big indicator. No one had ever been good enough for her according to Joe. Now she completely understood why.

While Joe showered, he began to wonder why everything was suddenly so clear to him. Sure, he had known how he really felt about her before tonight, but he had never had the clarity to act on it. Maybe seeing Rachel finally getting it right by dating Sam had opened his eyes? Whatever it was, he wished it would have happened sooner. Before he and Heather had been with other people would have been nice. *Maybe we would have done things physically that we would have later regretted, or perhaps, we would have hurt one another and not ended up together?* None of that would be an issue for them now. The timing may not have been there's, but Joe believed it must have been God's.

Joe also believed God had just forgiven them both for everything they had done outside of his will, but he fully understood that there was no erasing the consequences they were both dealing with as a result of the poor decisions they had made. He wished he had done things God's way so she wouldn't have to wonder how she stacked up to the others.

Since he had gotten such a late start, Joe was the last one to leave the locker room. After a quick trip to the trainer's room to pick up an ice pack, he headed for the gate he always met Rachel and Heather after his games. As was customary for him after a start, he had the trainers strap a big bag of ice to his shoulder. It was huge and looked pretty ridiculous, but it always helped him wake up pain-free.

He had always looked forward to seeing his girls waiting for him after his games, but this time felt very different. He felt like he was in junior high again. He was actually feeling nervous as he knew that Heather was the one person that could really hurt him. He wasn't accustomed to feeling so vulnerable; things were going to be very different now. Still, it was great; actually, it was amazing.

Heather had just brushed off another player that had tried to ask where she was going later when she caught a glimpse of Joe in the distance with his ridiculous ice bulge on his shoulder. The players all knew her through Joe, but none of them had any idea that she was the girl of Joe's dreams. Only Rachel, and now she, knew that.

She almost couldn't wait for him to get to her. "Put a move on it," she hollered at him when he was still quite a ways away.

With that, he broke into a jog. He loved her strong personality and knew that he needed someone like her to keep him in line. He too had a strong personality, but he knew Heather could definitely force him to stay on track. That had always been his problem, staying on track.

When he finally reached the gate, Heather jumped on him. "You are mine now," she screamed out as he snatched her out of the air and dropped his bag all at the same time.

"I know. I'm completely yours now, and you are mine now too, right?" He loved saying it almost as much as he loved hearing her say it.

"Yes, you are an owner!" She was so happy to finally be with Joe.

Then they shared their first real kiss as Heather's feet hit the ground. While they had lip kissed once when they were dating in junior high, and they had exchanged a friendly little kiss about half hour before when Joe was spilling his guts, this kiss was much more passionate. It was everything they both had hoped it would be. It was a kiss from their hearts.

Kissing the one that you have idolized and fantasized about for as long as they had both been doing so was not only relieving; it was also extremely exhilarating. Though it felt strange to be kissing passionately, it also felt right. It felt pure and real, and they were both feeling as if they were finally home.

Joe loved Heather's lips and had imagined kissing them for years. There were so many occasions that he had sat across from her just wondering how it would feel. Now that it was finally happening, it almost didn't feel real. He quickly realized that it wasn't her looks or the feel of her lips that mattered to him; it was her, her very being that mattered. Never had he experienced a kiss like this nor had she.

Heather was not the type to show weakness of any kind. Though she had felt the most terrible condemnation after aborting her baby, she never allowed anyone to see the scars it had caused. She was stubborn and had the ability to hide things from even those closest to her in a way that very few are capable of. Now, kissing her destiny, she knew this would be the one person she wouldn't need to hide anything from. This was real love, and she was kissing it like she had never kissed anyone before.

"Where are the love birds?" Joe asked when the kiss finally ended, and he had returned her to her feet.

"They are waiting for us at the car. Should we ditch them? They probably want to be alone anyway." She just wanted to be with Joe. It was nothing against them.

"Let's go get dinner, and then we can go to your place. We can go into your room to give them some privacy. I promise I won't try anything." He wasn't so sure of that though. Every inch of her was committed to memory. It was who she was that really mattered to him, but it was impossible for him not to think about her physique. She was tall, blonde, curvy, and very sexy. He had dreamed of her for so long that he was already beginning to worry about his recommitment to the Lord. He truly would need God's supernatural help to keep from falling into sin with her.

Secretly, Joe had saved dozens of pictures of her, which he kept hidden. He had pictures of her from a very young age as they had been in each other's company most of their lives. As much as he loved her body, it was her face that was engraved in his mind. Every time they were together, he found himself staring at her face and into those eyes. He had decided that God had given no one a better face than hers. There was nothing he would change about it; it couldn't be any better. Though it was always better in person, he had studied the pictures of her for years. Even his cell phone was full of pictures of her.

"Okay, but we can't have sex. If you try anything, I don't think I will stop you. Once we start, it will be too late. I will tear you apart if we start anything inappropriate. We have got to agree to not let that happen. Both of us have to swear to stop the other." With that, she gave him another very seductive kiss.

"How are we going to do this, especially with you kissing me like that? I want you so badly it feels like I may blackout midkiss. I guess it will have to be a short engagement?" He was absolutely serious. It wasn't like they were Rachel and Sam who had just met one another. They had been close friends all of their lives. Not only that, they were always around each other. There were no surprises. He knew she was the one, and as soon as he made his feelings known to her, she had admitted the same.

"I can't marry you if you are going to wear that stupid ice around all of the time though. You look ridiculous." This was the Heather he loved. She was tough and sometimes even mean. He knew that she would be able to round him out as he was the complete opposite and could never be tough or mean with any-one. He could joke around, but when things got ugly, his instincts were to appease and make light of the situation.

"I'll take it off in the car. Man, you really have this wifelike bickering thing down already." Before she could respond, he gave her another big wet kiss. She took and returned the kiss, but it didn't stop her from punching him.

"By the way, Heather, you may get tired of hearing this, but here it goes anyway. I love you."

"I love you too you big dummy." She couldn't help but call him "dummy." It had become a habit.

CHAPTER 9

The dinner conversation was fast and furious and filled with laughter. No onlooker would have believed the two couples were new couples. Heather and Joe were very physical, while Rachel and Sam were locked into one another with such undivided attention that any onlooker would believe that they were uninterested in anything else.

The conversation around the impending marriage started as a poking joke from Rachel but turned into a very serious discussion. When Joe turned to Heather and asked if she would marry him should he get drafted high enough in the draft to actually forego his senior year, Heather was so flattered she couldn't answer. After a few seconds, she finally got out a head nod, which Joe pumped his fist in the air at. "I love this woman," he proudly and somewhat loudly declared.

Turning to Sam, Joe bluntly asked the most pressing question he was dealing with. "My biggest concern is my desire to go back to the girl's apartment and have amazing mind-blowing sex with Heather. I'm sure that would be a mistake, so I'm not even going to ask if it would be okay. What I do need to know is what can we do, Sam?" Sam was a little put back by the question. It wasn't something he had anticipated being asked in front of the girls. He was surprised to see Heather leaning in for his response though. She showed no offence to what Joe had just said. He could tell she had the very same question in her mind.

At least, Rachel looked embarrassed. "You two have just recommitted yourselves to Christ. I can read you scripture about this, but I think you already know how God views sex outside of marriage. If you two went back to the apartment and went at it, I would suspect there would be consequences of some kind. It could even destroy what could have been a very strong marriage, but I don't know that for sure.

"Once we are his, it is much more difficult for us to sin as we are urged by the Spirit not to do so. If we press on with the sin in defiance, we will feel regret until we repent, change our heart toward the sin so that we hate it as God does, and then we are forgiven by God. Please remember, I'm talking about committed Christians that are allowing God to work in their lives. This type of Christian, which, by the way, is the only real Christian, has an active prayer life, reads the Bible, and wants to please God with his or her choices.

"Even with God's forgiveness, there are always consequences as a result of sin. Our sin will also be used against us by the enemy to taunt us and to make us feel that we are not good people or good Christians. Feelings of unworthiness are very common.

"At the very least, you two would regret it and feel condemnation for willingly sinning against God. I'm sure you can imagine how it would put a wedge in between you and God. He's our heavenly Father and requires us to obey him in response to his love and forgiveness. Only he can save us as it's he that created and controls everything.

"Please don't think that I'm judging you guys. I have the same feelings for Rachel right now, but I am committed to doing things God's way. That means I will take control over the desires of the flesh because God has promised to give me that ability if I'll only rely on him and do all I can to remove the temptation. Rachel and I will date until we are clear that God intends for us to be together in marriage. Then we'll get married, and then we will have that mind-blowing sex you are talking about.

"Our chances of staying together will be significantly higher because we will have done it God's way. If we were to do it the way the world tells us to, you know, 'just do it,' we would seriously decrease our chances of a strong relationship that would lead to a healthy God-blessed marriage. I think way too highly of Rachel to do it any other way. She deserves to be loved the way Jesus loved her when he gave up his life for her. The Bible actually tells husbands to love their wives the way he loves the church. He actually gave up his life for the church he loves so much. By the way, we, believers, are the church."

Sam knew his answer was revealing to Rachel. He wanted her to know that he wanted her, but he also wanted her to understand why he would not even attempt to sleep with her. The other two needed to hear the straight truth, no holds barred.

"Wow, that was pretty good," Joe said somberly.

"Look guys, I'm no expert in love. I've avoided anything that could make me stumble all of my life. Rachel is only the second girl I have ever kissed. What I do know is that God's way is always the best way. He made us, and he makes all of the rules. When we are disobedient, we deserve punishment. Since he is a righteous God, he cannot turn his head the other way when we sin." His honesty was what Joe had liked the most about Sam from day one. Both of the girls recognized the truth in what he was saying as well, and Rachel was becoming more and more attracted to him with every word he said. She was really starting to admire him and was growing surer that he was her future.

As Rachel began to think about where she hoped things would go with Sam, she started to realize that she had no experience dating a boyfriend like Sam would surely be. She sat there thanking God for bringing Sam to her and couldn't help but feel a bit unworthy. Hearing that she was only the second girl he had ever kissed made her feel very special. She loved the idea that he would have no one to compare her to if they ever got married and got to share intimacy with one another. She desperately wished she could offer him the same.

"I loved hearing that you want to have sex with me, Sam. I also like knowing that when we finally do make love, it will be the best you have ever had. I wish I had done it right like you have. Just so you know, I have only been with two guys. Joe and Heather can confirm that. I know it's two too many, and I wish I could go back and fix it, but I can't. Thank you so much for treating me like I'm pure. It means a lot to me." She spoke so everyone could hear, but she was staring into Sam's eyes and talking only to him. Her hand was in his below the table as they were on the same side, sharing a booth.

"Okay, we'll hold off on the sex then. Dang it!" Joe was only half joking. Heather was hugging him from the side, and he was doing his best to take his mind off of her left breast against his chest. *What a body*, he thought.

The rest of the conversation was around starting a Bible study. The four of them agreed to study the Bible together at least once per week. Joe had brought it up. It was something he had planned to ask Sam about even before all of these love connections started. There were lots of questions Joe wanted to ask, and he knew that Sam would likely have answers.

Joe picked up the tab with the money left over from his birthday money he had gotten from his father and from Rachel's father. With this meal though, he was almost tapped out again. He knew it would be difficult to say no to the major leagues if they offered him any real money. He was tired of always being broke.

When they got to the girls' apartment, Sam suggested that they all stay in the same room together since they were at all feeling tempted. Though they all teased him, they knew he was right and agreed.

CHAPTER 10

Their time together at the apartment flew by. They had left the restaurant at just before nine, and before they knew it, three hours had gone by. The conversation bounced around quite a bit, but it always seemed to come back to how Heather and Joe would soon be married. The future looked very bright.

Joe and Heather were incapable of keeping their hands off of each other. They sat next to each other on one end of the couch, while Sam and Rachel sat on the other. Heather eventually climbed into Joe's lap, and Sam couldn't help but comment.

"You two better have a really short engagement if this is going to work."

They all laughed, but Joe and Heather knew it was true.

At about midnight, Joe asked Sam, "Can our first Bible study be about getting some of our tough questions answered?"

Joe wanted to learn more about the Bible, his head was loaded with questions. He knew that much of what he had learned in school contradicted what the Bible said. Though he always inherently knew the Bible was true, he was hoping Sam could help him understand why science didn't seem to jive with the Bible. Secondly, he knew that Rachel and Heather had grown up in the same church as he had. They had heard all of the same Bible stories he had. Rather than start with stories, Joe was hoping to jump right into some real answers. In church, they never seemed to care much about all of the misinformation that was being taught. In Joe's mind, had they cared to discredit it, they would have preached or taught about the error of it all. Yet he had never heard any rebuttal of the world's contradiction of the Bible in church ever.

"It sure can. I'd enjoy that. We can spend lots of time on that. Actually, as we study any part of the Bible, we'll be faced with difficult questions. This is mainly true because there is an advisory to the truth. This advisory, the devil, has been at the game of trying to discredit God's word from the very beginning. He is the father of lies, and he is the master of deception. His ways permeate the culture of the world."

Sam was beginning to feel some pride, knowing that he possessed a breath of knowledge about God and his word that none of them had. For the first time, he was experiencing what some preachers must feel when they preach form God's word. The thought of being proud of this knowledge humbled him as he fully understood how God felt about this type of pride; he hates it. It was pride that brought about the devil's fall from heaven. The responsibility for these three young souls gave him pause so much so that he began praying to God for strength. He prayed for humility and the ability to speak the words God would have him speak to these renewed believers he was being entrusted to speak to. His praying was instantaneous and undetectable to the others. *What a heavy responsibility it is to be prepared to speak on God's behalf,* he realized.

"Cool. Tell me, Sam. How much of the Bible is true? How much is just stories, and how much has science proved is wrong?" Joe wanted to hear that the entire Bible was true as he had struggled with the implications of it not being true for some time. He had always wondered that if the Bible wasn't all true, then how do we know which parts to believe?

"The Bible and science are both 100 percent true, and science has not proven anything in the Bible to be false." He paused for a bit for that to sink in before he continued, "First of all, God made everything. He even created time. As the creator, no one knows how it all works better than he does. He was an eyewitness to it all. Additionally, God is also the divine author of the Bible. He calls it his 'word.' Each human author wrote under the inspiration of God. The Old Testament was in existence when Jesus walked the face of the earth, and he quoted scripture from almost every book in the Old Testament, thereby, confirming its authority and authenticity. If you don't believe Jesus would know that there are errors in any of the texts that he quoted from, you have far greater problems. If he was wrong about anything, he is not God and cannot save you from anything. The New Testament was all written within one hundred years of Jesus's time on the earth, and the authors were almost all firsthand witnesses to what they wrote about. Though many attempts have been made to prove inaccuracy in the Bible, at current, other than translations errors, there is no standing example of a proven mistake in the Bible.

"We can take some time going over the validity of the Bible in our studies. From the tremendous amounts of copies to archeological discoveries, it's actually harder to doubt the word than to accept it. Still, because there is an advisory to the word of God, it will always be questioned by people living in the flesh. Well, at least until Jesus returns and makes it all a moot point. The Bible actually says that every knee will bow, and every tongue will confess that Jesus is Lord when he returns." Sam knew that was a breathful, so he paused before going on, "There are some great resources we can use to study this subject. We'll work it into our study plan."

"What about your science statement? That it's 100 percent true." Joe was very interested to understand.

"True science is 100 percent true. Making assumptions about the past is not science. Assuming that things had to be a certain way to fit a theory is not science. Using our current conditions to interpret the past is not science either. The age of the earth is a great example. You see dating methods all make assumptions. For instance, by assuming that decay rates of today at atmospheric temperatures and pressures in our current environment are the state at which all things came about is a very poor assumption. Yet these assumptions are used by all of the current dating methods being used to say that things are millions of years old. Additionally, when a layer of earth is assumed to have been formed over long periods of time so many millions of years ago, then the fossils found in that layer are said to be that old. At the same time, the fossil types are used to tell how old the layer they were found in is. You may think that sounds crazy, but it's true. To most clear-thinking people, that is circular logic. However, to those that do not want to be accountable to a righteous God, it makes perfect sense.

"The Bible tells us that a worldwide flood drastically changed the earth's surface and that things were radically different afterward. Would this not lay down layers with all sorts of dead things fossilized in it as the water receded just like the Bible tells us it did? Does it not make sense that the smaller, less mobile living creatures are at the bottom, while the larger more mobile creatures are near the top as they likely survived longer? Also, what is a fossil? Isn't it something that was caught so quickly that it was preserved whole? How in the world can something die and not decay if this is not the case. It defies logic to think otherwise." Sam was starting to get a little emotional, so he decided to slow down a bit.

"What I'm trying to get at is that it all works together—the Bible and science. God created everything, and science is supposed to be based in observable, repeatable experiments of the reality we all live in. It's not supposed to be based on hunches and flawed logic. If God hadn't created everything as he tells us that he did, science itself would be useless. If everything were random as we are told it is, why would there be laws that things in the creation all adhere to? Things would not be repeatable, and we would not even be capable of rational thought.

"Evolution cannot explain morality or rational thought. The truth is that it requires a great deal of faith to believe in evolution as there is no verifiable evidence for the theory, and it violates all three of the laws of thermodynamics. There is quite a lot to study on this subject. It's one of my favorites, and I have tons of great resources we can use.

"Unfortunately, people have been lied to their entire lives about these things. They try to make what the world says and what God says work together because they actually believe the Bible has been proven to be wrong on many of these subjects. They are wrong, and they can't see the devil behind the lies. That's why he's worked so hard to get our schools and even our churches to teach his timeline. He too knows it's not true, but he wants us to doubt God's word. Through the use of potentially almost limitless time, the devil knows the human mind will believe almost anything could have happened by chance. If science was to agree to a six-thousand-year-age of the earth or even a worldwide flood, evolution would be dead. If they even agreed to million or fewer years evolution would be deal.

"Though some believe God created the cosmos and everything in it as we are told in Genesis 1:1 and then waited millions of years as he resides outside of our time before he began doing the work that the Bible picks up with in verse two, I personally do not. Though it does provide more time for what many believe is necessary for light to travel to the earth and a host of other things, it does not help any evolution argument as those millions of years would have to have been without death as death did not enter the world until man sinned. Death is a consequence of man choosing to sin.

"Satan knows that there are only two possibilities us humans will believe. Either we were created, which would mean we are accountable to that creator, or we came about by chance and are therefore accountable only to ourselves as we are at the top of the chain. The only other possibility is that we were created by something other than the God of the Bible who claims to have always existed without a beginning. He also claims to have created everything out of nothing. It's my belief that the lie that something else created us will be the lie that the Antichrist will use to deceive many. He could easily get people to believe he created us millions of years ago and planted us here on this earth and, therefore, we should worship him. Of course, this part is only my opinion."

"This is going to be great, learning the truth and why it's the truth. I knew there were answers out there, but I never got any at church." Joe was really excited about it, and by the looks on their faces, it looked like the girls wanted to hear more as well. He was also a bit disappointed in his church for not touching on any of this ever.

The four talked until about 1:00 a.m. before Sam pointed out how late it had gotten.

As they were getting ready to leave, Heather took Joe's face in her hands and told him to honor her by breaking it up with Ally before he came back to see her again. Since it was almost 1:00 a.m., she told him she was fine with him putting it off until the next day. He told her she was probably right since Ally would very likely be pretty drunk or already asleep by now. They exchanged another wet kiss followed by a big long hug before Joe headed out the door. "I love you" went back and forth several times as well.

Rachel and Sam exchanged a light kiss too; during which, Sam whispered into her ear that he was falling for her. Her response was quick and to the point. "I've already fallen for you, Sam." He couldn't have felt better about their future together.

Since Sam had been the driver for the evening, he had to drop Joe off before heading home. Thankfully, Joe's place was just on the other side of the complex. If it weren't for his bag of clothing and books, he would have likely walked home. The apartment complex was within walking distance of the campus, so Joe would be able to walk to the stadium to get his car in the morning.

Joe had a roommate named Mike, but the two had drifted apart as friends in recent months as Mike was practically living with his girlfriend. The two almost never saw each other anymore, though they had once been close friends that could have hardly been separated. Mike sightings had become so infrequent at this point that it was almost as if Joe lived alone.

Sam dropped Joe at the base of the stairs and drove off. The two were both filled with excitement about their futures. Neither one of them noticed Ally sitting on the balcony of Joe's apartment. She was waiting for Joe in sexy lingerie, which she had on beneath one of Joe's big T-shirts. She was also very drunk.

As Joe climbed the stairs, he began to type out a quick goodnight text to Heather. "You are the love of my life. Good night, sweetheart." He loved that he could say that now. What really felt great was that he wasn't just saying it to get some girl to sleep with him; he actually meant it. He knew Heather could hurt him in ways that no one else could. She had already done it to him once, and this time would be far worse should she choose to walk out on him again. There was no way he was going to give her any reason to do that. He had to handle things quickly with Ally.

Joe's apartment, like Rachel and Heather's, was on the third floor. When he got to his door, he was very surprised to find it unlocked. *Could Mike have actually come home?* he wondered. Before he pushed the door open, the other possibility popped into his head, *If Ally is here, what will I do?*

The door opened to an empty dark room. Before relief could set in, he heard her call him from the balcony. "I'm out here, baby."

Oh no, how do I handle this? He had been planning a good way to make the break, but her being drunk wasn't in it. Kissing or touching her in any way would seriously put him in jeopardy of losing Heather, the love of his life.

"I'm heading your way, but I need to take a leak first. I'll be right out," he yelled back. He dropped his bag by the door of his room and slithered into the bathroom to get his thoughts together. Ally wasn't helping him at all though.

"I need you badly tonight, stud muffin," she said through the door, which she was obviously repositioned at now.

Well, at least she's not yelling to the public any more.

Joe couldn't believe how nervous he was about breaking up with her. Since they had never really had a fight or anything, it felt pretty strange to be dumping her. Not that he wasn't convinced that he had to break up with her, but that it would have been far easier to do had he had some evidence that things were not working out between them. He really had none. All he could think of telling her was that he just didn't see them ever getting married and that he had always been in love with Heather. *Should I make it about Heather, though?* he wondered. He didn't want Heather to deal with any sort of retribution from any of this. She deserved better.

The other excuse he could use was that he could no longer have premarital sex because of his renewed commitment to the Lord. He was positive Ally wouldn't buy that one. There was no way she would be able to comprehend that in the condition she was in. After all, they had been very intimate for months now. How could he try to tell her he couldn't do it anymore? *God's way really is the opposite of the world's*, he decided.

To make it sound like he was actually doing something in the bathroom while he was stalling her, he flushed the toilet. Then he started running the water while he attempted to come up with a winning strategy. He didn't want to hurt her, but he couldn't back out of this breakup and run the risk of losing Heather by doing anything sexual with Ally. He had already decided that he couldn't start his relationship with Heather or his rededication to the Lord with anything like this on his conscience. He would have to get away no matter what.

For a while, he had heard Ally by the door. He was pretty sure she had slid down to the floor based on the last audible sign of her existence. *Is there any chance I could wait this out until she falls asleep? That would be ideal. I could talk with a sober Ally much easier than I can to this drunken mess that's waiting for me in the hall.* Boy, how he used to love it when she got that way. *How quickly things change*, he thought.

He decided to wait it out when suddenly his phone vibrated with a reply to his text to Heather. "You have been my dream husband for years. I love you, Joe. Good night." While it felt great to get her message, it made him question how to handle his current situation. After some thought, he decided to let Heather in on what was going on.

"I love you too. I'm in the bathroom alone. Ally was here waiting for me when I got home, but I think she just fell asleep on the other side of the bathroom door. What should I do?" *Was that a mistake telling her?* he wondered. Part of him felt that it had been a mistake, but he decided that he was more afraid of her finding out and being angry with him later than anything else. He didn't want to lie to her. Since he had time alone in the silence he was surrounded by now, he had typed out his text with enough info for her to know what was going on and that he wanted nothing to do with Ally.

"Get out of there, and come to me now." Read her quick reply. She couldn't believe it. His message had made her sit straight up in bed. This was really bad. Ally had to be drunk if she had him cornered in the bathroom and then fell asleep.

He knew she was right; he had to run. He quickly decided to send her a reply. "I'll sneak out and come to you. Can I sleep on your couch? I love you so much I can't wait to get out of here." Though his car was still at the stadium, it wasn't far to walk across the complex. Thankfully, he hadn't consumed any alcohol that evening. Quitting the drinking wasn't going to be a big challenge for him. It had never been something he needed anyway.

"Yes, you can sleep anywhere but where you are. Please get out. I can't wait to see you again tonight." She was trembling now with fear. Something told her this was a very serious situation.

To see if the coast was clear, he pressed his ear to the door, but he couldn't hear a thing. *It was time to move*, he thought. His first move was to shut off the bathroom light. *A beam of light could wake her.* The next step would be a little tricky if she turned out to be leaning on the door, so he very slowly cracked the door open. He was concerned when he didn't see or feel a thing.

To his surprise, Ally was nowhere to be seen, so he proceeded into the living-room hallway area. His eyes quickly adjusted to see her standing back out on the balcony, drinking the last drop of whatever drink she was working on. Just then, another text came in from Heather. "Please get out of there for us." He stuffed his phone in his pocket and attempted to head for the door.

Ally turned just in time to see him heading for the door. "Hey, I'm over here, silly. Where do you think you are going?" She was now heading his way, and it appeared to him that she was naked or at least in her underwear. Either way, she had shed the T-shirt she had been wearing when he got there. By the way, she was stumbling, along with the slurring of her speech. He knew she was really wasted. "I forgot something that I really need to get." It was all he could think of. Lie or not, he needed to get away.

"You can get it after you take care of me." She was on him now. He was in her grip, and she was trying to fondle him when he pulled back sharply.

"What's your deal?" she growled at him.

He made a crucial mistake next. Had he simply pulled away and left, everything would have likely turned out differently. Unfortunately, he made the cardinal mistake of trying to reason with a drunken person.

"Ally, I just don't want to hurt you." He meant it, but there was no way Ally was in any sort of mind-set to listen to or to understand what he was about to tell her.

"You would never hurt me, Joe. Come to bed now." She was incapable of processing data logically at that point, and Joe should have recognized it. He was too concerned about her feelings when he should have just fled.

"I've got to go, Ally. I can't be with you anymore." Though he was saying it as kindly as he knew how, it hit her like a punch in the face.

"You're my boyfriend. You have to be with me." Her expression quickly turned to one of profound sadness. She couldn't make sense of what she was hearing, and Joe hated what he was doing. He hated himself for what he was doing, but he also knew it had to be done. He was Heather's now, and he would not mess that up.

"I can't be your boyfriend anymore, Ally. I like you very much, but I just can't be your boyfriend anymore." She was holding onto his waste tightly now while he was continuing to try to free himself to get to the door.

"Don't you leave me, Joe! Who is she? Is it that Heather bitch?" Her sadness violently turned to anger. She knew it had to be Heather. She was no fool. Heather was always hanging around and flirting with Joe. She had noticed how Joe looked at her many times, and she was insanely jealous of her. Heather was easily one of the best-looking girls on campus, and Ally hated that about her. Oddly, her accusation surprised Joe. He had no idea how obvious his feelings for Heather had been to everyone.

"Yes, it's Heather. We have not done anything, though. Please understand, Ally, I love her, and I've loved her for a long time." He wanted her to know, but this wasn't the right time at all to drop something like this on her. Her tirade over Heather got very ugly very quickly, and the insults became filthy and plentiful. Joe was terribly conflicted throughout the entire tirade. He felt guilty for what he was doing to Ally, but he loved Heather and didn't like hearing Ally attack her the way that she was.

At the height of the profanity, Joe made a move to loosen her grip. He was able to break free and broke for the door as she fell to the floor. Before he could even get all the way out the door, she sprung off the floor like an angry cat and barely missed grabbing his arm though she did leave a long scratch mark that gave Joe a surprising sting. She had just barely made it to the door as she fell again with a hard thud. Her body landed with her hips in the doorway, and her legs still in the apartment.

Joe ran for the stairs as if he was being chased by a killer. When he turned to go down the first flight of stairs, he looked back to see Ally in a pile by the door. In that instant, he missed the step he was shooting for and fell head first into the concrete steps. It happened so quickly, and he was so distracted by the sight of Ally crumpled in pain that he couldn't even get his hands up in time to block his fall. He took the full force of the fall to his face and chin, and his body immediately went limp. He was gone.

CHAPTER 11

"**D**ad, are you still taking us to the movies tonight?" Joe never forgot a promise. Before Sam headed out the door for the day, Joe wanted to make sure Dad was still taking him and Robert to the movies later.

"Yes, your mother and Ms. Heather are going to dinner, and I'm taking you and your brother for pizza and to the movies. It's on the schedule, buddy." Sam loved being a father, but he loved being Rachel's husband even more. In the fifteen years since Joe Morgan's death, Sam and Rachel had found their way together. Unfortunately, Heather had not found anyone or her way.

"Dad never forgets a promise to you guys. You know that, Joe." Just saying her son's name brought back memories of Joe Morgan for both her and Sam. Joe's death had easily been the most difficult thing Rachel had ever been through. Not only was Joe one of her closest friends, his premature death had nearly pushed her closest friend, Heather over the edge. Heather's inability to accept Joe's death had consumed Rachel and Sam's lives for years. Even now, fifteen years later, Heather was a constant presence in their lives as she simply shut down the social part of her own life when Joe's fall ended his life.

Sam reached down and hugged his eleven- and nine-year-old sons. "I love you guys," he told them as he headed out the door. "I love you too, Mama," he said as he pulled Rachel in tightly to his out-of-shape body. He hugged Rachel every chance he got. Experiencing Joe's tragic early death had heightened Sam's sense of his own humanity. He savored every moment he had with Rachel, his beautiful soul mate. He never missed an opportunity to touch her or to tell her how he felt about her.

"Have a great day, Sam. I love you too." Rachel loved his admiration, and as long as they weren't in public, she always reciprocated any attempt he made at holding her. There was no safer place then in his arms. He had proven it to her over and over again. Rachel was convinced that Sam was the best person she had ever known. Being married to him was all she needed in life, though it came with much more.

Once Sam was gone, Rachel started preparing the boys for their daily homeschooling lessons. They would be done by lunchtime if nothing hung them up. To balance their lives, the boys were involved in sports and other programs, as well as being very active members in their church's youth program.

The decision for Rachel to stay home had been a difficult one. She had become a nurse shortly after she and Sam had married. Before they started their family, they decided it would be the best thing for the kids that they were planning to have to have their mother at home. With that plan in mind, she quit her job when Joe was born. Though they had discussed her going back to work once the kids were both in school, they later changed their minds in favor of putting the boys through a Christian-based homeschool program instead. Rachel would be an excellent teacher; Sam was sure of it, and he had been correct.

Losing Rachel's income had not been a big deal initially. However, as the years went by, it became a bigger and bigger deal. Sam had a good job as a process engineer at a chemical plant, but since they continually needed more money than he was making to get by, he decided to accept a high-pressure technical sales job to improve their finances. The money was better, but the stress was far worse and was now beginning to take its toll on his health.

CHAPTER 12

Heather woke up at 4:15 a.m. like she did every weekday. The alarm never woke her as she always awoke minutes before it sounded. As always, she was alone. Her routine was efficient and almost machine like. Nothing ever disturbed the routine, even her morning shake and health bar were mixed and eaten on schedule. She was in her workout clothes with her hair tied up and out the door by 4:35 a.m. Monday through Friday every week.

There was some slack in her schedule on the weekend as she got to sleep in a couple of hours Saturday mornings, and she always took Sundays off. Well, at least Sunday was the only day of the week that she didn't plan to exercise unless she had somehow exceeded her calorie intake for the day.

The drive to the gym was less than ten minutes. The first of three classes she taught each day was an advanced spinning class. The 5:00 a.m. class was for serious spinners only, and Heather was known for her hellish workouts. To make it through one of her advanced sessions was sort of a badge of honor for her students. Most students admitted that they didn't always press the way she did, though. Most were willing to admit they hadn't really adjusted their tensions as much as she had instructed or really gone 100 percent when she had instructed them to.

Heather was like an animal when she worked out, and she actually seemed to enjoy the pain. For those who dared to attend her 5:00 a.m. class, she rewarded them with an extra thirty minutes of class. The bikes were not needed for another class until 7:00 a.m., so Heather was given the freedom to push well past the 6:00 a.m. scheduled end time. Though her students often slacked off by not pushing themselves to do everything she instructed, Heather never slacked off and always did everything she preached.

Her natural strong, outgoing personality had crumbled with Joe's fall, but she had worked hard to pretend it had never left her. Now, fifteen years later, those who didn't know her well believed she really was as strong as she appeared to be. Those who knew her well though, her family, Sam, and Rachel knew differently.

Heather was nothing at all like she portrayed herself to be. She was an emotional wreck inside. To maintain her outward appearance of strength, she worked out four to five hours a day to create and maintain physical superiority over others. It made her feel as if she was still somewhat in control, but in reality, it was for everyone else; she knew how helpless and frail she actually was. Still, she needed people to believe she was strong. She couldn't let them know the truth. It had been fifteen years since Joe's fall, but the loss had changed her in a way she still didn't know how to accept.

In her quest to control everything external, she lived a celibate life. She refused to date in spite of almost daily advances. Not only would she not date, she even kept women at an arm's length. The only ones she ever really let in were Sam and Rachel. They had been with her the whole time, but she had let no one else in.

The night Joe died, Heather had been frantically trying to reach him. When he never returned her texts, she feared that Ally may have successfully seduced him. After almost an hour without a response, she knew something was seriously wrong. From the time he had left that night, she had been uncomfortable. The text from him telling her that Ally was in the apartment with him not only confirmed her concerns, but also put her into a state of panic. There was no way she was going to calm down until she knew that he was safely away from her.

Rachel was still awake texting back and forth with Sam when Heather knocked on her door that night. "I think something is happening with Joe. He won't return my texts or calls, and he told me Ally was at his place. I'm going over there right now. Can you come with me?"

"Yes, of course. Let's go."

They were out the door in less than five minutes, though it had been quite a while since Joe's fall.

On their way to Joe's apartment that night, Rachel texted Sam and told him what was going on. Though Sam hadn't been home long when he got the text, he immediately got dressed and headed to support Rachel and Heather. He would be fifteen to twenty minutes behind them, but he too sensed something was seriously wrong.

As Heather and Rachel approached Joe's side of the apartment complex, they began to see flashing lights everywhere. Heather freaked out as soon as she realized something had happened, and she began running toward the lights as quickly as her legs would carry her. Though Rachel attempted to keep up with her, she was no match for Heather's stride and superior condition. She was quickly left in Heather's dust, but sensing the flashing lights had something to do with Joe, she kept running at her top speed in spite of the distance being created between her and Heather.

When Heather reached the front of the apartment cluster that Joe's apartment was in, she noticed an ambulance and several police cars right in front of the stairs leading up to his apartment. Instinctively, she began screaming hysterically, "I knew something was wrong! I knew it!" As Rachel caught up to her, she was feeling the same way, but her nature kept her from showing it. Inside, she too was screaming. This was the worst possible thing either of them could ever imagine.

Heather's screaming got the immediate attention of one of the policemen. He stopped her in her tracks before she even got started up the stairs.

"That's my boyfriend up there. Let me go!" She was shaking with both fear and anger.

"I'm sorry, ma'am, but I can't let anyone up there." He knew Joe was gone, and it showed on his face and in his compassion for Heather. She could tell by his tone and expression that it wasn't good.

"Oh my God, is he okay? Tell me, is he okay?" She was grinding her teeth at him now and looked like she could take him out if she wanted to. To the bystanders, she was acting like someone who was having their life torn apart. It was a painful scene that no one that was present would ever forget, especially not Rachel.

As Heather began to refocus, she charged past the officer with what appeared to be superhuman strength only to be met by several paramedics carrying a body covered by a sheet. She immediately knew it was him and that he was gone.

"NO NO NO NO NO NO." She was crying and crumbling as she repeated herself over and over again on her way to try to hug who she knew had to be Joe under the sheet.

The policeman she had escaped from had to have assistance from several other officers to restrain her while Rachel passed out. Heather's screaming quickly died out as she noticed her friend hitting the ground behind her. With a dropping spinning motion, Heather broke free from the officers and made her way down to Rachel.

"Help!" she screamed while one of the paramedics rushed to assist.

The paramedics attended to Rachel's fallen body as it had landed hard on the concrete. Joe's body nearly passed right over the girls and was loaded into an ambulance and quickly shut in. Once Heather felt that things were in hand with Rachel, she began to feel a rage surge through her body. It had suddenly occurred to her that this was all Ally's fault. Without hesitation, she began screaming up at Joe's apartment, knowing Ally was up there.

It hadn't been Ally who had called the police. She passed out, not even knowing that Joe had fallen. It had been the downstairs neighbor who heard the terrible sound of Joe falling head first down the stairs. He opened his door only seconds after the fall, out of curiosity over the loud thuds.

When he saw Joe lying face down in a lump at the bottom of the top staircase, he called out to him but got no response. He quickly assessed the situation before making the emergency call. Seeing the way Joe's head had been cracked open and the amount of blood he had already lost, the neighbor immediately dialed 911.

Not knowing what to do while he was waiting, the neighbor climbed around Joe's body and up the stairs to find Ally half naked in the doorway of Joe's apartment. He had seen the attractive Ally come and go for months, so he decided to try to talk to her. Though he was able to wake her, she had no idea what was going on, and retreated into the apartment to lay down on the couch. The police found her there on the couch more than twenty minutes later, though she was found completely unconscious. She had no clue Joe had fallen but awoke as soon as she heard Heather's screaming from below.

"Is Joe okay?" Ally asked the police?

"No, I'm sorry. He didn't make it. He's gone."

Ally felt immediately sober and sick to her stomach. She ran to the bathroom, and with several policemen watching, she threw up several times. Sitting on the bathroom floor in her tiny underwear and with no shirt on, she looked up and said, "He ran away from me. He told me he loved Heather and that he had always loved her. When I tried to stop him, he ran away. I tried to grab him, and I even scratched him pretty badly, but he got away. I saw him go down the stairs, but I collapsed in a lump by the door when he left. I must have passed out. The next thing I knew you guys were waking me up, and I was on the couch. The whole thing feels like a bad dream." She was almost noncommittal as she spoke. She wasn't crying at all, but she seemed out of touch with the seriousness of what was happening.

Handing her a towel to cover herself with, the guy who appeared to be in charge began to question her, "So you two were boyfriend and girlfriend?"

Rather than answer his question, she came back with her own, "When you say he didn't make it and that he's gone, are you saying he's dead?" She was having trouble processing the data. Heather's screaming fit along with what they were telling her, but she just couldn't get herself to believe this was real. The only thing she was sure of was that the screaming voice belonged to Heather. There was no doubt about that.

"Yes, he is deceased, ma'am." The police officer had worked multiple fatality cases. He had seen every type of reaction a person could have to this type of situation. Ally was being investigated as she spoke, but no one was reading her rights. From what the neighbor who had called 911 had told them about where he found her along with what she was telling them now, Officer Jones was convinced that she had nothing to do with Joe's fall. From the evidence he had heard, it was just a horrible accident.

Heather's yelling seemed to get stronger and stronger. "I know you are up there, Ally. Why did you have to take him from me? If you did this, I will kill you!"

Just when things appeared to be calming down, Heather made a stupid mistake of yelling a threat in Ally's direction. She was immediately taken into custody for both her and Ally's safety. They needed to restrain Heather to be able to bring Ally down either way. Ally too had to be taken to the police station, but the two never saw each other again until the facts of what had transpired were known and reported to the public.

Sam arrived to find scores of people in the parking lot along with the ambulance and police cars. He hadn't heard a thing since he had been told that Rachel and Heather were heading to Joe's. The scene in the parking lot was the most terrifying experience of his life as he knew that it was his friends at the heart of it, since none of them had answered any of his calls or texts for sometime. He immediately began praying for everyone.

To avoid the congestion, Sam parked across the street and jogged across. He headed straight for the ambulance as it seemed to be the best place to start. Before he got there, someone screaming in the backseat of a nearby police car distracted him. He was shocked when he realized it was Heather. She had her face touching the glass and was hysterically screaming. He couldn't make out everything she was saying, but he thought he picked up something about someone killing Joe. He prayed that what he was hearing was wrong.

Though two policemen were between him and Heather, he miraculously managed to catch her attention in spite of her obvious hysterical state. "Where is Rachel?" he yelled at her. His voice startled several policemen. One of them even put his hand on his gun.

Surprisingly, Heather heard him and pointed to the ground over by the stairs. The squad car she was in was just beginning to pull away as she pointed the way for Sam. He saw Rachel lying on the ground. It was as if lightning had just hit him. He leaped toward her, noticing that two paramedics were attending to her. In a heartbeat, he was on his knees over her. The relief was immediate when he saw that her eyes were open. He could tell she noticed him as she stared right into his eyes, but she seemed to be in some sort of trance.

"Are you okay, Rachel? Is she going to be okay?" he asked her and the paramedics.

"She fell pretty hard, sir, but she'll be fine. We have a second ambulance coming for her. She landed hard on the concrete when she passed out. It looks like she may have seriously damaged her kneecap. It should be very painful, though she doesn't appear to be in any pain right now."

How could these guys be so calm about this? Sam wondered. He figured they must see this kind of stuff and worse all of the time. How they could do this sort of work day in and day out was beyond him, though.

"Can I go with her in the ambulance?" He wanted to be there for her. Why was she acting like this? Whatever it was, it had to be really bad? The only thing that made sense to him was that Joe must be badly hurt or dead.

"That's up to her." His lack of emotion made Sam shake his head in disapproval.

Rachel managed a wink and shook her head yes as relief rushed through Sam's body. Though he knew something terrible was happening, he couldn't help but feel encouraged that she wanted him with her. He was thankful for that, but his mind quickly turned to the mystery of what had gone on to put her on the ground like this.

The first ambulance was pulling out with Joe's lifeless body in it while Rachel's ambulance pulled in. Sam backed away a few steps and asked one of the bystanders what was going on. He was told that a dead body was taken away in the ambulance that just left and that Rachel had passed out while her friend got arrested for yelling at the girl in the other police car.

From where he was standing, he couldn't make out the face, but he was pretty sure it had to be Ally in the back of the police car the bystander had just pointed to. She wasn't sitting the same way Heather had been in the other police car, so he assumed she wasn't handcuffed. She didn't look angry either; she looked detached.

"Did that lady kill him?" Everything had slowed down inside of Sam, even his heart rate. The calm was unsettling, but it allowed him to focus his thoughts as if he wasn't in a traumatic situation.

"I don't think so. Derrick found the guy on the stairs, and I heard him tell the police that the girl passed out in the open doorway when he found her. I think the guy just fell down the stairs. I bet he was drunk or something."

Sam knew Joe wasn't drunk. *Was it possible for an athlete like Joe to just fall down the stairs on his own like that?* he wondered. Either way, he was thankful that Joe had just recommitted his life to the

Lord. Sam knew Joe was in heaven, but he also knew it wasn't going to be easy for those who loved him to accept. The thought of Joe being gone was almost impossible to accept. He was so much bigger than life and seemed almost indestructible.

That night seemed to never end, especially for Heather. For her, it would play through her head for years. It would change the course of her life. She would never be the same.

CHAPTER 13

After another long day of working out and teaching others how to take care of themselves, Heather came home to her empty apartment. She quickly showered and changed as to not waste any time. As usual, she was right on schedule.

As she entered the living room, a knock on the door startled her, even though she was expecting it.

"Who is it?"

"It's your date for the evening."

Heather slung the door open. "My favorite person in this Godforsaken world!" The two embraced. Rachel was the only person Heather ever hugged anymore.

"How are you doing, Heather?" Though they saw each other several times a week, they only spoke about feelings when they were alone. Rachel envied Heather's figure and work ethic, but she would never exchange lives with her. She loved being Mrs. Henderson, being a mother, and most of all, being married to Sam. She could honestly say she had never known a better man than him.

While Rachel had Sam and the kids, Heather had no one. Heather hadn't been with anyone since Kevin, and her one night with Kevin had been a huge mistake; it was the only mistake she had made with any man since Joe's death. That night had completely sealed her off from men and from ever trusting anyone.

Heather and Kevin had first gotten together several months after Sam's stirring speech at Joe's funeral. The speech had moved the audience in such a powerful way that Kevin, along with about half of the other funeral attendees, actually accepted Christ into his life. Not all of them were first-time conversions, some were rededications to Christ as Joe's had been the day he fell to his death.

Sam started his speech by sharing the last five hours of Joe's life with the audience. Once he got through Joe's rededication to Christ and his proclamation of love for Heather, he went on to say, "This is not a sad story. Joe is with his heavenly Father in heaven. He is where all of Christ's chosen will spend eternity. He's where there is no pain, no struggle, and only joy.

"It is all of us who need prayer now, not Joe. We all need to come to terms with God's timing in all of this. The Bible tells us God's timing is perfect, and I believe it. Joe's life and death will bring souls to the Lord. That was God's purpose in this. It's always his purpose. The Bible tells us that God loves us all and that he doesn't want any of us to spend eternity in hell, away from him.

"We will all struggle with this tremendous loss. Some in this room will be brought to the lowest of lows by this. In the end though, God's purpose will be done as it always is. Some of you sitting in this audience will realize who Joe really was. Though he was a sinner like the rest of us, he was also a force of nature. He affected us all deeply. You see, he was Christ's since he was in junior high. His rededication was very likely inevitable, and I'm sure God was working in his life all along. Could you not all tell by the way he treated us? He was full of God's love, and he couldn't help but spill it over into all of our lives."

The crowd was silent, except for weeping. Heather sat in her pew, feeling tremendous pride over her engagement to Joe. She loved that Sam had chosen to share it. What he was saying was true; she too loved that Joe was in heaven. She also felt secure in her decision to rededicate her life to the Lord. For a moment, the sadness faded away, and she actually was feeling comforted. She even began to feel God's love for her. She was sure that was what it was. How else could she be getting through this?

Sam had not even been a scheduled speaker. He had simply walked to the front and taken the mic near the end of the service. It was open-mic time, and Sam was the first to speak. He also turned out to be the last to speak.

Sam continued, "I ask that each of you look at your own lives. What are you living for? Joe was making a stand when he fell. Will you make a stand? If you want to know more about what Joe believed, I would love to tell you. Come down to the front, and we can talk about it. Let's not let Joe's death be a waste. Come up here and find out why he ran that night."

Ally was the first one to the stage. She fell to her knees and began shaking from her uncontrollable sobbing. The crowd quickly formed around her, but the first one to lay her hands on her was Heather. Though she never said a word to Ally, their peace had been made. Heather no longer blamed Ally for anything. God had given her a peace she couldn't understand. It allowed her to see the truth that Ally wasn't really to blame. It had truly been an accident. Heather could tell that Ally was feeling heavy guilt. It wasn't right, and she wanted Ally to know she had forgiven her.

Kevin too was moved by Sam's speech. Though inside, he wasn't sure of what he was doing, he recited the prayer Sam was instructing those who chose to make Christ the Lord of their lives that day. Unfortunately, he felt nothing as he was full of doubt. *Am I really in need of a savior?* he wondered. He told himself he wasn't a very bad guy; he'd probably go to heaven anyway. None of what Sam was saying about being a sinner and needing God in his life sunk in, though it had moved him to follow.

Kevin did love Joe though. He couldn't help but think, *If Joe needed God, maybe I do too?* That thought turned out to be enough for him to at least recite the prayer.

Heather noticed Kevin in the same huddle she was in. She had always considered him an operator, and she hated him for what he had done to Rachel. Seeing him being saved made her want to forgive him though, and being forgiven herself, she did just that.

Sam's joy over Joe's eternal destination had completely changed the tone of what had been the saddest occasion most of the audience had ever experienced. His altar call was in obedience to God's will, and it resulted in a plentiful harvest. Many of the conversions that day were genuine, but Kevin's was not. Too bad no one but God can see someone's heart as Heather's future may have turned out differently had she seen the truth about Kevin.

CHAPTER 14

Sam couldn't wait for his time alone with the boys. With only a half hour to go in the meeting he was in, he sent his brother Jack a text. "How's it going, Jack?"

The response came almost immediately, "Not so good."

It wasn't like Jack to be down. Even with the recent loss of his thirty-one-year-old wife to cancer, Jack always seemed to keep things positive. For him to say things were not so good wasn't good at all. Sam began to think it would be a good idea to invite him to join him and the boys for their pizza and movie night.

"Come to pizza and a movie with me and the boys tonight."

Why not ask Jack to come?. The kids love Uncle Jack, and he kind of acts likes one of them anyway. Uncle Jack was a youth pastor, and sometimes, it was hard to tell the difference between his behavior and the students.

Jack was very happy to get the invite. The fact that his brother Sam was easily his best friend, along with how much he loved to spend time with his nephews, made it a no-brainer to accept Sam's offer. Actually, Jack was the type of person who preferred to not be alone, especially when he was down. Being around friends and loved ones actually seemed to recharge him.

"Okay, when do I need to be at your place?"

Sam was really happy to hear he was coming. "Can you make it by 5:00 p.m.?" The movie will start at 7:00 p.m., and Sam wanted to make sure they had plenty of time for pizza, video games, and talking before they had to be at the theater for the show.

"I'll be there, old man."

That was more like it, Sam thought. Sometimes, the similarity between his brother Jack and Joe Morgan was uncanny. Oftentimes, Sam found himself thinking of his old friend when he was talking to his little brother. Though Jack was only being himself, his personality was eerily similar to Joe Morgan's.

Jack had been deeply in love with Tina. They had begun dating their senior year of high school, and neither of them had ever been with anyone else. Both of them were solid Christians, or as Jack preferred to call it, "Christ followers." They had chosen to dedicate their lives to serving God early in life and had been successful due to their constant reliance on the Lord for everything, including strength. Tina had been the organized one in their marriage. Now Jack was an unorganized mess without her. He felt completely lost without her.

Jack and Tina had tried for years to have children but had not been successful. When they reached twenty-six years of age, they started to look into why they couldn't conceive. Though they had gone in to find out why they couldn't conceive, instead, they found out that Tina had breast cancer. For the next five years, they suffered through many lows bottoming out when Tina passed away at the very premature age of thirty-one. Jack was only thirty when she passed away. He was left numb and alone.

Jack was amazing through the whole thing. Now, five months after her death, he seemed to be hitting a new low. As he often told his brothers, Sam and Tim, Tina had been everything to him. She was the only woman he had ever kissed, and he had never even dated anyone else. Since she passed away, his place had become a mess, and he seemed to be late for almost everything. She was his focus and the love of his life.

Sam and Jack had become very close in spite of their almost six-year-age difference. Though their younger brother Tim was much closer to Jack in age at twenty-eight, his serious demeanor and workaholic ways had taken him away to New Mexico. Sam and Jack rarely saw or even heard from Tim. With Tim out of the picture, Sam was Jack's closest relative. Dad and Mom were great, but they were parents, not peers. Sam was Jack's closest friend, a very wise one at that.

Sam and Jack's relationship really started to blossom after Joe Morgan's death. Though Jack was only fifteen and in the final month of his freshman year of high school when it happened, there was something in his personality that Sam needed to fill the void Joe left in his life. Jack made Sam smile, and after Joe's death, smiling wasn't something that came very easily.

Jack was a far-better athlete than Sam had ever been. Physically, he had grown into a taller stronger man than Sam. Jack's looks were well above average, and he got the type of attention that Sam remembered Joe Morgan getting from girls. The opposite sex had always been interested in Jack, but he never seemed to notice it or even care. His wife had been his sole interest in women, and there had been no signs of that part of him since her passing.

It wasn't an effort at all for Jack to captivate a room. It was just who he was. He was naturally funny, athletic, good looking, and very easy going. Thankfully, he was also very in love with the Lord. He earnestly searched for God's will for his life, and he fully understood that a life filled with joy could only come from serving the Lord. At fifteen, Jack was already committed to a life dedicated to Christ. As dedicated as Sam had always been to the Lord, Jack's level of commitment was even higher.

When Joe passed away, Sam had been living at home. With the crushing effect of Joe's death, Sam soon found himself in a very difficult position. With both Rachel and Heather struggling, he spent every moment he could with them, and it still wasn't enough. He stayed at their apartment until they had both fallen asleep every night, which was causing him to get home at 11:00 p.m. to 1:00 a.m. most nights. While he was there, he did his homework and stayed on top of all of his studies, but he wasn't able to keep up with his job, and he was struggling to keep his head above water.

Sam was forced to work long hours on Saturdays and whenever else he could find the time. Thankfully, the church allowed him to work whenever it was convenient for him. Half of what he did no one else could do anyway, at least not for that pay. Being away during the day seemed easier on the girls than not being there at night for them.

For just over a month, Sam practically ran himself into the ground. As summer began that year, Rachel and Heather begged him to move in with them. He agreed to a deal in which he would sleep in one room, while they shared the other. They also agreed to be as conservative as possible with how they dressed and to only use the shower after he had left in the morning. Due to his financial situation, the girls continued to pay the rent fifty-fifty, but Sam chipped in as much as he could for anything that he could. The three of them all agreed to have Bible studies on Saturdays and to attend church together on Sundays. Finally, they all agreed that none of them would drink alcohol.

The move in went against Sam's better judgment, but he felt it was necessary, considering what the girls were going through. Though his parents trusted his judgment, they questioned his moving in with the girls. He did it anyway, accepting the struggle he would surely face to not stumble. It was something he would never have recommended to anyone, and years later, he would admit that it hadn't been the right thing to do. By the grace of God, they made it work, and he never stumbled.

Sam's love for Rachel grew exponentially once they lived in the same apartment. They agreed to get married as soon as possible after graduation, which they did just a few months later.

Jack first met Rachel and Heather about a week after his brother moved in with them. Sam brought them home to meet his family and to shut his mother up. She had been driving him crazy with requests to meet Rachel. By the way Sam talked about her, she was sure Rachel would soon be family. She pushed and pushed until he finally asked the girls to come meet his parents. Rachel and Heather were very happy to go meet them, though Rachel was very nervous. She was sure Sam was the one for her, and she worried that his mother may not think she was good enough.

Jack would never forget the first time he saw them. As cool of a kid that he was, he was at a loss when he first laid his eyes on those girls. So much so that he came right out and said it. "Are we being punked? Where are the cameras?" Then he added, "Seriously, Sam, when are we really going to meet Rachel and Heather? When do you have to have these two knockouts back to the escort service?" With that, Sam put him in a headlock and said, "Knock it off you little pest."

The girls thought he was hysterical, and they both took an immediate liking to him. There was just something about him. His style was so easy, and his aim was clearly to entertain while poking at his brother. He showed no signs of disrespect, and neither of them felt uncomfortable around him. Actually, they were both flattered. It was clear he was impressed, and there was nothing creepy about the way he had said what he said. He maintained eye contact with both of them while he spoke rather than look them over. They had both noticed and would later comment to one another how sweet he had been.

When Sam visited alone a couple of days later, Jack actually asked him to pray with him about all of the impure thoughts he was having about them, both of them, but especially Heather. He was absolutely serious and insisted Sam pray with him. Sam was impressed with who his little brother was, and from that day on, they made praying together part of their relationship. The maturity it had taken for him to ask for prayer over something most kids his age would do constantly without any concern about the inappropriateness of it was almost beyond comprehension for Sam. He himself had done his best to avoid temptation, but he had never asked someone else for help.

Though Jack was very smart, he wasn't a particularly strong student. He understood people, and he instinctively knew how to interact with them. Though he never became the type of worker Joe Morgan had been, his basic way with and around people was dead on with Joe's. Sam had often wondered if Jack could have been as good at school and sports as Joe Morgan had been if that type of success had mattered most to him as it had to Joe.

Jack felt accountable only to God. God's Word told him to obey his parents and those with authority, so he did. He wasn't really trying to impress anyone, though. Honoring his heavenly Father was first in his life. It was in this area that Jack was different than most. So when Jack came to Sam to pray about the impure thoughts he was having about Heather and Rachel, Sam's admiration for his little brother swelled. Sam's admiration for his little brother would never wane, while Jack would forever look up to his older brother.

When Jack got his license early in his sophomore year, his favorite place to visit was his brother's place. He even called the place "Three's Company" after the old sitcom. Since the guy in the original cast's name was Jack, Jack often told Sam they should change places as he had the right name for the male role in their little show. As always, he was only kidding. He knew the battle he would fight living with those two beautiful girls would be too much for him.

Sam was always impressed with Jack's abilities with people, especially the ladies. From the very start, Jack had been at complete ease around Rachel and Heather, so much so that they both fell in love with him. They actually treated him like he was their little brother too. He was around enough to be family, and he made them all laugh so much that they missed him when he wasn't there.

On one occasion, Heather offered to rub Jack's back. His response got him both laughter and respect.

"Are you kidding me? Let a supermodel scratch my back with the Lord watching. I don't think so. You are like the woman Solomon was telling his son to avoid in all of those words of wisdom in the book of Proverbs." Then he gave her his best smile to let her know he wasn't putting her down.

Heather could see his strength in his ability to resist temptation, and she could also tell how attracted he was to her. She was both flattered by him and impressed with him.

CHAPTER 15

"Let's get out of here, Rachel. I'm tired of this apartment. Let's go get something that I'll have to work extra hard to burn." Heather meant it. Whatever she ate would be burned. She would count it, and before she allowed herself to go to bed, she'd get on the elliptical trainer in her bedroom and burn it off. She refused to go to bed with a calorie surplus. It went against everything she was teaching her students and her personal trainers. Heather made her living telling people how to live and how to eat to be healthy; there was no chance she wasn't going to follow her own advice.

"Sounds great. I'm really hungry! By the way, did I tell you that Jack is going with Sam and the boys tonight?" She knew she hadn't, but she couldn't help but let Heather in on it as she had always been aware of Heather's affection for Jack.

After a short pause, Heather shook her head no. Rachel knew more than anyone how deeply Heather felt for Jack. Though they were all aware of the pain he was in, Heather was dealing with more than feelings of sympathy for him.

"Sam says Jack's not doing very well. He's such a great guy. I just hate seeing him like this. He's still great with everyone else, but he seems completely lost without Tina. His place is a mess now, and he's late for everything, even in paying his bills." Rachel, like everyone else who knew him, loved him. Jack was kind to everyone and always went out of his way to make sure other's needs were being met. He was a natural entertainer that was just fun to be around. Though it was effortless and never had to be preplanned, he couldn't help but draw attention and laughs wherever he went. His sermons to the youth department were both hysterical and infectious. Some of his sermons had become legendary and were talked about among his young audience, even at school.

"Do you think he would come to one of my classes? I really feel a strong pull to help him through all of this." Heather absolutely loved Jack. She didn't just like to be around him, she deeply loved him. Though she had never really told anyone, not even Rachel, Jack was the only man she ever thought about.

Since her college days when he used to visit Three's Company to her time with him at Rachel and Sam's family functions, she had always been drawn to him. No one could make her laugh the way he did, at least not since Joe had passed away. She always felt excited to see him and considered him to be family and a great friend. It was much more than an innocent attraction, but she had been concealing her true feelings for many years as he was a married man. Her attraction to him had actually been a source of condemnation for her.

"I bet he would. He usually works out at home, but he hates being alone. You should ask him."

It wasn't like Rachel had never thought about the two of them together. On more than one occasion, she and Sam had talked about how perfect Jack and Heather were for one another. If Heather hadn't sworn off all relationships with the opposite sex, Sam and Rachel agreed that the two of them would have been a match made in heaven.

"I will then. I'll send him a text right now." She began to type while Rachel tapped out a text of her own.

"I'm leaving a free pass for you to come to my spinning class tomorrow morning. It starts at 8:00 a.m. Be there, and don't be late!" She had sort of a bossy way about her, which was exactly what a guy like Jack needed. Luckily for Jack, Saturday was a regular class rather than one of her advanced classes, though Heather always stayed a second hour for the more serious students.

Rachel's text to Sam simply read, "Make him go!"

The day Jack had refused the backrub from Heather was the same day Heather got the call from Kevin Todd seemingly out of the blue. Believing she had seen him accept Christ at Joe's funeral bought him enough trust for her to even speak to him after what he had done to her best friend, Rachel. Though he had never been Heather's close friend, he had spent a lot of time around her. He knew her through Joe Morgan who had always seemed to try to shield both Rachel and Heather from him. He treated them both like close friends, which had gotten him Rachel, but all he had ever garnished from Heather were dirty looks and confrontation.

Not only was Kevin not close to Heather, but also, he had been the target of Heather's anger several times. After he had broken free of Rachel, Heather had gotten in his face in public on two separate occasions. Both times were a result of how he had treated Rachel, and both had ended in her telling him that he never deserved her anyway. Of course she had been drinking on both occasions as had he.

Kevin, being the operator that he was, never returned her anger with anger. Instead, he honestly believed he would some-day turn her hate for him into an attraction and exploit the abun-dance of feelings she had for him for his own benefit. He even imagined his eventual breakthrough with her would lead to more passion than he had ever known. All of that hate she felt for him would explode into something very intense; he was sure of it. With those thoughts filling his head, he began to strategize how to get her into bed.

Early in the surprise phone call, Kevin established how badly he missed Joe and shared that he was struggling daily over it. Knowing it was their point of commonality, he would exploit their mutual suffering over Joe's passing to get her to see him. He knew it would be a challenge, and he even considered that it would require a "work of art" type of sales job to close the deal with her. It had been almost six months since Joe's death, and

Heather hadn't even been out on a date or otherwise since Joe's fall. She went to class, the gym, came home, and avoided all outside contact with others. Only Sam, Rachel, and occasionally Jack spent any quality time with her. She was almost catatonic most of the time and did all she could to avoid any contact with anyone, excluding her roommates.

Though others had struggled with Joe's absence, Heather had been changed by it. It was with her constantly, and she often struggled to see anything positive in her future. He would have been her husband and the father of her children. She had lain awake, crying and asking God why, more nights than not. His passing made no sense to her, and had it not been for Sam and Rachel's support, she may have taken her own life.

Unfortunately, Kevin was still the same guy he had always been. He played his conversion to Christianity to get Heather to believe he could be trusted. He had always had a thing for her, who didn't? When he realized that he had assumed correctly, and she actually did believe he was a changed man, he jumped on the opportunity to mislead her. He couldn't wait to collect his prize.

Though he never aimed to hurt her, he never gave much thought to what his gaming her would do to her long term. He never considered that taking advantage of her would damage her in an irreversible way. He never thought of what he was doing as bad, and he never considered himself to be a bad or mean guy. He was just a very childish and selfish guy, trying to have a good time with his life. What the heck, down deep, he knew she wanted the same thing he did, though he was dead wrong.

"My birthday is tomorrow, and I don't feel like being alone. Would you like to come over for dinner?" Knowing she was buying the whole conversion that was changing him thing, he figured it was time to take a shot. If she refused, he would continue until he got his way. As long as she was talking to him, he knew there was a chance he could get that gorgeous body in bed with him. The fact that she believed he was a new man worked to his advantage, but he knew he needed to close quickly before she caught him partying and sleeping around. In his mind, it wasn't all a lie as he really was missing Joe.

"I guess so. I hate that you are so down. Can I bring anything?" He had been using a monotone depressed-sounding tone since the call had begun. That along with her belief that he was now a changed man took her off of her usual game of suspecting that every guy was always trying to manipulate her. Before Joe's fall had crushed her the way it had, she would have seen Kevin coming. She was always looking for guy's angles and had never been foolish about what it was they were actually after. The pain from losing Joe had drained her so completely that she had avoided contact with outsiders, whom she called everyone but Rachel, Joe, and even Jack.

"Nope, just bring your smiling face. I'll see you at 7:00 p.m." Before she even answered, Kevin began developing his plan to land her in one night. Something told him he needed to close quickly. Manipulation and closing the deal were his two biggest strengths.

"Okay, see you then." She was filled with concern for him as she hung up. If Kevin was feeling even a small part of what she had been going through, she wanted to be there for him. She was so blind by her own misery that she never even questioned his motives. She had believed him about his conversion, and she felt everyone deserved another start. *If God had forgiven him and changed him, why shouldn't I*, she reasoned?

Since Rachel and Sam had left with Jack the night before, she had not seen them. She spoke to no one about her plans to have a birthday dinner with Kevin as she had left the apartment that morning before Sam and Rachel had woken up, and no one had been home since Kevin's call. Had Rachel, Sam, or Jack known about her plans with Kevin, she would have quickly been talked out of going. Wisely, none of them trusted Kevin.

Heather headed out to see Kevin that night, oblivious of what was actually going on. She thought he may need to cry with her, or perhaps, he would tell her about how he had been coping with

Joe's passing. Never did she consider that he was carefully crafting a plan to seducer her. After all, she believed he had changed.

When Kevin opened the door, he was in full character. He wore a tight shirt so he could tempt her with his well-proportioned chest and arms. He played her beautifully from the instant she first saw him, not allowing her to suspect his true motives. She was buying it all and suspecting nothing. His performance was so good that even he felt the feelings he was trying to portray. Before he knew it, he was actually sharing some of his true feelings. He was pouring himself out to her, but he never lost focus on the prize.

When she broke down, he even managed to manufacture some tears of his own and huddled with her so she couldn't see his smiling face. Had she caught a glimpse of his actual emotion, Kevin would have been lucky to walk away from the evening without a limp. She would have likely had superhuman strength had she caught him scamming her. Unfortunately, she never picked up on it.

When they had finished the meal, Kevin broke out some expensive wine. Though she resisted at first, she slowly broke down and agreed to have a glass with him on his birthday. What could it hurt? Sure she had sworn off drinking and was even in a pact with Rachel and Sam not to drink, but one drink couldn't hurt anything.

That one glass was never allowed to go empty as her tempter wisely kept pouring between her every sip. Her loneliness and brokenness along with the alcohol and his ability to say whatever needed to be said made a lethal combination he was able to ride into the kiss that led to the night she would regret for the rest of her life.

CHAPTER 16

Jack was with Sam and the kids at the pizza place when his phone buzzed as Heather's text came in. Just seeing her name on his phone got his heart racing. From the first time he had laid his eyes on her, he had been completely infatuated with her.

Her message read, "I'm leaving a free pass for you to come to my spinning class tomorrow morning. It starts at 8:00 a.m. Be there, and don't be late!"

Sam too was getting a text. His was from Rachel, "Make him go!" Noticing Jack reading a text, Sam asked, "Jack, did you just get asked to do something?"

"Yes, how do you know that?" He was somewhat blindsided that Sam knew that Heather had just asked him to her class.

"Rachel just sent me a text telling me to tell you to go. What is she talking about?" Had he just blown it by asking? Maybe he should have kept his mouth shut until he knew what was going on? If he needed to convince Jack to do something, this slip may have blown his chances. Sam had never been very good at playing games, and this time was no different.

"Heather just asked me to go to her spinning class tomorrow morning." He looked conflicted to Sam.

"Are you going to go?" *Please say yes*, the thought began running over and over in his mind.

"I'm not sure I can handle that." He had the look of someone that was shaken a bit. Sam wasn't sure what to think.

"You can't handle the exercise or Heather?" He wanted to make sure he knew what he needed to argue against. Heather was a perfect fit for Jack, and he also knew how Jack had idolized Heather all through high school. Heather was beautiful then, and she had done everything humanly possible to make her body perfect in every way since. If he was attracted then, surely he would be even more so now. It was very likely that Jack was intimidated by his attraction to her.

"I'm not sure I can handle either. I ride my exercise bike at home, but my pace is somewhat relaxed. Her class could kill me." Sam could tell he wasn't really that worried about the keeping up part. It had to be the Heather part of the invite that had him tied up inside. Jack went on, "On your other point, Heather has been the girl of my dreams since I first laid eyes on her. When I first started dating Tina, I had to constantly be in prayer over my attraction to Heather. I couldn't look at Tina without seeing her every flaw in comparison to Heather. She was inferior to Heather physically, but God helped me through it, and eventually, my infatuation with Heather subsided, and I was free to love Tina wholeheartedly. I've always loved being in Heather's company, but God has broken my longing for her. If I go to this class, I'm afraid of becoming a slave to her again. What if she is just trying to cheer me up, and I fall for her again? She's like part of our family, Sam. I can't go to anything we do as a family without seeing her."

Wow, Sam thought. He had no idea Jack had that type of thing for Heather still. "You might be right about that, Jack, but you are wrong about Heather. She's not asking you to come to cheer you up. She has been alone now for fifteen years. I've not seen her ask any man to do anything in that time, and now she's asking you to come to her class. Maybe you're her dream man?" The petrified expression on Jack's face caused Sam to briefly pause before he continued, "She is an amazing Christian woman that I honestly believe God may have been preparing for you all of this time. I'm not just saying this. Rachel and I have been talking about it for months now. Heck, we've been praying for it to happen."

Jack had almost begun to enjoy the sorrow he was dealing with. It was the simplest thing for him to wallow in his sadness. He had managed to function quite well in public and the church, and all of his young disciples were all amazed at how he had sustained himself through all of this. It was when he was alone that he was different since Tina passed away. He often found himself feeling lonely, and it wasn't uncommon for him to break down and cry over his loss.

Jack felt secure in where Tina had gone to spend eternity. That gave him peace of mind, but being alone without her wasn't easy for him. He needed to be around people to be happy, but he absolutely needed to be loved by someone to feel secure. Being alone was a tremendous challenge for him, and though it had only been five months since Tina passed away, he was really struggling. Tina's death came at the end of a long struggle that had taken part of Jack's playfulness away from him. Other women weren't even on his radar. He honestly hadn't even thought about moving on. It had only been five months, and he earnestly felt that God was using this time to draw him closer.

"Really, you believe she may have a romantic interest in me?" Jack thought about what Sam was saying and was hopeful that it was true. He felt a rush of hope about his future, followed by guilt. *Isn't it too soon to begin moving on? Tina was just been put in the ground.*

"I absolutely do, Jack. Since that mess with Kevin, Heather has been like a nun. God may have actually used that terrible time in her life to preserve her for you? Now she is asking you to do something with her, and I believe you owe it to her as her friend to go to her class. If she is God's choice for you, he will work it out. Don't worry about it. God is in control. It's not like she's going to jump you, Jack. Ease up, buddy." Heather had been like Fort Knocks for more than fifteen years now. She shared only with Rachel now as Sam had long since decided that it was inappropriate for him to be her confidante. Though they spent lots of time together, and Heather trusted Sam like no other man, she understood the risks associated with getting too close with any man. Sam was Rachel's husband. He could be no more than a close friend to her, and she respected him for that. However, as Rachel's husband, Sam heard just about everything Heather was going through anyway.

"All right, I'll go. I'd be lying if I said I wasn't scared though."

Typing a response to Heather wasn't easy. His stomach was in knots while he typed. "Against my better judgment, I'll be there. Thanks for asking me. Please don't kill me."

Though Heather rarely wore revealing clothes, at least not since that night with Kevin, it was impossible to conceal her figure. She never hid her body; she just didn't flaunt it. She worked harder than anyone else to look the way she looked, so she did have a measure of pride in what she had achieved. However, she was not trying to entice men, though it still happened frequently. Why she had to push herself to the edge of perfection had always been questionable behavior in Sam's eyes. Since he had gone the other direction and seemed to not even care to try to keep himself in shape, he kept his opinion to himself.

Even without makeup, Heather's face was naturally beautiful. It was as if God had given her all of the features, coloring, and shading in all of the right places. Where most women needed to use makeup to highlight or accentuate features, Heather simply had those attributes as a part of her natural complexion. She could get out of bed looking the way other women struggled to look. It was very rare for her to prepare to go out the way other women did.

Too bad she hated men so much.

CHAPTER 17

As they opened the door to leave Heather's apartment, Jack's response text vibrated Heather's phone. As he had felt moments earlier, Heather was now feeling the same excitement Jack had felt seeing a text from that one person out there, the one that could really hurt her.

"Good news, Rachel, Jack is coming to my class tomorrow!" Her excitement was unmistakable. Her face lit up like Rachel hadn't seen since their college days. It reminded her of the great times they used to have before Joe died. Heather hadn't been that person in years, and seeing her that way after so many years of blandness was both strange and exciting to Rachel. The reaction had been much more than expected, and Rachel couldn't help but think the chances of the two of them finding their way together was a very strong possibility.

Joe's death had really changed Heather. Through her struggles, which only intensified with Kevin's betrayal, Heather had become a loner. Though she renewed her commitment to the Lord, she chose to hide and internalize her struggles. Instead of working through her pain and anger over Joe's early departure, she just sucked it up. She went from being an undedicated student to being singly focused on her passion to exercise and to learn about good health and the body. It was as if a switch had been thrown and she no longer cared about stuff, prestige, the opposite sex, or anything else of this world, especially fun. She worked out, ate right, and spent the rest of her time reading. If it weren't for Rachel, Sam, and to a lesser degree, Jack, it would have been like she was living on an island. God was the only other thing in her life.

Heather's father had passed away when she was still quite young, and her mother eventually remarried and moved away with her new family only a few years after Joe passed away. Once her mother was gone, Heather really was alone. She never let anyone in and kept everyone at arm's length. Since she and her mother never saw eye to eye, they rarely spoke now.

Christ quickly became the center of her life after Joe's death, and she fully dedicated herself to studying his word. When everything in her life seemed to have lost meaning, she began to realize that God was always there and would never leave her. If it weren't for Rachel, Sam, and Jack, she would have fellowshipped with no one in those first few years after Joe's passing.

Almost immediately after Joe's death, Heather become overly organized in every way. Everything she owned was maintained meticulously. She cleaned constantly, and she managed her finances with an unusual commitment to detail and accountability to the Lord. She maintained a spotless apartment, and no one ever saw a dirty dish or spec of dirt on her floor.

Though she did everything to the best of her ability, nothing compared to her commitment to keeping fit. It really was an obsession. So much so that Sam and Rachel had often prayed for her deliverance from whatever it was that was driving her so hard in this area. Even hinting that it was an issue would make Heather very defensive. To her, it was part of who she was. Whether it brought honor to God was something she wasn't willing to talk about. It certainly hadn't brought her out of the funk Joe's passing had left her in.

To get closer to God after Joe's death, Heather began reading a chapter of the Bible every day along with her Bible studies with Rachel and Sam. After Sam and Rachel were married, she began teaching an eighth-grade girl's Sunday school class. Her passion was to keep young girls pure until marriage so they could avoid the pain and failure she and so many other women had been through.

Attending church was a chore for her as she preferred to keep to herself. Teaching a class assured that she would attend as she refused to not honor her commitment to those young ladies. It had kept her somewhat plugged into a church for almost fifteen years now. She smiled and shook hands outside of her class but never allowed anyone to really get to know her.

Heather's investment with youth brought almost continual heartache into her life. No matter how much she preached to them about the sanctity of marriage and that doing sex God's way was the right way, they just couldn't abstain. Sure, they would all agree with everything she said, almost every student she had ever had was willing to pledge to remain pure until marriage, but as she herself had done, none of them seemed to make it all the way. The casualty of their attitudes over sexual sin hurt her deeply over and over again, but her tough spirit and her heart to make a difference kept her there, year after year. She had also been around long enough to watch God work in many of their lives. No matter how much they went through, time and time again, Heather witnessed God pulling their lives back together.

From girls getting raped by "nice" boys to willingly giving themselves to boyfriends or even strange men, Heather's heart got broken each time. Being alone was the right thing for her, but seeing Rachel and Sam together made her burn inside for what they had. Unfortunately, she was just not able to trust anyone in that way anymore. She had decided the world was winning, both with these young girls and with her own life. Most of the time, she didn't struggle at all with her decision, but deep down, she was praying for God to give her a husband who would honor and cherish her in the same way Sam did Rachel.

Since she had made many of the mistakes the young girls she was mentoring were making, she truly ached for them. She had even had an abortion, and it seemed to haunt her more and more the older she got. Seeing others make the same mistakes while acting like it was no big deal was very difficult for her. Her minis-try was what she felt was God's calling on her life, but it brought her as much pain as it brought her fulfillment. It could just be so sad sometimes.

"Great, I'm so glad he said yes. He thinks the world of you, Heather." Rachel couldn't help but show her approval. Her smil-ing face and upbeat tone surely gave her away. Her positive words were just icing on the cake.

"Why am I so happy about this, Rachel? I love Jack, but he's like my brother. Getting his text made me feel like a little girl, though." This was exactly what Rachel wanted to hear. For years, she had tried to encourage Heather to find a man like Sam, but Heather had always responded with the same argument that God had given her the ability to remain alone. Christ was her man, she would always tell Rachel.

"Sam and I have been talking about this, Heather. We both believe that Jack is perfect for you. He is a great man, and he already loves you. He's also good looking, which I know you have always appreciated in a man." Rachel knew she was in dangerous territory. Even suggesting that Heather consider dating anyone was taboo. It had to be said, though.

When Heather went to tears, it completely caught Rachel by surprise. "What's wrong?"

"I think I've been waiting for Jack for fifteen years." Her sob-bing intensified.

"Really, I had no idea. I thought you had sworn off men?" For years, Rachel had believed that Heather would never date again. Hearing her startling admission was very revealing, had she really been holding out for Jack all of this time rather than simply swearing off all men?

"After my stupid mistake with Kevin, I set my heart on Jack. He always made me laugh, and I just felt pulled to him. He had just turned sixteen then, and I was twenty-one. He was just a kid, and I knew it was wrong for me to be attracted to him like that, but you've got to understand I didn't want to sleep with him. I knew I needed to wait, and I thought it would be three or four years before he would be old enough to have the courage to ask me out. The more time I spent around him, the surer I was that he was the one for me. When he started dating Tina, I was crushed. It was really Jack who gave me the ability to have no need of a partner. I knew inside that it was him I was supposed to be with. When he got married, I was set to live the rest of my life alone. I know it sounds crazy. Hearing myself say it out loud is embarrassing." This was completely unexpected. Rachel began to cry now as well. It just seemed so beautiful to her.

"He was just a kid, and it may have been crazy then. Now you are both adults, it's not crazy at all now. Why are you crying?" Rachel was trying to figure out why it wasn't joy that was coming out of Heather after hearing what she had just heard.

"I never prayed for her to die. I thought she was a great wife for Jack. I loved her too, just like everyone else did. I'm crying because I had hoped and prayed that Jack was going to be available for me someday. I hate myself for that." The two were back in the apartment in an embrace now.

"That's okay, Heather. You had nothing to do with what happened."

"I know, but I wanted it to happen. Once she got sick, I knew it was going to happen, and I started to think about Jack again. Not sexually. I have never thought of him that way. He makes me smile, and I feel like I did with Joe when he's around. He's different than Joe, though, and I don't love him the way I do because of Joe. I love him because I honestly believe God made him for me. I can't even look at him without feeling like we belong together. I have always loved him, Rachel. Since the first time he spoke, I was attracted to him. Am I a terrible person?" She was obviously feeling guilty. Rachel could sympathize but chose not to support her in her guilt.

"You are looking at this all wrong, Heather. God works in mysterious ways. The fact that you know Jack is the man for you is a blessing. God may have put this in your heart. I know this because I know you. You have been dedicated to the Lord for many years now. You have become an example to countless young ladies in Christ's name. Tina's death was part of God's plan. You have to just accept that. Jack is alone and unhappy right now, and you have to see if he is being led to you the way you are being pulled to him. You know Jack. He would never go after you for your looks. He's the only guy I can even compare to my Sam. He will only want you for you, and you know that." Her tone was almost forceful. Her conviction was infectious, and Heather's frown immediately turned into a huge smile.

"I can't believe I'm in love again. For so long, I thought this would never happen for me again. I've been thinking about Jack constantly since Tina got sick. When she passed away, I began to lie awake every night, feeling terrible for Jack and wanting to be there for him. He's been in my thoughts and dreams as if he were haunting me. Do you really think we may be right for each other?" She needed Rachel to reassure her. Hearing it the first time had really felt good.

"Of course, he will want you. You are perfect for him, and he already loves you. He needs someone to take care of him, someone to keep him on track, and you are that woman. I know you are. Besides, you are the best-looking woman I know. All men, including Jack, are attracted to you."

Heather couldn't contain her excitement any longer. "I love him!" she shouted. Her face was full of joy and tears.

Rachel was sure she was feeling God's presence in that moment. She had not seen Heather truly hopeful in years, and it was overwhelming. The circumstances were just too awesome for them not to have been orchestrated by God. With a sense of divine intervention in their minds, the two headed out for an expensive steak and what turned out to be one of the happiest evenings of discussion they had had in years. As they spoke, Rachel couldn't help but see her old, happy, strong friend sitting across from her. *This will change, Heather*, Rachel thought. She was sure of it.

Dinner had blown by for Rachel, while it had felt like a waste of time to Heather. Though she was excited to get things started with Jack, and she loved Rachel's company, she could hardly wait to get things started. Being the extreme driver that she was, patience was never a strength of hers. Heather did the best she could to enjoy their time together, but she couldn't stop thinking about Jack and how badly she wanted time to pass so they could be together.

Heather had been operating on a calorie deficit of 500 calories before dinner. When she was alone again in her apartment, she determined she only need to burn 250 calories to burn off the surplus she had taken in during her wonderful evening with Rachel. Due to the code she lived by, she could not go to bed without burning that surplus. Thankfully, 250 calories would only take her a few minutes on the elliptical. Since exercise always helped her think, she gave it an extra thirty minutes so she could plan her assault on Jack.

After a quick shower, she lay down in bed, and her thoughts drifted to that terrible morning when she had woken up next to Kevin.

"Why did we do this?" She was sitting up in bed, gathering her thoughts about what had happened as she spoke to the semiconscious Kevin. She had just woken up in his bed. She had a splitting headache, and she was already beginning to feel the anger that would be with her for years to come.

"We did it because we both needed to and we both wanted to." He was lying there, not even attempting to stop her from leaving. Heather knew immediately that she had been taken.

"I thought you had changed. I believed you were different now. I thought you were a Christian. I can't believe I fell for this.

I'm such an idiot!" She was standing over him now. Her headache was fading as her blood began to boil with anger.

"Come on, cut the crap. You wanted me because I turn you on. You can't honestly believe all of that God crap? I was moved that day because Joe was a great guy. I've woken up since, though, and so should you." Heather was furious now. She grabbed her stuff and left. Kevin was lucky she didn't turn her anger on him as it would have been very ugly. Though her every desire was to attack him, she quickly decided he wasn't worth it. She knew God would deal with him.

The two never spoke again, but the fall out of the encounter was near life threatening for her. She spent the next two months in such a bad place that no one could console her. She never drank alcohol or did drugs, but she did consider ending her life on more than one occasion. When she finally began to let Rachel and then Sam in, they convinced her to turn to God. She threw herself into God's Word. It fed her and sustained her, and then it began to restore her.

If it weren't for Jack's regular visits, she may have never smiled again. He was so much like Joe that she began to wonder if her attraction to him was really only some sort of translation of feelings or something. Whatever it was, it kept her from talking to other men. It was only a few months after they had first met when she decided he was the one for her. He had become all she thought about, and something inside of her kept telling her he would someday be her husband. From then on, Jack was the only guy she talked to other than Sam. She committed herself to wait for him and even wrote herself a contract to wait on him. Of course, since he was only sixteen, she knew she could never tell him what she had decided. Well, at least not until he was old enough to do something about it. *Maybe when he's eighteen?* she rationalized.

By Christmastime, Heather started working at the gym that she would go on to eventually become the most senior employee of. Exercise consumed her, which was what she wanted. She loved working out so much that she spent most of her day there. When she wasn't teaching others, she was pushing herself to be better.

By graduation, she had decided that she wanted to continue working at the gym for her foreseeable future. She made enough money to live on and was quickly gaining some of the best-paying personal trainees. Though she never stopped studying the body and good health, she had no intension of doing anything more than working at the gym at her current capacity. Money no longer held any sort of grip over her life.

While Sam and Rachel planned their wedding, Heather completely gave up on love. Well, at least anything outside of her fascination and future planning for her and Jack's future together. She knew she had at least two more years before there would be any chance for them to be a couple because of his age. Just thinking about how young he was made her feel ridiculous for believing they would someday be together. She even began to wonder if something was seriously wrong with her. No one she knew would have any real interest in someone his age. Knowing that her attraction to him was not predominately physical and that she never thought of them being intimate gave her some assurance that her thoughts were pure. Not that she wasn't physically attracted to him, she definitely was. It just wasn't the basis of her attraction. Sam and Rachel were married the summer after graduation, and they moved out of the apartment soon after. With them gone, the visits from Jack stopped, but she still saw him a fair amount at Rachel and Sam's place. Jack actually told her he would love to keep visiting her at the apartment, but he just couldn't because it would be inappropriate. This only strengthened Heather's attraction to him.

Before that summer ended, Heather decided to move closer to the gym, which would also be closer to where Jack lived. He was just turning seventeen at this point, but all she could think about was that he was one year closer to becoming an adult. She would wait for him as long as it took.

Though she saw Jack several times while visiting Sam and Rachel over the next year, it wasn't enough. Every time they were together, they always found a way to get alone where they could really talk. Not so alone that others couldn't see them but alone enough to have personal conversations. Heather was always amazed at how he thought and how naturally funny he was all of the time, while Jack completely idolized her. Since their time together was becoming less frequent since the move, she began to miss him and to plot how she could let him know how she felt as soon as he was eighteen. Common sense told her that he would still be too young to be her boyfriend at eighteen as she would then be twenty three and a half, but common sense had nothing to do with her feelings for him. Her feelings for him had become intense and undeniable.

Heather was certain her desire for him was coming from God as she had been able to completely ignore any and all advances from men since she had begun to know Jack. Her thoughts about him were almost never physical. She simply desired to be his and to be in his presence. Though, because of their age difference and his youth, she figured that his parents and society in general would not be able to accept the type of relationship she desired with him. Still she held on to hope, and down deep, she believed they would end up together.

Heather convinced herself that they didn't need to start dating as soon as he was eighteen, but she did believe she needed to let him know how she felt and about her willingness to wait for him on this birthday. It had to be done on his eighteenth birthday, lest she risk him meeting someone else.

Almost exactly one year after Rachel and Sam were married, Heather was invited to their house to attend a special dinner for Jack's eighteenth birthday. It was the birthday she had been waiting for. For weeks, she had planned how she would reveal her feelings for him. Finally, she decided to give him a note telling him how she felt rather than attempt to get him alone. In her mind, it would just be too awkward to tell him in person. Though she had no idea how her note's revelation would go over, she felt assured that Jack would be flattered and very interested. They had always been so natural together, and she could tell he was infatuated with her. He had even told her on several occasions how he had been praying not to look at her lustfully. These comments, along with his obvious attraction to her, made her feel confident that they would soon be together.

As she drove up to Sam and Rachel's little house, she was far more nervous than she had expected. As she pulled into the driveway, she saw Jack standing in the living room with some girl through the large window in the front of the house. She parked and ran up the walkway to see what was going on. It was a heartbreaking sight for her as Jack had his arm around a tiny little girl. She was a pretty little thing, and there was no mistaking that Jack was obviously with her; they were an item.

With a heavy heart, Heather turned and headed back to her car with every intention of driving away. As soon as she was alone in her car, sitting behind the wheel, her feelings overtook her, and she collapsed on the steering wheel, sounding her horn.

There was no way she could get away now without them seeing her. In a state of panic, she reached into the gift bag she had brought for Jack and pulled out the card. It was a normal birthday card with a note taped to the inside of the envelope that she planned to point out to him or to text him about later. The note itself had "Read when you are alone" written on the back of it. She had hoped no one but Jack would notice the private note. It was a risk that had been haunting her all day. Ripping it from the inside of the envelope was not easy, but she felt immediate relief as it tore free.

She stuffed the scandalous note under her seat and tried to pull herself together. As she refocused, she looked up and saw Jack and his pretty little thing heading down the stairs toward her. As they approached, she could see the joy on his face. She wondered if the joy was for her or for his pretty little girlfriend. Either way, she needed to gather herself so she could give a good reason to get out of there quickly. There was no way should could stay. Unfortunately, she had begun to cry already, and her body was trembling uncontrollably.

"Sorry, the horn was a mistake." Jack and little miss thing were already at her door now.

She had to come up with something as she was positive that she couldn't stay and deal with this. "I'm really sorry, but I'm only here to drop off my gift and to say happy birthday. I've got to head home to get ready for work." Jack's smile immediately vanished. He was very clearly disappointed.

"Too bad, I was looking forward to having you here." His disappointment was clear in his facial expressions, as well as his tone. "This is Tina. She's my girlfriend." He was trying to look happy, but Heather could tell he was very disappointed.

Why would he think there is any chance with me? Heather asked herself. *Why am I being so childish?* None of it was working though, no logic could. Her heart was breaking over this eighteen-year-old, and he didn't even know it.

Then the little angel spoke, "Hi, Heather. I'm so glad to finally meet you. Jack thinks the world of you." She stuck her tiny little boney hand through the window for a handshake so Heather gave her one. Though Tina was slight of stature, she was not weak. Her personality was quite strong, and Heather couldn't help but pick it up.

Wanting to assert her physical superiority over this tiny little flower, Heather felt a rush of adrenalin pulse through her body, and the tears and trembling were a thing of the past. She got out of the car to hand Jack his gift and to let this little thing see what she was up against. While she handed him the gift, she pulled him to her so he could feel her full breasts and taught muscular body. It worked, and anyone could have noticed that he was completely dumbfounded by the contact. He stood there without a reply, just looking into that perfect face and those deep blue eyes.

Heather noticed the effect she had on him and suddenly felt dirty and inappropriate. *What the heck am I doing?* To cover her foolish move, she reached over to Tina and gave her an identical hug. That worked too. Tina was completely intimidated. "Wow, you are like a supermodel with muscle everywhere," Tina said without thinking. Seeing Heather, who had to be over six feet tall in her heals, hug Jack had really bothered her. Not so much the hug but his reaction to the hug. Tina would never forget the look on his face that day. She never fully let it go either, knowing that Heather had some serious feelings for Jack whether he knew it or not.

Heather's strength shocked Tina. She had never felt a hug like Heather's, and it actually scared her a little. It had felt threatening as if Heather wanted her to know she could crush her. In a fraction of a second, she had made Tina feel completely inadequate. It was an encounter Tina would never forget and one she would never give Heather the satisfaction of knowing had gotten to her. Tina had an inner strength, one based on her faith.

"Thanks, I guess. Sorry I have to run. Please tell Sam and Rachel that I'm sorry I can't stay. Have a great birthday, Jack. You are a great guy. Heck, you are my favorite guy." She gave them a big smile, hopped back in her car and sped away.

Tina and Jack stood there clueless about the life-changing encounter they had just had with the bombshell. Jack was lost in his adoration of her, and Tina, fully realizing Heather was a serious threat to her and Jack's relationship, decided to never mention Heather's obvious infatuation to him.

Heather went home and cried until she couldn't cry anymore. The event had a lasting impact on her. It was the day that she knew she would be alone until Jack was either free of Tina or Jack or herself passed away. Everything in her had been telling her that Jack was the man for her. She had been praying to God to let him be, and she actually had believed that it was God's will. She had decided that she would wait for him, and it hadn't been difficult at all for her. The ease of waiting for him led her to believe that she should keep waiting for him. If Jack married this girl, she decided she would simply be alone for life. If Jack was who God wanted her to be with, as she believed all the way down into the deepest depths of her sole as he did, God would make it so.

Though she struggled a bit with why it was happening, she eventually decided it was God's will that she continue to wait. If Jack was meant to be with her, that would happen. If not, she would need lots of God's presence to not feel alone. Though part of her told her she would someday move on, at that point, she fully intended to wait or to be alone.

The only evidence of Heather's true feelings for Jack was in the note that she had hidden under her seat. That night, the note would be placed in an envelope and tucked away in a sacred space where it would remain sealed. Heather's prayer was that she would someday give it to him and tell him how she had intended to give it to him that day. Though she had no way of knowing it at the time, it was something she would think about for years to come.

Now, almost fourteen years after she had nearly pledged her love to an eighteen-year-old boy, Heather lay in bed, remembering it like it was yesterday. The birthday note was still in its envelope, and now she was sure it was finally the right time to give it to him. Almost unbelievably, her heart was still in the same place, and it was still his to crush. God had been keeping her pure for him. Sure she had been with guys before, but not since she had fallen for Jack. She had been so sure for so long about Jack that there had never even been a close call. There was no chance she was going to sleep tonight with what was about to happen between them the next day. It was finally here!

"Lord, please don't let anything stand in the way." She needed this to work out. It would kill her if it didn't.

At about two in the morning, Heather decided to get up and get the birthday note out of its hiding place. As soon as she had it in her hand, she felt calmness come over her. It was so reassuring that she fell asleep as soon as she hit the pillow. It was deep, restful, and refreshing sleep.

CHAPTER 18

Sam got home first and could hardly wait for his beautiful bride to arrive. He had already put the kids to bed and was headed down the stairs when he heard Rachel's key in the door. He instinctively hurried down the stairs to hide so he could scare her. Thankfully, Rachel was really struggling to get her key in the door. Her fumbling around gave Sam plenty of time to dive behind the couch. When the door finally opened and his slender wife quietly slipped in, he slowly crept around behind her in the dark and sprung at her. He succeeded in scaring her, but he failed in protecting himself from her violently swinging purse. It caught him in his private area and sent him to the floor.

Realizing it was Sam she had just struck, Rachel lovingly dropped down beside him and started apologizing, "Oh baby, I'm so sorry. Are you okay?"

Sam couldn't even speak for a while. He actually thought that he might throw up or maybe even pass out. He was just beginning to be able to move under his own control but couldn't yet speak.

"Oh, Sam, I'm really sorry. I'll prove it to you tonight. I can't wait to tell you about Heather." She had already started to laugh so Sam had trouble believing her apology was heartfelt. She was right to laugh though. It was pretty funny. He had gotten what he deserved for trying to scare her.

With her comment about Heather, he was able to get out, "Jack told me she has always been his dream girl."

"Really, you won't even believe how great that is?" She was on her feet now, trying to pull him to his feet. "Let's go to our room. If you can recover from my fury, I will give you the night of your life." She was absolutely serious. Her excitement over the possibility of Heather having a loving husband was the best news she had gotten in quite a while. She hadn't had a cause for celebrating in a long time. For years, she had been praying for Heather to have someone like Sam. Now she knew it was really going to happen.

When the pain had subsided enough for Sam to climb to his feet, he slowly pulled himself up by grabbing onto the back of the couch with his free hand while Rachel's light pull on the other stabilized his assent. Once he was on his feet, Rachel began to tempt him in an attempt to lead him up the stairs. He felt like carrying her up to their room, but he knew it wasn't a good idea to even try. While Rachel had remained very health conscious, he had really let himself go. Between the stresses of work and the weight of financial stress, Sam had developed a very unhealthy dependence on food and soft drinks. Whenever things got tough, Sam ate. If they got really tough, he hit the hard stuff like frosting. Things had gotten so far out of control that he was more than sixty pounds overweight. To add to his condition, he got practically no exercise.

For several years, he had been taking medication to keep his blood pressure in check. At this point, his condition was so poor that he could hardly keep up with the kids for even slightly animated activity. He hated being out of shape, but his level of fitness wasn't about to change as he continually quit on diets and exercise routines while eating like a growing teenager.

"Come on, baby," she said as she broke loose from the deep passionate kiss she was giving him and began pulling him up the stairs. Rachel had never felt comfortable being intimate anywhere but alone with him in their bedroom with the door locked. The thought of the kids catching them in action made it impossible for her to relax in an unsecured area like the one they were currently in.

They shared their news and enjoyed each other for almost an hour before falling asleep. Theirs was a perfect marriage. They almost never fought or even disagreed about anything. They raised their children as a team and made it a priority for their kids to know how deeply they were in love with each other.

Both Sam and Rachel were amazed at some of the things they saw in their coworker's and acquaintance's marriages. The attitudes about marriage of many married couples were so far from what their attitude about marriage was that they couldn't even imagine anything less than what they had. It was a marriage blessed by God, and they both knew it. They were both thankful for it. How much harder would life be without the security of a secure, loving relationship?

CHAPTER 19

Jack couldn't sleep a wink due to his mixed emotions over his date with Heather the next day. If she made a move of any kind, he was certain he would have no power to resist her. Not that he expected her to try anything physical, but it was possible that she may tell him she had feelings for him. If that were to happen, he knew he couldn't escape a permanent fall for her. Wasn't it too soon to even be thinking about replacing Tina? That question was haunting him from the time he had first gotten her text.

On the other hand, what if she only wanted to cheer him up? Could he even handle that? He was already feeling a tremendous feeling of hope over the prospects of them being together. *How much time had I prayed for that as a high-school kid?* he wondered. He was sure he could resist any advances from any other women in the world, but Heather was the one that he knew he could not resist. He also knew that he had already begun to imagine her as his wife, and he was positive that he would be deeply disappointed if she wasn't into him that way. That fact made him feel inappropriate since his wife hadn't even been gone for six months yet. It also made him feel certain that he would be in an even deeper state of brokenness than he was already in should she not have a romantic interest in him.

As much as he hated being alone, he didn't want to replace Tina, especially not this soon. Part of him didn't want to move on at all. *Didn't Tina deserve more?*

Though she had told him that she wanted him to move on after she was gone, they never spoke about it at length as it was such a sad subject to think about. Tina loved him deeply, and she fully understood that he would be a thirty-one-year-old man with no children. It would be unnatural for him to live the rest of his life alone. She continuously assured him that it would be okay for him to remarry. She knew he would do it right, and she had told him, "You are not built to be alone. You need someone to love you and take care of you." Still, it seemed really wrong to Jack to be thinking about someone else already.

He was sure of one thing, though. If he was going to move on, Heather was definitely the one for him. Since her text earlier that night, he had tough of nothing else but her; she owned him, and he knew it. Her beautiful outside was in his mind, but who she was in his heart from their past together is where the heavy feelings were coming from. This wasn't just a beautiful woman; this was someone who truly knew him, someone who he had a long history with.

Jack had sat through a movie with Sam and the boys but hadn't even followed the plot. His distraction was so consuming that he almost walked out in front of a car on their way out of the theater. Sam had noticed the state he was in and couldn't help but feel hope for his younger brother. For quite some time, Jack had been suffering like no other time in his life. Sam loved his younger brother, and he hated to see him going through such pain. This was Jack, the happiest person anyone had ever known. Seeing Jack in the state he was in that night encouraged Sam that the real Jack could be back soon. If anyone could bring him all the way back, Heather could.

As Jack lay in bed, thinking about his date, he was actually beginning to feel the pain he had struggled with as a fifteen-year-old boy. Heather had always been more of a dream to him than anything that he could believe he deserved or that he could ever call his own. When he was fifteen, he had felt like he loved her, but her beauty led him to believe it was mostly lust he was feeling. She was this gorgeous older woman, and he was this pathetic kid in love. He remembered feeling like he would have a chance with her when he got older. The memories came flooding in as he began to remember that time period of his life. At seventeen, he had felt that he was becoming an adult and that he would soon be considered an adult by her. He remembered imagining that she thought of them together as well and how he couldn't wait to grow up to be with her.

Like Heather, Jack had felt like they were meant to be together when he was in high school. He never knew she thought of him that way, but he did know that she liked his company. Whenever he came over, she spent all of the time he was there with him. They ate together, went to and rented movies together, and talked about God and everything else together. Sure Rachel and Sam were always around, but both Heather and Jack were there for each other, not for Rachel and Sam. Jack made everyone smile, but he did much more than that for Heather. They frequently caught one another staring, and it was this that had made Jack begin to wonder if she would ever see him as a man and not a boy.

For about a year, Jack spent most of his free time visiting his brother so he could be around Heather. When Sam and Rachel moved out, Heather and Jack still saw each other a couple of times each week at Sam and Rachel's place. Though Jack had tried to imagine a scenario in which they could be together, he just couldn't get past the fact that she was almost six years older than he was, but not only that, she was also easily the most attractive woman he had ever seen.

Through prayer and what he believed to be the facing of the reality of the situation, Jack was finally able to move on. Just before he turned eighteen, he decided to ask Tina out, though it meant he would have to give up on his dreams to be Heather's husband. At the time, he felt that he needed to move on and stop holding on to such a far-fetched dream. Jack had convinced himself that it would never happen between them. The age difference alone was just too much to overcome in his mind. He felt she could never take him seriously because of it. He told himself that it was better to start seeing her as only a good friend, almost family actually. Had he known her true feelings, he would have never even thought about dating anyone else, ever.

As he lay in bed trying to convince himself that it didn't matter if Heather only wanted to be his friend, his gut was telling him the opposite—he loved her, and her rejection would bottom him out. If she was about to make his dreams come true, it would be worth any unpleasantness he may be feeling, he finally decided.

Jack, being more and more aware that he wanted Heather to be his wife more than anything else in the world, became very nervous. He began sweating so profusely that he had to remove all of his covers. When he finally fell asleep for what couldn't have been more than a couple of hours, he could only stay asleep until about 7:00 a.m. He lay there motionless, thinking about her until he had to get up and get ready.

He chose to shower and comb his hair as he wanted to look as good as he could for her. He wondered, *Does anyone else going to a morning spinning class even care what they looked or smelled like?*

Had he known how Heather really felt about him, he wouldn't have gotten any sleep at all.

CHAPTER 20

Heather's usual routine on Saturday brought her in around 7:30 a.m. for her 8:00 a.m. spinning class. This Saturday was different, though, as Jack would be in her class today. Her excitement and the nerves she was dealing with brought her in early, so early that she was there to help the morning crew open the doors at 7:00 a.m. To get rid of some of her nerves and to kill time, she went to work on her upper body and midsection. She would need to be thinking clearly for what she was about to do.

From the moment she had entered the gym, she couldn't take her eyes off of the entrance. There was no way she was going to miss Jack coming through those doors. She had been imagining it for months. Actually, though she didn't want to admit it, she had been thinking about it since Tina passed away. Today was finally that day. It was actually going to happen, and there was no way she was going to miss it. For this reason, she chose only to do exercises she could do while maintaining constant surveillance on the front doors.

As she not so patiently waited for him, she began to wonder if it made more sense to let him make the first move when he was ready. She could just let him know she was interested and see where things went from there. His wife hadn't been gone for that long after all. *Maybe that was a better way to go?* she wondered.

Almost as soon as she was certain that the conservative approach was the way to go, she began coming up with reasons why it wasn't. *What if it took him a year or more to be ready? I've waited this long, it wouldn't kill me to keep on waiting.*

No, she decided things are different now. She was certain her patience was all gone. Waiting just wasn't a viable option. She was burning inside to be his, and the feelings had been steadily growing since Tina's death. In spite of the internal dialogue telling her otherwise, she knew now was time. Asking him to her class had already been the first move. *There is no going back now,* she told herself. Knowing him as well as she did, she knew it could take some real time before he'd actually make a move anyway. It had to be her pushing this thing, or she'd run the risk of waiting what would feel like another fifteen years.

With the decision to spill her guts affirmed solidly in her mind, she again began to imagine how she would deliver her soul to him. The plan she had been working out had her telling him that she had intended to give him the note she was now handing him on his eighteenth birthday. She would lay it all out in front of him and give him the power to reject her. She loved him, she had always loved him, and she was tired of hiding from it.

If he were to reject her, it would be devastating. She decided that it would be a sign from God that he wanted her to be alone. Just like she was prepared to do before Tina passed away, she would stay celibate the rest of her life if he didn't want her. He was the only man for her, and she knew it. She earnestly believed that her feelings for him were blessed by God. If that were the case, it would be like a fairy tale. If the feelings that were welled up inside her were not blessed by God, Jack would reject her, and she would accept it and keep living as she had been. How sad it would be.

She looked up and there he was. As usual, he wore a humongous smile, and she could see him trying to cheer up the rest of the morning crew at the reception desk as she got up and hustled his way. As she rushed to meet him, her feelings for him almost overwhelmed her as she felt more certainty with every step that he was her destiny. The wait to start that part of her life would soon be over. She wanted to be close to him so badly that she even considered hugging him right there.

"Hey you," she hollered to him as she excitedly ran toward him. The other gym employees were shocked that it was her voice when they turned to see who was hollering. It was completely out of her character. Not only was she not bubbly ever, but she was never this excited to see anyone, let alone a man.

"Hey, beautiful. I'm so glad you're here to save me. They were just about to begin an assault on my privacy." Heather almost melted hearing him call her "beautiful." His smile was so warming and caring that she just wanted to walk right up and hug him. It became an urge that she actually had to fight off. Knowing what he was going through in his personal life, it amazed her that he was still able to give others his very best. It was a reminder to her how unique a person he really was. *Oh yeah, I definitely love this guy,* she reassured herself.

"He's with me," she said to the twenty-something twinkie who was trying to hand Jack a clipboard with a sign-in sheet.

"Okay, Heather, he's all yours." The youngsters all treated Heather like she owned the place, which, after her many years on the staff, she practically did.

Heather almost said, "I hope he's all mine," but caught herself before anything came out. Though she had fought the urge, she lost to it and gave into it. Without any restraint at all, she gave him a warm full-body hug, which he returned remarkably smoothly. The embrace was not only intimate; it was also substantially long as the two remained in each other's arms without any thoughts of digression.

Jack was stunned that she had come at him the way she had but was also very excited to be hugging his dream girl. Only one woman had ever hugged him this way, and it had been quite some time since she had. His excitement for Heather was impossible to hide, and his face immediately betrayed any hopes he may have had of concealing his feelings for her. He had never felt so vulnerable.

The hug brought him back to the hug he had shared with her on his eighteenth birthday. That hug had haunted him for more time than he wanted to admit. That hug had been brief, but this one was not. With the way she was holding on to him, it was as if he had just returned from the front lines. This time was no different from the first in that it was something he knew he wanted to remember every detail of. Since the last one had been a one-time deal, he recorded everything he could in his mind in case this too was a single event.

As he held her he thought he felt her shudder a bit, but he wasn't sure. Just the thought of it made him fear where his insides were taking him. She definitely had the ultimate female physique and an unnatural power over him too.

Heather could not have cared less what anyone thought of her at that moment. Feeling his arms around her and catching a breath of his smell was almost too much for her. She quivered a bit in his arms almost as if she had gotten a chill. As she released him, Jack's smiling face said it all. He too was in heaven. As she had, he too had caught her smell and felt her desire for him. Their affection for one another was mutual, and they both new it. It was truly electric for both of them.

Before he could say a word, she pushed away with one arm, and with her other arm still around his waist, she led him into the heart of the gym. "We have time for some warmup before the class if you think you need it."

"Sure, you're the expert." He liked her being in control as he never liked to control situations. It had always been difficult for him to lead other adults. Students were a different story as he felt God would have him lead them. With adults, he simply had too much respect for others to control or push them in any way. Thankfully, as Tina had also been, Heather was the opposite.

Tina pushed and prodded people and always had a plan. Nothing was in the spur of the moment with her as everything seemed to be with Jack. Heather was exactly the same as Tina in this area, and it was one of the things Jack loved about her. In this moment though, neither were really in control of anything.

She put him on an elliptical for five minutes to get his blood pumping while she set up two mats for them to stretch on. After a little small talk, Heather decided to make her move.

"Jack, I really need to talk to you about something. Can we go get some lunch or something after the workout?"

"I'd like that, Heather. You can have as much of my time as you want. I have nothing else planned but you today, and I love being with you." He was feeling really good about her offer and hoped she was planning to tell him that she had always liked him. He'd definitely let her lead; she was good at it. If she told him that she liked him, it would be easy for him to tell her how he had always felt about her.

"Great. Let's go get you a good seat, mister." Her ascent to her feet was both effortless and impressive. It was as if she just stood up from the floor out of the stretch they were in. Jack was amazed and eagerly took the hand she offered him. She pulled him up like he was a child. The hug came back to mind as he felt her strength pull him off the floor. When she had hugged him, he had felt her amazing physique. Not only was she slender and chesty, she was also taut and powerful. It had actually been a bit intimidating, though he knew her too well and loved her too much to be too intimidated.

"Can't I hide in the back somewhere, Heather? I ride at home some, but I don't think I'm ready for your pace. I don't want anyone to know I'm with you because I'll probably embarrass you." Though he knew he was in pretty good shape, he knew he was no match for a workout junkie like Heather. She was a professional and a fanatic.

"This is my easy class. If you can keep up, you can stay for the second hour. I take it up a notch for my more advanced students in the second hour. You can either gear way down, rest some, or just wait for me to finish hour two. I can't let you hide in the back though. I want to be able to look you in the eye. You'll be right in front of me, and I would never be embarrassed of you." She had thought a lot about having him in her class. There was no chance he was ruining her fantasy.

"Okay, you win. I'll do whatever you tell me to do." He loved how she made things so easy on him. She was so strong and possessed all of the focus he lacked. He had never been a planner, but he loved to follow a good plan, and Heather obviously would always have one.

As she led him to the spinning workout room, things just felt right. Having him there made her feel like a better person. Her usual competitive nature seemed to melt away when he was around. Jack was what she needed in her life. He had always been her destiny.

Heather positioned him in the front of the class and helped him get his bike dialed in perfectly before she took her position on the instructor cycle about half a foot above the others. The class was quite full, and she had saved him the bike he was now mounted and strapped into. She had even provided him with a towel and water bottle, rightly assuming he would be completely unprepared. Seeing things prepared for him the way she had prepared them put him at ease as it reaffirmed that she really could fill the holes in his life.

Heather's bike was face to face with his. Her heart was so full of joy that she couldn't stop herself from making the announcement that made the rest of Jack's life. With a room full of students, Heather announced, "The man in front of me is Jack Henderson. I have waited fifteen years to have him in this class. He is the love of my life, and I want to spend the rest of my life with him." Everyone cheered, and a lady in the back of the class got off her bike and headed for the check-in counter where all of the other gym employees were congregated. Heather noticed her leaving and assumed she was going to break the news to the staff.

Jack stopped peddling while his jaw dropped open. He couldn't believe what he had just heard. She was pumping away and picking up the pace when she commanded him, "Don't fail me now, Jack. I've never started a class late, and today won't be the first time. Start peddling, lover boy." He couldn't even feel his legs, but he somehow managed to get them going. Everything she was saying was being broadcast over the loud speaker. This wasn't exactly private. Good for him that he had never had any reservations about being in front of a crowd. Actually, it had always been his specialty.

For the next hour, all of her intensity was directed at him. She pressed him to work harder than he had ever known he was capable of working. That stare with those longing eyes made him forget all about the pain as he followed her every command. He pumped away at the pedals knowing that he was looking into the eyes of the woman he would love for the rest of his life.

Jack couldn't believe it had already been an hour when Heather announced that they had reached the end of their scheduled time and that those that weren't interested in a more intense advanced session were free to go. Then she followed up that announcement, "Jack, you are not free to go, but you are free to coast as much as you like." She stuck her tongue out at him, and he did the same back at her.

Man she is pretty, he thought. *Not just pretty, she is absolutely perfect.*

His expression and wanting smiles assured Heather that he was hers. It had been fifteen years since she had kissed a man, and all the while, she had been waiting for this man. She wanted to be his wife more than anything, and now, staring into his eyes, she knew it was going to happen. God had finally given her Jack. It was His timing, and the perfection of it all was mind-boggling to her. Had she gotten her way, he would have been way too young for her. Now, everything was perfect. Age didn't even matter anymore. They were both old now.

The second hour passed even faster than the first had. Jack marveled at her tenacity. When he looked around, he noticed that absolutely, no one was keeping up. It wasn't just him who was slacking. Heather stood and peddled like she was Lance Armstrong dominating the hills of the Tour de France for most of the hour. As time wore on, the cyclers jumped off one by one. When it was finally over, he and four others were the only ones still left on the bikes. Jack had done his best to keep up where he could, but most of the time he was on low tension sitting in his seat just barely spinning at all.

"Have a great day everyone" she announced as she sat back, stopped peddling, and stretched her arms toward Jack in a welcoming gesture. The invite got him so excited he actually fell off of his bike on his way to her. His legs felt and acted like cooked spaghetti. Thankfully, Heather's legs were good as new. She was clear of her bike and pulling him up before he could get his own balance.

Heather scooped him up like he was a small child. Her powerful frame startled him a little at first, but her embrace was tender and loving, and he could hear her brokenness in her voice as she whispered, "I have loved you for so long, Jack." He was pretty sure that he had been right. She had definitely trembled in his arms earlier. It really touched him that she had.

Jack was touched but couldn't believe she had been attracted to him nearly as long has he had been to her. "You probably haven't loved me as long as I have loved you, Heather. It was practically from first sight for me." He was finally all the way up on his shaky legs as he continued, "You do realize that the only way to get me is to marry me, right?" In the background, they both finally noticed the clapping and cheering. The remaining class along with some of the early retirees from the beginner's class and most of the staff were in full applause. Those who knew Heather best gathered around to watch her express her feeling for someone as it had been an open debate for quite some time that such a thing was even possible.

Though no one ever dare say it to her face, everyone who knew her wondered if she would ever find someone. No one had ever seen her show any interest in any guy. Though she had gotten countless date offers from men and always had guys sending her flowers and other gifts, she never went on a date with anyone. She was so good looking that she had even had a couple of admirers who had gone so far that she had reported them to the authorities to get them to back off. The fact that she was undateable had become legendary around the gym. Seeing her with Jack was a very moving experience for anyone who knew her.

Noticing the crowd, Heather took Jack by the hand and led him through the crowd, ignoring everyone. Even those close to her didn't get as much as a nod or a wink. She took him straight to her private office where they could be alone. Being the most senior employee of the gym did have some privileges.

Shutting the door behind Jack, she brought him in close and told him, "I would marry you today if you would have me. I have literally been waiting for you since Kevin, who you know was my sixth and final. I wish I had never been with any of them. I'm sorry about that. I've waited for you since Kevin, though." He went in for their first kiss, and he almost lost himself in her heavenly lips before he caught himself and pulled away. It was like nothing he had ever experienced. Her lips were nothing at all like Tina's, and he had kissed no other's. Heather's lips were soft and tender, yet her ability to be seductive was new to him. A bunch of scripture, primarily from Proverbs, ran through his mind as he felt temped in a way he had never experienced.

As they pulled apart, he could feel a pull to go back at her. She was amazing and wanted him in a way he had never experienced before. Everything about her was without defect, and her body language and the look in her eyes told him that she wanted him now. All those helpless nights he had been through as a teenager dreaming and fantasizing about her were pushing him to take her right there in her office. Thankfully, the Holy Spirit would not allow it. He suddenly felt a superhuman strength allowing him to take over and pull back from his fleshly desires.

"I'm sorry, Heather, I have only kissed one woman in my entire life. You know what I do for a living, so you know I can't do this.

Believe me though, I am yours. I have been yours since the first day I laid my eyes on you. I used to have to pray to God to keep my filthy mind off your body. Even when I met Tina, it was you that she never measured up to. If it hadn't been for God helping me wash you from my brain, I would have never been able to date and marry her. He helped me push you out, and for the longest time, I only had eyes for Tina. Now that she is gone, God has put you back where you belong in my heart. I barely slept last night and prayed almost continually that you had invited me here because you were attracted to me. This is too good to be true, and although I don't want to hurt you, I have to maintain control here for both of us." The two sat down on the floor together, staring into each other's eyes.

"I don't want to have sex with you, Jack. I want to be your wife and have lots and lots of sex with you every night." She leaned into him and buried her head against his chest for a second while he put his hand on her head.

"Wow, I had no idea, Heather. I just thought you thought I was funny." He was more than stunned at this point.

"I have something for you, Jack. I've been waiting a very long time to give it to you." She leaned forward and reached into her desk drawer to produce the sealed envelope. On the envelope, she had written, "You are finally a man."

"Do you remember your eighteenth birthday, the day you introduced me to Tina?"

With a confused look on his face, he answered, "I sure do. It was the day I got the hug. I still think about that day, and I can remember how disappointed I was when you left without spending any time with us. Honestly though, your hug messed me up for a while. It made me realize that you were a full-grown beautiful woman, and I was only a pathetic boy with a huge crush. It killed my dream of being your boyfriend as I realized you had a real life, while I was still living at home and had another year of high school."

"Well, it's also the day you broke my heart. This is the note I planned to give you that day. I tore it from the birthday card's envelope right before you and Tina got to my car. I had been waiting for you to turn eighteen to tell you how I felt about you. Just read the note. It's the actual note I had planned to give you that day. It's been hidden in one of my drawers at home since then. I've never opened the envelope, hoping one day, I could give it to you." She could hardly wait for him to see what she had written him. It was thirteen years late, but this truly was the right time.

He sat up and tore open the envelope. *How cool is this*, he thought.

Upon opening the envelope, he immediately saw the writing on the outside of the note that read, "Read when you are alone." He gave Heather an inquisitive look and quickly unfolded it to read.

Jack,

I'm so glad that you are finally a man.

I've thought a lot about how to say this, but nothing seems to work, so I'll just come out and say it.

I want no other. You are the one for me. I am sure of it. Don't ask me how I know, I just do. If you will have me, I will wait until you are ready for me.

I don't care if I have to wait five or ten years for you to be ready for me. Today, I pledge to take no other until you make me yours. No matter how long it takes, I will be here for you.

When I'm with you, I feel at my best. My worries fade away, and I can't stop myself from laughing at everything you say. Your kindness touches my heart, and your smile and caring attitude are the most selfless I have ever seen. Other than your brother, I've not known anyone with as much faith in God as you have.

I've wanted to hug you for months now, and I can't wait until we get the chance to hug as boyfriend and girlfriend. I even imagine myself as your wife someday.

I AM YOURS IF YOU WANT ME. I can't say it any more clearly than that.

No, I don't think you are ready for me right now. All I'm hoping for at this point is that you will choose me and date no other as I will be doing for you. My best guess is that we can start to date the day you move out of your parents' house. What do you think?

I hope this note doesn't creep you out. If it does, I hope you will forgive me for being so naive. If you won't have me, I will be alone. That is what I have decided.

What I'm saying is true, and it's what I believe deep in my heart. If you think of me as a crazy old lady, I wouldn't blame you. As you know, I am already twenty-three years old and will be turning twenty-four before your nineteenth birthday.

If this is the only time you hear it, I need to say it. I love you, Jack Henderson!

Hopelessly yours,
Heather Thompson (Henderson?)

The letter was unbelievable to Jack. Just thinking about how radically it would have altered their lives put him in awe of God's timing in all of this. It truly was amazing. If he had gotten this letter, he was sure that Tina would have been on her final date with him that day. Jack wasn't sure what to do with those thoughts, but he was blown away how great he was suddenly feeling about his future.

"Yes, I will marry you. Am I enough of a man for you now?" He was overwhelmed with emotion but managed to bring his personality along for the ride.

"You sure are." She grabbed his face and kissed him like he was a man.

"Let's get married, Heather. We can do it at my church or yours. We'll invite our families but no one else, unless you want a big wedding? I'll leave it up to you. All I know is that I don't want to make you wait any longer. You poor thing, how have you managed without me?" Again with the humor. She loved it and his smile too.

"I don't care about the wedding. It doesn't matter at all. If we can do it right here right now, I'm good with that. I've waited patiently, and I don't want to wait anymore. Let's just make it happen. I want the marriage, not a wedding. I'm calling Rachel right now to let her and Sam know that we are about to be family." Jack couldn't wait to hear Sam's reaction. This was an amazing happening. No, it was a miracle.

"Heather, I don't want to be alone anymore. I know I can make the wedding happen at my church quickly. Our pastor will be shocked at how quickly I've moved on, but he'll understand, and he'll marry us as soon as we can get the license." She was already dialing Rachel but was able to agree with what he was saying before Rachel picked up.

"Hey, girl, you'll never guess what just happened." Heather could hear Sam's voice in the background, begging for her to put the phone on speaker, and based on the commotion, it sounded like she was doing just that.

"I'm here with the whole family. I'll put you guys on the speaker if that's okay? I'm not going to guess, just tell us. Are you two dating now?" Her excitement caught the attention of the boys, and they were all there quickly by her side to hear the news over the speaker phone.

"The speaker is fine. I want them all to here this." She could tell the phone was now on speaker before she continued, "Jack and I just decided to get married right away. Neither of us can wait, and we are going to have lots of babies while I can still have them."

Jack's voice came in, "Yes, at least a baby right away, though we haven't really talked about that yet." He looked into Heather's eyes and spoke directly to her, "You know, Heather, babies may cost you extra." Jack hadn't even thought about babies until now. Oh how he ached for children. This was all too good to be true. He couldn't stop himself from praising God out loud, "God is soooo good! Praise the Lord!" Jack hollered into the phone.

After the congratulations were over, Jack put his arm around Heather and said, "You are already thirty-six years old, gal. We better stop wasting time if you want to have kids." Heather gave Jack a half smile and told everyone she needed to hang up to deal with this situation. She promised them that she and Jack would come by around 4:00 p.m. to visit with everyone. When she finally hung up, she dropped the phone and pulled him to her mouth for the best kiss yet.

"Let's go get showers, something to eat, and find a place we can do some serious hugging." She was completely in control now, and Jack loved it.

"Yes, sir," came his sarcastic reply.

They stammered to their feet, exchanged another big hug, and began to head for their respective places to clean up. "How much time do you need?" Heather asked Jack.

"Can I pick you up in an hour?"

"Wow, what are you, some kind of girl?" Heather was trying to be funny now.

"Okay, I'll be there in thirty minutes." He loved her strength and was surprised that she didn't need more time. He knew she would look perfect when he showed up for her. When hadn't she looked perfect?

The Henderson family would always remember the excitement and the love and relief they heard through the phone that day. It was a moment none of them would ever forget.

CHAPTER 21

J ack had been right. The senior pastor at his church, Pastor John Dunkin, was concerned about him remarrying so quickly. It had been only five and a half months since his wife had passed away. His first question was what would the congregation think? When Jack explained to him that he had known Heather since he was fifteen, and that he would resign from the church if it was an issue for them, Pastor John immediately caved.

Pastor John was only acting out of love when he brought up his legitimate concerns about the timing of this union. As Jack had anticipated, Pastor John was not willing to lose such a gifted youth minister. It was because of Jack's appeal to youngsters, who in turn brought in their entire families, that their church was growing. Everyone knew it.

The ceremony went off without a hitch, and they were husband and wife only six months and two weeks after Tina's death. They kept the audience small and only invited immediate family and a few very close friends. All of the immediate family was there, even Tim, the youngest of the Henderson brothers.

Sam was almost six years older than Jack, and Jack was three years older than Tim who was two years older than their baby sister Katie. In spite of Tim's youthful age of only twenty-eight, he was already easily the most successful of the three by worldly standards. Though Sam had become an engineer, Tim went all the way and became a physician. After skipping two grades along the way, Tim graduated high school a year after Jack. At sixteen, he was a college freshman, and at twenty, he was admitted to the University of New Mexico's medical program. His residency began when he was only twenty-four, and he was offered a position at the University's Medical Center upon his graduation. His high IQ, calm demeanor, and relentless work ethic made him an ideal candidate for becoming a doctor. The universities medical staff recognized him early on as being more than just a superior student.

Like Sam and Jack, Tim was a very committed Christian. His knowledge and comprehension of scripture were as strong as any preacher's. His worldview was grounded in scripture, which he firmly believed to be truth. His devotion to becoming who the scriptures teach Christ followers to be drove him to seek God's will in all things. His beliefs, along with his gentle spirit, made him one of the most unthreatening doctors anyone had ever been around. Most patients were surprised to find out that he was a full-fledged doctor as he appeared to them to be completely without ego. His popularity grew so rapidly that he soon became the favorite of all of the nurses and the administration.

Unfortunately, due to Tim's tireless work ethic, he rarely visited his family. In fact, the occasion of Jack's wedding was the first visit in several years for Tim. He had not seen his parents or brothers and sister since his own wedding in New Mexico two years earlier. Tim had not been able to break free for Jack when Tina passed way, though he had spent several hours with Jack over the phone since the event. He had wanted to come but was detained on the day of the funeral, performing a surgery that had gone terribly wrong for one of his colleagues. He was so sorry about missing the funeral that he sent Jack a video of him and his wife telling him they were praying for him. He also made arrangements with Jack's favorite restaurant to have a weekly dinner brought to him every week for three months.

Even when Tim was around, he often got lost in the crowd due to his unassuming personality. While Sam was a bit of an extrovert, Jack was an extreme extrovert, and Katie was loud yet pleasant, Tim pretty much kept to himself. He usually did more listening than talking, and it was not uncommon for him to retire early to read. Everyone loved him and his big heart, but none of them had ever spent much time with him as he had left home for medical school when he was only twenty. They all had tremendous respect for him, though.

It was at Jack and Heather's reception that Tim very uncharacteristically stood up to make an announcement. "My family and I are very happy to be here for this most happy occasion. Thank you for giving my brother his happiness back, Heather. We believe the two of you are truly meant to be together." Tim's wife, while only twenty-seven years old, was the mother of three children. None of which were Tim's. He bonded with her when she came into the emergency room with a nasty head wound that her ex-boyfriend had given her with a punch in the face. Though the boyfriend was the father of two of the children, he never even lived with Mary nor had he provided for his children in any way.

Mary had recently moved out of her mother's and stepfather's house and was living alone with her three children in a one-bedroom apartment when Tim first met her. She worked hard to provide for her children, but her life was full of disorder. Though it was a life familiar to her as her friends and her extended family all seemed to be living under similar circumstances, Mary longed for something different. She often told herself she was different, but she found herself firmly in the life she never wanted. Having three kids outside of marriage with two different deadbeat fathers was something she had always sworn she would never allow, yet there she was.

Mary's family drank too much, looked for a good time too much, and always put themselves above their children. She always felt their ways were wrong, and she grew up telling herself she would never be like they were. The fact that she had become exactly what she didn't want to be had become the hardest thing to live with.

Tim continued, "I'm not much of a public speaker, so let me say what I need to say before I put my foot in my mouth. I have gotten an offer to move my family back down to the Houston area. I'll be interviewing for the position on Monday." He simply sat down and took Mary's hand.

Everyone was excited about his news, especially their mother, Jennifer. She felt she hardly knew Mary and the kids and loved the thought of having them around. She also knew how good it would be for Tim to get Mary away from her broken family and ex-boyfriends. From what she had been told, neither of the kid's fathers were at all involved in the children's lives in any way.

Before the night was over and the newlyweds hit the road for their honeymoon, Jack found time to break free to let Tim know how great it would be if they could move back. "Tim, we would love to have you back. I really want to get to know you, Mary, and the kids better. Please let us know right away as soon as you know. How soon would you move here?"

"If we decide we want the job, they have told me it's already mine. We will move here in less than a month, if Mary approves it. I plan to take her to a neighborhood in Pearland that I think she would really love to live in. She's really struggling with leaving her family, but we have been praying a lot about it, and we both think it's the best thing for us. Leaving her family is going to be very difficult for her, but it would also take a huge drain off of her. Please pray for us, Jack." As usual, Tim's voice was very soft and soothing. He never seemed worried or overconfident, just willing to accept God's direction in all things.

"I will, Tim. Can you believe I've just married Heather? She says she's been waiting fifteen years for me. I'm half afraid that she will kill me tonight." Jack could hardly talk to someone without some sort of joking.

"No, I really can't believe it. When Mom called with the news, I was shocked. Then after I had a little time to think about it, I knew it was God's plan for you. I'll never forget you asking for prayer about all of your improper thoughts about her. I even remember you praying to God for the ability to accept that she was just too old for you. Then you would say, 'If there is any way it can work, please, God, make it happen. Please make it your will.' When I recalled all of that, I was overwhelmed with how God answered your prayers. It made me break down, Jack. His timing is always better than ours. It's perfect."

Tim and Jack had often prayed with Sam and their father when they were young. Jack had never been the type to hide anything, even when it was about one of his weaknesses. He never held back when he knew he needed prayer for something as he knew God could free him when he had no strength to do it on his own.

"Man, I remember that now. All I remembered before just now was praying to God to keep my improper thoughts about her away. I had forgotten about asking for him to work it out. Imagine asking for it to be his will. Wow." *Was this really God answering my prayer?* he wondered.

"You got your dream girl, Jack, just like Sam and I did. It's really good to be a Henderson boy, isn't it?" Tim's stoic way always confused Jack, but this time, his big smile gave him away. Jack didn't have to guess; Tim was very happy for him.

As Heather and Jack prepared to leave for the honeymoon, Sam and Rachel gave them hugs and told them how much they loved them. Rachel couldn't help but think the moment they were having would have been very similar to the wedding between Heather and Joe Morgan that had never happened. How sad that was. In the end, it all worked out for the best though. Joe was now in heaven, and Jack and Heather would surely be happy together.

At no point after saying "I do" did Jack regret his decision to get married so quickly. Though it seemed improbable, he was fully ready to move on. He never forgot Tina. He kept pictures of her displayed in the house and truly cherished every moment they had had together. Heather fully understood and accepted Jack's past, but it was his future that really mattered to her.

CHAPTER 22

Heather and Jack left the wedding, heading for the San Antonio River Walk where they planned to spend the week, honeymooning. The restraint had been lifted with their vows, yet the lack of the restrainer didn't immediately lift the invisible wall between them. This car ride was the first time they had been alone together as a married couple. Since the day Heather had revealed her feelings for Jack, they had spent every free moment together. It had been a struggle, but they had somehow managed.

In fact, they had not kissed like their first kiss since the day they had revealed their feelings for one another. From that time on, they had agreed to not tempt one another, and though it had been a struggle, they had somehow managed. The urge to lie down together and wake up next to one another in the morning had been very strong. Though it had been difficult, they knew it was the only way.

Their conviction and commitment to doing things God's way, as well as their reliance on the strength God was giving them to wait until they were married never failed them. Each night, when they eventually separated and went their own ways, it broke their hearts. So dependent had they become on the other that they simply could not reframe from texting back and forth every moment they were apart. Due to her early morning classes, their routine became so taxing to Heather that she was forced to add a two-hour nap to accommodate it, which she gladly did.

Much of their conversations, text or otherwise, were effortless as they felt they could say anything to the one they were prepared to spend the remainder of their lives with. It wasn't like they had only been together for months; they had known each other for many years, and they had lots of history together.

In the weeks leading up to the wedding, they had begun discussing the fact that they would soon be together as husband and wife, which among other things, meant there would soon be physical intimacy. Though both of them looked forward to sharing themselves, they were both dealing with fears as well. Jack was not only intimidated by Heather's physicality, he was also very open about his uneasy feelings about being with someone other than Tina, especially so soon after her departure. Tina was all he had ever known, yet Heather had others to compare him to and that thought really intimidated him.

Though Heather completely understood how he was feeling, she knew he had nothing to worry about as she had never felt anything for anyone who could even kind of compare to how she was feeling for him. Though she looked forward to the physical part, it meant very little to her how "good" he was at it. Sharing this truth with Jack helped him, but hearing that it didn't matter how he compared because she loved him so much didn't totally satisfy his fear of failing her.

To assure Jack that he had nothing to worry about, she told him that even after they were married, she would wait as long as it took for him to be ready for her. Though he appreciated her attempt to take the pressure off, he knew there was no way there would be any waiting once they were married. He knew there was no way he would struggle once he was free to look at and touch that body. The worrying would be gone soon. He decided there would be new fears around that corner as well; that's just life.

Heather too had concerns. Her primary concern was that she may be doing something wrong by marrying him so soon after Tina's death. She couldn't help but feel that her desire to be with him had forced his hand and unfairly baited him into this rushed marriage. As many times as he had assured her that she had not done anything of the sort and that her timing had been perfect, it remained a stumbling block for her.

Heather was also concerned about their age difference. Being five and a half years older than Jack didn't feel like much of an issue anymore, but it sure had been when they were younger. For years now, she had been struggling with who she had been to have been attracted to him when he was only sixteen. It seemed to her now that it had been very unnatural, maybe even egregious, for a woman to be attracted to a boy the way she had been. She had been questioning herself for years over it, and it still bothered her. Thankfully, God had directed everything in such a way that a potentially very disturbing exposure of her infatuation with him on his eighteenth birthday had been completely avoided. If it hadn't, she was sure that they would have had no chance. Jack would have dropped Tina for her, but she would have been too mature for an eighteen-year-old boy at that time. Surely, God wouldn't have blessed their relationship the way he was blessing them now. At that time, when she was twenty-three, she would have been truly robbing the cradle.

Heather constantly brought up her doubts related to their age difference. Sensing that this was an issue that had been pushing her to question herself for fifteen years, Jack repeatedly told her that it had always been in God's hands. He explained his belief that God had kept them apart so that it would be right when it was finally time for them to be together. He was sure that the time was now, and even Heather was beginning to buy into it. "God's timing is not the same as ours," he often told her.

As the newlyweds sat side by side, heading into their new lives together, Jack's reservations vanished the moment Heather put his hand on her thigh as he drove. The fears he had about feeling guilty simply weren't there anymore. Whether or not he would compare favorably to her past lovers was far from his mind as well. All he could think of was his beautiful new wife and how blessed he was to have her.

As he sat and admired her, he promised himself that he would never give her a reason to feel that she wasn't the most important person in his world. She would be his partner in life, and he wanted her to feel completely comfortable and deeply loved. Her happiness would be above his own in all things. He would never hurt her, and he would do whatever it took to make sure no one else ever did either. His struggle with the guilt of marrying his dream girl and being happy in Tina's absence would not become a barrier of any sort as he was quite sure Heather deserved better than that. He would never allow those feelings to be perceptible in any way.

Heather could feel in the tenderness of his touch that he would never do anything to hurt her. His eyes told her he would lay down his life to protect her. Though he had never touched her thigh or anything else in a provocative way, there was noting at all in the way he was now investigating her upper leg that felt at all improper. It was clear he desired her, but she was quite sure it was all of her, not just her body, that he was after.

Jack needed her the way she needed to be needed. He just loved her more than he needed to be with her physically. His primary desire was to honor her and make her happy, and she could actually feel that in his touch. Their connection was so strong that they didn't even need to speak to share their emotions, or at least it felt that way.

As he caressed her while they sped down the highway, Heather began to feel that her life was finally going to be the life God had been planning for her. Though she knew there would always be struggles, she would do anything in her power to make Jack happy until the day he died. As his fingers crept up her thigh, she began to feel an excitement that caused her to let out a low moan that got all of Jack's attention.

"We better pull over before I run us off the road."

"Sorry, Jack, I hate to cause us to stop. I just want to get you alone in our honeymoon bed where I can do some real damage. Slowing us down was not in the plan." He had pulled his hand out of her lap while he spoke.

It was the only stop they made as neither of them wanted to prolong the trip. Jack needed to cool off a bit, and they needed gas and bathroom break. They had changed clothes before they left so they weren't wearing anything formal.

"Let's get out of here, Jack. We need a room now." *We're not kids anymore we should act responsible and drive safely and not distracted*, she told herself. *Maybe I shouldn't rev him up so much? Nah, it's too much fun.* She leaned in and licked his ear to really get him going.

"I hope my heart doesn't stop tonight, baby. Please take it easy with me. I want to be around for you more than one day. You have waited too long for us to be together to take me out tonight."

"Do you want me to drive, honey? I need to get you alone, and you have been driving like a little old lady." She was right in his face, demanding he either drive the remainder of the way like he wanted her, or he get out of the driver's seat and allow her to set the pace.

"You got it. I would love for you to drive the rest of the way. That way, I can stare at my beautiful wife the rest of the way." He turned and unlocked his door then realized she was doing the same.

"I'll go around. You just slide over." She popped out and jogged around the car before he could even respond. Jack watched in amazement at how quickly and smoothly she moved. It all looked so effortless. He was so captivated that he was unable to get moved in time as his eyes were glued on her glorious body bounding around the car.

"Get over, dummy. Don't make me move you." Her smile told him she was only kidding, though it did cross his mind that she may actually be able to move him against his will.

He maneuvered himself over to the passenger seat while she hopped in and leaned into him for another sensual kiss. "You know you are only the second girl I have ever kissed, right?"

"You know that you are the first guy I have kissed in fifteen years, right?" It even amazed her when she said it.

"I love that about you, baby. You'll never have to kiss anyone other than me the rest of the way." He was smugly smiling at her while enjoying his view of her.

For the rest of the drive, Jack could not keep his eyes and thoughts off of her. The unveiling would be something he would never forget. She was his wife now, so he felt that it was acceptable to think about her that way, and he did little else the rest of the way. As much as he had fought the urge to think about it before they exchanged their vows, he had not been very successful.

Heather loved the way he was looking at her. For years, she had covered her body and avoided attracting men with her sexuality. Down deep, she loved that she could attract them, but she had fervently fought her instincts to temp them. As good as it felt to be adorned by them, she was quite sure it only served her and was therefore not Christlike. Now all she could think about was how badly she needed this one man to want her. The thought even entered her head that she would not always be able to be the most attractive woman in the room. Would she be able to handle that? After all, had she not been trying to do just that all of these years? Trying to be the best-looking woman who no one could have had become her obsession. *How sad*, she decided.

She was sure of it; Jack was absolutely gaga over her. No, her husband was gaga over her. It felt really good to be admired by him. *Finally, a good reason to look like this*, she thought.

Something in her shift in demeanor told him she needed to know he wasn't with her solely for her looks. Though he had been telling her some derivative of what he was about to say, he was quite sure she needed to hear it again. Why wouldn't someone as beautiful as she was wonder what would happen should her looks betray her?

"Heather, you are the most beautiful woman I have ever known. Though I have always been attracted to your beauty, it's your love for and commitment to the Lord, your personality, and your character that make me want to be your husband. You may someday lose your looks, but those other things are eternal as is my love for you."

Tears immediately came to her eyes. "Thank you, baby. That means the world to me. I am so lucky to have you."

Even with Heather's torrid pace, the remainder of the trip seemed to take forever. It was almost painful for both of them.

As Heather pulled into the roundabout in front of the hotel, she commanded Jack to go check in, and she'd park the car and bring the bags.

"Please let me check us in, and come back out here so we can bring the stuff in together, baby. I don't want you to be alone in the dark out here or have to struggle with all of the bags. Can you please wait for me?" He wasn't giving her a test; he was just concerned.

"Okay, I'll be here waiting for you, handsome."

When he challenged her about the bags, she immediately chose to follow his direction. Though it wasn't a big deal, it meant a lot to Heather to respect her husband. Her nature was to push people around, but she had quickly accepted his refusal to do what she had said. What made her feel good was the fact that she had enough respect for him to let him lead. She thanked God as her inability to allow others to lead had been another fear she was having. Could she let him lead their family? This small incident gave her hope that she could. The fact that he was concerned about her well-being touched her as well.

The rest of the evening exceeded both of their expectations. They just fit together perfectly in every way. The two were amazed at how much they actually agreed on. It was as if they were sharing a conscience. They attributed it to their mutual knowledge of God's Word, and their commitment to being Christ followers.

It was the little things that amazed them the most. For instance, Heather liked the right side of the bed, while Jack preferred the left. Heather was a very early riser, while Jack was a bit more of a night person. It allowed them to take advantage of each other's natural preferences for things like shower schedules and alone time. While Heather questioned everyone she met, especially men, Jack always seemed to see the good in people. Together, they got a much clearer picture. In every sense of the cliché, they completed each other.

However, the biggest area that they completed one another in was their personality types. Heather was a very organized person in everything she did, including planning, managing money, diet, and every other area of her life. Jack was much more extemporaneous. He was tons of fun for everyone around him, but he was often late and ill prepared. It had always been Tina who had kept him in line. She had even paid all of their bills. Heather would become an even stronger foundation for Jack than Tina had been. Her ability to grind through anything and overcome anything in her way made the effort necessary to keep Jack on track minimal for her.

Actually, it wasn't even an effort at all for her. On the flip side of the equation, Jack brought the fun and laughter Heather's life was missing. He treasured her as his wife, and he gave her just what she needed—joy in her life. Her face seemed to have been surgically reconstructed into a permanent smile since they had come together.

They would later find that they had conceived during their honeymoon. Based on the delivery date the doctor would later give them, it was likely that they had conceived during their first opportunity that first night in San Antonio. Since they had decided to try to get pregnant as soon as possible, the news that they had succeeded was another great reason to praise God. Only months earlier, they had both been struggling. For Jack, it had only been a few months, but it had been an unbelievable loss he was suffering from. For Heather, it had been years of loneliness as if she had been in some sort of emotional prison.

From the moment the two had said "I do," it felt as if they had no problems anymore. The sadness Jack had been dealing with was gone, and Heather was a completely new person.

The overwhelming sense of good fortune or blessing in their lives quickly became an ever-present reminder to be thankful.

CHAPTER 23

Three days into the honeymoon, Jack and Heather decided to invite Sam, Rachel, and the kids to spend a full day at Sea World with them. Sam and his crew were a big part of both Jack and Heather's lives before the marriage, so there would be almost no transition into new routines after the marriage. Sam and Jack had actually discussed the possibility of such an invite before the wedding, so the invite was not a total surprise.

Sam and Rachel agreed to take a day of vacation so they could spend Friday at Sea World with the newlyweds. They reserved a room at the same hotel on the River Walk that Jack and Heather were in for Thursday and Friday nights. The boys were almost as excited to stay in a hotel and eat out every meal for two days as they were to get to go to Sea World.

The minute the four came face to face, Rachel was overcome by a feeling of familiarity of the moment. It was almost like a flashback of some sort. It instantly reminded her of the final night the three of them had with Joe Morgan. Sam had led them all back to Christ, and Joe had made his love for Heather known. Heather had even agreed to be his wife that night.

Rachel hadn't realized how similar Jack actually was to Joe until that moment. The feelings choked her up a bit before she caught herself and remembered that Jack and Heather were together now. Joe Morgan had been Rachel's closest friend and protector right up until the day he died. Without him, she would have never met Sam, and Heather would have never met Jack.

The feelings had really caught her by surprise, but she managed to gather herself before Jack and Heather were close enough to notice her condition.

"You two look great together," Sam let out before they were close enough to shake hands or hug. The boys were trailing Mom and Dad but started to overtake them as soon as they saw Uncle Jack and their new aunt.

"Tell me something I don't know." Jack's face looked like it was about to explode. He was so obviously happy.

The four exchanged hugs, and then let the kids in the mix. Little Joe called Heather "Aunt Heather" for the first time, and everyone let out an "awww." It was cute.

Since it was already after 9:00 p.m., Sam told Rachel he'd get them checked in and go hang out with the boys, while she went to spend some time with Heather and Jack. She accepted and asked Heather and Jack if they were up for that. "We sure are," came the reply, and the three of them set out to find a place on the River Walk where they could sit outside and talk.

Though Sam would have liked to have spent some time with them, he always put Rachel first in situations like this one. He knew how badly Rachel wanted to catch up with her best friend, and he felt like she deserved the time alone with the adults more than he did. As she always put it, "At least you get to go to work." Rachel was alone with the kids all of the time, and Sam felt that she deserved all the breaks he could give her.

In almost two hours, Rachel was back in the room with her family. The time she had spent with Jack and Heather had left her feeling fortunate to have someone like Sam. Sam was the most loving man she had ever known, and watching the powerful, young love Jack and Heather had for each other for the past two hours had made Rachel appreciate that she had someone like Sam who loved her as much now as he had during their honeymoon. When she climbed into bed with him, she was very happy he was still awake.

"It's just great seeing those two together. They are just boiling over with joy. Honestly, I was a little uncomfortable with those two pawing at each other out there. Still, it made me want to come back to my wonderful man. Did you miss me?" She had brushed her teeth, removed her makeup, and taken out her contacts. As usual, as she climbed into bed, she was wearing one of his oversized T-shirts and her panties.

"You are a very beautiful woman. I still can't believe I get to be married to you. I'm really sorry how out of shape I've gotten. I have definitely not held up my part of the deal." It was something that was really bothering him. No matter how many times he tried to start a diet or to start working out, it just wouldn't take. He simply couldn't stop binge eating. He didn't have to be hungry at all to eat. Hunger actually had nothing to do with it as he was almost never hungry. More often, he was sick to his stomach. Eating unhealthy food and drinking Coke had become his drugs of choice, and they were easily his biggest vices.

"Honey, I think you are perfect the way that you are. I do worry about your health, though. I want you to be around for us. I think you are very sexy. You know I do." She really didn't like the way he treated his body, but she knew it was something he was losing the battle against, and she knew he was well aware of it without her constant hounding him about it. Instead of nagging him, which seemed to be the appropriate response to how he neglected his health, she prayed for him and his health constantly. She had not lost her attraction to him because of his out-of-shape body, and though it seemed kind of crazy to her, she felt even more attracted to him knowing that his unhealthy lifestyle had more to do with the stress he was feeling to provide for their family than anything else. She understood how he could feel that way though as he had really put on a lot of weight. It had never been his looks that made her want him, but she knew telling him that wouldn't help at all.

"I'll start again when we get back. I'm not going to start a diet when we are on vacation." She had heard it so many times that she had to hold back her laughter.

When the alarm went off in the crowded hotel room, only Sam was willing to wake up and get going. Within a minute of his alarm sounding, he was in the bathroom, starting a shower. As soon as he was through in the bathroom, he shook the boys and Rachel, and they all began scrambling to get ready. As usual, Sam had it all planned out perfectly, and they were able to show up right on time to meet Jack and Heather for breakfast. By 9:30 a.m. they had all climbed into the SUV and were on their way to Sea World.

By mid-afternoon, it had gotten so hot that the gang was ready for the water park. Sam and Jack took the boys to the locker room to change while the girls headed to the ladies locker room to do the same. While Sam and Jack prepared, Sam told Jack how happy he was for him as this was their first time alone since the wedding a few days earlier. Jack appreciated Sam's comments but shared some concerns he was having regarding his inability to feel he deserved to be this happy so soon after his wife's death.

"That's only natural. Those feelings are exactly why Heather loves you so much. You have to accept that this is God's plan for you so you don't hurt Heather, your wife. She has never been this happy, and you have given her joy that she has never experienced. Since I've known her, I've never seen her this way. You are her answer to prayer. Love her the way she deserves to be loved, the way she loves you."

"Thanks, Sam. I know you're right. I just can't believe I get to be with her. She is too beautiful and perfect in every way. I just can't get over how beautiful she is."

"I feel the same way about Rachel, and I've felt like that about her since our first date. Enjoy this happy time in your life. I love you very much, Jack. Rachel and I are both so happy for both of you. Don't waste your time feeling guilty. You have no reason to be guilty."

As they walked out of the locker room, they found a table, and the four of them sat down to wait for the ladies. Sam scrambled to push all of the extra clothing he was now holding into the small backpack they had brought along when he realized it would be much easier if he pulled out the towels first. "I'm going to get a locker. Do you and Heather want to put your stuff in there too?"

Before Jack could answer Sam's question, Heather and Rachel emerged from the ladies' locker room. Jack's inability to answer Sam's question had everything to do with the state of shock he was in watching his amazing wife exit the ladies locker room. The boys were jumping around with excitement, but Jack and Sam were frozen and staring.

Rachel was a beautiful woman with an above-average figure, but Heather's figure was a show stopper. Her figure seemed almost unreal as if it could only exist in a cartoon of some kind. Everything seemed to have been accentuated beyond believability. Jack had not felt threatened by Heather's beauty publicly before this moment. Sure, when they were together, he notice men looking at her. He had even noticed women noticing her with what appeared to be a look of jealousy on their faces, but he had never felt that the stares were violating her in any way until this moment.

From the moment she had come out from the ladies locker room, in what Jack considered a conservative bathing suit, he couldn't help but notice everyone staring at her. No suit could possibly conceal her figure; there was just no hiding God's design and all of those years of hard work. Though she wasn't overly muscled, she was toned beyond belief. She looked as if she were some sort of fitness beauty contestant. Actually, she looked more like she was the hands-down winner of such a contest.

Heather was painfully aware of the stares she was getting. Though she took staying in shape very seriously, the attention she was getting quickly made her feel self-conscious, and she feared that it would make Jack uncomfortable. She was his now, and it seemed really wrong to be attracting so much attention. As she got close enough for them to hear her, she said, "I'm not sure I can do this. I feel very uncomfortable. Would you guys mind if

Rachel and I went and had an early lunch on our own? You guys can join us when you and the kids are through."

Jack was proud of her but couldn't help but feel like covering her up. His happy-go-lucky personality allowed him to almost never experience any sort of jealousy, but this was an entirely new experience for him. Though it made him feel awkward, he didn't want Heather to feel like she had done anything wrong, so he replied, "No problem. We can meet you later, but we would all love to have you with us. I don't want either of you feeling uncomfortable, though. It's not your fault you are the best-looking women in the world."

Both of them smiled, but it was easy to see that everyone was uncomfortable. Truth be known, the attention they were getting bothered Rachel even more than it bothered Heather. Not only did Rachel hate the attention she was getting in her own bathing suit, she couldn't stand to see men looking at Heather the way they were. It made her want to cover her up.

"No, we're sure. Give us a call or text when you guys are done. Have a great time." Rachel was already walking away as she spoke. She wasn't even going to give Heather a chance to reconsider.

After the girls left, the boys stayed for almost two hours without any distractions. Heather and Rachel were happy to get a little alone time together, although they chose to not leave the water park. They dressed and found a bench where they could see all of the action. As they sat and watched the boys enjoy themselves, Rachel asked Heather what her plans were for church.

"Now that you two are married, I guess you'll be officially leaving our church for Jack's? Since you two started dating, you've gone there every week. I've heard you stopped teaching the girls' class too." She was more curious than anything.

"My place is with Jack, but there is some news we haven't yet shared with you guys. Jack has been in touch with Pastor Cook about a position." Pastor Cook was the pastor at Heather, Sam, and Rachel's church.

"Really? I hadn't heard anything about this. What position?" She was really surprised as their church already had a youth pastor.

"Well, he told me not to get too excited about it as the deacons and church would have to vote on it before anything happens, but it looks like Pastor Cook is ready to retire. Jack would be his replacement as the senior pastor. Jack's been working toward his doctorate for some time now with the intent of becoming a senior pastor. He's on track to have it in less than a year, though he says it's not a requirement for the job." Jack had told her that he planned to tell everyone later in the day and that she could tell Rachel whenever she wanted.

"No way, I can't believe it! That would be wonderful. I can't believe he's never even mentioned it to any of us, only his wife. How cool is that?" She was blown away in a very good way. If he became the pastor, he would have his own parents in his congregation. It was the church Jack and Sam had grown up in.

"It's very cool. We do need to keep it quiet, though. Jack told me I could tell you, and he plans to tell both of you tonight. He also plans to tell his parents when we get back. Even if it happens, he would not step into the role until this time next year." She was so proud of Jack, and it showed. Most of her life had been spent knowing he was the only man for her. Now that they were finally together, everything that she had ever imagined he would be was being confirmed daily for her. His selfless love for her and his family, as well as his desire to do God's will in everything he did, made him the best possible husband she could have ever imagined.

Rachel was too excited to not break the news to Sam right away. She even waived him over when he looked over to see how the two were doing. He too was very surprised and even more excited than Rachel had been. He knew Jack would be a great pastor, and that the excitement Jack would bring along with his passion for God's will could rebuild their slowly dying church. He and Rachel, along with his parents, had been praying for their beloved church to rebound after more than a decade of decline. Jack would be God's answer to this prayer; Sam was sure of it.

The rest of their time together at Sea World and on the River Walk would remain in all of their memories as some of the happiest memories of their lives. The kids loved being around Uncle Jack almost as much as his new wife, Heather, did. Sam and Rachel remained in awe of God's perfect timing, and they marveled at the joy they were now seeing in both Jack and Heather.

Jack and Heather felt invincible, and they knew they were being surrounded by God's love and blessings. Jack had been through a tough couple of years before these recent events, and Heather had been in hiding for almost fifteen years in preparation for Jack. She finally felt like she was living again. Heather never felt so loved, so right, and so safe as she did at that point.

CHAPTER 24

Mary awoke mysteriously in a hospital bed. Having no recollection of how she had gotten there, she began to panic. In her confusion, she was fumbling around to find her cell phone, which was nowhere to be found. As she started to get her bearings, she was relieved to see a familiar face in the room.

"Stella, wake up." Her closest friend, Stella, was asleep in a chair next to her bed.

Stella woke to see Mary's swollen and confused face staring at her.

"Hey, how do you feel?"

"Not great. How did I get here?" She had been so pumped full of pain medication that she couldn't feel the pain from the enormous gash that had taken fifteen stitches to close on the back of her head.

"Danny punched you right in the face, and you fell backward onto the barbecue pit like a dead person and passed out. It was terrible, and I started freaking out when you wouldn't wake up. I wouldn't have even been able to get you into my car without help from Carlos and Rudy. They helped me bring you to the emergency room and stayed here until you were sewed up and we were told you would be okay.

"He hit you and then just walked away with his skanky little girlfriend by his side. You hit the pit so hard I thought you were dead. I hate that guy." Stella too was trapped in a similar lifestyle with two kids of her own and no husband. Her disgust for Danny was based on more than the events of that evening though; there was plenty more evidence to go on.

Mary began to remember what had happened to lead up to the knockout punch after Stella finished filling her in. At twenty-three years of age, she already had three boys. Her oldest son was already six years old as Mary had given birth to Richard just a couple of days after her seventeenth birthday. The other two boys were Danny's boys; Ben was three, and Victor was only ten and a half months younger.

Richard's dad had been Mary's high school boyfriend in her sophomore year. When they first started dating, he already had a drinking problem, though he was only sixteen. In his family and in the culture they were both a part of, no one considered his drinking a problem, not even at the age of sixteen. They all drank as he did, both Mary's family and his. Actually, most everyone they knew drank until they were drunk every weekend, and some did it every night.

As a child in the culture in which they lived, it was perfectly normal to see fighting, hear all kinds of foul language, and see all sorts of unnatural lust among unmarried people. Parents allowed their children to be exposed to all kinds of evil without even considering what it could mean to their child's future. Though some children felt loved, all of them felt secondary when the adults were having "fun." The worst part was that no one seemed to think this type of dysfunction and destructive behavior was at all out of the ordinary.

Families stayed close in this culture, yet drama was the norm. Someone was always doing something that hurt everyone around them and acting like it was their own business. Someone was always cheating on someone or threatening someone. Kids were often hurt by preventable accidents due to the carelessness of those who were older and should know better. It always seemed like there was some sort of scandal to talk about or impending crisis of some kind. Drama and turmoil were expected.

Mary's first pregnancy had caused her father to disown her. He refused to speak with her as he had continually warned her about Jamie, the father of the baby. Though he had been right, his refusal to deal with her in a mature manner pushed the two apart and fed her anger and bitterness toward life and men. As her father had predicted, Jamie wanted nothing to do with her once she was pregnant. Though he did attempt to get her to sleep with him again several times, he never even pretended to care about their baby.

Mary had a very sharp mind, but the demons she had been forced to live with had successfully convinced her that she too would be doomed to live like the rest of her family had always lived. Since she had never really seen life done any other way, she hadn't even considered that there was any other way. At sixteen, she just didn't have the perspective to believe it could be any different for her.

Without the support of her father, she had no other alternative for support than her mother and slimy stepfather. Her stepfather had made more than one pass at her over the years, though she had never told anyone. By the time she was sixteen, she had already threatened to stab him in his business if he ever tried anything again, but being the coward that he was, he heeded her warning and stayed away from her. Mary had actually begun to look forward to stabbing the big slob in the groin if he ever touched her again. How would her mother deny what a piece of trash he was with a massive groin wound as a result of an attempted rape of her daughter? Sadly, Mary was pretty sure her mother would find a way to deny and ignore it.

Mary had the body of a fully mature woman at the age of fifteen, but she wasn't at all flirtatious because of it. Oddly, she had almost no sexual attraction to the opposite sex at the age of sixteen when she had gotten pregnant. She had only wanted someone to put her first and soon found Jamie treating her like she was special. Though he wanted only one thing from her, she was too desperate for someone to love her to listen to her father's warnings, or to notice for herself. She freely gave herself to him, believing that he loved her and that he would always be there for her the way he constantly told her that he would be. Unfortunately, what he had for her was never love as Jamie wasn't capable of loving anyone more than he loved himself. Mary was simply too young to have any idea what love looked like. She had never even seen a good example of love in her life.

It was Mary's desire to be loved that had made her susceptible to Jamie. The lack of a role model in her life caused her to wonder if what she was getting from her family was really real love. Though she figured her father loved her, the fact that he could not love her through what she was going through made her wonder. Clearly, his love for her came with conditions, and she was clearly failing him. Not that she felt he should approve of what she had done, but where was the forgiveness? In her mind, no one really loved her.

Mary was ill prepared for the emptiness and hopelessness of life. It's what had made her susceptible to Jamie's flattery. Her rapidly maturing figure had begun to draw lots of attention from boys and men, but she was not emotionally prepared to be desired that way at such an early age. Her naivety had left her pregnant and alone. She would eventually learn that men were willing to say and do anything to get what they wanted from her. Unfortunately, it would be too late.

Mary's first pregnancy led her to the difficult decision to drop out of high school so she could start working full time to support her soon to be family. Abortion was never an option for her. She instinctively knew how precious life was, and to her, there was no decision to be made. She didn't want to rely on other people, and she wouldn't parent the way her parents had. She would put her child first, and she would be solely responsible for the child's welfare.

Before Richard was born, Mary was able to save up quite a bit of money by working a full-time day job, as well as a part-time night job. Her mother and stepfather were boarding her while she was pregnant, but she desperately wanted to move out as soon as she was able. She wanted her baby to have a real chance and for him to know that his mother would always put him first. No child of hers would ever feel as unloved as she did.

When Richard was born, Mary was only seventeen. She had not finished high school but was a hard worker who had already established herself with her employer. Mr. Thompson had never had anyone work harder or smarter than Mary did. For this reason, he had been very agreeable to his young secretary taking some time off to have her baby. Though she was only seventeen, she was very smart and great with customers. Though he had no idea that she was pregnant when he hired her, he valued her efforts and abilities so much that he decided to give her two weeks of vacation after Richard's birth without showing any signs of disappointment in her obvious deception. He saw the honor in what she was doing, and he fully recognized her potential.

For Mary to get back to work, she would need someone to take care of Richard. After exhausting all of her other options, she finally called Jamie's mother. His mother, Sally, didn't know about the baby, but she knew Mary quite well and was available as she was home all day every day.

As Mary had anticipated, Sally was more than willing to help, but Mary knew there would someday be consequences. It was Sally who had created the father of her child, Jamie. Jamie was the worst sort of person in Mary's eyes as he was completely incapable of seeing or telling the truth. It simply wasn't in him. Everything Jamie did was ultimately for his own pleasure. Amazingly, he never saw it that way and would go through the remainder of his life complaining about everyone else when things continually went badly for him as a result of his own poor decisions. Jamie later fathered two more children but was never married.

With Richard being watched during the day, Mary went back to work full time so she could maintain her benefits and earn a living to provide for Richard. For two years, she never entertained dating or even befriending a man. This way, there was no chance a man could hurt her or the baby.

Within weeks of turning eighteen, she had moved out of her mother's place and into a small one-bedroom apartment. At this point their lives were simple, and Mary was prepared to keep it that way. Though she took Richard to family functions, she kept him from the late-night, out-of-control drunkenness part of family time. She did her very best to shield Richard from all of the dysfunction. Unfortunately, what she couldn't control was the indoctrination that Sally was giving Richard all day long.

Richard's young mind was being molded by a self-absorbed person who had created two sons who had not and would not ever function properly in society. As much as Mary tried to recalibrate Richard at night, she was losing the battle, and she knew it. The signs were there as Richard was beginning to have a false sense of worth based on looks and possessions. Mary could see it in her son even at only two years old but wasn't sure how to irradiate it.

Then Danny came along. He was the sweetest guy Mary had ever met, or so she thought. Though she was cautious at first, he slowly worked his way into a date with her. She liked that he had goals and ambition as he had real plans to do something with his life. Though he came from a very similar family and culture, he seemed to want to escape as badly as she did. He was attending college at the University of New Mexico, and, though he was only a freshman, she believed, with all of his focus, that he would someday graduate.

Mary's mother babysat Richard the night of their first official date. When she later found out that her mother had taken Richard to a smoky bingo game, she threw a fit that her mother seemed incapable of understanding. On another occasion, her mother left Richard with a thirteen-year-old girl so she could go out dancing. Her mother just couldn't say no to her stepfather or even to her own interests. It was no different than it had been when she was a kid. In fact, Mary had been left to watch her younger brothers and sister without any food or promise of a meal many times. If she was presented with an opportunity or request from her husband, Mary's mother just simply couldn't act for the children's best interests.

By the third date with Danny, Mary was beginning to believe he was someone she could trust. Maybe he could fill the void she was feeling, the need to have someone truly care for her. She was very wrong about that but wouldn't find out until after she was pregnant again.

The first time they slept together was the result of too much alcohol. The second time she had gotten both drunk and high. Though these were both things she had sworn to avoid, she began to find herself surrendering to them when she was with Danny. Before she knew it, she was being sucked into the life she had always promised herself she would never be a part of. It was almost as if some force was pulling her there.

Soon, leaving Richard with her untrustworthy mother became a common practice. Not because her mother's behavior had changed in any way, but because Danny was changing her.

When Danny started visiting her in the middle of the night, she never refused him, and it always resulted in sex and him falling asleep on her couch while Richard slept in the next room. Though he was always drunk, high, or both, she was always completely sober for these visits. Each visit opened her eyes a little more to what he actually was, a fraud. Though he may have once had ambition, his character was simply too weak to achieve any of the goals he constantly bragged about.

As time went by, Mary began to see him as the self-centered person that he really was. She would soon realize that his kindness toward her in the beginning had only been an act. From time to time, he would turn it on again, but the closer they got to one another, it became less and less frequent. Soon it was much more common for him to be cruel than kind. Though they had once spent lots of time together, it was becoming rare for her to see him except for when he wanted something from her. Most of the visits were late at night after he was done doing whatever it was that he really wanted to be doing. She began hearing rumors of him with other girls, and she had no doubt they were all true.

Finding out she was pregnant was devastating. She had already decided to break clear from Danny before her store-bought pregnancy test came up positive. Being pregnant would only complicate things, but she knew for sure there was no other alternative. The fact that he was failing out of school would also complicate things. She had been very wrong about him.

After thoroughly thinking it through, she decided to break up with him without letting him know she was pregnant. She reasoned it would be easier that way, and she didn't want any part of him trying to stay around because of the baby. He was definitely not parent material.

The evening of the positive test, Danny showed up at Mary's door at two in the morning. As usual, he was stumbling drunk. As she attempted to get him to leave, her refusal to sleep with him created the situation she was trying to avoid. She would have to try to break up with a drunken guy. It was the last thing she wanted to do, but she felt there was no alternative unless she was willing to give into him one more time.

When she began to explain to him that it was over, things quickly escalated. Almost immediately, he began to threaten her. His jealousy over the thought of someone else touching her got the best of him as he felt she was his property. No matter how convincingly she assured him that there was no one else, he wasn't having it. Being the insecure macho type, he was incapable of allowing her to call the shots. Who did she think she was?

In the heat of the moment, she suddenly realized that her fear that he might stay because of the baby was a really long shot. With that in mind, she decided her best option was to just come out and tell him. The baby would likely make him run like it had with Jamie.

"I'm pregnant with your baby, but I don't want you in its life." She screamed it at him so loudly that Richard actually woke up in the next room.

Danny slapped her across the face so hard it knocked her to the floor as he stormed out yelling curses at her. Though the slap was painful, she was happy to see him go in hopes that it was over. Unfortunately, she was wrong as he continued to show up mostly late at night and only when he was drunk. More than once she was forced to call the police on him, which eventually led to a restraining order.

Once Ben was born, Mary softened a bit and removed the restraining order. She felt it was unfair to not offer Danny the opportunity to be a part of his son's life. In only a few weeks, he had succeeded in getting her pregnant again. When he wanted to, Danny could be very convincing. Though she had no intention of ever allowing him to touch her again, in what she would later decide was a moment of weakness, he had fooled her for the last time.

Though Mr. Thompson had given Mary time off after Ben's birth, that time was about to expire. Learning that she was again pregnant and not wanting to ask Jamie's mother to watch Ben let alone the baby she would be having in nine months, Mary requested a meeting with Mr. Thompson only a few days before she was to return to work. Knowing that he was a resourceful man, she decided, if anyone could, he may be able to help her.

She had been correct; he was able to help. Once she fully explained her situation to him, he was eager to help as he had long been a fan of her work ethic and generous personality. Though he hated to lose her, he felt compelled to help her. Having a client who owned a daycare center provided a workable solution for Mary. He recommended her for a job, and she was immediately extended an offer.

She would be able to take both Richard and Ben to work with her, and she would no longer need to count on her mother and Richard's grandmother to care for them during the day. Thankfully, she didn't even have to take a cut in pay as the position was full-time and came with some limited benefits. All of her hard work for Mr. Thompson had paid off. The job had truly been a blessing, and Mary was very thankful to have a way to manage her single-mother show. As she was sure he would, Danny took off the day she told him that she was pregnant again. Life would not be easy, but that was just how it had to be. She had made many mistakes, but she owned them all and was prepared to accept the consequences.

Victor was born only ten and a half months after Ben's arrival. Richard was three, Ben was about to turn one. She loved her little ones more than anything, and the trauma of her life and consequences of her stupid mistakes had completely transformed her. Mary no longer drank or did drugs at all. She stayed home with her kids every night, and she left her family's parties anytime anything got out of hand. She began living her life entirely for her children and soon began to wonder why things had to be so hard. *There has to be more to this life. There has to be some meaning somewhere. With people only looking out for themselves, it can't all be pain and struggle, could it?* Mary thought.

Mary quickly became an avid reader as the kids were always watching kiddy stuff on TV, and she needed to have something grown up to do. Her love of reading gave her the confidence to take and pass the GED test so she would at least have a high school equivalency. It gave her a measure of pride, but inside, she was very disappointed in where her life had taken her. If she hadn't been such an idiot, she felt pretty confident that she could have gone to college and made something of herself. Her feelings about her poor circumstances in life were mostly regret. She had no one else to blame for her poor choices. She didn't pity herself that helped no one. Instead, she chose to learn from her mistakes.

Mary met Stella through her daycare job. They immediately hit it off as they had lots in common, including the fact that they were both single mothers with totally absent fathers. They quickly became close friends. The two shared many common struggles, and soon, Stella began to push her church on Mary as it had been a big help in her own life.

Being brought up as a Catholic, Mary wasn't sure if she was comfortable going to a non-Catholic church. Still, Stella was doing such a good job selling her that she finally broke down and went. The kids were now six, three, and two at the time of their first visit. Mary was only twenty-three.

After two Sunday services, Mary agreed to visit Stella's single's class. It was where Stella had met Bob, a like-minded man she was now happily dating. Mary wasn't agreeing to go to meet men but to support her friend and to learn some more about the God of the Bible. Stella had told her that the class was much more in-depth than the general services. Mary longed for more depth, knowing instinctively that only God could fill the emptiness she was feeling. It was amazing to her how little she actually knew about scripture. Her family only sparingly attended church her whole life, and no one in her family ever read the Bible.

When she walked into her first single's class with Stella, Tim spotted her and immediately felt a pull toward her. He simply couldn't look away. He had never been the type to stare at anyone, and his rather average build and looks kept him from ever assuming that any woman would welcome his stare. Mary was special, though. He could tell. The fact that she was young and attractive intimidated him, but he almost didn't care. He couldn't wait to hear her speak, so though completely out of character for him, he walked right up and introduced himself.

"Hi, I'm Tim. It's really nice to have you join us." His calm nature and unassuming personality immediately set Mary at ease. His stare didn't feel unusual at all as she could tell he was truly someone who cared for other people. It was in his eyes, his voice, and even his handshake. He seemed so calm and at peace that it made Mary feel completely at ease. It didn't hurt that he only looked into her eyes, nowhere else. It was an undivided attention like she had never felt before.

"I'm Stella's friend, Mary." She couldn't help but give him a sheepish smile, but she did her best to conceal it.

"It's great to have you with us, Mary. Stella talks about you quite a bit. She thinks the world of you and has been telling us you may join us. I'm so glad today is that day. Please sit wherever you like. I hope you don't mind me asking Stella to introduce you to the class?"

"Not at all." Mary would have never guessed Tim was the teacher she had heard so much about. She had heard so many good things about him from Stella that she assumed he would be a much-older man. Stella had built him up so much that Mary expected someone much more imposing than Tim was.

From Tim's appearance, Mary would have never guessed that he was any sort of scholar as he appeared to have no ego. He seemed very peaceful and unassuming. There was something else, something that made her feel valuable. She wasn't sure, but she thought it may have been love. *Is it possible this guy is radiating love?* It made her feel like he already respected who she was as a person without any trace of judgment of any kind. How much he knew about her from Stella, she didn't know. *Maybe he'd be acting differently if he knew everything*, she thought.

Stella quickly found Bob, the man she had begun dating. Mary had previously met him, so they said hello to one another, and the three sat down together. Bob was a really nice guy who had been through an ugly divorce. Thankfully, there had been no children involved. As soon as they were seated, Stella leaned in and whispered to Mary, "That was Dr. Henderson, the Tim I'm always telling you about. He's a surgeon and probably the smartest man I've ever met."

With Stella confirming that the kind man they had just met was Tim, she sat in amazement, waiting for the class to begin. The doctors she had met had been arrogant or at least somewhat detached from people like her. This guy was very different. He seemed meek to her as if he wasn't a threat to anyone. She had not been around many men that were not at least somewhat macho. If a man was even somewhat nice to her, she was very suspicious. Danny had taken her innocence in this area of her life.

Most of the men in Mary's personal life had been dishonest and self-serving. Just about all of them had been slaves to alcohol or worse vices. With the exception of Mr. Thompson, she had relatively little exposure to men who did things for other people. Tim was different; she could sense it from the very beginning.

Tim started the class by asking Stella to introduce her friend. The introduction was very brief, and they soon found themselves into Tim's lesson. He took them into God's Word right away. He wasn't just reading scripture though; it was like a history lesson. From what Mary could see, he read directly from the Bible and had very few notes. He knew the material inside and out. She quickly decided that everything Stella had said about Tim's knowledge of the Bible had been true. Though it may not have taken much to impress her as she had very little Bible knowledge herself, Tim seemed to instruct the class from within as if he didn't even need his notes for guidance though he rarely quoted scripture without reading it straight out of the Bible.

As the class went on, Mary began to wonder if he even needed the Bible. It even crossed her mind that he was only reading it from the Bible to demonstrate to the class how to treat God's Word. He was clearly showing that it was not his word but God's. It seemed to her that he was honoring the written word by reading it rather than simply lecturing them.

Mary was most impressed with how he encouraged participation and never made anyone feel like their point of view or interpretation was of less value than his own. Clearly, he had a much-deeper understanding of every subject they spoke about, but he never once flaunted it. Instead, he often expanded upon their idea with support. He handled every member of the class with love by not discounting anything anyone had to say and never interrupting them. Though she had little exposure to men who loved others in this way, she immediately admired that about him.

While he taught the class, Tim could not stop looking into Mary's eyes. For years, he had concentrated on nothing but his studies and his relationship with the Lord. Now he was feeling something new, something bigger than him. It was a sense of responsibility that he couldn't understand, but he soon would.

Though neither of them knew they were only three weeks away from Mary needing Tim's professional care, they did both feel a connection. The timing was perfect, as God's timing always is. The evening that brought Mary into the ER started when a wasted Danny and his latest drugged-up girlfriend showed for Ben's third birthday party. Mary had told him about the party so he could come by and wish his son a happy birthday. She had not expected him to show up drunk and with a girlfriend.

Her anger over him showing up drunk for the party led to her getting confrontational when he refused to leave. Her attempt to lead him out of the house triggered the punch to her face that landed her in the hospital. He had swung full force, and his fist connected squarely with her face. She had not been looking directly at him when he had begun his swing so she didn't even attempt to get out of the way of the blow. As his fist collided with her cheek, she flew backward so quickly that he almost fell on top of her as she fell. Her head collided with the iron bar-becue pit, and she was out like someone had flicked off a light. Danny grabbed his half-naked under-aged girlfriend, jumped in his broken-down old car, and sped off while he let loose with the obscenities. He did nothing to help her. In his mind, he had done nothing wrong, and it had been Mary's fault. He couldn't believe she had tried to tell him what to do. Who did she think she was?

Bob, Stella's new boyfriend, was not at the party. Thankfully, Carlos and Rudy were there. Their presence helped scare off Danny. They were also needed to get the unconscious Mary to the hospital. Sadly, the three-year-old Ben saw the whole thing go down, while Victor and Richard only saw the blood on the grill after their mother had been taken away to the hospital.

Tim was the ER doctor on duty that night. When he realized who the patient was, his heart began beating extra time. It crossed his mind that the unusual pull he had felt for her since he had first met her may have had something to do with this moment. Whatever the outcome, he was now sure that his feelings for her were very real as he had never been so fearful of the fate of any patient. There was no way to deny that God had put something in his heart for her.

When Tim first saw her blood-stained white blouse and hair, it frightened him more than anything else had ever frightened him. Her appearance caused a panic in him he had never previously felt. Though seeing traumatic injuries was nothing new to him, seeing Mary like that definitely gave him some new feelings. Upon examination, he quickly confirmed that the wound itself wasn't as life threatening as it had first appeared to be. As the fear had been, the relief was excessive too. While he was already drawn to her, the feelings he experienced seeing her injured solidified his belief that he needed to investigate what they could be to one another. It was much more than a physical attraction; he was sure of that.

When Tim learned through Stella what had happened, he went immediately to the Lord in prayer. How could anyone do this, especially to the mother of their children? He just couldn't understand it. Though he saw many sad things on a daily basis as a result of his profession, he had never experienced it firsthand before. It had always been someone else's loved one, never his own. The thought of Danny punching her turned his stomach, and it brought an anger to him he had never previously dealt with. Though he prayed for peace, it didn't come initially.

Mary was treated and heavily medicated that evening, but she didn't wake up until the next day.

Waking up in a hospital with Stella by her side was initially very curious to her. After a short discussion, she quickly began to remember the previous night's events. Though she had never even seen his fist coming as he had sucker punched her, she had felt the punch and the falling sensation before her head hit the grill and the lights went out. The fact that he had just left without even trying to help her up spoke volumes about where Danny was at this point in his life. The thought that this man was the father of two of her children brought her to tears.

"I hate what I've done to my life and my kids, Stella." She wasn't looking for advice; she just needed to share her disappointment in her life choices with someone who actually cared for her. She didn't need help either, just someone to listen.

"I know how you feel, Mary. I feel the same way." Mary knew Stella understood her situation and that her own life would allow her to sympathize.

"Why do we have to keep making things so hard on ourselves? I should have never called that loser to let him know about the party. He never spends any time with the boys and has never given me a dime to help raise them. I don't want him to spend any time with them from now on. Why am I such an idiot?" The tremendous pain and regret she was dealing with were overwhelming for her, and Stella could feel for her like no one else.

"Hey, guess who sewed you up and brought you back to life last night?" She wasn't sure if Mary would be happy to hear it was Dr. Henderson or if she would be embarrassed.

"Oh no, was it Tim? I'll never get him to marry me now." She was only kidding, but she really was disappointed that he had been exposed to her ugly life. Though she was not sure of it, she had been feeling that he was attracted to her. She was sure he was too good for her, and she was pretty sure that this look into her life would eliminate any interests he had in her. What a wonderful person he was, and what a mess she was. That's how she saw it. He was way too good for her, and any previous thoughts she had entertained about him showing interest in her were definitely only fantasy.

"It sure was. He even came by this morning to check if you were okay. He told me to text him as soon as you were awake. I'm doing it now." She was already tapping away. It had been her hope that Dr. Tim Henderson would take to Mary. He was perfect for her, and how could he help but be attracted to her? He may be out of her league in every other way, but she was clearly the more attractive of the two. It wasn't even close.

"Wait, let me get myself together first." It was a dead giveaway of her interest in him, but she didn't care.

"Sorry, I already sent it," she said, pushing *send*. She wasn't going to wait at all as she figured Mary would try to stall and to maybe even talk her out of it.

"Dang it, I bet I'm a mess?"

Before she could worry anymore about it, she realized she hadn't asked about the kids. "How about the kids? Are they all okay? Are they still at my mom's place?" The incident had happened at her mother's house.

"Yep, they are all fine. Ben saw the whole thing, though. He was very upset. Your mother told me he said he hated his Dad." Hearing Stella talk about her three-year-old son hating his father broke her heart. She felt all of the guilt for the situation they were all in, it really was all her fault. Why hadn't she been smart enough to stay away from Danny from the very beginning?

Then Stella's phone shook. "I just got a text back from Tim. He said he's taking a quick shower, and he'll be here as soon as he can. I bet he hasn't slept at all, poor guy." Stella was sure of it now; Tim had a romantic interest in Mary. The guy had just worked all night and was willing to turn around and come back in. She began thanking God for him as soon as she stopped speaking. He could completely change Mary's life. Not just because of his income as a doctor, but as a loving father and husband. He would be a rock for her, Stella was sure of that.

"I hate that for him. Text him back, and tell him I'm okay. Let him know a visit is unnecessary. Why do you think he feels he needs to check on me like this?" She was thrilled inside that he wanted to come see her, but she was also embarrassed of her life and what she imagined she looked like. Though they had washed and cleaned her well, she hadn't had a chance to fix her makeup and hadn't even combed her hair. She had woken up during the stitching, but they had her so sedated to keep her from dealing with the pain that she hadn't been aware of anything. After all of the stitches were in and she had been thoroughly cleaned up, she fell asleep like a rock.

"No way. You can tell him to leave once he gets here if you want to."

Before either of them expected him, he was walking through the door. Mary had lived a tough life, but seeing the concern for her on Tim's face gave her a new hope. *This guy definitely is into me.* Though she still felt bad about how she probably looked, and she was embarrassed about her life, she was too strong to let those things blind her to what her heart was telling her. In that moment, it didn't matter that she wasn't good enough. He was there for her anyway, and she was positive he had real feelings for her.

"I'm so sorry I wasn't here when you woke up, Mary. How are you feeling?" His voice and his eyes were full of concern for her. He didn't know why, but for whatever reason, she was already very important to him.

"I'm fine. Thanks for saving my life. I wish you would take care of yourself now, though. Have you slept at all?" He was holding her hand and couldn't help but feel that they were much more than new friends already. His concern for her was actually scaring her a bit. No one had ever cared for her the way he was making her feel he did. It wasn't like family cares; it was much more complete. It felt like love, the love she had been longing for. The love she had been chasing after with Jamie and again with Danny. Neither of those guys was capable of the type of love she was looking for, but this guy oozed it. *Maybe it's just the way he is,* she told herself.

"I'm so glad to see you doing so well, Mary. I was shocked when I realized it was you last night. It was terrible to see you like that. I'm not sure I deserve any credit for saving your life, though, as any one of our physicians would have done the same as I did.

It's our job. Honestly, the injury wasn't really life threatening. I'm just thankful that you are going to be okay. I want you to know that I've been praying for you since the second I realized it was you. I've also been thanking God for giving me a chance to get to know you better. I'm really looking forward to that. You have been on my mind since we first met." He was speaking slowly and softly but very directly and sincerely. Though Stella was in the room, he spoke very directly to Mary as if they were alone. It was heartfelt, and Mary could tell. Oddly, he had never been very forward about his attraction to any woman before. It just happened naturally with her to his delight.

Mary was touched that he cared and couldn't help but feel unworthy. She was shocked to see tears in his eyes as he spoke. There was no mistaking it; he really wanted to get to know her better. It was a little too much for Mary, so she quickly decided to burst his bubble.

"Really, you don't even know me, Dr. Henderson. My life is a mess. That's how I got in here last night. My ex-boyfriend punched me in the face right in front of my family. My, no, our three-year-old son saw the whole thing. Did you know I have three children?" She wanted to make sure this guy had all of the facts before he started building up some fantasy about her in his mind.

"No, I didn't know you had three children, but I don't see why that matters. You are who you are, and I have no choice but to accept that. I have an attraction to you I simply cannot understand. I believe it is God's will for me to get to know you better. If your life is a mess, maybe that's why God has brought us together? My life is as structured and as under control as anyone's. My family is without scandal and full of love. Your kids need a father who will put them first, and I may be that man. God knows what he is doing, and he's laying you on my heart. I want to know why. Can you afford me that opportunity?" His demeanor never changed. It was as if the outside stuff and circumstances didn't matter to him. He seemed sure that God was leading his feelings for her, and she was quickly convinced. The peace she felt about him told her everything would be okay.

Tim had never spoken to a woman the way he spoke to Mary that day. It actually surprised him, but he felt good about what he was saying and hoped Mary could see how sincere he was. Nothing was ever hidden with Tim, and Mary would soon learn to trust him in ways she had never thought possible.

Mary had an enormous amount of respect for Tim already. Her only issue was her feelings of inferiority. This guy was amazing. Not only was he a Bible expert and a physician, he also seemed to be without baggage of any kind. He was from some other world, someplace without pain, fear, and all of the other baggage of the world. She began to wonder if it was just her looks he was after, but that didn't add up either as he now knew about her children and what a mess she was. He couldn't overlook all of that because of her looks; she wasn't that good looking she decided.

Tim had taken a full time position at UNM's Medical Center after he completed his residency. The offer to stay on full time was based on his tireless work ethic, his abilities as a doctor, and his unusual way with patients. Stella had told Mary that it was public knowledge that he didn't have a girlfriend and that he had never even attempted to pursue anyone. Everyone in the singles' group believed he was someone that had chosen to live a single life.

"Yes, I'll give you a chance to find out why God is making you want to get to know me. One day with my kids should help you pretty much figure me out. I have some pretty strange feelings for you too. I guess I'd like to figure that out as well. I've never known anyone like you. You are such a good and knowledgeable person that I just can't imagine you will still want to be around me once you've figured out how little there is here." This guy was just too smart for her to pretend around with. He would know the truth anyway, she was sure of that. It made things very easy for her as she felt she could and should tell him exactly how it was.

"You are wrong about that, and I look forward to convincing you of that fact. I know God is in this. I don't know if you are my soul mate or what's going on, but I do know you are different and special. God loves you, and I know he has a plan for your life. If he's brought us together, we don't want to miss it." Tim was feeling a strange surge of emotion for her now. It was most definitely a love interest, and he began feeling thankful and even started thanking God in prayer while he stood over the woman he was quickly beginning to believe was his future.

The two quickly came together spiritually. It was completely effortless. The connection was undeniable. Though Mary had not even finished high school, her constant reading and sharp mind made her a perfect match with Tim. She was far more intelligent than she ever gave herself credit for. Though she was nowhere near as well read as Tim nor did she have anywhere near his breath of knowledge, she was quick witted and a natural critical thinker. She challenged Tim's interpretation of scriptures, and it always brought a deeper understanding to both of them when they put their heads together.

They were different in many ways, yet they quickly began to think alike on the important things. Tim grew from having someone so different from him in his life, as did Mary. She believed in him and appreciated him in ways that no one else could have. Part of it came from her dysfunctional past, and the rest came from her thankfulness to be with a man of God that would always put her first in everything he did. They fell fiercely in love.

In two year's time, after Mary had become a Christ follower, they were married. Tim had never been with a woman. He had never even kissed one before Mary. During their two-year courtship, they kept their relationship nonphysical by maintaining strict boundaries. It wasn't always easy as they had a natural desire to be together, but their respect for one another and their commitment to do things God's way helped them make it to their wedding night without betraying their commitment to wait for intimacy until after they were married.

The kids quickly took to Dr. Tim. They liked him from day one. With time they loved him as he loved them. They were eight, five, and three when their mother married him. Since the younger boys' father was completely out of the picture, Tim formerly adopted them. Richard was a different story, though. Grandma Sally had been successful at pulling her son Jamie in just enough to keep Richard's last name different than the rest of the family. There were four Hendersons and one Martinez in their household as a result.

Tim moved the family into a very average home in a fairly nice neighborhood and immediately took to being a father. He loved it, and he wanted nothing more than to have another child with her. Unfortunately, Mary had no interest in having more children. The three they already had felt like more than enough to her.

After two years in the new home, Tim felt a calling to return home to Houston. Though he knew part of it was driven by his desire to get Mary away from her dysfunctional family, it was really more than that. He wasn't sure why, but he felt that his family needed to be a part of the boys' lives. He also believed that Mary would change her mind about not having a fourth child if he got her away from all of her reasons for not having more children.

Mary knew what a mess her family was, but she couldn't help but love them. Her father and she had rebuilt their relationship since she had married Tim, and she didn't want to leave him alone. Her younger brothers and sister were struggling through life, and none of them knew the Lord. Mary wanted to be there for them as well. Unfortunately, her mother and she never seemed to connect. Because her mother had always chosen her stepfather over her and everyone else, Mary had trouble believing she meant much to her. For that reason, along with her mother's noncommittal style, Mary and her mother only coexisted. They had little in common and almost never shared any deep thoughts. It was very disheartening for Mary who craved a deeper connection.

CHAPTER 25

I t was Friday, around 2:30 p.m. Heather had just finished her last personal training appointment for the week and was headed home with the home pregnancy test she had purchased earlier that day. She had missed her period and had already waited a week before talking herself into buying the home-test kit. Though she was hopeful that the test would yield a positive result, she had tried not to get too excited until she knew for sure that she was pregnant. Having a child would be the answer to both her and Jack's prayers. Just being married to each other felt too good to be true, and adding a baby to complete the family would almost be too much. Heather was afraid to think too much about it to avoid any let downs.

Maybe her cycle was just being thrown off by all the passion she and Jack were sharing? She had not been active for fifteen years prior to their honeymoon. Since they had both said "I do," it had almost been continual.

She began to pray, "Please God let me give Jack a baby." It was such a big wish for both of them that she wondered how disappointed she would be if she weren't.

The positive sign came up quickly. It was one of the best moments of her life, and she loved knowing that she would get to tell Jack. The realization that it was actually going to happen—she and Jack were starting a family—made her shout praise to the Lord. She was so happy that she burst into tears, feeling over blessed. She even felt a little lightheaded from her flush of emotions.

While she was still sitting on the toilet, holding the positive test, she quickly came up with a plan. She tapped out a text to Jack, "Meet me at Salt Grass at 7 p.m. I have a surprise for you. I won't be at home, I'll see you at the restaurant." She knew he would come home to get ready, so she grabbed the new very sexy dress she had bought for this very occasion and began to plan her escape.

Jack's response came back quickly, "Sounds great! What's the occasion?"

"Wear something nice. I'll give you the news then." Being a youth minister, he owned several suits. None of which were very fancy or stylish.

"Okay, see you at seven. I love this, and I love you." He always ended any conversation with Heather by telling how much he loved her. She loved hearing it.

"I love you too!"

She wondered if he had already guessed what the surprise was. Then she decided he probably hadn't as he told her that he believed he was the reason that he and Tina had not been able to have children. The doctors had told him he had a low sperm count and that his chances of conceiving were very poor. It made her news that much better. This was a miracle. It certainly felt that way to her.

She quickly dialed up Rachel.

Rachel answered, "Hey, Heather."

"Can I get dressed at your place for a big dinner with Jack? I have a really big surprise for him, and I don't want him to see me in the sexy dress I'm planning to wear. I'm giving him some really great news." The excitement in her voice peaked Rachel's curiosity, and she immediately knew what it was.

"Are you pregnant?" It was more than hopeful thinking. She and Sam had been praying nightly for them to have a child. Everyone knew how badly Jack wanted children, especially Sam and Rachel.

"Yes, can you believe it? I'm so excited. I can't wait to tell Jack." She was practically screeching she was so excited. Rachel could hear it in her voice that this was one of the greatest things that had ever happened in her life. It was really strange to think back to only a few months ago when Heather was completely alone with no prospects. For years, she had been partially closed off to life. Now she was this bubbly, happy, soon-to-be mom. It was truly amazing. The changes in Heather's disposition were undeniable. She was truly blossoming.

"This is wonderful news. I am so happy for you guys. When will you be here?" Rachel couldn't wait to see her best friend, her sister-in-law. She was so excited that she couldn't wait to hang up so she could go tell Sam.

"I've got to pick something up on my way, but I should be there about four or so. Will that work?" She couldn't get her mind off of her plan. She would stretch it out and make him suffer over dinner, then she would give him the real gift—the small wrapped box with the positive test inside. It would be perfect.

"I'll be waiting at the door for you. I'm so excited. Can we tell Sam when he gets home? I expect him about four thirty." It was such great news that she couldn't wait to hang up and start thinking about it.

"Yes, we can tell Sam. See you soon, Rachel. Good-bye."

When she arrived at Rachel's, the two embraced and cried a little bit. It was such a happy time, and they both new that this would totally change Jack's life. He loved children, and having one of his own had been his dream for years. Had Tina not gotten sick, they would have eventually gone hard after adopting a child.

Rachel loved Heather's plan and even chipped in with a couple of suggestions. To Rachel, it didn't really matter how Heather told Jack. The news itself would be the reward. However, she completely understood why Heather wanted it to be so special. Rachel was convinced that it didn't really matter what Heather did or how she did it, Jack would always remember it. Of course, he would know that it was from God, and it was definitely a gift for both of them. What a miracle having a child actually is.

Sam arrived around four thirty, and they jumped him with the news. He too was ecstatic. It was his number-one prayer for his brother now that he was married. Nothing could have been sweeter news. "Man, I wish I could be there to see his face. Make sure you let him know I knew before he did." He was only kidding, but he did think it was pretty cool that he already knew and Jack didn't.

"Very funny, Sam." Heather tried to smile, but it actually did bother her a bit. *Should I have let Jack know first?* she began to wonder.

"I'm texting him to see what he's doing tonight. I'll tell you what he says." Sam couldn't wait to mess with Jack a bit over this.

"As long as you don't tell him anything that could help him guess that Heather is pregnant. Don't say anything that would bring him over here either. He doesn't even know Heather is here." Rachel loved seeing Sam so happy about anything. She loved how much he loved his brother, and the fact that they were so close had always been something she respected about them. Their family was very tight, and all of them earnestly loved one another. It had all started with their parents' God-centered, loving relationship.

"Hey, Jack, what are you up to tonight?" Sam's text to Jack read.

"I've got a big date with Heather. How about you?" He was hoping that Sam and Rachel weren't hoping to get together. Based on Heather's message, she was set on her plans. He was sure she wanted them to be alone. It could be almost anything as she was involved with so many clients. Maybe something good had happened for one of them? Still, he couldn't help but hope that she was pregnant. It would change his life if she were. He was sure of that.

"I was hoping you could go to a movie with me and the boys? We could give the ladies some girl time." He loved messing with Jack. He knew Jack never liked to say no, especially not to the boys.

"Not tonight, Sam. Heather is set on going out alone. How about tomorrow night?" As expected, Jack hated saying no so badly that he offered a compromise.

"Man, you are whipped, brother!" He was smiling ear to ear now.

"I know," came the reply. Sam just let it die rather than run the risk of giving anything away or causing any disruptions in Heather's big news. It killed him to do so, though. Later he would tease Jack about it.

Around six o'clock, Heather disappeared into Sam and Rachel's bedroom to get dressed. After almost thirty minutes, she emerged with her makeup perfect and the sexy red dress painted on her magnificent frame.

"Whoa," was all Sam could get out.

"You look amazing, Heather. I've never seen you dressed like that." Rachel was impressed and even felt a little intimidated. Heather's beautiful face and long blonde hair were enough to make women envious, but her body was ridiculous. It almost didn't look natural as if she was some artist's rendition of the perfect female physique. Everything that was supposed to stick out stuck out, and everything that shouldn't didn't. None of it was out of place. She was really kind of a freak.

"Thanks, guys. I feel kind of self-conscious in it, but I wanted to make sure Jack didn't forget tonight." Since Kevin had violated her trust, Heather had avoided tempting men with her body. She had kept it covered when possible and rarely wore anything that drew attention. Being human, she couldn't help but feel proud when she caught someone admiring her body, though.

Heather had always told herself that her work ethic and interest in health were her primary motivations to push herself to perfection. Down deep, she loved feeling beautiful, and she liked that others were impressed. She had lied to herself for many years, believing that her obsession with her own body wasn't unhealthy. Being married to Jack had really opened her eyes, and she now saw her behavior in a new light. She had come to the realization that it had always been her desire to be admired for her looks. Though she had always told herself she didn't constantly work on her physic and health to tempt men or to make women feel physically inferior, she now realized that wasn't entirely true. Going forward, she would strive for modesty first and foremost. It was the best way to honor her husband and herself.

Now she belonged only to Jack, and she didn't want anyone but him looking at her lustfully. Though she struggled with showing off her figure in public, tonight was a very special occasion, and she had come to grips with her feelings of discomfort. Even if Jack felt uncomfortable with the attention she would get, for one evening, it was worth it if it created a memory that stayed with him.

"I would say that you need a body guard in that dress, but you look like you could probably beat the crap out of anyone that bothers you, so I won't." Sam was paying her a compliment, but he realized how he sounded, so he quickly added, "You are the second most beautiful woman I have ever laid eyes on, Heather. Jack is a lucky guy." He was reaching for Rachel as he spoke. She was rolling her eyes at him in response to his ridiculous claim.

"If I had that body, I would probably kill you myself, Sam." Rachel was only half joking, and he could tell.

"Well, now I feel better. Seriously, guys, should I wear something else?" She didn't want to be stared at by other men all night. She just wanted to make Jack drool. The public location was necessary to keep him in suspense and to keep him from tearing it off of her. In public, he would have to spend time thinking about what was to come.

"No, go with this, and then retire it. I bet Jack will want to frame it. You are doing him a big favor, and he will love you even more for letting him drool over you in it tonight." Sam spoke with assurance in his voice. It made Heather feel more comfortable and Rachel a little jealous.

"Okay, I'm heading out then." She looked excited yet nervous.

Rachel gave her a big hug and immediately noticed that Heather was about six feet tall with her heels on. It really was a strange feeling to be in her presence when she was dressed like this. Not only did she have the perfect female body and the face of a movie star, she also had the height and power of a professional wrestler. Though it was intimidating to Rachel, she knew Jack, at six foot two, would love her like this. Besides, he always commented on how nice she looked in heels when she dressed up for church functions. Of course, she was always far more conservative with the dress choice for church.

As she drove into the parking lot of the restaurant, Heather saw Jack's car and chose the spot next to it. Before she cut off the engine, she noticed him still in the car sitting there, waiting for her. He was almost fifteen minutes early, which was very unusual for him.

They rolled down their windows, and he spoke first. "Hey, beautiful, I'm early. I couldn't wait for you to get here. Wow, you look amazing." All he could see was her perfect face and the low-cut top of her skin-tight red dress.

She smiled back and put her window up before climbing out. He did the same and almost passed out when he saw how she was dressed. *Why would this creature want to be with me?* he asked himself.

"Oh my goodness! You are not human. Take me to your leader." He was joking around like usual, but he couldn't look away either. He walked up to her and gave her a big hug and kiss, completely engulfing her in his embrace. To make sure he would always remember her in this dress, he stepped back and took several pictures of her with his phone while she protested and cringed.

"Stop it, and get over here." She wanted him to help cover her up. If she was going to pull this off, he would have to help her. She needed him to keep her attention off of the looks she would surely get. She really hated those looks now. They made her so uncomfortable. She even wondered if it hurt Jack to have men notice her.

"Boy, I'm suddenly having a lot of trouble thinking about dinner. Are you sure you don't want to just go home, and I can eat off of that beautiful body of yours?" He wanted to be alone with her desperately, but he also wanted her to enjoy the evening, and he knew she loved this restaurant. He was only giving her options. His hopes that she was about to tell him she was pregnant were now at an all-time high. What else could get her to dress like this?

"No, you are buying me dinner first, buddy. Then you can unwrap me. I promise it will be worth the investment." Her innuendo was working. She could see his struggle to remain focused. She was holding a gift in her left hand, and he had not even noticed it.

"Pay to play, I get it."

All through dinner, Jack could think of nothing but the certainty of their encounter later that evening. Though he asked about the good news several times, he never pressed her. At no point did he mention the gift bag she had with her. She was surprised that he hadn't noticed it but decided that the dress was working even better than she had hoped.

When the meal was over, she put a small gift bag on the table. "What's this?" he asked.

"It's just a little something for us. I think you are going to like it." She pushed it across the table to him, and he reached in and pulled out the tiny outfit. It was two pieces of tiny black cloth, but he immediately knew what it was.

"What the heck is going on, Heather? You are killing me here. Not only are you dressed in the sexiest dress on the face of the earth, now you are passing me sexy undergarments right here at the table. I can't handle this. What's happening here? Is this lingerie the surprise?" He was very confused as she was usually very cautious with her appearance when they were going to be in public. Now she was handing him a bag with sexy panties in the middle of a restaurant.

"The surprise is yet to come. I want tonight to be a night that you will always remember. Is it working?" She could tell that it was, but she needed to hear it from him. Having his child in her belly was making her so proud.

"No, you're ugly. Are you kidding me? Of course it worked. I'll never forget how you look tonight. Never ever. You are the most perfect woman I have ever seen anywhere—TV, movies, anywhere. I love you for lots of other reasons, but your perfect body doesn't hurt either. Can we go be alone now so I can prove to you how well this has all worked?" He had already paid the check, so he stood and reached for her hand.

As they walked across the restaurant, Jack couldn't help but notice everyone staring at his wife. It had been the same when they came in, but he just hadn't been able to notice due to the obvious distraction. Heather noticed the stares too, but she didn't let it stop her from strutting for her husband.

"I bet people think I'm cheating on my wife with you. Who's actually married to someone that looks like you?" As usual, he was in awe and immensely proud of her.

"Race you home," Heather said as she pushed him away.

"What about the big news that got you dressed up like this? It's not just the dress and sexy gruds, right?" The suspense was killing him. She was just going too far for this to be anything less than her being pregnant. *Could it really be that?* he wondered.

"I'll tell you at home. Let's get out of here." She had her key out and was scrambling to get it in the keyhole before he could get a jump on her.

Realizing that she would beat him home and take the one slot in the garage, Jack turned and began to run for his door. He jumped in and they raced home. As usual, Heather won. She had taken a different route than the one she knew he would take, and she was a far more fearless and focused driver.

Heather was already closing the garage as Jack drove in. Not only was he a much slower driver than she was, he also wanted her to have the garage. He never liked the thought of her climbing in and out of her car outside. Her car belonged in the garage, not his.

Seeing that the garage door was already closing as he pulled in, Jack hit his garage door opener button to see if he could catch her getting out of the car, but she had already gone in the house.

He had hoped to find her waiting for him in that dress, but he knew he was too late and that she was obviously in a big hurry to get herself situated for whatever she was planning. As he began to feel some excitement that she might be running ahead to put on that little slingshot deal she had presented him with at dinner, a text came in from her, "I'm preparing in the bathroom. Get ready for me and wait for me on the bed."

This was all very exciting. Could it be…was there any chance she could be pregnant?

He walked in to find only the kitchen light on. He quickly used the guest bathroom and headed to the master bedroom. In his excitement, he stripped down and climbed into bed. "I wanted to take that dress off of you myself. How long will it be, baby? I'd hate to fall asleep, waiting for you." If it had taken her two hours, he would have still been wide awake, and he knew it, but he wanted to hurry her along.

"I'm almost ready, honey. I hope you have the lights on. I want you to see every inch of me." She was already in the string outfit and was happy to see how stretched the tiny pieces of fabric were. She was sure he would go crazy as she paraded around for him. The second gift was now ready to go, and her body was all stuffed into the sexy lingerie so she opened the door with the gift bag hanging from her fingers.

Although he had been admiring her amazing body for six weeks now, this time was different. She had kind of an oily appearance and seemed to have a darker complexion than usual. Somehow, he managed to notice the gift amongst all of the curves. Maybe because she was spinning it around in a circle in front of his face.

"Wow, all of this and another gift?" He still couldn't believe she was really his.

"Please don't touch me until I touch you." She instructed him to sit up on the side of the bed and walked in between his legs to set the gift bag on his thigh. "Don't open that until I give you the signal."

Jack shook his head yes but could do little else. As her powerful body stretched and contorted in front of him, he wasn't sure he could handle it. "Baby, I really need to touch you."

She stood up and gave him a glimpse under each piece of fabric and then told him to open the gift. She was convinced that she had done enough to make sure he would never forget the evening, and she was right about that. She was also pretty sure that she would never again do what she had done for him tonight. Though she was never shy or ashamed in any way with her body when they were alone, she wasn't much of a temptress and didn't really need to do anything to get him going for her. Though she had a strong personality, she was not much of an entertainer. Dancing in front of him had been very uncomfortable, and she had actually felt kind of stupid doing it.

He reached in and pulled out the tiny box and shook it. "It sounds like a toothbrush." She was still teasing him, so he ripped the box open, and the test fell to the floor. As it popped out, he saw what it was, and he realized what it meant.

He stood straight up into her and lifted her toward the ceiling. The two collapsed onto the bed, and the joy filled the room. Jack jumped out of bed and hopped around a bit before he attacked her. It was another beautiful moment in their young marriage, and as Heather had hoped, the moment would never be forgotten.

Life was very good for Jack and Heather.

CHAPTER 26

Jennifer and Mike had just climbed into bed when the phone rang. Though it was only 9:00 p.m., early evenings were a common practice for them as Jennifer liked to read, while Mike watched TV until it was lights out. Though they had different interests, they liked to do things together, and going to bed early was one of those things.

"Mom, it's Jack. Is Dad with you? I have some really great news!" His excitement surprised his mother. Though Jack always seemed excited about something, she could tell this was something significant.

"Of course, we were just going to bed." Mr. and Mrs. Henderson had been strong examples to their children. Not only did they put God first in everything they did, they put each other second and then the rest of the family third. It was them that had made the three Henderson boys into the great husbands all three of them had become. Even their baby sister had found a good Christian man to marry. All four of their children were in strong, healthy, God-centered marriages. It was exactly what they had prayed for all of their lives.

After retiring early every evening, the two did their own thing for an hour or two before spending time together in prayer. They always prayed for each one of their children and grandchildren immediately after turning out the lights. This had been their routine all of their married lives. Though they had both grown up in a Bible-believing church, they had seen many families in the church fail. Many of their closest friends had lived through difficult times, dealing with tragedy and pain from their spouse or primarily from one of their children making poor decisions. From early on, the Henderson's had decided that their family would be God's family. They prayed for his blessings over everything they did and over all of their loved ones. Though they occasionally had hardships, their lives, as well as the lives of their children, were richly blessed because they put God first. Though there were not at all impervious to trials, they always kept their faith in God and were always brought through them.

Even with the blessings, they knew they were not immune to this world's fallen, sinful nature. Ugly things touched their family like anyone else's family. It was the way they always went to God for strength and rallied around each other that set them apart. Mom, Dad, and all four kids chose to live life God's way. None of them were perfect, but they were forgiven when they stumbled. Sure they suffered consequences when they sinned like everyone else did, but they understood why they were suffering consequences and always accepted them and repented and turned from their sins.

"Heather just told me that she is pregnant! We are going to have a baby in seven and a half months." He could barely contain himself. He was so excited.

"That is great, honey." Jack could hear her telling Dad, "Heather is pregnant." Then she continued, "Boy, you two didn't waste much time." Jack heard almost nothing from his father and was a little put off by it. Not long ago, Jack had told his parents that he was the problem and that he didn't think he could ever have his own children.

Shouldn't they be more excited? he thought.

"We didn't want to wait, Mom, and we can hardly believe it's happening so soon."

"We are both so happy for you, honey. This is really great." She was very supportive, and he could tell she was excited but not as excited as he had expected. She went on to add, "Is this some kind of miracle?"

"It may be. They never told me I couldn't have kids, but that the odds were definitely against it." It was starting to hit him now how prefect the timing actually was. If he and Tina would have conceived, things would have been far more complicated.

"Honey, I have some good news for you too. You'll never guess what it is." Jack's mind couldn't even imagine anything outside of what he was trying to process about the baby he and Heather were going to have. He always wanted to hear good news, but he had no interest in guessing what it might be. In the back of his mind, he was beginning to feel a little let down that his parents had not been more excited about his news.

He put his hand over the phone to speak with Heather. "They have good news for us." She asked him to find out what it was, so he took his hand off the phone and said, "I don't want to guess, Mom, but I do want to know what it is." He clicked the button to switch the phone to speaker. "You're on the speaker now, Mom."

"Hi, Heather, I'm so happy for you guys."

"Thank you, Mom."

Jennifer continued, "Tim called a little while ago to let us know that he and Mary have decided to take the offer. They will be here next week to start looking for a house. He'll start working at the hospital in less than a month." She couldn't hide her excitement over Tim's return. He was the baby boy, and they were all proud of his success. They all admired his intelligence, his ability to work and study tirelessly, his love for the Lord, and his kindness toward everyone. Everyone in the family wanted to get to know Tim better now that he was completely grown up, and now, it would finally be possible.

"That is fantastic! I was hoping he would take that job." This really was great news. Now he knew why Tim had called and left a message while he and Heather were celebrating earlier. Jack hadn't remembered to check the message after seeing the call come in because he was so sidetracked by Heather's seduction.

"Since tomorrow is Saturday, your father and I would like to have you and your brother over. I already talked to Sam, and he and the whole crew are coming at 3:00 p.m. Can you and Heather come at 3:00 p.m.?" Jack looked to Heather for the answer.

"Sure, we can make it. I have a morning class, which Jack always comes to and a couple of private training sessions, but I'll be done by 2:00 p.m. We can easily make it by 3:00 p.m. I was supposed to see my mother tomorrow night, though. Are you okay with me inviting my parents? Also, what should be bring?" Jack was glad she did the talking. In most cases, he would agree only to find out she already had something planned. Having her on the call took all of the pressure off of him. She always knew both of their commitments, while he usually even forgot his own.

"No problem at all. We would love to have your parents. Please don't bring anything. I'm sending Dad to the grocery store tomorrow morning. He'll get everything we need for a barbecue. We'll see you guys at 3:00 p.m. tomorrow." Then she remembered something. "Oh yeah, you don't need to call Tim about the baby. We have already talked with him. Just so you both know, Sam told us and Tim that Heather is pregnant an hour or so ago. Sorry, I'm already all cried out over it. Dad even cried. What great news!" She was kind of smiling now.

"That son of a gun," said Jack. He finally understood why they hadn't been more excited when he had broken the news about Heather's pregnancy. Heather was still holding on to him while she began to giggle a bit about the situation.

Though his parents were still on the phone, he began to speak directly to Heather. "I bet he liked having all of this information before I did. That jerk even tried to get me to go to a movie with him and the kids when he knew you were planning to break the great news to me tonight. I guess I deserve it for all of this kind of stuff I've done to him over the years?" Jack had always been the fun one in the family. He pranked everyone, all of the time. It was rare that he was ever serious about anything, even about serious things.

Heather said nothing but pulled him in tightly with a big smile on her face.

His mother decided to end the call. "You definitely had it coming, Jack. See you kids tomorrow. Dad and I love you both. Good night." They hung up, and Jack and Heather were alone again.

"Are you ready for round two, Jack? That was a pretty big dinner. I need to burn some more calories before I go to sleep."

"I better help you stay in shape before your body starts to bloat up." He was only kidding, and he hoped his kidding wouldn't hurt her feelings in any way.

"You will pay for that, skinny." She grabbed him and manhandled him flat to the bed.

He didn't mind being dominated by her at all. It did make him wonder if he could escape if he wanted to, though. He was pretty sure he could, but it would be close. He was definitely stronger than her in the weight room, though she was superior physically in every other way.

CHAPTER 27

Tim and the two youngest boys, Ben and Victor, were headed for Grandma and Grandpa's house. The boys had only seen this set of grandparents twice in their lives—first at their parents wedding and once when Grandma and Grandpa Henderson had visited them in New Mexico. Their mother, Mary, and their older brother, Richard, had gotten up and left their new Pearland home early that morning with two escorts: Heather and Rachel.

Tim's family was now officially living in Pearland, Texas. Mary had struggled mightily with the decision to leave her family behind in New Mexico, but now that they were settled in their beautiful new home, she was beginning to feel that they had made the right decision. Though it had only been a couple of days since she and the kids had been in the new home, she sometimes felt guilty for leaving her family in New Mexico, so much so that she was already spending countless hours on the phone with all of them.

By the way Tim treated them and interacted with them, no one would have ever known that they were not his biological children. It was only their Mexican features that could have tipped anyone off, but even then, their mother was Mexican, so it wasn't unreasonable that they could be a product of their marriage. While the younger boys were treating Tim like he was their father, Richard was not. In the two years Tim had been married to their mother, Richard called Tim "Dad" but did little else to accept him as his father.

Mary believed it had a lot to do with Richard's biological father's mother, Sally. Her son, Jamie, had almost no interest in his son. However, anytime something threatened the way Sally thought it should be done, she would flex her muscle by getting Jamie to call Mary to complain or by getting Richard himself to complain to Mary.

Mary was constantly worrying about Richard's fate. Though the younger boys were also born out of wedlock, they seemed to accept Tim and were full participants in their new family. Tim loved them all, but Richard was pushing him away. He just refused to be a full participant in their new family. Additionally, Richard seemed to be strangely detached from his feelings. All he seemed to care about was his own needs and wants. Even his mother's feelings didn't seem to matter to him.

At ten years of age, Richard was only the size of a normal six- or seven-year-old. His lack of size made people believe he was far younger than he actually was. He would often get praise for being so grown up as they often didn't realize how old he actually was. He was already beginning to require constant praise to feel adequate as his Grandma Sally had constantly filled his head full of material and vain concepts of self-worth.

At ten, things weren't too out of line in his life. Only his mother and Tim ever noticed the signs of things to come. Unfortunately, they were right about where things were going.

As Tim and the two younger boys pulled into Grandpa and Grandma Henderson's place, they were greeted by their excited grandparents, Sam and his boys, and Jack. They were all in the front yard, waiting for Tim and the boys so they could make them feel at home. Rachel, Mary, Heather, and Richard were all shopping and would be gone for at least a couple more hours. Even though he would be the only boy with the ladies, Richard had refused to go with Tim and his younger brothers that morning.

Sam's oldest son, Joe, was eleven years old and about to be twelve. His younger son, Robert, would be ten in a couple of months. The boys had only met Uncle Tim a couple of times and had only met his boys once at Tim and Mary's wedding. Only Tim and Mary had come for Jack and Heather's wedding.

As soon as the car was parked in the driveway, Ben and Victor rushed out to greet their grandparents. Soon, they were playing with Joe and Robert as if they were all old friends. It wasn't hard to see that the boys were picking up Tim's trusting ways. Ben was now seven, and Victor was six. Tim had been officially their father now for two years. Before that, Tim had been around constantly while he and Mary got acquainted and fell very deeply in love. Tim had been the steady man in their lives since they were only three and two years old. They called him "Dad" because that's who he was to them, not because that had to.

Tim loved Mary very deeply, and the boys knew it. They had benefited from Tim and Mary's love as it had given them a sense of security. Ben and Victor felt as if Tim was their real father, and since the other guy wasn't around and couldn't have cared less, Tim had adopted them and was now officially their dad. His love for the boys and their love for him was all quite healthy.

Tim's marriage to Mary was pure gold. Due to Mary's difficult childhood, she had very low expectations of Tim. Actually, Tim not getting drunk every weekend was enough for her. Not lying to her or cheating on her were also nice benefits of being Tim's wife. She appreciated these things more than any woman without her background ever could have. The fact that he was much more than she ever dreamed of in a man made her feel blessed to be with him. Tim seemed to put her and the boys first in everything. Though he worked lots of long hours at the hospital, he would do whatever it took to spend time with all of them. She simply couldn't doubt his commitment to their family.

Still, coming from her background, Mary would always be suspicious of men. She would also always look at things with a critical eye. In her world, no one could be trusted. Believing anyone about anything would almost guarantee that you would be the taken advantage of or made to look like a fool when the truth surfaced as it always eventually did. Tim was now the only man she trusted. It wasn't easy or natural at all for her though.

As the kids played in the yard, the Henderson brothers and their parents moved inside as their baby sister and her husband pulled up. Katie was now twenty-six and had been married to Tom for two years. They had no children and never would.

Jack, as usual in a crowd, was shining brightly. His excitement over having their family back together and the fact that he would soon be a father had him in a state none of them had ever seen before. It was both intoxicating and contagious. Not that he had ever been one to focus on his troubles. Actually, it had always been a struggle to get him to worry at all about his troubles or anything else for that matter. Things were really good in his life right now, so much so that he seemed to not have a care in the world. He was suffering from excessive happiness. As a result, he was making everyone laugh constantly, and his love for all of them was gushing everywhere.

Tim—though full of relief over finally having his new family away from the world Mary's family was trapped in—was really beginning to struggle with Mary's fears about Richard, as well as his own concerns about him not accepting him into their family. All of Mary's problems seemed to stem from her fears over Richard's direction and future. Anything Mary felt affected her ability to function with others, and no one felt it more than Tim. He instinctively knew that the issues they were seeing with Richard were only going to get worse as he grew older, and he had no clue how to fix them. He prayed constantly about it, but nothing seemed to change. Being in a new job and being the tireless worker that he was gave him very little free time. As usual, he had thrown himself into his work from the time he had taken the new job. When he was at home, he was playing with the younger boys or spending quality time with Mary. Richard got nothing from him as he chose to be alone and to push him away.

Sam had always been Mr. Consistent. He was always looking out for everyone else. These qualities had made him a wonderful husband, father, and employee. What these qualities didn't give Sam was the ability to relax. Though his faith was strong and he deeply believed that things were in God's hands and that God would always look out for him and his, Sam was engulfed in fear. No one could have known it. Though the outward signs were there, high blood pressure, the inability to lose weight, and the irritability over things and circumstances out of his control, Sam often felt like he was a step away from failing his family. No one ever noticed because he never complained about his circumstances or the pressures that were eating at him. The only one who ever heard a thing about his cares was Rachel. She knew everything, and she worried constantly about his health because of it. She prayed for him constantly and always tried to encourage him to think more about his health. To him, though, it was just another thing to worry about.

As the three Henderson brothers enjoyed each other's and their parent's company, the girls and Richard pulled into the driveway. As they scrambled to get out of the car quickly, it appeared at least to Grandma that they were on some sort of mission. Grandma made an observation to the group, "It looks like they have something up their sleeves, boys." She was notoriously difficult to pull anything over on. She always saw it coming. It was probably a result of having four kids who were always up to something.

Tim immediately noticed that the girls were rallying around Mary. Well, everyone but Richard who looked pouty and alone. *What was going on?* he wondered.

The giggling ladies opened the door for their new resident sister-in-law so she could make her grand entrance for all to see. Though nothing was strange about her appearance, her smiling face and a small gift bag in her right hand were both tells that something was going on.

"What's going on?" Jack let out.

Heather put her finger over her lips as Mary walked up and handed the perplexed-looking Tim the gift bag. He pulled it from her hand and dug his hand down into it until he found a tiny item of clothing with a tiny hanger on it. He quickly pulled it from the bag to see it was an infant's outfit. Leaping to his feet, he attacked his wife with an enormous, loving hug. "We are having a baby!" he hollered.

CHAPTER 28

Richard was unreachable by phone, and Mary was beside herself after finding out that he had once again lied about where he had spent the night. If it had been the first time, she would have been surprised, but Richard's lying had now become the norm. It had gotten so bad at this point that every word from his mouth had to be assumed to be a lie. Your odds of being right were far better that way.

Summer was almost over, and school was right around the corner. It would be Richard's senior year, while Ben would be a freshman, and Victor was going into the eighth grade. Their baby sister, Tina, was soon to be seven and would be going into first grade the following school year. Though Tina was the only biological child of Tim's, Ben and Victor were every bit as loved. Tim also loved Richard, but it was much different. It was mostly one way, and Richard acted as if he wanted no part of it.

Since he wouldn't answer his phone, Mary dialed Richard's girlfriend to see what she knew about his whereabouts. She figured he had asked to spend the night at a friend's house with the intent of going to his girlfriend's place or some party or something. The act was getting old, and Mary was getting very tired of it. Each time she caught him, Richard would lie from beginning to end. Even when his mother knew the truth, Richard would continue to lie. It was like peeling an onion of lies, and one could only navigate through them by knowing the truth and pushing through each layer to get there. Even then, it was a certainty that there was more to the story.

At this point in his life, Richard seemed incapable of telling the truth. Every time Tim and Mary gave him the benefit of the doubt, it backfired. They both felt that they needed to allow him to prove himself and knew they couldn't always be there to guide him every time he was presented with a tough decision, but it was getting to the point where they were both sure he would always chose the wrong thing. It was almost as if he wanted to lie about everything, as if he really believed he could get away with it.

The rest of the family was quite functional. Ben and Victor were becoming fine young men, and they fully appreciated the dream lives they were now living. Tina, though only seven years old, had become someone other kids loved to be around. She was kind and always seemed to be smiling.

Tina's best friend was her slightly older cousin Maria. Aunt Heather and Uncle Jack's daughter, Maria, had been born only a few weeks before Tina. The two were inseparable and seemed to be the primary target for Richard's hatred. From the time Richard had learned that his mother and Tim were having a baby, he began expressing feelings of jealousy and anger. The target for his angst was always his mother.

Richard could not have had a more displeasing personality. Not only was he a liar of the worst sort, his attitude was terrible all of the time. It was as if he was always looking for conflict in everything he did. In his mind, nothing was ever his fault. He could accept no blame; it simply wasn't in him to be responsible for his own actions. It was always an excuse with him when something went wrong. You could count on it; in his eyes, he had done nothing wrong.

Mary, having actually lived through difficult times, had zero patience for her eldest son's ridiculous insistence that his life was so terrible. Though Richard had been given everything anyone his age could ever want, including an iPhone and a car, he still felt his life was tragic. Not only that, he felt that his parents loved his brothers and especially his baby sister more than they loved him. Though he didn't understand it, he was actually destroying his family and driving a wedge between himself and all of them. Sadly, it was all because he cared more about himself and his own feelings than he did about any of them.

Richard's biggest flaw was his inability to honor women. He was becoming more and more disrespectful to his mother, which drove Tim crazy, and kept the two constantly at odds. Though it hurt Mary, it made her feel disgust for her son who brought a heavy burden of inappropriateness; he was her son after all. Though he had not spent any time with his biological father, Richard had picked up many of his faults. Of all these faults, the way he treated and though about women was the most difficult for his mother to accept. Mary simply would not put up with Richard treating women the way his biological father did.

By this time in his life, Richard thought so highly of himself and had such a low opinion of women that he began using his lying ways to wiggle his way into relationships with girls with low self-esteem. Though he wasn't targeting the ones with low self-esteem, he was naturally attracted to them unconsciously. Just like his father, he believed that he was a nice guy and always portrayed that to his prey. Once they were involved, he began to manipulate them and eventually made them feel that they were lucky to have him, as he truly believed they were.

Going into his senior year, he had already slept with several girls and messed around with quite a few more. He would say and do anything to get them to be with him, and he loved how good he was at doing it. Of course, he never respected any of them, but that never crossed his mind. In fact, he spent all of his time trying to meet and hook up with other girls, regardless of whether he had a girlfriend or not.

The hardest part for Mary was that Richard seemed to think there was nothing wrong with what he was doing. In spite of the constant preaching about God's ways he got daily from Tim and his mother, he discounted their warnings of the consequences of doing things the world's way. He thought of them as simple and closed minded and often laughed to himself while they were lecturing him. How stupid Tim had been to not sleep with his mother before they got married he decided. *He could have had her any time he wanted,* he thought. Tim's example had meant nothing at all to him.

Richard craved attention and drama. He was skilled at dragging people into his mess of a life to achieve just that—attention and drama. Normal friendships were almost nonexistent in his life. In most cases, he had a very short window of time before his new best friend would get tired of his act and run from him. If he managed to maintain a relationship with another guy for more than three months, there was likely something wrong with the friend. Most of them were seriously flawed, but Richard always thought they were good friends early on. Of course, that feeling never lasted as they never were good people if they hadn't seen the train wreck that was Richard coming.

Richard so craved drama in his life that he became an expert at achieving it, though he never developed the maturity to realize what he was doing. If he didn't have enough uneasiness in his life, he would simply crank it up a notch. Yelling and screaming was something he simply needed in his life. Without it, he felt like no one cared. Though he didn't understand why he felt so empty and worthless, he blamed it on everyone else, mainly his mother. Sadly, it was his mother who had given up so much all of his life to make things better for him than they had ever been for her. It was his mother who would always be there for him, and she was the only one who would always care about him. It was his mother who picked up all of the pieces every time he destroyed everything around him. Of course she was supported by Tim, but he was more in it for her sake. Tim felt that Richard needed to hit bottom before he would ever start looking up.

Richard's lies ranged from small, seemingly inconsequential lies to monster lies. Time and time again, the truth eventually surfaced, and each time, more credibility was lost. The eventual exposure was always painful and usually left scars on everyone involved. Just when things appeared to be getting better, the next usually even more shocking lie would be exposed. Everyone in the family was praying for Richard to change. No one wanted this for him, his mother, or their family. Unfortunately, it was just who he was, and he saw no reason to change.

On this occasion, the friend whose house Richard was supposed to be staying at admitted to Mary that Richard had never even been to his house that night. When Richard's girlfriend wouldn't answer her phone, Mary left her a message that she would call her parents in twenty minutes if she didn't hear back from her. Mary wasn't positive they were together but assumed they were and was quite sure Emily wouldn't want to get caught in a lie by her parents either. Almost immediately after the threat, the string of lies began coming via texts from Richard. Not knowing how much his mother knew, he started by saying he was at his friend's house and would be heading home right away. It was the same old routine again.

Tim and Mary had both had enough. When Richard finally got home, they didn't even attempt to get the truth out of him. Instead, they laid out the new rules. Essentially, all trust was gone as was his car and his freedom to go out on his own until after graduation.

Not surprisingly, the sentence didn't go over well with Richard. His only card left to play was his usual threat to go live with his "real" father. They had heard it before, but clearly this time, it was different. Richard was actually foolish enough to go though with it. Being annoyed at the years of lying and the false accusations that had brought the police to the their home on more than one occasion, Mary called Richard's bluff and arranged a flight back to New Mexico for him to live with Jamie, his real father.

Knowing that Jamie was as much if not even more self-absorbed than Richard, Mary and Tim were sure that the new living arrangement would not be the final solution. Mary feared much worse as she knew Jamie was a heavy drinker and likely a drug user. She feared the move could lead to even more worldliness and despair for Richard. She even feared that living with Jamie could get Richard in serious trouble or maybe even get him killed.

Jamie partied all the time, had fathered other children without ever being married, and chased women all of the time. It would be like Disneyland for someone like Richard. To her, it felt like the last thing he needed. However, Tim didn't agree. He felt that Richard had been listening and that he would eventually find his way back to the correct path if he were exposed to all of the ugliness of the life he was choosing to live.

This had been Richard's decision, and they needed to let him pay the consequences of his choice if they ever wanted him to learn anything. All they could and would do for him is pray night and day. They were both frustrated, but neither had given up on him. Praying for him and giving him the freedom to make his own decisions was the best thing they could do for him. They both agreed it was, though Mary struggled considerably with it.

As was always the case, the younger boys and Tina had been suffering while Richard had selfishly kept their mother burdened with the chaos of his life. Many a night had Mary lay awake worried about where Richard was or what he was doing. On multiple occasions, she had taken late-night drives to check to see if Richard was where he told her he would be. Most times, he was not, and as a result, Mary was constantly conflicted inside, leaving almost nothing for the rest of the family. Tim hated what was happening to her as her happiness was one of his top priorities.

In less than three months' time Jamie had enough of the disrespectful and devilish Richard. He threw him out, vowing to never want to see his face again. He sent Richard to his mother's, Sally, house and vowed to never speak with him again. Richard had only completed a few weeks of his senior year of high school when his father threw him out.

Though Richard had never shown any respect to his mother or to Tim, spending time with Jamie had created some of what had not been there previously. His acts of defiance with Jamie had gotten him punched in the face and thrown out. If nothing else, Richard now realized that he had left a perfect situation with two loving parents, all the support he could ever need, his own car, and all of the comforts that came with being a Henderson.

Grandma Sally lasted even less time with Richard than his real father had. In less than a week's time, she was on the phone with Mary, telling her that Richard had to go. Sally would not allow anything to disturb her safe little life. Since her husband had died, she enjoyed having only herself to worry about and wasn't about to take on the mess that was Richard. Her complaining over the years had come naturally, and her meddling and prodding had been without consequence to her. Now that there was a consequence, namely Richard, Sally wanted nothing to do with it.

After some begging from Richard and many assurances that things would be different, Mary and Tim agreed to take him back. The deal was that he would pay off the car they had bought him, pay his own cell phone bill, and go back to finish high school. None of which ever happened. Tim and Mary never really expected it to, though they both desired it.

CHAPTER 29

Sam lay in bed next to his wife. At forty-three years of age, Rachel was actually getting better looking every day in his eyes. Though she wasn't the workout fiend her best friend and sister-in-law Heather was, Rachel took very good care of herself, and it showed. She, Heather, and Mary all walked together three to four times each week, and sometimes Katie, Sam, Jack, and Tim's baby sister joined them as well. Rachel and Mary also did one of Heather's spinning classes at least twice a week.

Sam loved everything about Rachel. One of the many things he admired about her was her commitment to remaining fit. Not only did she exercise regularly, she also watched what she ate. Unfortunately, he had not done the same. He had not even really tried to stay fit for her, and that fact only added more stress to his life. He couldn't help but feel guilty for not even trying.

As Sam thought about his good fortune in having such a great wife and listened to her soft snore, he got a text from his youngest brother, Tim. "Richard is coming back. Please pray for us." Tim had sent the message to both Sam and Jack as they were both his best friends and prayer partners. With Jack as their pastor, Tim leaned pretty heavily on him for advice and prayer. However, it was his big brother Sam who Tim really connected with. Tim had grown up admiring Sam so much that no one could ever have a bigger impact on him than he did. Actually, both of his younger brothers always went to Sam first for advice and even for prayer.

It was very late, but getting a text from Tim at any hour wasn't unusual. His duties at the hospital could have him there pretty much any time, day or night. He would often spend time with his family when they were available and then go back in to check on patients, study, or fill in for someone doing ER. Tim was somehow able to function on very little sleep. Six hours was the longest he ever slept, while four or five was really all he ever seemed to need. His burden to help others pushed him to always be on the lookout for an opportunity help someone. When he wasn't helping someone, he often felt guilt for not doing so.

Tim's caring for others had a huge impact on everyone he encountered with the exception of Richard. Tim had given up on any expectation of Richard accepting him any time soon, but long term, he believed there was still a good chance. He figured Richard would learn everything the hard way until he was mature enough or broken enough to realize that his ways were flawed. Hardship and defeat would someday get through to Richard, and then they would have a chance to bond. Unfortunately, as things currently stood, Richard was just not capable of seeing through the fog he was living in.

Though all of Richard's anger seemed to be aimed at his mother and his siblings, he seemed to have almost no regard at all for Tim. Since Tim believed that all things are possible with God, he never gave up hope that Richard would turn. Richard had no choice but to learn God's Word, and Tim firmly believed it would have an effect on him. So much so that he never stopped praying for a miracle, and he never allowed himself to condemn Richard's entire future based on his struggles as an adolescent. Tim's love for others and ability to forgive others was a product of his faith, which was firmly based on God's Word. The fact that he had read about many great men and women who had come from less-than-ideal circumstance to do great things added to his unwillingness to give up on Richard. The Bible itself was full of flawed people doing great things for God.

Sam said a short prayer after reading Tim's text about Richard's return and typed back. "I'm praying for you guys, brother. Hang in there, and let us know if you need anything." *It is such a shame, Sam thought. Will it ever get better for Tim and Mary? Will it ever end?* Tim was one of the wisest people Sam knew, and yet he just couldn't come up with anything to change Richard. Nothing seemed to work, and neither Sam nor Jack had an answer outside of prayer at this point. They were all sure that continued prayer was the only solution, and they all understood resolution would come in God's appointed time.

Sam's youngest son, Robert, was only a few months younger than Richard. The two were in the same grade, but they had no common friends and no classes together. While Robert was a strong student and an extremely friendly person, Richard was the complete opposite. Robert had friends he had grown up with, while Richard had none that had been his friend for more than a few months. Every time things got ugly with Richard, Robert was the first to find out. Being who he was, he refused to talk behind Richard's back but frequently found himself in between the stories and the truth. Things had gotten so bad for him that he had done everything he could to avoid crossing Richard's path. He even had to stop reading anything Richard posted on Facebook or any other form of social media.

As Sam's thoughts drifted back to his own problems, he began dwelling on his son's college tuition. Joe was very soon to be nineteen and was in his second year at the University of Houston. The money Sam and Rachel had saved for college was already about gone, and they still had three more years for Joe and four years for Robert who was now in his senior year of high school. Financial burden wasn't a new thing for them, but it was a heavy one for Sam. So heavy that Sam thought and worried more about it than anything else, especially his own health.

Though Rachel had homeschooled the boys, she had gone back to work as a nurse two years earlier to help pay off debt and to save for the boys to go to college. It was Tim who had found her the position, and she now worked three to four days a week to get her forty hours in each week. It was good money, but she never really enjoyed the work or being in a hospital. With her standoffish personality and her preference to be in the background, she struggled to work with doctors and patients. It was a real struggle for her, and it only added to the stress Sam was dealing with. He hated that she had to do something she didn't like, and it added a considerable amount of stress to his already overstressed system.

As Sam lay there, thinking about how they could get out of the hole they had dug themselves, he began to feel pressure in his chest, and his arms were tingling just a little. The pain came for a while and then went. Shortly, it was back again. Though he didn't think it was serious, he decided to send Tim a text to see what he recommended. It had only been a few minutes since Tim had sent him a text, so he figured he was still awake. It was 11:38 p.m.

"I'm having some pressure feelings in my chest, and my arms keep tingling. What do you think?" Sam would have never sent the text if he thought Tim was asleep as he really didn't think it was anything serious.

The reply came quickly. "Get dressed. I'll meet you in your driveway in three minutes." Tim had been really worried about Sam for quite some time. Though Sam never complained about his stress level and always tried to stay positive for everyone else, Tim knew he was struggling. With Sam being seventy to eighty pounds overweight, Tim feared for the worst when Sam's text came in.

"Wow, are you sure it's that serious?" Sam was really surprised Tim would react this way. It was probably a false alarm. *Maybe Tim just needed to talk?*

"I'd rather be on the safe side. I won't knock." He wanted to see Sam either way, but it wouldn't take much to check him out.

Sam quietly climbed out of bed, being careful to not wake Rachel. He didn't want her to worry, so he dressed quietly and snuck out. Tim was already in the driveway and out of his car when Sam opened the front door. He was standing there behind Sam's car with a small bag he was setting on the closed trunk.

"Thanks for coming, Tim. I don't think I'm having a heart attack, but I'm glad you are here to check." He was actually really concerned that something like a heart attack was going on, but he didn't want to seem like a hypochondriac. By this time, he was starting to feel really clammy and faint, and the chest pain kept coming and going. The pain felt like a tightening of some sort.

"Let me do a couple quick checks, and then we can talk." As usual, he was very calm and under control. It was reassuring to Sam as it always was for Tim's patients.

As Sam drew close, Tim pulled some equipment out of his bag. In a matter of minutes, he had run several tests and asked all the questions needed to decide what was going on with Sam. Without much explanation, he instructed Sam to get in the car. Before Sam could object, the two were on their way to the hospital.

"Sam, you have too many symptoms for us not to go to the ER. Let's be on the safe side with this as you will be fine if we catch it before it hits hard. In the worst case, we would have to do surgery tonight. I can do it myself tonight if needed." Though he was still calm, he was suddenly very serious.

"This is freaking me out a bit, Tim. I'm not resisting, but it's just scaring me. I know this is what you do, and I'm sure you're doing the right thing. Should I let Rachel know what's going on?" Suddenly, all he could think of was Rachel. What if he never got to hold her again? She had warned him that he needed to start taking care of himself. Though he always listened, he obviously hadn't been able to honor her by getting himself into shape for her and the boys. Now on the way to the hospital, he felt terrible about all of it.

For years, now he had been using food and soft drinks to relieve his stress. When things had gotten tough, he ate and drank more. Whenever he tried to stop, something stressful would come up, and he would become depressed until he would break down and enjoy the immediate relief he always got from a big Coke or from junk food. He never doubted that it was heading to this moment. He had always wanted to get out of this world and onto the promise, but he knew it was wrong to make it happen prematurely. At this moment, he was feeling that it was really cowardly to be doing it this way. He couldn't help but feel like a big foolish failure. His only option at this point was to pray for God's mercy to save him so he could be there for his family.

"I'll leave that up to you. If you let her know, I'm sure she'll head this way right now. When is she working again?" Tim felt pretty sure that he could fix Sam up without much damage, but since he could not tell the future and any surgery involving the heart was risky, he was not about to tell him to not have Rachel by his side for this if it turned into surgery.

"She goes on duty at 7:00 a.m. tomorrow. Can you send her a text if I have to stay tonight?" The conversation was completely without emotion, very professional. It felt odd to Sam as it was outside of their normal relationship to talk emotionless facts the way they were, but he fully understood the reason for his brother's professionalism.

"I will."

They were already pulling into the hospital at this point in the conversation. Tim continued through the parking lot into the emergency room roundabout. They parked, and Tim walked Sam in right through the waiting room and into an exam room. One of the administrative assistants saw them and asked if she could help.

"Can you please have someone move my car out of the drive? Here's my key. Please send Tammy to room 115. Thanks." Tammy was one of the most senior nurses on the staff. Tim had just left the hospital a few minutes earlier, so he knew who was working.

Things progressed very quickly and, as promised, as soon as he knew what needed to be done, Tim sent a text to Rachel. "I am doing a triple bypass on Sam tonight. He should be okay. He loves you."

Rachel awoke to the sound of the text coming in. It had long been one of her biggest fears that she would get a text in the middle of the night about one of her boys being in an accident or something. When she realized that it was 2:00 a.m. and that Sam was not next to her in bed, she scrambled for the phone, fearing the worst. The news was shocking, and she suddenly felt her life coming down all around her. Sam was everything to her, and she knew that she simply could not do life without him.

"I'm on my way. Don't let anything happen to him." Her text made it back to Tim quickly, and he shared it with Sam.

"Thank you, Tim."

"Please don't take him, Lord. We all need him. I cannot live without him, Father." Rachel prayed out loud as she rushed to get dressed. Her mind was racing, but nothing she thought about was being resolved. She decided against waking the boys as they were nineteen and seventeen now, and they both had transportation. She decided it would be better to make contact once she knew more as the hospital was pretty close by.

Before she could finish applying her makeup, she began to feel a panic she would never forget set in. Seeing her own eyes staring back at her in the mirror brought her to tears, and her entire body suddenly felt week as she slumped down to the floor for a good cry. Only through prayer and her desire to get to the hospital to be by her husband's side was she able to regain her bearings and get herself made up and dressed.

The drive to the hospital was very difficult for her. She was crying and convulsing so hard that she was having trouble keeping her eyes on the road. It was more of a blur than anything else. Her mind kept telling her that nothing mattered if Sam didn't make it, and fear of the worst was all she could think about. That thought was too much for her to bear, but it wouldn't leave her head. Tim had said he would be okay, but she had known this was coming, and she had feared he would leave her early. For years, she had been worried about losing him, and now it was happening. How could she live without him?

She got to the hospital so quickly that the procedure had not even begun. She quickly found the operating room due to her familiarity of the hospital. Rushing to his side, she and Sam held hands while he lay on the operating table.

Sam was thankful to have had every second he had with her as he feared he could expire that very night. Again the condemnation of failing her and his family filled his head. Seeing her cry and the fear on her face was too much for him.

Tim was off preparing for the surgery when Rachel had come in. He had been waiting for her as he was sure she would be there in no time when he saw her quick text response. Tim gave Sam and Rachel some time together before he instructed her to go to the waiting room so they could get the room ready and do the procedure. Being a nurse herself, she knew the protocol and fully understood that she needed to leave the room. The surgery would take around four hours to complete. She gave Sam a big hug and a kiss and started to leave as tears ran down her face.

Before she could get out of the room, Tim caught her. "Rachel, I've called Heather to come sit with you. She told me she would be here as quickly as possible. Pray for us. Pray that God will be with us." He seemed so calm that it actually helped Rachel begin to feel some relief. No one knew more about Tim's abilities than Rachel. She worked with him and knew his reputation as the best heart surgeon in the hospital. In the seven years he had been there, Tim had built a very strong reputation and was respected by everyone in the hospital, especially Rachel.

"Thank you, Tim. I wouldn't want anyone else working on him. He's my whole life." Her eyes were filled with tears, but as usual, Rachel never made a big scene in public.

"I hope I'm doing the right thing, Rachel. I've always believed that it was somewhat unethical to perform surgery on one's own family as a situation could arise where I may not be able to maintain the proper objectivity. The only exception I can think of would be when the surgeon is the doctor with the surgical skill and ability to successfully perform the procedure better than anyone else available. I hope I'm not being arrogant Rachel, but I feel that that is true in this case. If you agree, I will proceed. If not, I'll get Dr. Andrews in to do this procedure." Tim hated saying that he was the best man for this job, but he wasn't going to let his feelings get in the way as he actually believed it was true.

"Tim, you know that I know that you are the very best. Everyone does. No one would ever argue that. Get in there, and save my husband." She showed absolutely no signs of doubt, which made Tim feel confident that he should proceed as planned. She gave him a big hug and told him she loved him.

Heather was walking into the waiting room just as Rachel came out of the operating room. They walked into each other's arms and then headed for a private waiting room where they could be alone. As they sat down, Rachel noticed Jack sitting alone in the larger waiting room. "Hey, is that Jack over there?"

"Yes, he told me he couldn't stay home with this going on. We can go get him now or later. It's your call." Heather was so proud of how much Jack loved Sam. They were both great men in her eyes.

"What about Maria and Marcus?" Jack and Heather now had two children. Marcus was two years younger than his big sister Maria.

"Samantha came over to watch them." Samantha was their neighbor's nineteen-year-old daughter. She had grown up in the church they were all members of. It was actually the church Jack was the Sr. Pastor of too.

"Get him over here." She stood to her feet and began waiving, but Jack wasn't looking their way.

Heather sent him a text, and he was there in a flash. For just over four hours, they talked, prayed, and even tried to rest. Heather nodded off for a while, but Rachel and Jack could not. So traumatic was the experience for Rachel that she felt an anxiety building inside of her that made her pray that she too wouldn't soon need medical attention. Her world was crumbling around her as the fear of losing Sam was dominating her every thought.

Sensing her crushing fear kept Jack fully engaged, which really helped Rachel get through the excruciatingly long surgery.

For years, Rachel's life had been perfect in her eyes. She had worried about nothing but her husband and her children. Sam was an incredible father and an even better husband. The boys had both kept really clean in spite of all of the filth and worldly lusts all around them. Rachel had been amazed at how strong her boys had been as all of her friend's kids had been through spats with drugs, stealing, premarital sex, and just about everything else. Amazingly, Joe and Robert had been in almost no trouble, and both of them had been strong students and hard workers. She truly was living a blessed life.

Though Rachel had seen what was going on with Sam for many years, she never knew how to help him. Going back to work was the only thing she could think of that would help him as she knew the financial stress was his heaviest burden. She had hoped he would stop feeling the deadly stress that was destroying him when she started working again, but like everything else she had tried, it hadn't helped. He actually seemed even more stressed with her working.

Outwardly, Sam was still the same guy he had been when she first met him, and the more she thought about it, his insides hadn't changed either. Most people just didn't see that part of him as he always gave others his best all of the time. He was good with people, and he always pushed himself to stay away from talking about his problems. He would rather be there for them than burden anyone. It was the way all of the Henderson children had been brought up to behave. "Love your neighbor as yourself" was scriptural and, therefore, was what they were taught. Though each had a different style, they all strove to put others before themselves.

Sam had always been someone driven by worry. It was the reason he had always worked so hard. He had done more with only average intelligence than anyone could have ever expected.

He was wise in many ways due to his foundation in God's Word, but his inability to let go and completely trust God in everything kept him prisoner to his fears. Though he had always known it to be true that he had no reason to fear, he struggled with letting go and letting God. For that reason, he used excessive effort to achieve things in life and was always harder on himself than anyone else could ever have been on him. Though it was an admirable quality, it was killing him.

Sam's biggest vice was food. He rarely ate because he was hungry but because it was his drug of choice. He had only drank alcohol once or twice back in college, but he had felt uncomfortable and afraid of the mistakes he might make while intoxicated. Food seemed more acceptable, and though it may have been a slower and more conservative way for him to destroy himself, it was working now. Whenever things got stressful, when most people would have had a drink, he chose to eat. If something was bad for his waistline or his health, he hungered for it. Icing was his favorite pill, and to get it, he would buy day-old cakes to get it cheaply. Though he wasn't a coffee drinker, he got his caffeine from drinking lots of Coke. He drank it from sun up to sun down. It even slept next to him in a giant mug every night.

Sam continually talked about losing weight and had started and failed diets hundreds of times over the years. His failure had very little to do with a lack of effort or that his diets weren't sound ways to lose weight in a healthy way; instead, he never lost weight and kept it off because he really didn't want to lose the weight. He never understood why, but he knew it was true.

The results of his recklessness had finally caught up with him. Sitting there in the waiting room, Rachel was sure she couldn't accept it if Sam didn't make it. It wasn't something she was willing to even imagine. Though she was scared of it, it only existed as a fear that she would not allow herself to think about. Still, part of her kept telling her he would die. She just refused to listen.

Just before 7:00 a.m., Tim came out of the operating room and into their waiting room. Rachel felt immediate relief when she noticed the inviting smile and the look of satisfaction on his face.

"It went very well, and he should be just fine. He was very clogged up, but we got it all." Though Tim had not slept in twenty-four hours, he looked amazingly good and somewhat well rested. Days and nights like this were not uncommon to Tim, so it wasn't a stretch for him to function at a high level even under these circumstances. What he had almost no previous experience with was working on someone this close to him as the time he had sewn up Mary hadn't really been a life and death situation. Emotionally, this was an entirely new experience for him, and though it was not written on his face, he was completely drained. Thankfully, the relief of the success of the operation was giving him all he needed to deal with it.

"Thank God," Rachel exclaimed as she rushed to Tim for a hug. Her relief overwhelmed her, and she began thanking God over and over in her thoughts. All the things she would no longer take for granted were also flooding her thoughts.

"Yes, thank God. I know he was in there tonight, and he was definitely there when Sam texted me about his pain earlier tonight. Who knows what could have happened had he not done it when he did. If he had gone to sleep, he may not have woken up. Maybe now he'll start to take care of himself better?" Tim knew what he had just said was harsh, but it was the truth. Sam needed to take his health more seriously.

"I am going to make him my number-one student. That will be my gift to him, Rachel. Please encourage him to work with me. There is no reason he can't outlive all of us if he gets it together. I don't want to see you go through this again." Heather had her arm around Rachel and was almost as relieved as she was. "Deal. We'll all go after him. He can't do this to us anymore. I'm a train wreck. He had my heart in his hands tonight, and I don't want to live without him. I can't do it." She was exhausted and couldn't understand how Tim could still be going so strong.

For the next five days, Sam constantly had visitors. The nurses were constantly running people out of his room so they could give him his treatment. The outreach from the church and from his friends was significant. While the love from the church and his friends was overwhelming, the love from his family was even greater. His failing heart had brought them all even closer together, and they all vowed to help him get and stay healthy.

Surviving and getting a second chance to be there for his family helped refocus him. His priorities changed, and he began to look at everything differently. He decided that it was irresponsible for him to treat his body the way that he had for so long, and he committed to change from the way he had previously lived his life. In the end, the changes actually improved his marriage, which both he and Rachel thought was impossible.

God had shown Sam through the whole ordeal that though life here on earth is short, he has a purpose for every day of it. Not taking care of your body is not really an option as it's only an attempt to quit on God. God gave us everything—our bodies, our talents and abilities, everything. If we try to cheat him by dying early so we can avoid having to face the difficult things of this life, we are not honoring God. Everyone who cares about you gets hurt when you don't honor the body God gave you. Eating too much and not exercising was no different than drinking too much alcohol or taking drugs. All of them can be destructive as doing anything of this world to excess is sin.

After six weeks off from work, Sam began to work with Heather three days a week at the gym. The three days eventually turned into six. Three of them were with Heather, and the other three were with Jack. Within a year, Sam was down nearly eighty pounds. He was truly a new man with a new lease on life. He had never felt better, and Rachel's attraction to him and respect for him reached new highs, as well as his boys respect for him.

Almost losing his life turned out to be the only thing that could reach him and change him. He would no longer use food to deal with stress, and he would no longer choose to be a slave to it.

CHAPTER 30

After only a couple of months with his real father, Richard returned home. Tim and Mary had enjoyed the first month or so of the break from Richard's constant mess of a life, but things had gotten progressively uglier with each incident between him and his father, and they soon began hearing grumblings almost daily from Jamie, but most came through his mother, Sally.

Though Jamie had fathered two more children since Richard, none of them lived with him. Only he and his drug-addicted girlfriend were in the apartment while Richard was staying there. In the end, the fact that Richard had been able to coexist with Jamie for almost two months surprised Tim and Mary. Their selfish personalities were repelling the other so powerfully by the time Jamie sent Richard packing that they both expected and preferred to never see the other again. Richard had that effect on a lot of people.

Unfortunately, Richard hadn't changed from the experience of living with his father. He had learned a lot about real life while he was there, but he was only sure of one thing: he didn't want to become like his father. Beyond that, he was still completely self-absorbed, incapable of telling the truth, and thought of women only as objects. Though he pretended to be a believer if his parents or someone at church or in the family asked him if he was, inside he was very confused about what he actually believed about God.

He carried lots of anger with him, was incapable of seeing his own part in his many failed relationships, and his confused belief in God inspired no obedience.

Even though his parents had been able to get the school to readmit him for his senior year, he dropped out and, instead, promised to get his GED. He claimed it was just too much for him to return to a school where everyone knew him and would judge him. Two years later, he still had no GED and had worked for no one more than a few months at a time. He had ventured back out of the house, but this time, on his own. However, like everything in his life, he would run out on his responsibilities, leaving behind unpaid bills and everything his parents had given him for the apartment.

After a few weeks at a friend's house, he was again thrown out on the street. This time, it was for sleeping with his friend's girlfriend. With nowhere else to turn, he returned home and quickly found another job that he would soon quit because of some scandal. To get to and from work, Tim and Mary agreed to buy him another car, though neither one of them were quite sure what had happened to the last one. This time, Richard had agreed to own the car and the insurance himself. In an attempt to hold him accountable, they drew up a contract in which Richard would pay them back for the car at a very low monthly payment with no interest. Though they both knew they would never get the money back, they tried to make Richard realize that life wasn't easy and that we all have to pay our own way. As predicted, he made one payment, stopped for six months, made another payment after his car had a bunch of work done that his parents paid for, and then seemed to forget about it indefinitely in spite of the constant reminders. Richard never seemed to follow through on anything, and he never saw things how they really were.

When he got a seventeen-year-old girl pregnant around his nineteenth birthday, Mary hit a low that would put her in an almost permanent state of anxiety laced with anger. In less than a week, Richard told everyone that the pregnancy hadn't taken.

No rational explanation was given as to why the pregnancy hadn't taken, only that it was off. Unfortunately, the relief was temporary.

Only nine months after the first scare of a pregnant girlfriend, Richard found he had done it again. This time, the pregnancy took, but his girlfriend promptly dumped him after an incident where he actually punched her. She wisely wanted nothing to do with him, and thankfully for Richard, chose not to press charges. However, her parents refused to not call Richard's parents to tell them about the punch and the pregnancy. Tim and Mary were broken by the news and told Nina's parents they would help financially and be involved in any way they could, regardless of Richard's involvement.

Within a week, Nina's parents visited to tell Tim and Mary that Nina had agreed to put the baby up for adoption. Tim and Mary agreed that adoption was by far the best solution, knowing that Richard was completely incapable of being a loving parent or a loving anything else. Nina was a senior in high school and was in no way prepared to be a mother. Though the adoption made the most sense, it was a terribly painful situation for everyone, especially for Nina. Only Richard seemed unaffected.

Had Nina chosen to keep the baby, it would have been her parents raising another child. She was in no way capable emotionally or financially to raise a child. Tim and Mary knew that Richard's immaturity would not have allowed him to deal with his parents giving so much attention to a baby that he wasn't even willing to father either. The adoption would alleviate this potential but would likely leave them with a feeling of sadness and loss.

From the time Mary found out about the pregnancy, she felt her feelings for her son had changed permanently. She became distant and unavailable for days. Knowing she wasn't giving the boys, Tina, and Tim the time or attention they deserved was eating her up, but she was feeling like she had nothing left for them. Her anger and dislike for Richard hit an all-time high, and she felt like Richard was the worst kind of person on the face of the earth. She felt he had become even worse than his real father.

Mary couldn't help but feel responsible. She blamed herself for everything, feeling that it had all started because of her failures. Had she not gotten pregnant in the first place, Richard would not be who he was. If she could have done things God's way, she would have never had children until she met Tim.

She often wondered if Richard's faults were a result of her sin or if they were simply a result of Richard's poor character and choices. Why had the younger boys turned out so well, while Richard was such a mess? Maybe it was just genetics? The boys did have a different father, though he to had a mess of a life too.

Tim hated seeing Mary so conflicted. He told her that the past was the past and assured her that she had been forgiven. He didn't want her beating herself up over something he was sure God had forgiven her for. It was something she couldn't do anything about as it was in the past. He assured her if it was a parenting failure, they were both equally guilty. He even tried to get her to believe that Richard would grow up, and all of this would be behind them.

Unfortunately, Mary was inconsolable over Richard's continual self-destruction and self-imposed depression. She became so conflicted that she became dependent on sleeping pills to get any sleep at all. Even then, there was no guarantee of a good-night's sleep as she felt she always had to be ready for the next big event. *How bad will the next thing be, and who else will he hurt?* she thought.

Tim firmly believed that the two biggest factors in Richard's character issues were his genetics and his early life programming, which was done by Grandma Sally who had gotten similar results with both of her own sons. Both of their lives were disasters as they cared only for themselves. There had to be something there. The constant ego-building style of Grandma Sally likely led to Richard's superficial values. If a person does not understand that this life is temporary and that we are here for God's purpose, not our own, they have no chance of understanding their true value as God's most precious creation. We are made in his image, and he desires relationship with us. If we focus on ourselves, we will never fill the God-shaped hole we all have in our lives. Loving God and others is what we are commanded to do. It's the only thing that brings fulfillment, loving self brings only destruction.

The saddest part for Tim was Mary's fear that Richard would never change. They had felt that Richard was improving on several occasions, but each time, they had been wrong. Still, he always had it in the back of his mind that nothing was impossible for God. With that belief in his heart, he never completely lost hope. It may take what felt like a long time to him and Mary, but he felt confident that God would eventually get to Richard and change him. It would be in his perfect timing though, not ours.

CHAPTER 31

Joe, Sam and Rachel's eldest son, was ecstatic that Tiffany had said yes. He had asked her to go see a movie with him, and her acceptance was no sure thing. His excitement over her yes was so great that he couldn't wait to call his mother to tell her about it.

"Mom, remember that great girl I was telling you about?" He was still living at home and would be home later that evening, but he just couldn't wait until then to tell her. At twenty years old, he was just starting his senior year at the University of Houston.

"Tiffany?" Rachel remembered all right. How could she forget? Joe had gone on and on about her for weeks. Not only did he think she was beautiful, he thought she was everything he ever wanted in a girl. It wasn't in his nature to get this way over a girl, though. He had bought his father's teaching about dating only to find a wife, so Rachel knew that her eldest son's interest in this Tiffany was very serious.

Joe and Tiffany had been in a class together and had studied together ever since that class. She was dating a guy who was a star on the football team, so Joe felt that he would never have the chance to let her know what he thought of her. Thankfully for Joe, her boyfriend cared more about his own desires than Tiffany's convictions.

Joe had been suspicious of Tiffany's boyfriend since the beginning. Since he had become such a close friend of hers, she had begun to tell him more and more about Alan. Soon, the things she was telling him began to make him wonder if Alan respected her at all. It bothered him to hear the manipulation Alan was trying to pull off with Tiffany. To Joe, she was too special to be treated that way, and it was bothering him so much that he had even spoken to his mother about it several times.

A couple of weeks earlier, Tiffany had called Joe very late at night. She was in tears because her boyfriend had tried to get her to have sex with him against her will. Joe rushed to her side, and she completely opened up and shared everything with him. She told him that she had been saving herself for marriage and that her boyfriend had known that from the very beginning. She couldn't understand why he was making her feel like she didn't care for him because she wouldn't sleep with him. Did he not believe she would wait until marriage?

That night, she told Joe that she was now sure that Alan had no long-term plans with her. She was positive that he only wanted sex, and she was feeling like a fool for not seeing it earlier. She told Joe the story of how he had shown up at her place drunk, and how he had tried to get her to sleep with him in spite of her strong resistance. When she got passionate in her refusal, he made some very hurtful comments to her and told her he would go get some from one of the many other girls who really wanted him.

Tiffany and Joe shared the same conviction of saving sex for marriage. They shared their beliefs that night, and it made Joe even more attracted to her. So much so that he had been floating on a cloud ever since. Though she was really broken and deeply hurt by the betrayal she was feeling, Joe couldn't help but feel hopeful about his chances of getting to tell her about his feelings for her. Had she called him only because she thought of him as a friend, or had she called him to talk because she knew he really cared about her? She hadn't called her best girlfriend; she had called him. It made him feel very hopeful.

He hated to see Tiffany hurting, but he loved the idea of her being single. She was different from every other girl he knew in so many ways, and he couldn't think of anyone else since he had met her. Seeing her in pain and hearing her revelation about staying sexually pure until marriage had given him hope that there may be a real chance for them. More than anything, he was extremely excited and encouraged that she had not been with anyone. The thought of her with anyone made him feel sick to his stomach. *How can people sleep around like so many do?* he wondered. It was more than inappropriate to Joe. It was appalling. Was there anything more personal?

Joe knew she was the one for him, and for the last two weeks, he was feeling he may actually have a real chance with her. He had already decided she was a problem for him as he could think of nothing else, but since their long, deep conversation, he had a reason to believe that she could be the one for him. It was almost too much to handle, and he already feared losing her.

During their deep conversation, Tiffany explained that early in her relationship she had, believed her football star boyfriend was sweet, and when she told him she was a Christian and that she was waiting until she got married to have sex, he had told her he too was a Christian and that he would wait for her. Though he never pretended to be waiting himself, he did promise to wait for her. Joe could understand why he had agreed to wait as she was that beautiful; anyone would wait. Through several weeks of dating, they became very close, and she had believed that he really was falling in love with her as she was falling for him.

Though he assured her he would wait until they were married, she began to notice inconsistencies in his behavior. He always seemed to stare at good-looking girls, his language around the other football players was terrible, he drank, and sometimes she felt that he was fooling around with other girls. Since she didn't like to go out much and hated parties, he usually went alone, and she often heard rumors, which he always denied. They were all warning signs, and that night, she told Joe that she felt like a fool for being so gullible. Alan had been really smooth and had always acted like such a good, sweet person when he was around her.

Joe took it all in that night. For the past two weeks, he had been feeling terribly sorry for her yet believed a separation was the best thing for her. Not only for his own cause, but also because this guy would have hurt her worse than he had if things would have gone any further. Tiffany had dodged a bullet.

Thankfully, Alan had not been able to convince Tiffany that he loved her and that they would always be together. Had that happened, he may have been able to convince her to have sex with him. At least, that's where Joe believed it could have led. Joe wondered if he would ever get to that point with her. Would I try to get her to sleep with me? He hoped not. However, in the past, he had felt how easily passion could remove inhibitions. He decided he wouldn't even temp himself with Tiffany or anyone else. Doing it right was that important to him, and Tiffany definitely deserved to be treated right.

Joe was happy to hear his mother respond with Tiffany's name when he had asked if she remembered that girl he was always talking about. It was great to have such a loving, caring mother. Joe was a bit of a mama's boy, and her being supportive of anything he was into was really important to him.

"Yes, Tiffany. I asked her out, and she said yes. I told her I really like her, and that I want to get to know her better. She told me she liked me too and that she knows she can trust me." His voice was full of emotion, almost to the point of vulnerability. Though he was excited, it sounded like he was fighting back tears as he spoke. She had seen this coming for a while now.

"That is great, honey." She was a little worried inside, though. Joe was such a good kid that she always worried that people would take advantage of him. Now that he was so infatuated with this girl, she would have the ability to really hurt him. Ever since Joe was a little boy, Rachel had always worried that he would get hurt emotionally, not because he wasn't emotionally strong, but because he cared more about other people than anyone she had ever known. Sam too was built this way, but Joe was to the extreme.

"Tiffany says her dad played baseball for Houston, and he's told her that he knew you and Dad back then. His name is Kevin Todd. Do you remember him?" Rachel felt like she had been punched in the stomach. Tiffany's dad was the jerk that had broken her heart and destroyed her best friend, Heather, by pretending to be a Christian so he could sleep with her. Hearing his name sent a chill down her spine as she suddenly realized that she had never really forgiven him. To that very day, she hated Kevin Todd more than anyone or anything in the world. Rachel began to feel her legs failing her and slumped down onto the arm of the couch without saying a word in response.

After a long pause, Joe broke the silence, "Are you still there, Mom? Are you okay?" He thought he could hear her breathing or maybe even gasping for air. Although he had no clue it had anything to do with the revelation he had just made about his beloved Tiffany's father, he could tell something was seriously wrong.

"Sorry, honey. I'm here. Is Tiffany a Christian? Is her father a Christian?" *Had Kevin changed, could that piece of trash ever change? How could anything that came from that guy be sweet or good?* Tiffany had to be a lie, just like her father. How could she tell Joe that he was wrong about this girl he worshiped? There was no chance this could go well for him. She could come to no other conclusion.

"I think he is. I can ask her. I know Tiffany is a really good Christian. That's why she is so perfect for me. I bet her dad is too. She had to have had good Christian parents to be the way she is." Joe could feel that something was going on. His mother had always been there for him. She had always been supportive in all things, but he wasn't hearing her usual support in this. He was sure something was wrong, but he still hadn't put his finger on it.

All through high school, Joe had hung out with his church friends, but he had avoided dating because of his father's constant warnings about what might happen if he put himself in a tempting situation with the opposite sex. Sam had done such a good job convincing his son that God would bring someone to him that he had been patiently waiting his entire life. Actually, Sam had convinced both of his sons to do so. He told them many times that the reason he and their mother were so happily married was the fact that they married the person that God had brought them. They both believed their father, and they committed themselves to do it the same way their father had. It hadn't been easy for either of them, but they had both been successful.

"Her father wasn't a Christian when we knew him. In fact, he wasn't a really good guy at all. He was a teammate and good friend of Joe Morgan's, though." She didn't want to burry the guy in her son's eyes, not knowing what had happened in Kevin's life over the years. Still, she was feeling a hate for him that had been lying dormant in her subconscious for more than twenty years. Somehow, she would need to find a way to give him the benefit of the doubt. *Maybe God had changed him?* She had told herself that she had forgiven him, but now that she knew he could potentially reenter their lives, she was quite sure she never really had.

"I'll find out if he's a Christian, Mom, but please don't hold anything her father did back then against Tiffany. I know she's a great person. I've spent a lot of time with her, and I know she's special. It's not just her looks, Mom. Yes, she's attractive, but she's much more than that. I like everything about her, especially how I feel when I'm with her. You know I've been waiting for God to bring the right girl into my life just like Dad did to get you. This may be the one for me, Mom. I really think she might be, and I really want her to be." He had thought of nothing but her ever since he first met her. It truly had been love at first sight.

When Joe and Tiffany first started talking after class and studying together, Joe knew right away that she was different. She seemed valuable to him and not just because she was good looking. Everything she said and did seemed unique as if no one could have said it or done it better. She was smart and funny, but more than anything, she seemed to be kind. When he learned that she was a Christian and that they shared the same convictions, it really began eating at him that she had a boyfriend.

For months, Joe had been praying for a change in Tiffany's relationship status. He had met her boyfriend, and he could sense that he was not a good guy. At first, he wondered if it was only his attraction to her that was making him feel that way, but the longer he spent around her and heard about the things Alan had said to her, the more sure he became that he was a fraud. The kindness Tiffany thought she saw in him was only an act. *Why couldn't she see it?* he wondered.

The thought of her being hurt by that jerk had been really bothering Joe. Now that things were finally turning in his favor, Joe couldn't help but feel that their breakup was answered prayer. He wanted someone to be happy for him and to share in his excitement. He had been sure his mother would be, but she clearly wasn't, and it was really throwing him.

"I'm sorry, honey. I just don't want anyone to hurt you." She already feared ever seeing Kevin again. He was the last person she ever wanted to see. If God had changed him and saved him, he would have to be different. Even then, she had no interest in ever seeing him again. If he tried to apologize to her, she wasn't sure how she would feel about it. Then she started to wonder how difficult it would be for Sam. How would he feel about this?

"I want you to get to know her the way I have, Mom. She is great. She's smart and funny, and she loves the Lord. We've talked about the Bible a lot, Mom. She's been in church all of her life, and she reads the Bible every day. We have had great talks about scripture. I'm convinced she is the real deal. I have no questions about her, and I know you will love her." His mother's reaction was really bothering him. He wanted her to be behind this so badly that he was beginning to doubt himself. Maybe she knew something, or perhaps God was giving her this pause for some reason? All his life, she had always put his dad and her boys first. She always wanted them to be happy. Dad analyzed things, but Mom could just feel when they were right or wrong. Hearing the apprehension in her voice, even though she wasn't attacking Tiffany or her father, was enough for Joe to feel uncomfortable.

"I'm sure I'll love her if you love her. If you think she is a great person, I'm sure I will too." She could sense Joe's disappointment and realized she was out of line. She had been forcing him to defend someone she had never even met, and she could tell he had already fallen hard for Tiffany. Rachel knew that she needed to trust her son's judgment and that he really needed her support. She knew Joe needed to hear that she was happy for him, but it wasn't coming easily.

"Well, I'm taking her to see a movie tomorrow night. She knows I don't have much money, so she offered to feed me at her place before the movie. She's really nice, Mom. You will love her. I think I already do." Oops, he immediately regretted saying that. His mother knew he had an addictive personality, and she had always warned him not to jump into things with such a foolish, trusting heart the way he always seemed to do. Telling her he loved Tiffany would only make her think he was acting on impulse rather than sound judgment. He knew what he said was true and that it was more than some impulsive feeling, but he shouldn't have volunteered the information to his mother so soon. He was so excited about her and their future that he just couldn't contain himself.

"You will have a great time, Joe. You are a wonderful person too. Don't forget that, and be careful, honey." His whole life, he had been impressed with his mother's ability to support their family even at her own expense. He had inherited that quality from her, yet his impulsiveness was not at all a part of who she was. That part of him really scared her.

Rachel loved her eldest son's big heart but feared him getting hurt because of it. The fact that he was a bit of a mama's boy endeared him to her but also made her worry more about him. His desire to gain her approval made her feel like she could always step in to breathe some reality into any situation before he got trapped going headlong into something that would surely hurt him. His younger brother, Robert, also had a big heart, but he was far more independent with far thicker skin. Robert was her baby, but Joe was always the closest to her heart.

"I'll be careful, Mom. I've got to go. I've got a study group in a few minutes, but I'll be home tonight. Do you think Dad will think it's too soon for me to fall in love?" He was doing it again. Why couldn't he keep his mouth shut?

"Your dad understands love better than anyone I've ever known. If you love her, he will support you. Please try not to get hurt by this girl, though, Joe. I want her to feel like you do, but it's hard for anyone to love someone the way you do. You have your father's gift for loving others, but most people don't have it, and I don't want you getting hurt because of it." She didn't want to let Joe down, but hearing that this girl had been dating a superstar on the football team made her wonder what she was really all about. Rachel's history with Kevin may have been behind her distrust of Joe's judgment in this more than anything else though, and she was well aware of that fact.

"I love you, Mom. I want to make you and Dad proud of me. I need you guys to approve of her. She's perfect. You'll see." He always told his mother he loved her. She had always been there for him, and he had always told her everything. Not only did he love her, he trusted her judgment and intuition. What he had just picked up from her about Tiffany's father had to be something major by the way she was acting. Everything inside of him was telling him mom was wrong, though.

"I love you too, sweetheart." As she was hanging up, she pulled herself up off of the couch. She had to let Sam know about this Tiffany. How could she be Kevin's daughter? It didn't seem to add up to her. How was this possible? For Kevin to have a daughter the same age as Joe, she would have been born only four years after Joe Morgan died. Could he have changed that much that quickly?

Rachel felt terrible inside for not supporting Joe better over the phone, but she felt even worse about her unresolved hatred for Kevin. Now that she was off the phone with Joe, she could think of nothing else but Kevin and what he had done to both her and Heather. When she tried to begin preparing dinner, she found herself unable to concentrate or focus on anything other than that terrible man. Her mind was cluttered with questions about Kevin. Would she and Sam lose the intimacy they had always shared over this? How would she and Sam ever accept Tiffany or the evil Kevin into their family?

CHAPTER 32

A t 9:00 p.m. Jack and Heather were just getting ready to climb into bed. Getting to bed early wasn't unusual at all as Heather's typical day started with a 5:00 a.m. class. As she was curling up next to her gloating husband, she heard her phone vibrate with a text.

"Do you have time for a short call?" The text from Rachel read.

Heather told Jack she needed a minute for a call with Rachel and snuck out of the room for the call.

"No problem. I'll check on the kids."

Jack stuck his head in the kids' rooms to see if their seven-year-old daughter, Maria, and their five-year-old boy, Marcus were asleep. They both looked to be asleep as Jack's heart filled with thankfulness for the family God had given him. As quietly as he had snuck in, he snuck back out and headed to the master bedroom.

"Hi, Rachel, what's going on?" Just asking made her begin to wonder. The nature of the text was a big mystery to Heather. Was Rachel just trying to set something up that couldn't wait, or was there something wrong? It was pretty unusual for Rachel to want to talk at this hour as she was fully aware that Heather and Jack would be climbing into bed about this time.

In the few minutes, Heather had to think about why Rachel needed to talk, she had decided that something had to be wrong. Just asking Rachel what was going on felt awkward to Heather. She feared mostly that one of the boys had gotten into some kind of trouble. For years, Heather had been waiting for terrible news about something one of the boys had done or that had been done to them, but it had never come. Those two boys were just different, she had decided.

From Heather's experience teaching Sunday school to high school-age girls, her perspective of what could possibly be wrong was very broad. Seeing firsthand how the enemy was having his way with young people had opened her eyes. She had seen lives of very young girls ripped apart by sexual sin, abuse, drugs, and alcohol. She had learned that anything was possible from anyone as we all have a fallen nature. We are all tempted by our desires, and we all succeed to sin. Heather had decided to work with young girls after being hurt repeatedly by her own poor decisions. She had learned that there was no guarantee of success or failure based on our parents or our social economic stature or anything else. In many cases, there seemed to be no rhyme or reason why someone had failed and chosen sin over life. Everyone was susceptible, and everyone needed God to help them through temptation and to defeat its grip on their lives. Bad situations and unfavorable circumstances result in higher levels of sin in our lives, but even when someone seems to have all of the right stuff in place, sin still happens.

"I spoke to Joe earlier tonight. He's got a big date tomorrow with a girl he's head over heals for. He's very serious about her and is even saying that he loves her. I'm calling you because it turns out that her father is Kevin Todd." She paused for a few seconds in case Heather had a reaction. When she heard nothing, she continued, "I haven't been able to calm down since Joe and I got off the phone. I haven't even told Sam yet. It's really messing with me. I can't get past how much I still hate that guy. How could anything good come from him?" She was really struggling with the feelings she was having. They felt too big for her, and she was well aware that she would not be able to hide them. She felt anger but mostly anxiety. The thought of coming face-to-face with Kevin was unbearable. It wouldn't take Sam long to figure out something was wrong with her, so she would speak with him next. She was hoping that confiding in her best friend, Heather, would help her calm down before her talk with Sam, who would likely handle thing much better than she was.

"Wow, I haven't heard that name in a long time. I hope he's changed." Heather hadn't felt the same anxiety that Rachel was feeling. Actually, she wasn't feeling much of anything. She had only concern for her friend as she could hear the fear and pain in Rachel's voice. Even though it was Kevin that had pushed her over the top and kept her from dating for all of those years, she couldn't help but feel like it was part of God's plan for her. If it weren't for Kevin, she wondered if she would have had the strength to stay alone for all of those years it took for Jack to be available. Their marriage was the best thing she could have ever hoped for. Not a day went by when she didn't thank God for her wonderful husband. *Had Kevin been part of God's plan?* she wondered. Maybe not, but she felt fairly confident that the Lord had used what had happened to calibrate her to that purpose.

"I'm a wreck, Heather. I thought I had forgiven him, but I'm sure I haven't now. I'm feeling lots of anger. If I had never seen him again, it would have been too soon. Now I don't see how I can avoid that nightmare. Joe really likes his daughter. He says she's a very committed Christian. How can that be?" If anyone could understand how she was feeling, she felt it would be Heather. Heather had just as big of a reason to hate him as she did.

"He may be totally different now, Rachel. I've forgiven him whether he's changed or not. I pray that he has changed though. If his daughter is someone Joe likes and cares for, I'm sure she's everything he believes her to be. You know Joe is just like Sam. Would Sam be wrong about her?" Heather had always been amazed at how similar Joe and his father were. Since Sam had first come into her life, he had been the most stable person she had ever known. His heart attack had been the first time she had ever worried about his future. Joe idolized his dad so much that he had become a younger version of him, almost a carbon copy. The only major differences were gullibility and maturity. Both of which would likely come with time.

"I know you're right. I think this is really more about me having not forgiven Kevin. I hate that it will make me feel so uncomfortable to be around her. I don't see how it won't. I think I already let Joe down when I reacted strangely over the phone when he told me that the girl of his dreams was the daughter of someone who hurt us both so deeply. Can you pray with me?"

The two spent another twenty minutes praying and talking before Jack finally came out to see if everything was okay with Heather. She told him she would be right up, and she and Rachel ended their call a minute or two later.

With the prayer and all of the thinking she had done behind her, Rachel decided to let Sam know she was ready for bed where she would break the news to him. He agreed to head to bed, and shut off ESPN as he started for their bedroom.

From the time he had first gotten home, he had known something was wrong by the way Rachel was acting. Since she would not admit it to him, he had decided to wait it out as he had learned was always the best way to handle this type of situation with Rachel. If he pushed her, she would only get angry with him. If he waited, she would tell him what was bothering her when she was ready. He was pretty sure that she was not angry with him and almost certain that it was something pretty important to her. At this point in their marriage, Sam could read the all of his wife's signs. Guessing what was actually wrong though, he could not do.

As he left the living room, Joe came through the front door. He hollered into his parent's room, "I'm home, and I'm going to bed." It was getting late, and he was on such a high because of his impending date with Tiffany that he chose not to engage his mother before they had both slept on whatever was bothering her. Though he wasn't positive, he couldn't imagine it could be anything other than Tiffany's father.

Rachel heard him and responded, "Good night, sweetheart." She was thankful he wasn't pushing her to talk about Tiffany or her worm of a father. She would talk to Sam about it before she decided how much to tell her son.

As Sam began to brush his teeth, he noticed that Rachel was acting like she was about to tell him whatever it was that had been clamming her up all night, so he came right out and asked, "Are you okay, honey?"

"I don't know. I just found out that the girl of Joe's dreams is Kevin Todd's daughter." There it was, just like that she had said it. She knew Sam would likely tell her everything would be okay and that he wouldn't have a big hang up with Kevin. In the past, he had always been so quick to forgive people. What she assumed would be his reaction bothered her almost as much as telling him. She wanted someone else to be appalled at the thought of ever seeing Kevin again. Heather's lack of disgust in her situation hadn't helped her at all. Oh yeah, she definitely had not forgiven Kevin.

"Really, how do you know that?" Though he wouldn't let on to how it made him feel inside, Sam immediately thought about his perfect wife with that terrible man. He hated how Kevin had treated her, and he knew he would always feel something between them should Kevin become a part of their lives. He was sure of it, and it actually hurt him to think about it. Rachel was number two in his life right behind the Lord but by far the first person. Anyone who made her angry or hurt her in any way was immediately his opposition. His instinct was to protect his wife from anyone who would cause her pain, and Kevin was number one on that list.

"Joe called to tell me that the girl he's always talking about, Tiffany, agreed to go to a movie with him. He told her how she feels about her, and she revealed that she has strong feelings for him too. Then he told me that her dad says he knows us. He played baseball for Houston, and his name is Kevin Todd. I got really quite, and I know I freaked Joe out a bit. Just hearing

Kevin's name again made me feel really angry and dirty. Joe could tell by my response. I think I really let him down today." She looked really broken and hurt, so Sam walked over and put his arm around her as he gave her a big hug.

"I'm so sorry, baby. What do you know about this Tiffany? I thought she had some big-time football player as a boyfriend?" He wanted to get some information and was hoping that Tiffany wasn't someone that matched up to Joe's high standards. Seeing Kevin wasn't something he wanted any part of either. Though he felt he had accepted Kevin for what he believed he was, he wasn't sure he was actually over his feelings of jealousy and anger. The thought of having to forget the past and to accept the new Kevin wasn't something Sam wanted any part of.

"According to Joe, she's the most perfect creature that ever walked the face of the earth. It's like listening to you talk about how you felt about me when we first started dating. He says she's beautiful, and yes, she was dating a star football player. Apparently, that's over now. Joe goes on and on about how he knows she's special, and that he has a very strong desire to be around her and with her. The hardest part for me to believe is that he claims that she is a great Christian and that she grew up in the church. How can that be? The worst part is that Joe told me he loves her." She could tell that Sam was feeling as uneasy as she was about this. He seemed to want it to go away just like she did. His face gave him away, though she could see him trying to be strong for her.

"Joe would know if she's really a Christian or not. He's very mature spiritually, and he knows what a strong Christian is. If he says this Tiffany is a good Christian, I'm sure she is. Kevin must have really changed, or maybe he doesn't even live with them." It was kind of a backhanded remark, and Sam knew it and immediately regretted it. Sam knew exactly what Rachel was feeling without her explanation. He too wondered if it were possible for someone as morally bankrupt as Kevin had been to change. His suggestion that Kevin may not have lived with her really meant that maybe Kevin had nothing to do with her upbringing. It just didn't compute for Sam, and he hated that he had shown such disbelief that Kevin could have been saved and changed. Who was he to judge someone he hadn't seen in over twenty years?

"I don't want to see Kevin ever again. I just told Heather about this, and all she could say is that he's probably changed and that she has completely forgiven him. Can you believe that? I wanted her to tell me what I needed to hear, and she came at me with her forgiveness toward Kevin. What kind of a Christian am I?" Heather had helped her by praying for her, but she was having trouble understanding why Heather didn't feel like she did about Kevin. Was she not the good person and good Christian she believed herself to be? She knew she was a sinner, but now she was wondering how far from God's image she actually was?

"She's right to forgive him and to give him the benefit of the doubt. We need to forgive him too. The fact that we haven't shows how human and flawed we are. I think we need to pray about this before we talk to Joe. If Joe likes this girl as much as he's telling you he does, we will end up face to face with Kevin soon. Let's start praying for strength and for the ability to forgive and move on. I hate this for you, baby, but I know you can handle it." He felt really sorry for her, and he hated how he was feeling too. Most of all, he hated this for Joe as he knew Joe would suffer if he and Rachel couldn't get over the past.

They prayed and held hands until Sam fell asleep. Rachel never really slept that night.

At Heather and Jack's place, there were lots of heavy prayer. They were praying for Rachel and Sam mostly, but they also prayed for Joe, Kevin, and Tiffany. They knew what Rachel was going through. Heather had never had the feelings for Kevin that Rachel had had. In her case, it wasn't that he had hurt her so badly; it was that he had shown her that she didn't need men. He had given her the strength to wait for Jack. Though it felt like she would stay single the rest of her life not long ago, she was at peace with the mistake she had made that night. She never really hated Kevin the way Rachel had, though. If anything, she hated him for what he had done to Rachel, not for anything he had done to her. It had been far easier for her to move on and forgive him than it had been for Rachel. Actually, Rachel obviously had not forgiven him at all.

Jack was so moved by what he believed God was doing through this situation that he decided to change the coming Sunday's sermon to talk about forgiveness, not only for Rachel and Sam, but because it felt like it was what God was leading him to do.

CHAPTER 33

Tiffany tapped out a text to Joe about an hour before they were to meet at her place for dinner the night of their first official date. They could really be alone at her place, and she felt safe enough with him already to do so. She didn't even consider anything out of her will could happen, not with Joe.

Her text read, "I'm very excited about tonight! I talked to my dad today. He told me that your parents might hate him because he was a real jerk when they knew him."

She had spent the afternoon with her father. Knowing that his daughter was a perfect match for Joe based on all she had told him, he decided that he better let her know some of the history between him, her mother, and Joe's parents. He started by telling her that he had been a really selfish guy when he was in college. He explained that he had done a lot of things that were out of the character that she had always seen in him. He even got a little emotional and told her that he was very embarrassed by who he once was. Then he told her not to be surprised if Joe's parents hated him for the things he had done.

Kevin went on to tell her that it was Joe Morgan that Joe Henderson was named after. Joe Morgan had tragically died in a freak accident in the prime of his life. Joe had everything going for him and was even headed for the major leagues when the accident happened. He was running away from a bad situation when he fell headfirst down a flight of concrete stairs.

He explained that Joe Henderson's parents were very close friends with Joe Morgan, as was he. Then he added that the bad situation had actually been a drunken girlfriend and that that girlfriend had in fact been, Ally, her mother. This revelation dropped Tiffany's jaw, but she pressed her father to continue, and he did.

Kevin went on to explain that Joe Morgan was planning to break up with her mother for a girl named Heather. It was Heather who Joe really loved, and when he told Ally she became very angry with him and attempted to keep him from leaving. He broke free from her and ran out, only to trip and fall down the stairs.

He explained that it was this tragic event that had brought him and her mother, Ally, together. If it weren't for all of these events, he explained that he and her mother may have never gotten together, and they may not have ever been saved either.

Then he got into the reason why the Hendersons likely hated him. He explained that he had been a womanizer, and that the Hendersons knew all about his escapades. He decided against telling her that he had slept with Joe's mom, Rachel, or that he had been with Joe Morgan's girlfriend Heather. He wasn't sure it would help anything to tell her, and he worried that it would make it impossible for him to ever reconcile with Rachel, Sam, or Heather. For all he knew, Heather was not even in the picture anymore, though he reasoned that she may be. He had never been close to any of them but Joe and knew nothing of what had become of any of them. He only knew Sam and Rachel were still together because of Tiffany.

Kevin reasoned that Joe's parents may not want their son to know the ugly history. If Tiffany and Joe ended up together, things could get very uncomfortable. Though he said nothing at this time, Kevin decided he would be completely honest about all of it should she find out the details through Joe. It was the least he could do to let Joe's parents make the decision.

Tiffany had begun telling her father how great Joe was several months earlier. When she told him his name was Joe

Henderson and that his parents had both gone to the University of Houston, he immediately suspected that Joe was Rachel and Sam's son. After seeing those two together at Joe's funeral and then having Heather tell him how happy they were the night of his birthday, he had always assumed they were going to remain together. Though he didn't know Sam well, he was well aware of Sam's friendship with Joe Morgan. He knew Joe had looked up to Sam, and he had been deeply moved by Sam's speech at Joe's funeral.

When Tiffany showed her father a picture of Joe Henderson, any remaining doubt that he was the son of Sam and Rachel Henderson was removed. Though Joe was not a clone of either of his parents, he did show a resemblance to both of them.

The conversation with her father had left Tiffany feeling somewhat dumbfounded. What were the odds of her father knowing Joe's family so well? How was it possible that she and Joe had been so drawn together? Was this all something God had orchestrated to save them all back in their college days and to bring her to this great guy? She wasn't sure why, but she already knew that Joe would become her best friend, and that she would end up as his wife. It seemed kind of silly to her think like that, but she couldn't help it. Joe was already a close friend, and tonight was the first step between them becoming an inseparable couple. She could tell he felt the same way by the way he treated her and by the way he stared into her eyes whenever they were together. Even when she was still in her unhealthy relationship, she had begun to feel that Joe was her destiny.

Though her father hadn't told her that he had once dated Joe's mother or that he had also slept with the woman that Joe Morgan had been leaving her mother for when he fell to his death, she sensed there was more by his obvious embarrassment and regret over how he had acted back then. Thinking about what it was that might make them hate him worried her. *Could he have slept with Joe's Mom?* she wondered. It never crossed her mind that he had slept with Heather, Rachel, and her mother.

The fact that Joe Morgan was Joe Henderson's namesake and that her mother had been his girlfriend blew her mind. It was strange yet exciting to her as if it was prewritten history that they end up together. It seemed too big for her to comprehend, yet she knew it was more than coincidence. Nothing could explain the attraction she was feeling to be with Joe. Sure he was attractive, but her desire for him was unexplainably strong. *Was God behind all of this?* she wondered.

Joe was just getting out of the shower when the text from Tiffany came in. All his mother had told him was that Mr. Todd hadn't been a very good guy in college. He had no idea about all of the history, though he had many times been told about Joe Morgan. Though he had no clue that Joe was running away from a woman when he had fallen, he had been told how tragic and unexpected his fall and death had been. In his earliest memories, they had been telling him what a great guy Joe Morgan had been, and that Aunt Heather had been engaged to be married to him when he had his terrible accident. Joe actually believed that Heather had been single all of those years because of Joe Morgan and not because of Kevin or Uncle Jack.

"Yeah, my mom acted really weird when I told her who your Dad is. I can't wait to see you, Tiffany!" All he could think about was the time he was about to spend with her. Things were so different now that she was free. The concerns about his mother's reaction to hearing Tiffany's dad's name were way in the back of his mind at this point, but they were not gone.

"I'll tell you what I know tonight. If you want to, come early." She couldn't wait to see him. Though she had just suffered through the betrayal of her ex-boyfriend, she was feeling very excited about her future with Joe. Hearing that he was named after this Joe Morgan who had dated her mother made her want to share everything her dad had told her. She felt like all of the coincidence wasn't really coincidence at all but fate instead. She couldn't help but feel all of the past had led to her and Joe being together. *Is it only for us or for our whole families as well?* she wondered.

"Okay, I'll get dressed and head your way." This was great. He couldn't wait to get there. Knowing she wanted him to be early made him even more excited.

Joe pulled on a pair of jeans and a nice polo shirt while he was rushing to get his hair combed and his teeth brushed so he could hit the road. Suddenly, there was a knock on his door.

"Yeah?" He figured it was his mom, but he was in a big hurry and didn't have time to stop what he was doing to answer the door.

"It's Mom. Can we talk for a second before you go?" Rachel had lain awake all night thinking about the situation. She finally decided that she better tell Joe everything before he got too far into this relationship. She didn't want him to think she had held anything back from him after he had told her who Tiffany's father was. It would jeopardize all of the years of honesty between them, and she wasn't willing to risk losing his trust.

"Okay, but I'm really in a hurry. Tiffany is waiting for me." He was really rushing and couldn't wait to get out the door. He didn't want his mother slowing him down.

She walked down the hall from the bathroom Joe was in and sat down on his bed and prepared what she was going to say. She had decided to hold nothing back. If he knew everything, he would be far better off. As hard as it would be, she would tell him everything. She always had in the past, and she knew this situation required her to be upfront, or it would result in a far worse discussion in a few weeks or maybe only days from then. If she didn't do it now, how could she expect him to tell her everything going forward?

In less than two minutes, Joe came bursting through the bathroom door and down the hall. Seeing his mother sitting on his bed caught him by surprise. "Hey, what are you doing?"

"Joe, I've decided to tell you about Tiffany's dad. If you know everything, you'll better understand how your father, Aunt

Heather, and I feel about Kevin Todd." She hated doing this, but she and Sam had always made it a point to be as honest as possible with the boys. They had always involved the boys in their decisions as well.

"Okay." He couldn't think of anything else to say. He didn't even sit down.

For the next few minutes, Rachel told Joe everything. She explained how she had dated Kevin and that they had had premarital sex together. It was the most difficult thing she could ever say to her son, but she felt he needed to know to fully understand who Tiffany's father had been. When she told him, Joe stopped what he was doing and sat down beside her. It felt to her that he wanted to comfort her. Rather than acknowledge his concern, she chose to continue in spite of the regret and embarrassment she was feeling.

She told him how his father had forgiven her and accepted her even though he knew about her unhealthy relationship with Kevin but that Kevin kept on living the same way even after pretending to accept Christ into his life. She went on to tell him that Aunt Heather had been seduced by him and that she hadn't dated anyone since him until Uncle Jack. She even explained what had happened the night that Joe Morgan had fallen to his death. Her emotion was mostly anger, and Joe could hear it in her voice and see it in her face. It actually frightened him a bit as he had never seen her like this before.

When she finally finished, Joe looked her in the eyes and lovingly said, "You have got to confront him and forgive him, Mom, so you can move on. I bet he's a totally different guy now. Tiffany sent me a text today saying that her dad told her that you and Dad might hate him because he was such a bad guy back then when he knew you guys. Why would he admit to all of that if he hasn't changed?" He could clearly see that she had unforgiveness in her heart.

Rachel went to tears in response. She hated that she had been holding anger toward Kevin for all of these years, and she was embarrassed about what she had just told her son. He was probably right; Kevin was likely not at all like he had been. Not that Joe had defended Kevin, but that he now knew about her failures made her feel like a piece of trash for what she had done.

"You may be right Joe. I just can't control my feelings about this guy. I just hate everything about him, and I assumed I could always think of him as a lost soul. Maybe I like having him to hate?" She felt so uncomfortable and childish sharing all of this with her first-born child.

Joe scooted closer to his broken mother and held her under his arm while he spoke, "Mom, it's okay. You have good reasons to have these feelings. You and I both know that God can do anything. At least hear his story before you write him off. Tiffany is great, and she's close to her dad. I'm sure he's part of the reason why she is so grounded in the Word. I can tell by the way she speaks about him that he is not who you remember him to be. He is probably a totally different person than when you knew him." He had almost forgotten that he needed to get going. It suddenly popped back into his head and he again felt the need to go to her right then.

"Mom, I hate to leave in the middle of this, but I really need to get going. My future is waiting."

"I know, honey. Sorry about laying all of this on you. I just wanted you to know everything before you started figuring out things on your own. I am so sorry I slept with that man. I was so stupid. It makes me feel like trash that I did that with him. Your father saved my life, Joe." She had settled down quite a bit, and she was now forcing a smile for him. She was so proud of him for loving the Lord the way he did. Imagining him making a mistake the way she had at his age seemed almost impossible. Sam had been so strong when she met him, and now she was so proud of his son that was clearly equally strong in his faith. *Thank God*, she thought.

"I love you, Mom, and I will always respect your opinion. I'm telling you now that Tiffany is amazing, and I'm betting her dad is not at all the way you remember him. I can just feel it. Please don't be embarrassed about your past. It's what made you my mom, and it led you to Dad." He seemed confident and very enthusiastic.

"I just wanted you to know everything. I'm sure she's all you say she is. Try to have a good time. I'm sorry if anything I said ruins your time with Tiffany." She stayed seated as Joe jumped up and ran out the door. She was so proud of the man they had raised. Tiffany didn't know how lucky she was. Joe was going to treat Tiffany just like Sam had always treated her. That's what made her most proud.

As he left the room, he hollered to her, "You're the best, Mom. Thanks for always telling me the truth. Don't worry!"

After he was gone, she lay on his bed in admiration of him while she continued to wonder what type of person Kevin had become. "Lord, please protect my baby, and help me forgive Kevin."

Joe drove the fifteen minutes to Tiffany's apartment full of excitement about the time he was about to spend with her, yet concern for his mother was battling with his excitement. How strange it all seemed. All of that history between his parents and Tiffany's dad, yet they had only known each other a few months. Was this meant to be? He sure hoped it was.

Joe was at her door knocking about ten minutes early. If it had not been for his mother's revelation, he would have been even earlier.

Though she had been in the kitchen when she heard him knock, she was across the tiny one-bedroom apartment so quickly that Joe thought she must have been sitting by the door, waiting for him. Her voice came through the door like a knife through his heart. "Who is it?"

"It's Joe." He was so excited to be there that hearing her voice made him suddenly nervous.

She unlocked the bolt and quickly pulled the door open. As usual, Joe was impressed. Her face was all he would look at as he had been praying to God for strength to not violate her by staring at her body. Still, he could see her long tan legs in his lower periphery as she was wearing jean shorts. *Don't look at her legs*, he told himself. Her shirt was conservative as usual, but it simply couldn't hide her curvy body. Again, he told himself to maintain eye contact.

"You look great, Tiffany. You always look great." He was happy to see her shy smile at his comment.

"I couldn't wait for you to get here, Joe. I'm not sure what's going on, but you are always on my mind." With this comment, she was more than happy to see his face blush. It was very clear to her that he was infatuated with her. In their few months of friendship, she had gotten to know Joe pretty well. They had even spent time discussing the Bible. She knew he was the type of guy she needed to be with, and now, with all of the history she had heard from her father, she was feeling like they were meant to be together.

Tiffany couldn't wait any longer. If he was just going to stand there at the door, she would have to act. She reached out for him and brought him in and shut the door to her apartment with a big hug. It was their first real contact, and Joe knew immediately that he would never forget the moment. She smelled so sweet and pure, and she felt so vulnerable in his arms that he felt a chill go through his body. His conscience stepped in and reminded him how important it was for him to honor her with his thoughts and actions.

The way she had brought him in to hug him in private behind a closed door reminded him of his mother. As deeply as his mother loved his father, she only showed affection for him when they were alone. To him, that was very sweet as he knew it wasn't because she was embarrassed of anyone seeing them but because no one needed to see as it was between them and no one else. That's what his mother had told him once, and he was glad to see that Tiffany was like his mother in this way.

"You smell amazing, Tiffany." He said it without thinking first and immediately feared that what he had said would make her feel uncomfortable.

"Thanks. Sorry I grabbed you like that. I just wanted to hug you to see if there was any magic there. Lucky for you, it was all magic." She gave him her best smile and pulled him by his hand into the kitchen to show him what she had been working on.

What she had just said made him smile hard while his heart and mind filled with hope. As she pulled him toward the kitchen, he realized she could pull him anywhere and he would follow. *Would I even be able to resist her if she were to try to seduce me?* he wondered. Thankfully, he was sure he would not have to find out. What if she didn't have a commitment to stay pure? Would he stumble? The thought crossed his mind, and it made him feel very uncomfortable. Maybe he wasn't as strong as his father. Maybe he would fail that test.

"What's that?" He was pretty sure it was a bread machine, though he had never really seen one. What she had just said about the magic had him kind of in a stupor, and he wasn't really all there yet. He was trying to regain his faculties but was in a sort of stupor as he held hands with the angle of his dreams.

"It's a bread machine, and it's just finishing up on a batch of pizza dough. Have you ever made your own pizza from scratch?" She had turned to him when she had gotten to the bread machine, and he was in awe at how absolutely adorable she looked with her big smile cranked all the way up.

Staring into her eyes, he was incapable of answering her question. Instead, with his mind still stuck on her comments about the magic she had felt when they hugged, he came right out and told her how he felt.

"Tiffany, I know I've already told you that I am attracted to you and that I think we are a perfect match for each other. What I haven't told you is that I think you are the one for me." *Holy crap, did I just say that out loud to her? What was I thinking?*

"I know, Joe. I've been wondering the same thing." She tightened the grip she had on his hand and leaned in and took his other hand. Then she asked if they could get their first kiss out of the way. Joe was shocked but incapable to resist. He didn't answer right away, but when an unexplainable calm came over him, he spoke confidently.

"We sure can, but you need to know that I have very little experience kissing girls. As we've discussed, I've been saving myself for marriage. There's a good chance I'll disappoint you." He was completely serious. It was actually a fear of his. Though he had kissed a couple of girls, he had never allowed anything passionate and had never been in a situation like he was currently in with someone he felt as strongly as he did about Tiffany.

"You better not disappoint me." She reached up and put her hands on his shoulders to pull him down to her. Her lips tasted really sweet to him, and they were softer and felt fuller than he had expected. It was the perfect first kiss. He was blown away, and Tiffany, feeling Joe's innocence and tenderness, knew instantly that he was her future. Her heart told her so, and her mind kept telling her how sweet it was that he was so unsure of himself.

"You can relax, Joe. That was not at all disappointing. You love me, don't you, Joe? I definitely felt love in that kiss." It was only their first date, but she was falling for him and could tell he had already fallen for her. She was pretty sure he was quivering now that their kiss was over, and it seemed really sweet to her.

"I do, Tiffany. I really do. You are everything I've been praying for all of my life, especially since I was old enough to want to get married. You may be too good looking for me, though, and that's got me really intimidated. I'm so glad you decided to give someone as average as me a chance." He saw her as way too good for him, so he wasn't being false with her when he said what he had just said.

"You are not average, Joe. You're really good looking and above average in every other way I can think of. From the time I have spent with you, I believe you are a great person. More than anything, I love that you love the Lord." She spoke to him almost as if he were already her husband. It felt natural and real and quickly put him at ease.

"There are some things I need to tell you. My dad told me some stuff about the past earlier today, and I want to see what you think and hear what you know. I think he was holding back information to protect me or you or maybe your parents or something." She wanted to let him know what her father had told her as it was part of the reason she was feeling like he was meant for her.

"My mom told me everything before I left to come here. When I say everything, that's exactly what I mean. I'm betting I know more than you do, and I want to tell you everything too. I want us to always be able to trust each other." As his parents had always done with him, he always chose to share the truth as soon as possible. It always came out either way, so he liked to share it right away to avoid any accusations of withholding information or lying. Hiding the truth was always futile as it always came out eventually. No matter how difficult it was, it was always better to deal with sooner than later.

"Really, did she tell you that my mom was Joe Morgan's girlfriend?"

"No, she didn't. She must not know that. She told me it was some girl named Ally. Is that your mom?"

"Yes, she was a pretty wild woman when my wild father met her. My dad tells me they became a couple because of Joe Morgan. Tell me something you know now." Her curiosity was really getting the best of her. She was glad that she wasn't the only one with information.

"Well, apparently my mom was your dad's girlfriend, and he was one of two men she slept with before she met my father." He doubted her dad had told her that.

"No way, really? Are you making that up?" She seemed amused by it more than shocked, but inside, it made her feel really uncomfortable. Would it be a problem between their parents?

"Yes, it's true. They were broken up for about a year when your mother witnessed Joe Morgan fall down the stairs the night he proposed to marry my aunt Heather." She had given him some information that he did not have, but he was sure he knew much more than she did as he was sure his mother hadn't held anything back. The look on her face told him he had been right.

"My dad didn't tell me any of that. He told me he had lots of partners before my mother as had she. They both live like such saints now that it's really hard for me to imagine either one of them acting that way. They don't drink alcohol or anything. It's really strange to think of them as wild college kids. So does your family hate my dad?" She was starting to feel that there would be some harsh feelings from both of Joe's parents over all of this. If Joe Morgan was close enough to them to name their first son after him, all of this stuff was major in their lives. Suddenly, she was feeling really uncomfortable. She decided that her father hadn't told her everything to protect Joe's mother, but it kind of hurt her that he hadn't.

"Only my mother does, but she told me tonight that she wants to stop hating him. She needs to forgive him. I think they will have to all come together and get to see the changes in each other before they can put it all behind them. My mother is tied in knots over this, and she knows that it's because she has not forgiven your father. I think you and I coming together is part of God's plan in all of this. It's kind of neat when you think about it." Tiffany was following along and nodding at everything he said. He could see she was in complete agreement, but he could also tell she was feeling kind of bad for her father and possibly about meeting his mother and father.

Just then, the bread machine light changed colors, indicating that the dough was ready. She reached in and pulled out the dough and plopped it onto the counter she had prepared with flour. She pulled off a small lump and a larger one, which she handed Joe. Then the two of them started spreading out the dough on the countertop. She was showing Joe what to do but didn't speak much. To kill the silence, Joe attempted to change the subject back to them.

"This is great, Tiffany. I'm so happy to be here with you. I was starting to think I would never get a chance with you." He didn't really understand God's plan in all of this, but he was sure of his feelings for her. Losing her now would seriously hurt him, so he wanted to let her know how glad he was to finally be on a date with her.

"I'm happy too, Joe. Somehow, I think you were going to get a chance with me sooner or later either way. Honestly, you have been the first thing on my mind for longer than you know. Just thinking about you makes me happy." She had been struggling with her feelings for him for a while now. There would be no period for getting over her boyfriend as she had already been on to Joe for some time. She actually didn't need to get over her ex; Joe was all she thought about whether she fully understood it or not.

As they prepared their pizzas with all of their favorite toppings, the two joked and poked at each other, though the thoughts about their parent's pasts were still in the back of both of their minds. When the pizzas were ready for the oven, Tiffany slipped them in and started the timer. They sat and talked while they waited for the pizza to be ready, and they were both surprised how quickly the buzzer sounded.

They talked about everything else Rachel had told Joe while they ate their pizza. The commonality that their parent's pasts brought them made them both feel their being together was fate. As uncomfortable as they both were about how to bring their parents together, they were in this together. It seemed so easy to talk and relate that they felt as if the other was inside their head, and they were right.

After an hour of talking, they decided to skip the movie. Tiffany lived alone, so they would have no one interrupting them. Though her apartment was tiny, the apartment complex was really nice as was all of her furniture, including a really nice flat-screen TV in the living room and another in her bedroom. Sam had been impressed by her new car when he first met her, but the more he got to know her, the less of the material things he seemed to notice. He was never the type to care much about clothing and things. Had he known much about them, he would have likely been very impressed. Tiffany definitely came from money.

The two talked for the remainder of the evening. Being in each other's presence was all either of them wanted. Not only did they get each other's sense of humor, they connected on almost every level. They never even turned the TV on, and they were shocked to learn that four hours had gone by when they had decided to go back into the kitchen to make some cookies and saw the time on the microwave. Neither of them had even glanced at their phones in spite of the multiple vibrations they were both getting.

As Tiffany began to mix the dough for the cookies, she asked Joe when she was going to get to meet his parents. He was surprised she was asking as he feared that she would want to avoid that meeting. To encourage her, he wasted no time by responding, "How about tomorrow? Do you want to come hear my Uncle Jack preach? He's the guy married to Heather."

"I would love to go with you. Can you give me the address and let me know when to be there?" She was really excited to meet these people she had been hearing about. She wanted her father to be forgiven by all of them. If they only knew who he was now, they would forgive him. She was sure of it. He was a great guy, a committed Christian, loving father and husband, and someone she was very proud of. Unfortunately, she was also feeling a fair amount of fear that Joe's family may not accept her because of him. Still, she wanted to face this head on.

"My Uncle Tim is having us over for a barbecue after the service. We'd love to have you stay for that." As he spoke, he wrote the address to the church on a napkin. "You can meet me at 8:45 in the parking lot, or I can come pick you up? We have a Sunday school class at 9:00 a.m. that I'm dying to show you off in. The service starts at 10:30 a.m." He wasn't lying. There were people in there who had gone as far as to taunt him and his brother for not liking girls. The truth was that both he and his brother feared everything that could cause them to stumble. Dad had driven that fear into them. Dating or even spending significant time with a girl were things both he and Robert fled from.

"I'll meet you there. I'm not sure I'm worthy to be 'shown off,' though. I better get you out of here by 11:00 p.m. so I'm not late tomorrow. We have an hour until then. The cookies should be ready in about twenty minutes, and you'll be out of here by eleven easily." She didn't want him to leave, but she wanted to make sure she was well rested for church as she would be meeting his entire family. It was starting to really bother her that her father was hated by them for what he had done so long ago. She began to wonder if Joe's parents would be able to get over the past and forgive him. *What if they have trouble accepting me because of him?*

"So this isn't a sleepover?" He was only kidding, though it did bother him that she was setting a time for him to leave. *Why does she want me out?* he wondered.

"Not if you want me as a wife, it's not." She sounded tough, but Joe loved hearing her say something about being his wife.

"I'll leave right now if it helps me become your husband someday?" He loved how they could be so open with each other already.

"No, I don't want you to leave before you have to leave. I'm only setting a time because I'm nervous about meeting your family. I hope your parents don't hold their past with my father against me? I want them to like me, and I need them to forgive my dad for what he did to them. They would really like him if they knew who he was now." She had sensed that Joe didn't want to leave and that he was concerned that she was setting a time for him to leave. Being attentive to his feelings would be easy as he was so easy to read. Letting him know why would hopefully make him feel better about it.

"My mom will love you. She will forgive your dad with time. You are amazing, and I've already told her that I love you." Again, this was amazing, being able to say exactly what he felt all of the time. She was great.

"I hope she will. You love me?" Why he couldn't keep his mouth shut was a mystery. He was unable to respond.

After what felt like a long time, she spoke again, "I think I love you too." She had been thinking about nothing but him for weeks. Even when she still had a boyfriend, she was deeply attracted to who he was. Being in Joe's presence made Tiffany feel comfortable and at ease.

Joe stood from the kitchen table to embrace Tiffany who was up and working on the cookies. "I'm a little scared. You are the first girl I've ever said 'I love you' to. You could really damage me if you choose to."

"I feel the same, Joe. I've known you were the one for a while now. If you reject me, I would be a mess too." She was squeezing his midsection and enjoying the feelings of security she felt with him. Joe was there to protect and care for her, and he would respect her too. She was sure of that.

The cookies were some of the best Joe had ever eaten. She had made them from scratch, and Joe appreciated the extra effort that took. By the time they had each eaten a few of them, it was almost 11:00 p.m.

"I'm texting my mom to let her know you are joining us tomorrow." He tapped out the message as he spoke to Tiffany.

The text shook Rachel's phone as she and Sam were watching the end of a movie. She had the phone in her hand as she was hoping to hear from her son. The vibration startled her, but she was anxious to hear from him, so it was a welcome startling. After reading the text, she pressed pause on the movie and told Sam.

"Great, it will be good for us to meet her. Ask him if she can come to Tim's too so we can all get to know her a little."

"I will. You're right, this is good. I hope God helps me forgive her father and keeps me from holding what he did to me and Heather against her." She turned the movie back on while she typed her response.

"Great! Please invite her to Uncle Tim's after. We want to get to know her." She wanted to sound as positive as possible.

In what felt like only seconds, Joe was reading his mother's response out loud to Tiffany. He was so proud of his mother for putting her feelings aside for him like this.

"See, you have nothing to worry about. They will love you. My brother won't believe you would ever date me, but he'll love you too. The rest of the family will love you too. By the way, my mom said that Aunt Heather had already completely forgiven your father when she spoke with her last night." He didn't want to break the string of telling her everything he knew. He hoped to always be able to communicate with her in this way. She seemed to like it, and it seemed natural for her to tell him things as they were as well. He really liked that about her.

"Should I wear something nice? Will I wear it all day, or do I need to change after church to go to your Uncle's house?" She was already planning what she would wear, and being the planner that she was, she had been thinking about bringing a bag full of alternative cloths just in case something came up that required something less formal.

"Well, my Uncle Tim has a really nice pool with a great slide. Most of us kids swim when we visit, but we don't have to. Everyone usually goes home to change after church when we do this kind of thing. You can change at our house if you want to?" He really wanted to see her in a bathing suit but knew it was a lustful thought. If she wanted to swim, he would respect her by not staring. *Could I even do that?* he wondered.

"I'll bring my suit, but I'll only swim if you do. I can put it on under some shorts and a T-shirt at your place after the service. I'm so nervous, Joe, but I really want to be there with you, and I really want to meet your family." It was really strange to her that she felt this way about him so soon and that she was so nervous. The thought of him checking her out in her bathing suit never crossed her mind. It wasn't consistent with everything she had seen from him so far. He respected her too much to violate her in any way. Every other guy she had ever dated had pushed her to have sex with them, but she didn't expect that to be an issue with Joe. With Joe, the pressure to have sex before marriage simply didn't seem like it would ever be an issue. Kissing and hugging him that night had shown her what type of boyfriend he would be. He kissed back but made no advances. He had actually seemed scared when they were touching, and she was sure he would respect and honor her purity.

"Great! I can't wait for you to meet all of them. My uncles and aunts are all amazing. I think you will really like Uncle Jack's preaching style too. It's almost eleven now, so I better go. Can we text until midnight?" He wanted to get her permission before he kept her up all night texting. If she agreed to text until a certain time, they would go until then but no longer.

"Midnight is good. I need to know you have made it home safely now that we are an item and all. Are you going to introduce me as your girlfriend tomorrow? Will you think about me tonight?" With that, she moved toward him again and started to close her eyes and pucker her lips again for a good-night kiss.

Seeing her invite, Joe brought her in for the final hug and kiss of the evening. It was easily the best. This time, he felt the warmth of her body and got a deep whiff of her magnificent odor. "I can't believe that you like me this way. I'll think of your smell all night. Not only will I think of you, I'll think of nothing else. I'll call you my girlfriend tomorrow, if that's what you are?"

"Yes, that's what I want if you want me the same way? I hope you understand how serious this is? If you really like my smell so much, let me give you this shirt so you can lay with it tonight."

"Of course I want you the same way, girlfriend." It was blowing his mind that they were now together. Before he could put much thought into it, she ran to the bathroom, grabbing another shirt from a laundry pile to change into. In what seemed like the blink of an eye, she was out of the bathroom and handing him the shirt as she clung to him like before.

"Thank you so much, Tiffany. This is the greatest gift you could have given me. I will make it my pillow tonight, and I'll sniff it so hard that I'll suck all of your smell out of it." He was extremely excited to have the shirt in his hands.

"Can I give you mine? I have another one in the car. I'll run down and get it if you want it?" Feeling so excited to have her wonderful smell with him, he didn't know whether or not she would have any interest in having something of his. After asking her if she wanted his shirt, he began to feel a little strange about the offer, wondering why anyone would want to smell a stinky guy's shirt.

"Please, I'd love that." She loved his smell, though she hadn't shared that with him. Though she was pretty sure he used no cologne, his natural odor mixed with his shampoo, soap, and the detergent his mother used was the smell she was sure would always make her feel safe and loved.

Joe ran with a power in his legs he had never felt before. He had left so quickly that it had actually startled Tiffany. As he ran, he felt like he could run through a wall for this girl. Reaching the car, he was thankful he had left a coat in the back seat. It had been there for quite a while in spite of the fact that it hadn't been cold enough for a coat of any kind for several months. His shirt was off, and he was pulling on the coat so quickly that it even amazed him how quickly he was done and on his way back to her.

Tiffany watched him run to the car and back and had just enough time to formulate a plan. Before he was back in the apartment, she started laying it out for him. "I want to know you are holding my shirt tonight while we're texting. Here's the bad news, you have to give my shirt back tomorrow. I'll give you the shirt off of my back every time we are together so you always have me with you at night. I've never done anything like this before, but I want to be with you in this way. This will be our thing. I want you to think of me as much as I'll be thinking about you. If you'll do the same for me, we can be together all of the time. Is it a deal?" She loved the thought of Joe smelling her. She knew it wouldn't be anything sexual or creepy between them. It was much more than that to her, and she was sure it would be to him as well.

"I love this idea. I always want to have your smell with me. This is a terrific idea. I absolutely love it. I hope you will wear my shirt while I'm using yours as my pillow cover? I better honor your schedule and get going as it's after eleven now." They were holding hands again.

"I sure will, Joe. Don't text me until you're home. I'll be lying in bed, waiting for you. Hurry home for me." She was giving him her most inviting smile, which led to their final kiss of the evening. It was soft and tender and touched both of their hearts.

They pulled away from each other, and Joe left feeling like he was floating on a cloud.

The drive home was painful as he wanted to let her know he was constantly thinking of her the whole time. Having her shirt around his neck was almost too much for him. Before he knew it, he was home, and his nose was drying out from the constant heavy sniffing. She had been right about swapping shirts; it really did feel as if they were still together. It was a great feeling.

All of the lights were off in the Henderson house when Joe got home. Not wanting to wake anyone, he quietly ran up the stairs to his room typing his first text of the evening to his perfect new girlfriend. As he had the entire trip home, he was hugging and sniffing the shirt she had just given him. It was rich with her smell; it too was perfect.

The texting went on until 12:00 a.m., but stopped right on schedule. Amazingly, it had not been a dream. Tiffany was actually telling him she loved him in writing, and they were officially girlfriend and boyfriend. He told himself he would never erase the proof she had just given him. Strangely, Joe fell asleep almost immediately after the texting stopped in spite of his fear that he would not be able to sleep at all after his life-changing experience with her that evening. He felt so completely comfortable, knowing that Tiffany's feelings were mutual with his that falling asleep had been effortless.

When the texting had ended, Tiffany struggled for a while with thoughts about meeting Joe's family. What she had heard about the past had her somewhat confused and tied in knots. She eventually fell asleep when she realized Joe would protect her from any unpleasantness. She could tell that he would defend her in any situation. There was no questioning who he was as a person and that he truly loved her. He was like no boyfriend she had ever had. Wearing his shirt and smelling his smell made her feel loved and secure.

CHAPTER 34

Tim awoke early Sunday morning to complete the lesson he had been working on for his Sunday school class. Though Tim was the regular teacher, when something came up at the hospital, Sam would usually fill in and teach his lesson. This week, he would be teaching his usual "married with children" class, and Sam and Rachel would be in the audience. Today would be the day the family all came to his house after church as well, so he wanted to walk the property before he headed out for church.

Tim was all set to cook both beef and chicken fajitas, while Mary would prepare green enchiladas with the chili from New Mexico that her father sent them every year. The entire family had learned to love both the green and red versions of the famed Hatch chilies. More than anyone, Sam loved them, especially the green.

As part of his normal routine, Tim stuck his head in Tina's room to check on her. He had almost forgotten that she was not alone as her cousin and best friend Maria had slept over and was asleep in the bottom bunk of the bunk bed. Tina was eight years old now, and her cousin Maria was only two months older. They attended the same school and were in the same class together. Though their personalities were different with Tina being the more aggressive and driven one, they were inseparable. The two girls were so close that Jack often used them as an example of friendship in his sermons.

The next door in the same hallway was the boys' room. Ben had just started his junior year of high school, while Victor was now in his sophomore year. Though the boys looked nothing like Tim, he couldn't have felt more like they were his own. Their biological father had completely abandoned them years ago, and the boys had been his adopted kids ever since they could remember. He was as proud of both of them as any father could be. They were both great students and outstanding young men. Both of them played football and baseball, and Tim did whatever he could to make it to their games.

Ben was becoming a very strong baseball player, and his coaches thought he was on the path to getting some college offers to play shortstop. Victor was much more sturdily built than Ben but didn't seem to have developed into the athlete Ben was becoming. Instead, his strength lied in his academic achievement. Tim was sure Victor would go on to be a doctor or something as he had the ability to study and a thirst to really understand things.

Finally, he came to Richard's room at the end of the hall. Though Richard had come back to live with them again, he had not changed all that much. He had bounced in an out for several years now. Not that he ever really disappeared as he constantly texted his mother. Over the last couple of years, Richard had become a heavy drinker, and Tim and Mary were very suspicious as to whether he was using drugs as well. Thankfully, there had been no major events for quite some time. Tim was thankful for that but was pretty sure things were bound to get worse for Richard before they got any better. Unfortunately, he was right about that.

After checking on the kids, he came back down stairs to get a quick shower and to take a quick look at his sleeping wife. He loved her so much that he was constantly looking for ways to make her happy. Though he knew she believed that he loved her, he always sensed that she wondered why he would value her so highly, and why he had chosen her over everyone else. To him, it was kind of funny as he felt that she was the more attractive and that he was lucky to be with someone so beautiful who loved him so completely. He was filled with confidence that her love for him was pure and infinite but worried that she sometimes questioned why he would love her.

He prepared in the quiet of the morning. Though he had no way of knowing about his nephew's, Joe's girlfriend, he somehow knew that today would be an important day.

CHAPTER 35

Jack awoke Sunday morning to find his beautiful wife, Heather, working out on the floor at the base of the bed. It always amazed him how she remained so committed to maintaining her physique every day. She had even done so through the birth of their two children, Maria and her fourteen-month younger brother Richard. As she had many times told Jack, "It is easier to stay in shape than it is to get back into shape."

So dedicated had Heather been to fitness that she had actually written and published a book about staying fit while having a child. It had been fairly successful, and the whole experience of getting the book on the market had been very rewarding for her. Since she had very little interest in becoming a writer, it had ended as quickly as it had started. Her passion would always be teaching and training people how to take care of and how to rehabilitate their bodies. She even had the kids doing exercises with her every night before they got into bed.

Jack could not remember a time when he had gotten out of bed before her. She was like a machine while he was all over the place with his schedule. His playful, fun style was in complete contrast to her grinding regimented style. Together, they were truly far better than either could ever be alone. In spite of their six-year age difference, they hit on all cylinders when it came to their beliefs and priorities. God was number one for both of them, and he was a huge part of their marriage and every decision they made.

Not being a morning person, Jack typically stayed up Saturday evenings, preparing his sermons once Heather had fallen asleep. He would get up just early enough to go over it once before they headed for church. In most cases, his notes were just a jumbled-up mess. His preaching style was somewhat free form as he was blessed with the gift of public speaking. He could get up in front of the congregation with only a few notes on a napkin and speak for hours. Jack actually found that his sermons were far more impactful when he simply let God lead him while he was on stage. Since he spent hours in the Bible every week, the scripture was all there in his head just waiting to be called on.

Jack's style was so filled with emotion that it wasn't at all uncommon to hear people going to tears or breaking out in laughter throughout the congregation when he was on stage. His ability to connect with the audience and to reach into their hearts and thoughts had grown the church year on year since he had taken over. It was Jack's fear that people may come only for the experience of hearing him speak so he worked very hard to stay as confrontational as possible to challenge them to seek God's will in their lives. He didn't want the congregation sitting on the sidelines on any issue. If God addressed it in the Bible, Jack felt compelled to do the same. He felt that every Christian needed to read the Word daily and that they needed to have likeminded Christian friends to help them grow and to remain accountable to God. We were made in God's image, and he desires relation-ship. For this reason, Jack worked tirelessly to find leaders willing to take on this task of getting people involved in each other's lives. Jack was fond of saying, "Faith is a work in progress, and like business, it is either growing or dying."

Jack also felt that it was important to preach all of God's word. He made it a point to drive home that the Bible is always right. It is only man's limited ability to understand things along with our foolishness to trust man's fallible thinking over God's word that gets in the way. Jack fully believed that it was one of the enemy's strategies to make people believe they could not understand the complicated things of science and that they should therefore listen to secular scientists and accept their flawed conclusions as fact rather than question everything for themselves. Through his word, Jack believed that God gave us the answers we need to answer the difficult questions all around us.

Jack's refusal to take liberty with God's word did occasionally drive people and families from the church, but Jack firmly believed that it was God's church and not his or theirs. It was not about growing the church membership and budget, but instead, it was all about winning souls and growing God's kingdom. Jack took that very seriously, and the criticism from the liberal thinkers in the congregation had been very harsh. Being as carefree in his personality as he was, he simply took it all and kept on rolling along. He feared only God, who could give him the second death—not man or the devil—who could only take the things in this world from him.

Sharing God's love and forgiveness was Jack's primary focus, while forcing the praise he constantly got from the congregation out of his head was his biggest challenge. There was simply no place for pride with Jack. As the Bible says, pride comes before a fall. Loving others as we love ourselves was his primary message to his congregation. To him, there were really only two choices— love from the Father or fear from the enemy. Everything else about a person stemmed from which of these a person chose.

This morning was really no different than any other Sunday morning. Heather was stretching away on the floor, and his alarm had just woken him at his usual Sunday time. What was different was all of his thoughts. Instead of his head being filled with ideas about his sermon, he seemed preoccupied with thoughts of Rachel and Sam. He was pretty sure they were both struggling with the thought of coming face to face with Kevin again, and it was creating an unusual burden for him.

"Good morning, beautiful," he said as he stretched his way out of bed.

"Hey, baby."

"Did you sleep okay?"

"Not really. I woke up and started thinking about Rachel."

"Oh yeah, what were you thinking?"

"It's this Kevin thing. She has never really forgiven him."

"She will. If Joe keeps dating his daughter, she'll have to. I'm sure Kevin is very different guy now."

"I bet you're right, but right now, she's tied in knots."

"It's gotten to me too. Today's lesson was inspired by the whole situation. Let me get a quick shower, and I'll give you a preview."

"I'll go get the kids started, and I'll be back in a flash."

"Deal. If you hurry, you may get lucky and catch me still in the shower."

CHAPTER 36

Joe heard his phone buzz and rolled over in bed to see what it was. He was excited to see it was a text from Tiffany. He continued his roll over all the way onto his back with the phone in his hand while reading her message. It was only two minutes before his alarm was set to go off at 7:45 a.m.

"I woke up at six thirty and couldn't go back to sleep. I'm scared and excited about today. I love knowing you're my boyfriend and that you love me, and I'm still wearing your shirt. See you at eight forty-five, good looking."

He loved hearing that she was thinking about them and that she was sticking to the whole boyfriend-girlfriend thing. The good-looking comment helped him a bit, but he still felt out of his league with her. *Does she really think I'm good looking?* he wondered. He had been a late bloomer but was now about six feet tall and was in pretty good shape. Unfortunately, he couldn't help but compare himself to her ex-boyfriend. Her ex was a pretty muscled-up guy that Joe was pretty sure could get girls who looked like Tiffany any time he wanted. If he had to guess, Alan was about six foot four and probably outweighed him by forty or fifty pounds.

Joe thought about what to say before typing back, "You are amazing, Tiffany. You're very pretty, really smart, and totally perfect in every way. I love my perfect girlfriend! You have nothing to be scared of. Everyone will love you. I've got your shirt on my pillow and smelled it all night." It was a long message and took some time to type, but he felt all of it was necessary. Saying he loved her and getting it in return was pretty strange and felt very premature. Still, he actually felt like he was in love with her, so it wasn't a lie.

The answer came back quickly, "Thanks, Joe. You are sweet. I loved sleeping in your shirt. We can exchange shirts when we part at the end of the day again. See you in a bit." She loved every word they had ever spoken or texted to one another. He was always so complimentary of her, and she could tell how important she already was to him. She had even told her dad, Kevin, that she had never met anyone like him. Earlier that morning, she had texted her father to let him know that she was going to go to the Henderson's church that morning. He told her simply that he loved her and that he was sorry that his past had made this difficult for her.

She had been up for quite some time and had tried on everything in her closet; that was saying a lot. She knew that how she was dressed wouldn't really matter that much, but she was so nervous and excited that she nervously went through her entire wardrobe before she finally settled on something. She had settled on a nice conservative dress for church and to wear her bathing suit under a pair of jean shorts and a nice T-shirt for the afternoon at Joe's Uncle Tim's place.

She was feeling somewhat uncomfortable at the thought of wearing a swimsuit in front of Joe's family, though. It wasn't that she didn't have a great body, but her father had always told her to not display it. He had been the type that preyed on young, attractive girls, so he knew firsthand what men would be looking at if she gave them an opportunity to do so. For some reason, it felt like that's what she would be doing by wearing a suit in front of them.

Feeling uncomfortable about the situation, she gave her dad a call as texting just wasn't a good enough way to communicate the way she needed to with him. Almost as soon as he picked up, she was into the details of what was going on between her and Joe. She even confessed that she knew that he had slept with Joe's mom and his aunt Heather. Her revelation brought a sense of failure Kevin hadn't expected. It affected him deeply, and he wasn't able to hide it from her. Not even on the phone. He hated who he had been and felt responsible for what it was now doing to his daughter's life. The last thing he wanted was for his daughter to be punished for his sins.

Kevin was surprised to hear that Heather was Joe's Aunt and asked some questions to better understand all of the relationships. He hadn't even known that Sam had brothers. All he knew was that Rachel was an only child and that Joe Morgan had been like her brother. He repeatedly told Tiffany how sorry he was for all he had done, and she kept assuring him that God and she had forgiven him. She told him he hasn't been that guy in a long time and that he shouldn't continue to beat himself up over it.

Kevin was filled with embarrassment and regret over his past. The person that he now was had no resemblance to what he had once been. He had many times prayed for forgiveness and was sure God had forgiven him. Yet he was dealing with feelings that he hadn't ever experienced before. It wasn't God's forgiveness he was worried about at this point as that was the only thing he was sure of. It was his daughter, Joe, and Joe's parents' forgiveness he was fearful of. If his daughter was going to have a healthy relationship and life with Joe, they would all need to forgive him. What if they couldn't?

Kevin knew he would be forced to face his past in the form of Rachel, Sam, and Heather. He also knew Ally would have to deal with his past through all of this, and he hated the thought of putting her through any of it. Why did any of them need to pay for his sins, especially his wife? He had always been a loving husband to her, but he knew there were consequences he was going to have to deal with that would hurt the woman he lived for. Ally meant the world to him, and he hated himself for any pain and discomfort this was going to cause her.

Kevin assured Tiffany that everything would be okay with the Hendersons and that all of this uneasiness would be behind them at some point. He admitted to her that he too was scared to face Rachel, Sam, and Heather. He even preached to her that this was all a result of doing things his own way instead of God's way. The sins of his past, though he was forgiven and assured to live in heaven forever with Jesus, still carried consequences here in this world. These consequences were not only his to bear, and he felt terrible for what he had brought on all of them.

Tiffany told her father she loved him and decided she owed it to him to be strong and to support him. She would not allow who he once was to cloud who he is now. She was proud of him, knowing he was the great man who had loved her and her mother, not that child he had been. The call had given her the confidence and strength to face what she was heading into. She would fight for her dad's honor if need be.

After a morning of getting everything just right, she headed down to her car with a bag full of clothing. The church was only a few minutes from her apartment, and she didn't want to be late. She was never late for anything.

Even with her newfound strength, she felt like her stomach was tied in knots.

CHAPTER 37

Joe got dressed and was headed for the stairs when Robert came from behind him and pretended he was going to push him down the stairs.

"Very funny."

Robert was following in his father and Joe's footsteps by going to the University of Houston and studying engineering. He was at least an inch taller than Joe and had been far more popular most of his life. Their personalities could not have been farther apart as Joe was far more like his mother, while Robert took after his father. Robert had a little bit of Uncle Jack in him as well, and as his father often jokingly said, "All you need is a little bit of Jack in you, and it will spoil the rest."

"I hear we are all going to meet your sweetheart today." Robert had a way of getting to Joe. This morning was no different. Robert had been up a while longer than anyone else as he had become a morning jogger. After his run that morning, Sam had told him that Joe's girlfriend was joining them for church and that she would be coming to Uncle Tim's place as well.

"Yes, she's meeting us at church. She'll be in our college-age Sunday school class with us today as well. Please don't embarrass me." He really didn't care how Robert acted, though. It just seemed like the right thing to say. Although Robert often drove him nuts, Joe always admired his way with people and his ability to make people feel special. He always wished he had part of what Robert had when it came to dealing with people, but it simply wasn't his thing. Joe also admired his younger brother's ability to attract girls. Thankfully, Robert too believed every word of their father about respecting women and only dating to find someone to marry. If he didn't, Joe was sure Robert could have been a real playboy.

"If she's hot, I might steel her from you, big guy." He was only joking as he had heard how head over heels Joe was for this girl from their mother. Even if she was the most beautiful thing he ever saw, he would never do that to Joe. Still, as the younger brother, Robert felt it was his job to rile Joe up whenever the opportunity presented itself.

Joe never really liked his younger but bigger brother calling him "big guy," but he did feel like Robert respected him and was only teasing him. Though they got on each other's nerves a fair bit, the boys always got along. Their friends were in different circles, but they managed to do quite a bit together anyway. They were actually quite close, and they both admired each other for their differences and strength. Both of them were fully committed Christians as well. Sam and Rachel had very successfully brought them up in the fear and adoration of the Lord, and it permeated their characters.

"You wish. She likes the quiet, caring type, not the loud, annoying type." He was all the way to the base of the stairs now when he turned back to see Robert enjoying their exchange. Robert loved people, and he seemed to get something out of every exchange. He was the master at remembering people's names and went out of his way to meet them. He couldn't be in public without talking to someone. He made new acquaintances everywhere he went and with anyone who would listen. More than anything, Robert loved family and friends. He had a true knack for knowing what everyone needed and always seemed to be there for them when they needed him. He never missed an opportunity to give someone a hard time either.

"She sounds boring. Good luck with that." He was still kidding around, and Joe knew it. He also knew that no one would be more impressed with Tiffany than Robert would be. He fully expected Robert to tease him that she was way too good for him once he had seen her. Though he agreed that she was out of his league, he didn't feel that she was too good for him, just way better looking than he was. Still, Joe was sure Robert would be blown away by Tiffany's looks. He couldn't help but feel proud of her, though he fully understood that her real beauty was who she was inside. He at least liked to believe that he would not have fallen for her the way that he had if she were only beautiful on the outside.

Mom was in the kitchen taking some sausage out of the oven when Joe walked in. She had also made a big pan full of scrambled eggs. Rachel loved making a sit-down breakfast for the family Sunday mornings. As usual, Dad was sitting and eating already, while he and Robert hadn't even made it down to the kitchen yet. Since he had lost all of the weight, Dad never missed breakfast, though he ate far less throughout the day.

"Today is the big day huh, Joe?" Sam couldn't keep his mouth shut about it. Knowing how reserved Joe was, Sam always enjoyed prodding him a little. Sam never ceased to be amazed at how remarkably similar Joe's personality was to his mothers. They were both the type of people that Sam had always taken to—the type he really understood. They both kept to themselves and enjoyed only deep, meaningful relationships. Neither of them enjoyed going parties or being in large groups either.

"Yes, Dad, she's meeting us in the parking lot in about twenty minutes." He was suddenly feeling very awkward about the whole situation. He could only imagine how Tiffany was feeling. "I know you guys will love her. She's great."

"I'm sure we will. Mom tells me she told you our history with her father. Did you tell her everything Mom told you?" Sam wanted to make sure they knew exactly what she did and did not know.

"She knows everything, but you guys don't." He kind of liked having info that they didn't have.

"Tell us, Joe." Rachel couldn't wait one second to find out what it was. She didn't even allow Sam to respond.

"Her mother is Ally. She says you guys knew her too. Also, her Dad is not at all like he once was, and she says he's really embarrassed and ashamed of his past. I won't have you guys holding her father's past against her." He was very uncharacteristically assertive with his last statement.

His parents were shocked at the news and surprised at Joe's last statement. Sam couldn't hold in his thoughts. "That's how he got saved then. It was Ally who saved him. I knew her conversion was real that night. They must have gotten together, and then she brought him to the Lord?" It just had to be that way. He had seen how broken Ally had been that night. It had left a permanent memory etched in his mind. Of all of the people on that stage at the funeral, it was Ally who had looked the most broken and the most in need of forgiveness. He remembered praying with her and feeling the impact of her prayer. He knew it was real then, and he was sure now that Kevin had changed.

"This is all so strange to me," Rachel said softly as she stared at the table. "I can't wait to meet her Joe. I know she will be all that you say she is." She quickly refocused and established eye contact with Joe.

"Neither of us will hold anything against her, Joe. We have some forgiving to do, but we won't let that stand in the way of loving her." Sam had to get this straight for everyone. It had to be this way, and he was sure Rachel would be with him on this.

"That's true, honey." Rachel immediately backed up Sam's statement with her confirmation.

Robert got to the table as Joe was shaking his head in acknowledgement to his parents promise. They had all eaten and were ready to go in just a few minutes after Robert's arrival. The boys helped their mother clean the table and get the dishes in the sink and the leftover sausage and eggs put away. The dog scored a few scraps as well.

The drive to church took only a few minutes. As they pulled in, Joe spotted Tiffany's car in the parking lot. Since they had been exchanging texts, he knew she was there already, and he knew just where to find her. "Dad, she's right there in that blue SUV." His excitement was growing just knowing she was close.

"That's a pretty nice car. Is that her Dad's?" Sam was surprised to see her sitting there in such a new-looking top-of-the-line vehicle. *How does a college student drive a Lincoln Navigator?* he wondered.

Before the car was even in park, Joe was out and headed toward Tiffany. As he hopped out, all he said was, "No, it's her car."

As he walked toward her car, he began to wonder if she would feel comfortable hugging him with his family watching. He quickly decided he would let her decide.

Tiffany opened her door and stepped out just as Joe was approaching. Without giving it any thought, she buried her head in Joe's chest and gave him a big hug. "I'm so glad we are back together. You better keep me safe today."

As he took her in and sucked in her wonderful smell, he began to assure her. "You will always be safe with me, Tiffany. You look so beautiful in that dress. I can't wait for my family to meet you. They are going to love you. Are you ready for this?" He was so proud that she was his girlfriend. Not only was she one of the prettiest girls he had ever seen, she was also surely his soul mate. He had known it for quite some time now.

"Sure. I'll just leave my stuff in the car and drive to your house to change after the service. Are they all watching us?" She had let go of him now, but he was standing in between her and his approaching family so she was unable to see for herself.

Joe took her by the hand and turned around to see his parents and younger brother coming their way. "They sure are. Let's go."

Joe had been right to think Robert would be impressed with her. Actually, he was more than impressed; he was blown away. In fact, he was so impressed that he couldn't stop himself from blurting out, "No way. This girl really likes Joe?" Only his parents heard him, and they both told him to shut up under their breath.

"Mom, Dad, Robert, this is Tiffany, my girlfriend. Tiffany, this is my mom and dad, and my kid brother Robert."

As he spoke, Tiffany extended her had to Rachel first and said, "Nice to meet you, Mrs. Henderson." Then she went on down the line greeting and shaking hands with each of them. They were all smiles, and Rachel and Sam were both relieved that they felt no ill will toward her.

Robert was completely incapable of keeping his mouth shut about her looks. "Wow, why did you tell us she was plain looking Joe. She's not plain at all. She's beautiful."

Tiffany's head turned immediately toward Joe who replied, "Very funny, moron." Robert was already smiling ear to ear when Tiffany turned to look back at him. She understood what was going on and instantly knew that Robert was the instigator in their brotherly dance.

"Did I hear you right? Did you just call her your girlfriend?" Robert couldn't help but point out what Joe had just introduced her as.

"Yes, he said that right, Robert. I am his girlfriend." She reached around Joe's back and gave him a squeeze right there in front of his family. She wanted him to be assured that her feelings for him were real. She knew they were but needed him and his family to know as well. Doing this in front of people she had just met was completely out of character for her, but she was feeling an odd sense of confidence that she would soon realize would always be present when she was with Joe.

Joe's pride swelled inside of him while a sheepish grin came across his face. He wrapped both of his arms around her and lifted her from the ground in acceptance of what she had just said. There was no chance he would leave her exposed to any uncomfortable feelings. He would return her affection any time she gave it.

When the awkwardness was over, Rachel spoke, "It's such a pleasure to meet you, Tiffany. Joe has been talking about you for so long it feels like we already know you." Rachel had promised to be supportive no matter what but was very happy to have it coming so naturally. Being in Tiffany's presence was making it clear that everything her son had been saying about her was true. Tiffany was different. Though she was beautiful, she was also somehow very humble and grounded. More than anything, she could see that Tiffany's feelings for her son were deep and very real. Rachel was rarely wrong about these types of things, and though they had just met Tiffany, it was clear to Rachel that none of what she had worried about would be an issue.

"Thank you so much, Mrs. Henderson. Your son thinks the world of you and your husband. I couldn't wait to meet you guys. You've done a great job raising Joe. He's so kind and smart and caring." She wasn't trying to lay it on or anything; it was just coming out.

Joe stood there, admiring his soul mate as she spoke to his parents. While he watched their faces, he could see them being won over by her. She was so adorable and genuine that Joe knew his parents would have to love her, regardless of who her father was. Her communicating so confidently with his parents really impressed him. How could anyone find fault with her. She was the most perfect creature he had ever known.

Finally, Robert spoke up as they were running out of time, "Unless we want to sneak in late to our Sunday school classes, I better escort these two lovebirds to our class." Joe was only mildly amused, while Tiffany quickly noticed the differences in Joe and his brother. She could tell that Robert was at ease in a group and around girls, while Joe was always a little uncomfortable around both groups and girls.

Still, Robert seemed like a kind person to her. He hadn't come off as arrogant at all, just confident and sure of himself. She also noticed that he was taller and more athletic than Joe was. He was different in a lot of ways physically, but they both had similar facial features. Personality wise, Joe was the type of person she got along well with. Robert was the type she usually tried to avoid. It was just too much for her to be around someone like him. Spending half of the time worried about what they may say or do next was just too much for her.

When the youngsters had gone, Rachel turned to Sam and started in, "Can you believe how much she looks like her parents? I can see her dad in her face and her mother in everything else. It's amazing." Whenever someone who knew Tiffany saw her dad, they always knew he was her father. There was no denying it. Her physique right down to the long blonde hair was clearly her mother's image, though.

"Wow, I couldn't believe it either. It was like a female Kevin. Thankfully, I didn't feel anything negative for her, did you?" He too was amazed at her appearance, but he was even happier that he didn't feel anything that made him uncomfortable from either Tiffany or Rachel. The fact she was driving such an expensive vehicle was hard to ignore as well.

"No, I felt nothing but joy for Joe. She's an angel. I can't wait to get to talk with her later. She seems really into Joe. She'll either be his wife or break his heart forever. Did you see how he was around her?" Her primary feelings were relief and amazement. Her relief had to do with her lack of bitter feelings or discomfort around her, and her amazement was due to Tiffany's stunningly similar facial features of her father.

"I sure did. How could I have missed it? He's in deep already, honey. There is no going back for him. Luckily, I think she feels the same." He felt some concern for Joe, but knowing Joe like he did, he was pretty sure things were going to work out. How could anyone not be overwhelmed by his son's ability to love with all of his heart? Joe's love for others was a gift straight from God.

"What about this car?" Sam said, pointing to the brand-new, top-of-the-line vehicle they were still standing next to. "I guess

Kevin is still rich." Rachel responded as she turned and began heading toward the church.

The boys and Tiffany were entering the building on their way to the college-age class, while Rachel and Sam hurried off to meet Heather and Mary in Tim's class. Jack had other obligations but made it a habit of frequently popping in and out of Tim's class.

As Rachel and Sam entered the meeting room, Tim spotted them and noticed how quickly they moved to the table where Mary and Heather were sitting. It was a bit unusual as Sam normally came right to the front to chat with him before joining the ladies at their customary table.

"Hey, guys, what's going on?" he said as he came over and sat down at their table.

Rachel explained everything as quickly as she could as the rest of the class socialized and enjoyed refreshments and doughnuts. Before she was through, she promised them that they would all get to meet Tiffany during the service and that Tiffany would be coming to Tim and Mary's after.

"You will be blown away how much she looks like her father, Heather," she promised.

Tim's class, as usual, was very good. Since he believed in respecting people's time, he always let them out right on schedule. The Hendersons left as a group for the sanctuary shortly after Tim let the class out. Just before they entered, Heather spotted a familiar face. It was Kevin's face on a beautiful young girl.

Heather stopped in her tracks after seeing Tiffany. Instinct took over as she broke away from the group to head Tiffany and Joe off. She caught them quickly but had fallen in behind them. Instead of yelling to get their attention, she pulled Joe's arm toward her lightly, which also caught Tiffany's attention. Though she had their full attention, her eyes were glued on Tiffany as she spoke, "Wow, you look exactly like your father."

Though she was used to hearing how much she looked like her father, this time was very different. No one would have to tell her who this was; it had to be Heather. Her dad had just told her how beautiful Heather had been when he knew her. This had to be her.

"Yes, ma'am. I get that all the time. You must be Heather? I'm Tiffany, Joe's girlfriend." What she hadn't expected was Heather's beauty. Though her father had made a point of how beautiful she had been, Tiffany would have never imagined that Heather would still be anywhere near this attractive. Though she was very impressed that her father had dated someone who looked like this, she felt instantly sorry for her mother. From what she had been told, it was Heather that Joe Morgan had left her mother for.

Though Joe's mom, Rachel, was an attractive woman, Heather was stunning. Her face, hair, eyes, and everything else was just so overpowering that she couldn't help but feel a little intimidated. Heather seemed huge and powerful to her as well. It crossed her mind that her mother would feel very inferior to Heather if she were there.

"Yes, I'm Heather, Joe's aunt. It's so nice to meet you. I'm so glad you could make it today. My husband is the preacher, so I'll be sitting with you guys." Heather could sense that Tiffany was feeling a bit challenged, so she backed down and fell behind the rest of the family as they all arrived from behind her. She even chose to sit on the far side of the pew to make sure Tiffany didn't feel uncomfortable the way she was picking up on. As she walked away, the rest of the family came by and introduced themselves to Tiffany one by one. She and Joe stayed at the end of the pew while the others came in, greeted Tiffany, and kept going down the pew to sit down.

When they had finally all passed, Tiffany pulled Joe down and whispered into his ear, "Heather is scary good looking. Between her and your mother, I feel really sorry for my mother. They are both really beautiful women. I've never seen anyone as good looking as Heather, though, ever. No one at any age, let alone, however old she must be." She looked to be somewhat overloaded at this point, and Joe could see the discomfort in her eyes. He put his arm around her and held her as they sat together at the end of the pew. As if meeting his parents wasn't enough, she had just met Heather and everyone else in their family, even his grandparents.

After the worship portion of the service, Jack leapt up on stage like a bolt of pure energy. Tiffany was immediately drawn in. His enthusiasm and passion was infectious. He spoke so effortlessly and without notes. It seemed as if he was just talking with them one on one. Though his subject was forgiveness, he found ways to make the audience enjoy the subject, and more than once, the congregation erupted in laughter.

Though she held hands with Joe, she was so involved in what Jack was preaching that she almost forgot where she was. What he was saying made so much sense to her that she began to feel that Joe's family really could forgive her father for what he had done to them. Had Pastor Jack actually prepared this message for his own family, knowing that she would be there today? The more he spoke, the more she was convinced that he had.

Jack pushed deep and challenged everyone in the audience to examine themselves for signs of unforgiveness. He told them that it was a sin for someone who had been forgiven by God to not forgive someone, especially if that person had been changed by God into a new creation that God himself had forgiven. Jack went on to explain that forgiveness is revealed in our hearts. When we haven't forgiven, any remembrance of the offense will feel like salt in a wound to us. If there is pain, the forgiveness we have extended has not been complete. Forgiveness is a conscious decision we have to make, not just a feeling.

He explained that unforgiveness was the hardest on the person holding onto the offense, and oftentimes, the unforgiven isn't even aware of the offense. Why people choose to beat themselves up over an offense had more to do with a false sense of value each of us puts on ourselves. If we get the focus off of ourselves, Jack argued that we would more easily forgive and forget.

At the end of the sermon, when he pleaded with the congregation to forgive so they too could be forgiven, Tiffany noticed that Rachel was crying and that Sam was consoling her. Jack went on to explain that when we don't forgive, we create a barrier between ourselves and God. Because he loves everyone and has wiped away the sins of those that he has forgiven, he cannot tolerate our disobedience when we do not forgive others. This rebellion, stubbornness to not forgive, leads to more struggles until finally the sinner begins to drift away from the Lord.

When he was through with his message, he offered to pray with anyone who felt they needed prayer. He directed them to come down front right then or to come down when the service had concluded. To Tiffany's surprise, Rachel and Sam were the first ones on their knees at the altar. Jack was hugging and praying with them as the music started to play. As the three huddled together, several others made their way to the front where the other church staff met and prayed with them.

"I want to go down there for your mom, Joe." She felt too uncomfortable to just go on her own but felt it was something she needed to do. She was hoping he would lead her down so she wouldn't have to do it alone.

"Let's go."

That was all she needed from him to get herself out of the pew. Tiffany stood and exited their row with Joe close behind. The rest of the family, including the kids, followed.

Tiffany and Joe walked down together. When they got to Joe's parents, Tiffany put her right hand on Rachel and her left on Sam and began to pray. Joe put his hands on his parents as well and also began to pray for them and for Tiffany. The rest of the family filled in around them, but Rachel immediately sensed that Tiffany and Joe had come to support her, and it began to strengthen her as she felt their understanding and forgiveness. It was in her hands to forgive Kevin, but now, she had all of them praying for her. For the first time, she finally felt that she was ready to forgive Kevin, and she did as she completely fell apart.

The remainder of the day convinced everyone that Tiffany and Joe were destined to be together. She was truly the girl who

Rachel and Sam had always prayed that God would bring into their son's life. She was a perfect fit for him in every way, though it was her faith in God and commitment to living her life to honor God that stood out the most to them.

Even Richard, in spite of all of his anger toward the family, agreed that Tiffany would be great for Joe. Not even he could find fault with her. No one did.

CHAPTER 38

The time Tiffany spent with Joe's family had cemented him into the role of Tiffany's full-time boyfriend. That day had been perfect in every way. Rachel was drawn to Tiffany, and they connected in a way that had made Rachel feel as if she were her own daughter. For the course of the day they had spent together, Rachel and Tiffany sat by one another and shared things neither of them could have imagined they would be sharing with any new acquaintance. The bond was so strong that Rachel felt it was God himself blessing them and her son with Tiffany. Tiffany felt the same about the whole thing.

That day had also reassured Tiffany that Joe was the right guy for her. She couldn't take her eyes off of him that day, and his every action convinced her that he was the right guy for her. His giving personality could be seen in his interaction with everyone he encountered. He played with the younger children, always seemed to be in a good mood, and cared for his mother and the others in his family by serving them throughout the day without ever being asked to help. It was easy to see that he was the "giver" type her father had always told her he wanted her to be with. As the day went on, she couldn't help but fall deeper and deeper for him.

The two were in constant communication the week following Tiffany's intro to the family. Joe spent lots of time at Tiffany's place, and the two agreed to set some ground rules around physical contact to make sure they wouldn't mess up and destroy each other's purity. The shirt exchange happened every day that week, but that was as close to sleeping with one another either would allow. It felt really great to Tiffany to be with someone who was as serious about their commitment to stay pure until marriage as she was. It was far different than having a boyfriend promise to wait who himself had not waited. Everyone before Joe had pushed her to sleep with them, arguing that they would be married someday, so what's the difference? She was thankful she had known better and was very thankful to finally be with someone else who shared her conviction.

When they weren't together, they missed the other so much that they texted one another continually. Thanks to the shirt exchange, neither of them was ever without some sort of physical evidence of the other. When they were together they felt whole, but when they were apart, they ached for the other. Both were constantly thanking the Lord for the other, and they often told each other about it. Nothing was secret between them. No matter how private or embarrassing, they shared everything.

Though it was only their first week as a couple, things were moving very quickly in the relationship. The two began discussing marriage and what their life together would look like. It never felt premature to either of them. They were so serious that they even began to set dates and plan how the whole thing would be executed.

Friday of their first week as a couple, Tiffany asked Joe to come to her parents' house the following evening to meet them. Though her parents lived only an hour or so from where Joe had grown up, he had only been in the area once or twice in his lifetime. They lived in an exclusive neighborhood in the Woodlands, Texas.

Joe felt slightly uncomfortable as they drove up her parents' driveway. He was suddenly appreciating what she must have felt the previous week. The neighborhood itself was intimidating, but when he saw her parent's ridiculously huge house, he suddenly felt very small. His Uncle Tim's place had been the nicest thing he had ever seen, but this was easily twice the size and twice as nice.

"I can't believe how worried I am that they won't think I'm good enough for you. How could anyone be good enough for you?"

"Joe, please don't worry about that. They know how I feel about you, and they know you are a great guy. My dad even says your dad was one of the best people he ever knew. They will love you. Trust me, I trusted you last weekend with your family." She gave him a wink, the one he had already grown to love. It was something she had picked up from her father, and Rachel had noticed her doing it to Joe several times when they had been together the previous Sunday. Every time Rachel saw her wink at Joe, it made her think of Kevin. As if Tiffany's face alone wasn't enough to constantly remind her of Kevin, her wink and other mannerisms were all directly inherited from her father. They were constant reminders to both Rachel and Heather that Tiffany was in fact Kevin's daughter, but to Joe, they were just more reasons to fall for her. They were things he would later notice in her father, but for now, they were her traits, and he dreamed of them constantly.

"Okay. You're right. You were very brave. I can't even imagine how you must have felt meeting my family." He really was amazed at how willing she had been to meet them so soon. He had already begun to admire her ability to handle herself around strangers. It definitely wasn't an area of strength for him. Actually, it was his preference to listen and watch others rather than participate. He was a very analytical type of person, having inherited his mother's personality.

The evening turned out to be much less stressful that he had anticipated. Their home was immense and decorated with what appeared to be the best of everything, though none of it was overdone or arrogant. Her parents were exactly as she had described them.

Her father was in great physical condition. Joe could see why women had been attracted to him. His features were strong, and he seemed handsome, even to Joe. He couldn't help but see Tiffany's face in his either. What was more impressive than his looks, his home, or anything else was his ability to put Joe at ease. It seemed as if Mr. Todd had no worries at all. It was as if there was nothing weighing him down. His calming personality allowed Joe to relax just enough to forget about his circumstances.

Tiffany's mother was beyond friendly. She seemed to have an affection for Joe that made him feel welcomed right away. Though she had once had an amazing figure, at this point in her life, she showed no signs of it. Though she was still an attractive woman, she looked nothing like the woman Rachel, Heather, and Sam would remember. Since Joe had never known her as a young woman, he saw no similarities between her and her daughter outside of her hair coloring.

The conversation was very light, yet Joe could feel Mr. Todd skillfully working him for information. Though it never felt uncomfortable, he was well aware that Mr. Todd was looking out for his daughter by prodding around. Since Joe had nothing to hide, and his intensions were pure, he didn't worry much about Mr. Todd's line of questioning. Actually, he found himself being impressed at the man's discovery skills. He was truly gifted in this area, and Joe couldn't help but be impressed.

Joe would later hear the story behind her parent's money and the circumstances that had brought them together. As it turned out, Kevin's father had been the CEO of a major US oil company. When Kevin started college, his father was already sixty years old, and he was on his second marriage. His stepmother was only thirty-five years old, while his biological mother was fifty-five. Kevin's dad died at seventy due to all of the stresses associated with climbing to the top the way he had. His failures as a husband and father didn't help with his stress level either. As an executive, he had been a dynamo, and he was well compensated for it.

Kevin was his father's only child. Unfortunately, he and his father were never close. Kevin had gone through life, feeling like he simply didn't measure up to his father as his father never showed him any signs of approval. When Kevin graduated college, his father was sixty-four years old and was still too busy to get to know his son.

Kevin graduated a year after Joe Morgan passed away. Though his father was at the ceremony, Kevin knew his father had wanted him to graduate with something other than the business degree he had achieved. Actually, it was quite clear that his father thought he should have studied to be an engineer and later gone back to get a business degree if and when he needed one. Kevin never had to guess about his father's disappointment in him as his father never hesitated to come right out and tell him how he was failing right to his face.

Prior to graduation, Kevin was drafted in the later rounds of the MLB draft as a catcher. He signed a contract to play in the minors and chose not to tell his father. It wasn't until the night of his graduation that he felt the courage to do so. His father's response had been, "Go enjoy yourself while you can. I'll still be here doing real work to provide for my loved ones when you are done clowning around and decide to grow up and provide for yourself." The comment had cut Kevin deeply, but it wasn't anything new to him.

It was later that evening that Kevin and Ally first slept together. Though Ally had accepted Christ into her life at Joe Morgan's funeral, she had fallen away since due to a lack of support and a bout of depression. Since Joe's death, Ally had spent the summer alone with her family in San Antonio. Though they were not believers, they lived a quiet life and kept to themselves. She was able to hide from life all that summer.

When she returned to school, she began struggling with her new way of living as all of her friends were still hitting the party scene. Though she had known Kevin well when she had dated Joe, she never really knew him personally. After several weeks of coming over to his house with her friends, he asked her to hang around to talk about some things he was dealing with regarding

Joe's passing. She agreed, knowing his reputation full and well, but feeling a strong desire to be around him anyway.

To her surprise, Kevin was really a mess inside. Though he may have had some designs on getting her into bed, it didn't take her long to see that he was really dealing with something that seemed spiritual to her. The way he was living his life and his inability to please his father were creating an emptiness that he knew could not be filled. Though he had pretended to be a Christian to get his way with Heather, he was now constantly thinking about his need for God in his life. He began to realize that he really had wanted Christ in his life when he had prayed that prayer at Joe's funeral. *Can anything else fill the void?* he wondered.

Kevin was hurting over Joe's death at that point more than he ever had in the past. Joe had been such a close friend that he was feeling a huge hole in his own life without him around. He and Ally talked about the fact that they had both accepted Christ in their lives at Joe's funeral, and Kevin admitted to her that he had used Joe's death to sleep with Heather. At first, Ally enjoyed hearing it as Heather was the reason she was about to lose Joe before his fall. Soon, she realized that Joe was leaving her because of who she was, not just because of Heather. Additionally, she and Heather had buried the hatchet that day at the funeral. She could sense that Heather had forgiven her, though she knew she had not fully forgiven Heather. The forgiveness did eventually come, but it was years later as it seemed to slowly fade away. As they say, time heals a multitude of sins.

Ally had been very reckless prior to Joe's death. Not only had she experimented with just about any drug that was put in front of her, she also had been with many partners. Though she never cheated on Joe, she had gotten around before they started dating. For that reason, she was able to accept Kevin's past and understand that he was in a battle against his sinful desire to sleep with everyone he could. She felt his pain and began to develop a strange desire to be there for him. He, more than anyone else, seemed to understand what she was going through, and she completely understood him. Additionally, she was strongly attracted to him. Though she was now saved and trying to live her life differently, she still had strong urges to be with him.

The more time the two spent together, the closer they became. Early on in their courtship, Ally was celibate, but Kevin was not nor did he pretend to be or try to be. They were not boyfriend and girlfriend but were becoming best friends. Ally became a true confidante and eventually his closest friend. By Christmastime of that year, they were always together, and Kevin was no longer sleeping around. He wanted only to be with Ally, and he told her so. At that point, he would have felt he was cheating on her had he continued to sleep around.

When their romantic relationship began, Ally, knowing how easily Kevin could slip up and have sex with someone else, made Kevin agree to not have sex with her or anyone else. She promised him they would be over if he did. For months, things went well, and they both cut way back on their drinking and completely stopped thinking about anyone else but each other. When they did have people over, Ally always sat with Kevin. The two worked together to completely avoid any mistakes with the opposite sex. They kissed frequently and openly, and everyone knew they were a couple. They were both proud of that fact.

When Kevin was drafted into the MLB, no one was more proud of him than Ally was. She wanted Kevin to succeed at whatever he chose to do but had no expectations of him that made him feel he could fail her. Knowing he loved baseball, she agreed to follow him wherever he went and to give him every chance at succeeding in baseball. Her offer so touched him that he fell even deeper in love with her, hopelessly so. He had never felt that anyone could love him the way he was sure she did, and it began to change him. No longer was he out for himself in this world; he was out for them now. No longer did he sit around, stewing about his father, instead, he actually began to want to please him.

Ally read the Bible day and night. She talked constantly about it with Kevin, and the two had great discussions about it. Though he had repeated the prayer at Joe's funeral, Kevin knew inside that he wasn't really a Christian. He had not really believed nor had he chosen to follow Christ; he had only said the words to see if it somehow changed him. Ally didn't feel the same about her conversion. Hers had been real, and her heart was telling her that God had forgiven her and really did love her. Unfortunately, neither of them felt the need to attend a church nor had they developed any relationships with other Christians.

The night of their graduation, both he and Ally got their degrees in business. Ally had been there when his father told him that he should have been an engineer, and she saw the pain, disappointment, and anger on Kevin's face. When he told his father he had signed a contract to play professional baseball, she was shocked that his father wasn't proud. It was at that moment that Ally decided to make love to Kevin that evening. She loved him deeply at this point, and she needed to take his mind off of his jerk of a father. The consequences didn't matter anymore to her.

Kevin's father had just made his remark about being there for Kevin when he failed to make a living playing baseball when Ally took Kevin's hand and said, "Let's go." Kevin turned and looked into her eyes before turning back to his father and saying, "Dad, this is Ally. She has been my girlfriend for a while, and I love her. I plan to ask her to marry me tonight. I was hoping to get your blessing, but now I realize that is not possible. I don't think I even want it anyway."

Ally was in complete shock. She had no idea this was coming. Kevin turned to look into her eyes again. "I love you with all of my heart, baby. You are the one for me. I have never loved anyone but myself until now, but you have changed me. Will you be my wife?"

She reached up and grabbed the back of his head and said, "Hell yes, I'll marry you!" Then she pulled him down for a big wet kiss.

With Mr. Todd standing right in front of them, they walked away without even waiting to see his reaction. They never even looked in his direction. They went immediately to Kevin's house and made love and talked all night long. From that moment on, they were inseparable. Nothing would ever come between them. They were both completely cured from whatever it had been that had made them both so promiscuous. Neither desired anyone but the other from then on.

Before Kevin had to head out to report to his minor league baseball team, they went to Las Vegas and got married. Later, they would regret not waiting until that day to share the most intimate gift they had to give to each other. As it turned out, it would have only been a few more days. From that moment, they began praying that their kids would be stronger than they had been, and that they would wait until marriage for sex. From their own painful experiences, they both knew how damaging it could be to not wait until you were married to the person God picks out for you.

For several years after their wedding, they travelled around with one minor league team after another, trying to make it to the majors. When Ally got pregnant with Tiffany, they decided to give up on Kevin's dream of playing in the majors and returned to Houston to start their family.

After a few months of struggling, they swallowed their pride and asked Mr. Todd for help. He was more than willing to help and thoroughly enjoyed lecturing them for the next three years until he died in his sleep from a heart attack. Being the only son, Kevin inherited a fortune. Rather than work for anyone else, he and Ally decided to start several businesses. With his ability to lead others and to drive people to success, everything Kevin touched became successful. In almost no time, Kevin turned his father's fortune into real wealth. Had his father been around to see it, he may actually have finally been proud of his son.

Almost immediately after his father's death, Kevin and Ally were invited to attend a close friend's church. Since both he and Ally wanted to learn more about God and both knew they needed something in their lives, they agreed to attend a Sunday service. They also felt that young Tiffany, now three years old, should be brought up in the church. They both had the highest regard for Sam Henderson and often used him as an example when discussing their reasons for first going back to church. It was Sam's example and his willingness to speak about God's will that had first led them to accept Christ into their lives. How had they stayed away for so long was a mystery to both of them?

The one visit turned into a new church family, and some of the closest friends in their lives sprung from that decision to attend. Their rededication and ability to see how God had worked in their lives made them valuable new additions to their new church. Eventually, they were both baptized after their emotional surrenders and rededications to God's authority in their lives. It was almost as if someone had turned on a switch, and now, they both were new creations. From that moment on, they both dove into God's word and never looked back.

Though they both wanted a larger family, Ally never conceived again. They tried all of the latest technology to get pregnant again and even considered adopting before they finally decided that Tiffany would be enough for their family.

Kevin's biggest regret since trusting in the Lord was that he had not done so sooner so he could have spoken to his father about his faith. He was sure his father had not accepted Christ, and it really bothered him that he had been ill prepared to witness to him.

CHAPTER 39

Sam sat up in his hospital bed. As usual, Rachel was sitting in the chair by him, reading a book. "Go home, baby," he quietly slurred.

"You're awake. How do you feel?" She reached out and took his hand.

"Okay. I love you." He was very hard to understand, but she knew what he was saying. The last few months had been pretty tough as Sam had been in and out of the hospital several times. As hard as it was to see him this way, they had had such a wonderful full life together that Rachel felt mostly grateful for the time they had had. After all, they had been very happily married for fifty-six years now.

Sam looked up at the love of his life, wondering if this could be the last time he ever saw her. It amazed him how she had managed to remain so beautiful all of these years. Even at the age of seventy-eight, she was still someone men noticed; well, older men at least.

"I love you too, Sam. Get some more sleep, and I'll be here with the grandkids in the morning." They now had five grandkids—three from Joe and Tiffany, two boys and a girl; and two from Robert and Kathy, one boy and one girl. Rachel wasn't talking about them though. She was talking about their great-grand-children. Joe was now fifty-one, and Robert was forty-nine. Joe's eldest was now twenty-six and had two young children. Robert's eldest was twenty-three and had a one-year-old baby girl. Rachel's plan was to come in with all three great-grandchildren in the morning. Robert's wife, Kathy, would be with her as well.

"Kevin?" Sam and Kevin Todd had become the closest of friends since their reconciliation as a result of Joe and Tiffany dating and eventual marriage. Kevin had been in the room with Rachel when Sam had fallen asleep earlier.

"He stayed, and we talked for almost an hour, but he left when you didn't wake up. He told me to remind that you two are watching a movie together in the morning. He'll be here early and promised you two would be done before I get here with the kids." Kevin had lost Ally eight years earlier. Since then, he had been completely alone. To keep himself busy, he had been doing anything and everything his church needed him for. Almost immediately after Ally's death, Kevin bought a house in Pearland to be near the rest of his family, the Hendersons. The move from the Woodlands only saved him an hour of travel each way, but especially at his age, driving felt like a waste of time. He needed to be near his family, and the Hendersons were his family.

"Good. Love you." He gave her his best smile and squeezed her hand as hard as he could so she would know he was really okay.

"I love you too. Good night, sweetheart." He seemed so peaceful that it made her feel comfortable leaving him for the night. She gathered her stuff and gave Sam a hug before she left.

Once she had gone, Sam lay in bed, thinking about his life. God had given him the best life he could have ever imagined. Not only had he had the best family he could have ever imagined, he had also had some of the best friends anyone could have ever had. Thinking about Kevin's return in the morning made him think about the blessings he and his family had all gotten through Joe Morgan.

It was through Joe Morgan that Sam had met Rachel, Heather, Kevin, and Ally. Rachel had become his wife and given him more love than he could have ever hoped for. Heather had been one of his and his wife's very best friends, and she had become a part of their family when she married Jack. Ally had become a huge part of their lives and had been instrumental in the foundation of her daughter, Tiffany, who had become their son Joe's wife and given them three grandchildren and two great-grandchildren. It was Kevin, though, who truly amazed Sam. In spite of who he had once been and how he had hurt both Rachel and Heather, it was he who had really had the biggest impact on Sam's life.

After Joe Henderson and Tiffany Todd were married, Kevin insisted on handing over one of his businesses to them as a wedding gift. Joe and Tiffany worked together to quickly double sales by bringing in Sam to run the sales department. Sam was able to bring in some of the sales people he had worked with as a sales engineer, and they all brought a strong customer base with them. The engineering group grew quickly, and within ten years, they were bought out by a monster company as they had been eroding that company's customer base year on year. Joe, Tiffany, and Sam were the three main partners, and the deal left them in a financial position that allowed them to have true financial freedom.

Joe eventually started another business but was more interested in enjoying himself than making money. He did both—working his consulting business and taking lots of family time off while he allowed his more-than-capable team to run things.

Sam retired after the buyout at the age of fifty-seven. He and Kevin attended every sporting or other event any of the kids and grandkids got into after that. They played golf together several times each week and spent most of their free time together with the family; even vacations were spent together. They were also very active volunteers in various ministries.

Kevin loved all of the Hendersons and spent much of his life trying to make up for what he had done to Rachel and Heather. Both of them, along with Sam, had long since forgiven him. Unfortunately, it was many years before Kevin finally forgave himself the way God had long ago.

Of all the things Kevin had done for their family over the years, his role in bringing Richard to the Lord and to God-centered living was the most amazing.

Richard had hit rock bottom in his mid-twenties. He drank like a fish, couldn't hold a job or a girlfriend, and found himself in trouble with the law constantly. For nearly ten years, he stayed at rock bottom, and on numerous occasions, Tim and Mary had to call the authorities to get him off of their property. His addictions had gotten more and more expensive, and anything they gave him only supported his habits. Though he had been arrested several times, everything he had been arrested for had been relatively minor.

One night, when Kevin and Ally were going out for dinner at an expensive steak restaurant, their paths crossed with Richard's. As they were walking from their car to the restaurant, they heard someone call, "Mr. and Mrs. Todd." It was Richard. He didn't know them well, but he knew them well enough to remember them.

"Hey, Richard, what are you doing here?" Kevin knew who it was right away as he had been asked to pray for him many times.

"I'm dropping off my girlfriend. She works here." His car was making lots of noise, and Kevin found himself feeling for him and how bad his life was. For years, he had been hearing about his struggles. Tim and Mary had been going through a living hell over this kid. Kevin quickly decided to do something about it.

"Here is my card. If you want to start over, give me a call." He handed him the card while maintaining eye contact so he could see and try to get a read on where Richard was by his reaction.

Richard reached for the card but immediately felt embarrassed. "Thanks." Though he was embarrassed, something told him Kevin could really help.

He had been spiraling down lower and lower in his own self-loathing, but his defiance and stubbornness kept him from giving in to what he knew was the right thing to do. Things were starting to change inside of him, though, and he really hated where he was in life and that he had destroyed his relationship with his family. The realization that his parents had always been right and that they would forgive him was creating hope he hadn't had before.

When Kevin took his hands off of the door of his car, Richard drove away and began crying almost immediately. He knew this was a chance from God. Kevin could really help him. Was this the chance he had been praying for? Part of him felt that it wasn't even worth trying as he would surely fail, but his desire to end the worthless life he was leading was just too strong for him not to try.

As Richard drove off, Kevin turned to Ally and asked, "When he calls, can we take him in under some strict rules? He'll be out if he breaks one of them. I feel that God is laying this on my heart."

"Let's draw up the rules over dinner. You are always right about this kind of stuff. Besides, I think I feel the same way about this." She loved Kevin's heart for others. He had not been this way at all when they first met, but his yielding to the Lord and his emersion in God's Word had created a giving spirit in him, and Ally adored that about him.

When Richard called Kevin the next day, it was easy to tell that he was a broken person. Kevin invited him to their house to meet with him and Ally, and the two of them laid out all of the rules. If he followed them all, including the daily Bible study, they would put him through college, buy him a car, and pay all of his bills while he lived with them. There would be a legal contract that he would have to agree to sign that would require him to pay them back for everything without any interest and at a very small monthly amount. They explained to him that they were not his parents and that this was a business arrangement, not charity. They were getting into the business of Richard and reserved the right to end the deal if any of the conditions of the terms agreed to by both parties were broken.

Richard agreed to everything and signed the agreement. He had to break all ties with his former life, completely quit using drugs and alcohol, have no girls in the house, come home every night, and absolutely no arrests would be tolerated.

Kevin and Ally cleared everything with Tim and Mary, who were hoping and praying every step of the way as was the rest of the family. This time things seemed different to Tim, though. He just had a feeling that God was ready to change Richard. He prayed ceaselessly that he was right.

Though Tim had initially believed that everything Richard had been through had been a product of his circumstances—being born out of wedlock; having been trusted to his grandmother's care, the one who had messed up both of her own boys; and the fact that his father had abandoned him, Tim no longer believed that Richard's fate was only a product of circumstances. He had seen too many examples of kids who had absolutely no reason to chose to destroy themselves do it any way. Each of us must choose our own path and whether or not we will choose to believe. Circumstances may play a big role, but anyone, regardless of how good they have it, is susceptible to this sinful world and our sinful nature. It simply cannot be predicted if someone's child will stray or not. However, keeping your kids in God's word greatly increases their chances of getting it right or at least eventually returning to the way.

In less than a year with the Todds and their strict contract, Richard chose to recommit himself to the Lord. He literally became a new creation in Christ over the next few years and began to repair his broken relationship with his parents.

After four and a half years with the Todd's, he graduated with a nursing degree and was immediately hired by the hospital Tim worked for. Rachel was still working there at the time, and the two began to develop a friendship. Aunt Rachel eventually became a role model for Richard. Not only a role model for how to be a nurse, she became a role model for how to live life as well.

While working at the hospital, Richard grew to admire Tim in ways that just hadn't been possible before. The two became very close, and Richard's mother, Mary, finally had the biggest burden of her life taken away. All the years of worry about Richard were finally over, and Mary was finally free. Though there were other problems and trials in her life, Richard's return to their family completely changed things for all of them.

Rather than hold Richard to his financial commitments, the Todd's forgave him of his significant debts after only a handful of payments. He was now a man of God and was soon to meet the woman who would become his wife. Had he not been transformed, he would have never attracted and won over someone of Lisa's character.

Richard's recovery and what he became was truly a miracle in Sam's eyes. Kevin had done many things for all of them, but it was what he did for Richard that transformed Sam's admiration for Kevin into genuine love. Kevin became Sam's closest and dearest friend, and the two were never far apart from then on. Sam had already benefited in so many ways from Kevin, but seeing Kevin's heart in what he did for Richard made Sam need to know him better. For Kevin, his feelings and admiration for Sam had always been there.

As his thoughts left Kevin and began to drift off into thoughts about the rest of his family, more than anything, he felt grateful about the life God had given him. He felt he had been blessed beyond anything he could have ever imagined. Though he had been through many struggles throughout his life, including a period of time when he was afraid they may go bankrupt, the good had clearly outweighed the bad in his life, and he was very thankful for that.

Sam knew he wasn't worthy of the life he had been blessed with, and though it had bothered him that he had never truly suffered for his faith as it seemed like he had never had to bear his cross the way many others have had to, his heart went out to all of the Christians worldwide who had lived with real persecution. As he lay there, thinking about his own life, he now realized how foolish he had been to worry about the things he had worried about. It was easy now to look back and see God's hand in it all. How truly blessed he had been.

As he recollected the trials in his and his families' lives such as Joe Morgan's death, his heart attack, his near bankruptcy, Jack's loss of his wife, Heather's near suicide and years of living in pain,

Tim and Mary's struggle with Richard's life choices and the attitude that almost destroyed him, Sam could now see God's timing in it all. At this point, he could finally see why it had all happened the way it had all happened, and how it had all shaped them into stronger, more loving believers. Every event, no matter how horrible and painful it had been to live through, had resulted in someone new being brought to the Lord.

Knowing that what needed to be done had been done, not by him, but by the savior, Jesus Christ, took away any fear of passing that he could have had. He knew he had lived a blessed life that he didn't deserve, but even more awe inspiring was the salvation he would soon enjoy thought he didn't deserve it.

Why people chose to lean on their own understanding rather than on God's word had always troubled him. The flawed logic many used to speculate whether someone had or would go to heaven or hell had always bothered him. Many times he had heard people say that someone had been a good person and was definitely in heaven because of it when scripture was very clear that there was nothing anyone can do to earn their way into heaven. How someone could live their entire life without consulting God's word on the subject was beyond him.

Being so near the end of his life, Sam couldn't wait to start eternity. He hoped that God would say to him that he had been pleased with how he had lived his life, and he hoped his life had the type of impact for the kingdom his heavenly Father had expected of him. As he began to worry, he was suddenly calmed when God's living word, which had become a part of him after so many years of study, reminded him that God is love and that he was forgiven. There was no place for worry, only a strong sense of relief that the hard part was almost over.

Knowing those closest to him were saved helped him feel a peace he was very thankful for. He felt he had been obedient in leading them and others to the Lord, though he fully understood that God had saved all of them, not him. Still, he knew there were many opportunities he had missed, and along with all of the needless worrying he had done throughout his lifetime, it was one of his only regrets.

When he shut his eyes, he had no way of knowing that they would never open again.